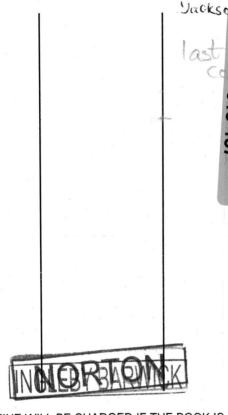

Dear Readers,

I am honored to once again participate in a MILLIONAIRE'S CLUB continuity.

No two people needed each other more than Zeke Travers and Sheila Hopkins, and getting the couple to realize that fact was both a challenge and a joy. Zeke and Sheila's story is a special one, and I hope you enjoy reading it as much as I enjoyed writing it. And I'm always excited when I can reunite my readers with characters from past books, such as Darius and Summer from *One Night with the Wealthy Rancher*.

I want to thank all the other five authors who are a part of this continuity. I enjoyed working with each of you.

Happy reading!

Brenda Jackson

TEMPTATION

BY
BRENDA JACKSON

Published in Great Britain 2012
by Mills & Boon, an imprint of Harlequin (UK) Limited,
Eton House, 18-24 Paradise Road, Richmond, Surrey TW9 1SR

© Harlequin Books S.A. 2011

Special thanks and acknowledgement to Brenda Jackson for her contribution to the Millionaire's Club series.

ISBN: 978 0 263 89169 0
ebook ISBN: 978 1 408 97764 4

951-0512

Harlequin (UK) policy is to use papers that are natural, renewable and recyclable products and made from wood grown in sustainable forests. The logging and manufacturing processes conform to the legal environmental regulations of the country of origin.

Printed and bound in Spain
by Blackprint CPI, Barcelona

Brends Jackson is a die "heart" romantic who married her childhood sweetheart and still proudly wears the "going steady" ring he gave her when she was fifteen. Because she's always believed in the power of love, Brenda's stories always have happy endings. In her real-life love story, Brenda and her husband of thirty-eight years live in Jacksonville, Florida, and have two sons.

A *New York Times* bestselling author of more than seventy-five romance titles, Brenda is a recent retiree who now divides her time between family, writing and traveling with Gerald. You may write Brenda at PO Box 28267, Jacksonville, Florida 32226, USA, by e-mail at WriterBJackson@aol.com or visit her website at www. brendajackson.net.

To the love of my life, Gerald Jackson, Sr.

To the cast and crew of *Truly Everlasting—the Movie*,
this one is especially for you! Thanks for all
your hard work!

Though your beginning was small, yet your latter end
would increase abundantly.

—Job 8:7 KJV

One

Some days it didn't pay to get out of bed.

Unless you had a tall, dark, handsome and naked man waiting in your kitchen to pour you a hot cup of coffee before sitting you in his lap to feed you breakfast. Sheila Hopkins smiled at such a delicious fantasy before squinting against the November sun that was almost blinding her through the windshield of her car.

And the sad thing was that she had awakened in a good mood. But all it had taken to spoil her day was a call from her sister that morning telling her she wasn't welcome to visit her and her family in Atlanta after all.

That message had hurt, but Sheila really should not have been surprised. What had she expected from her older sister from her father's first marriage? The same sister who'd always wished she hadn't existed? Definitely not any show of sisterly love at this late stage. If she hadn't shown any in Sheila's twenty-seven years, why had she assumed her sister would begin showing any now? Not her sister who had the perfect life with a husband who owned his own television station in Atlanta and who had two beautiful children and was pregnant with her third.

And if that very brief and disappointing conversation with Lois wasn't bad enough, she had immediately gotten a call from the hospital asking that she come in on her off day because they were shorthanded. And of course, being the dedicated nurse that she was, she had agreed to do so. Forget the fact she had planned to spend the day working in her garden. She didn't have a life, so did it really matter?

Sheila drew in a deep breath when she brought her car to a stop at a traffic light. She couldn't help glancing over at the man in the sports car next to her. She couldn't tell how the rest of him looked because she could only see his profile from the shoulders up, but even that looked good. And as if he'd known she was checking him out, he glanced her way. Her breath caught in her throat and her flesh felt tingly all over. He had such striking features.

They were so striking she had to blink to make sure they were real. Um…a maple-brown complexion, close-cut black hair, dark brown eyes and a chiseled jaw. And as she continued to stare at him, her mind mechanically put his face on the naked body of the tall, handsome man whom she would have loved to have found in her kitchen this morning. She inwardly chuckled. Neither she nor her kitchen would have been able to handle all the heat her imaginary lover would generate.

She saw his head move and realized he had nodded over at her. Instinctively, she nodded back. When his lips curved into a sensual smile, she quickly forced her gaze ahead. And when the traffic light changed, she pressed down on the gas, deciding to speed up a little. The last thing she wanted was to give the guy the impression she was flirting with him, no matter how good he looked. She had learned quickly that not all nicely wrapped gifts contained something that was good for you. Crawford had certainly proven that.

As she got off the exit that led to the hospital, she couldn't get rid of the thought that she didn't know there were men who looked like him living in Royal, Texas. Not that she knew all the men in town, mind you. But she figured someone like him would definitely stand out. After all, Royal was a rather small community. And what if she had run into him again, then what?

Nothing.

She didn't have the time or the inclination to get involved with a man. She'd done that in the past and the outcome hadn't been good, which was why she had moved to Royal from Dallas last year. Moving to Royal had meant a fresh start for her. Although, Sheila knew that where she lived was only part of the solution. She had reached the conclusion that a woman didn't need to be involved with a no-good man to have trouble. A woman could do bad all by herself. And she of all people was living proof of that.

Ezekiel Travers chuckled as he watched the attractive woman take off as though she was going to a fire or something. Hell, she wasn't the only one, he thought as he watched her car turn off the interstate at the next exit. Whoever was trying to ruin his best friend, Bradford Price's, reputation had taken things a little too far. According to the phone call he'd received earlier from Brad, the blackmailer had made good on his threat.

Someone had left a baby on the doorstep of the Texas Cattlemen's Club with a note that Brad was the baby's father.

Grabbing his cell phone the moment it began to ring, he knew who the caller was before answering it. "Yeah, Brad?"

"Zeke, where are you?"

"I'm only a few minutes away. And you can believe I'll be getting to the bottom of this."

"I don't know what kind of sick joke someone is trying to play on me, but I swear to you, that baby isn't mine."

Zeke nodded. "And a paternity test can prove that easily, Brad, so calm down."

He had no reason not to believe his best friend about the baby not being his. Brad wouldn't lie about something like that. He and Brad had gotten to be the best of friends while roommates at the University of Texas. After college Brad had returned to Royal to assist in his family's banking empire.

Actually, it had been Brad who suggested Zeke relocate to Royal. He'd made the suggestion during one of their annual all-guys trip to Vegas last year, after Zeke had mentioned his desire to leave Austin and to move to a small town.

Zeke had earned a small fortune and a great reputation as one of the best security consultants in all of Texas. Now he could live anywhere he wanted to, and take his pick of cases.

And it had been Brad who'd connected Zeke with Darius Franklin, another private investigator in Royal who owned a security service and who just happened to be looking for a partner. That had prompted Zeke to fly to Royal. He'd immediately fallen in love with the town and he saw becoming a business partner with Darius a win-win situation. That had been six months ago. When he'd moved to town, he hadn't known that his first case would begin before he could get settled in good, and that his first client would be none other than his best friend.

"I bet Abigail is behind this."

Brad's accusations interrupted Zeke's thoughts. Abigail Langley and Brad were presently in a heated battle to win the presidency of the Texas Cattlemen's Club.

"You have no proof of that and so far I haven't been able to find a link between Ms. Langley and those blackmail letters you've received, Brad. But you can bet if she's connected, I'll expose her. Now, sit tight, I'm on my way."

He clicked off the phone knowing to tell Brad to sit tight was a waste of time. Zeke let out a deep sigh. Brad had begun receiving blackmail letters five months ago. The thought nagged Zeke's mind that maybe if he had been on top of his game and solved the case months ago, it would not have gotten this far and some kid would not have been abandoned at the club.

He of all people knew how that felt. At thirty-three he could still feel the sting of abandonment. Although his own mother hadn't left him on anyone's doorstep, she had left him with her sister and kept on trucking. She hadn't shown up again until sixteen years later. It had been his last year of college and she'd stuck around just long enough to see if he had a chance in the NFL.

He pushed that hurtful time of his life to the back of his mind to concentrate on the problem at hand. If leaving that baby at the TCC with a note claiming she was Brad's kid was supposed to be a joke, then it wasn't funny. And Zeke intended to make sure he and Brad had the last laugh when they exposed the person responsible for such a callous act.

Once Sheila had reached her floor at the hospital, it became evident why they'd called her in. A couple of nurses were out sick and the E.R. was swarming with patients with symptoms ranging from the flu to a man who'd almost lost his finger while chopping down a tree in his front yard. There had also been several minor car accidents.

At least something good had resulted from one of the accidents. A man thinking his girlfriend's injuries were worse than they were, had rushed into the E.R. and proposed. Even Sheila had to admit it had been a very romantic moment. Some women had all the luck.

"So you came in on your off day, uh?"

Sheila glanced at her coworker and smiled. Jill Lanier was a nurse she'd met on her first day at Royal Memorial and they'd become good friends. When she'd moved to Royal she hadn't known a soul, but that had been fine. She was used to being alone. That was the story of her life.

She was about to answer Jill, when the sound of a huge wail stopped her. "What the heck?"

She turned around and saw two police officers walk in carrying a screaming baby. Both she and Jill hurried over to the officers. "What's going on, Officers?" she asked the two men.

One of the officers, the one holding the baby, shook his head. "We don't know why she's crying," he said in frustration. "Someone left her on the doorstep of the Texas Cattlemen's Club and we were told to bring her here."

Sheila had heard all about the Texas Cattlemen's Club, which consisted of a group of men who considered themselves the protectors of Texas, and whose members consisted of the wealthiest men in Texas. One good thing was that the TCC was known to help a number of worthwhile causes in the community. Thanks to them, there was a new cancer wing at the hospital.

Jill took the baby and it only screamed louder. "The TCC? Why would anyone do something like that?"

"Who knows why people abandon their kids," the other officer said. It was apparent he was more than happy to pass the screaming baby on to someone else. However, the infant, who looked to be no more than five months old, was screaming even louder now. Jill, who was a couple of years younger than Sheila and single and carefree, gave them a what-am-I-supposed-to-do-now look as she rocked the baby in her arms.

"And there's a note that's being handed over to Social Services claiming Bradford Price is the father."

Sheila lifted a brow. She didn't know Bradford Price personally, but she had certainly heard of him. His family were blueblood society types. She'd heard they'd made millions in banking.

"Is someone from Social Services on their way here?" Sheila asked, raising her voice to be heard over the crying baby.

"Yes. Price is claiming the baby isn't his. There has to be a paternity test done."

Sheila nodded, knowing that could take a couple of days, possibly even a week.

"And what are we supposed to do with her until then?" Jill asked as she continued to rock the baby in her arms, trying to get her quiet but failing to do so.

"Keep her here," one of the officers responded. He

was backing up, as if he was getting ready to make a run for it. "A woman from Social Services is on her way with everything you'll need. The kid doesn't have a name…at least one wasn't given with the note left with her."

The other officer, the one who'd been carrying the baby, spoke up. "Look, ladies, we have to leave. She threw up on me, so I need to swing by my place and change clothes."

"What about your report?" Sheila called out to the two officers who were rushing off.

"It's completed already and like I said, a woman from Social Services is on her way," the first officer said, before both men quickly exited through the revolving glass doors.

"I can't believe they did that," Jill said with a disgruntled look on her face. "What are we going to do with her? One thing for certain, this kid has a nice set of lungs."

Sheila smiled. "Follow procedure and get her checked out. There might be a medical reason why she's crying. Let's page Dr. Phillips."

"Hey, let me page Dr. Phillips. It's your turn to hold her." Before Sheila could say anything, Jill suddenly plopped the baby in her arms.

"Hey, hey, things can't be that bad, sweetie," Sheila crooned down at the baby as she adjusted her arms to make sure she was holding her right.

Other than the times she worked in the hospital nursery, she'd never held a baby, and rarely came in contact with one. Lois had two kids and was pregnant with another, yet Sheila had only seen her five-year-old niece and three-year-old nephew twice. Her sister had never approved of their father's marriage to Sheila's mother, and Sheila felt she had been the one to pay for it. Lois, who was four years older than Sheila, had been determined never to accept her father's other child. Over the years, Sheila had hoped her attitude toward her would change, but so far it hadn't.

Pushing thoughts of Lois from her mind, Sheila continued to smile down at the baby. And as if on cue the little girl stared up at Sheila with the most gorgeous pair of hazel eyes, and suddenly stopped crying. In fact, she smiled, showing dimples in both cheeks.

Sheila couldn't help chuckling. "What are you laughing at, baby-doll? Do I look funny or something?" She was rewarded with another huge smile from the baby. "You're such a pretty little thing, all bright and full of sunshine. I think I'll call you Sunnie until we find out your real name."

"Dr. Phillips is on his way and I'm needed on the fourth floor," Jill said, making a dash toward the elevator. "How did you get her to stop crying, Sheila?" she asked before stepping on the elevator.

Sheila shrugged and glanced back at the baby, who was still smiling up at her. "I guess she likes me."

"Apparently she does," a deep, husky male voice said from behind them.

Sheila turned around and her gaze collided with the most gorgeous set of brown eyes she'd ever seen on a man. They were bedroom eyes. The kind that brought to mind silken sheets and passion. But this wasn't the first time she had looked into those same eyes.

She immediately knew where she'd seen them before as her gaze roamed over his features. Recognition appeared in his gaze the moment it hit hers as well. Standing before her, looking sexier than any man had a right to look, was the guy who'd been in the car next to hers at the traffic light. He was the man who'd given her a flirtatious smile before she'd deliberately sped off to ditch him.

Evidently that hadn't done any good, since he was here, standing before her in vivid living color.

Two

This was the second time today he'd seen this woman, Zeke thought. Just as before, he thought she looked good…even wearing scrubs. Nothing could hide the wavy black hair that came to her shoulders, the light brown eyes and luscious café-au-lait skin.

He wondered if anyone ever told her she could be a very delicious double for actress Sanaa Lathan. The woman before him was just a tad shorter than the actress, but in his book she was just as curvy. And she was a nurse. Hell, she could take his temperature any time and any place. He could even suggest she take it now, because there was no doubt in his mind looking at her was making it rise.

"May I help you?"

He blinked and swallowed deeply. "Yes, that baby you're holding…"

She narrowed her eyes and clutched the baby closer to her breast in a protective stance. "Yes, what about her?"

"I want to find out everything there is about her," he said.

She lifted an arched brow. "And you are…?"

He gave what he hoped was a charming smile. "Zeke Travers, private investigator."

Sheila opened her mouth to speak, when a deep, male voice intruded behind her. "Zeke Travers! Son of a gun! With Brad Price as quarterback, you as split end and Chris Richards as wide receiver, that was UT's best football season. I recall them winning a national championship title that year. Those other teams didn't stand a chance with you three. Someone mentioned you had moved to Royal."

She then watched as Dr. Warren Phillips gave the man a huge bear hug. Evidently they knew each other, and as she listened further, she was finding out quite a lot about the handsome stranger.

"Yes, I moved to town six months ago," Zeke was saying. "Austin was getting too big for me. I've decided to try small-town life for a while. Brad convinced me Royal was the place," he said, grinning. "And I was able to convince Darius Franklin he needed a partner."

"So you joined forces with Darius over at Global Securities?"

"Yes, and things are working out great so far. Darius is a good man and I really like this town. In fact, I like it more and more each day." His gaze then shifted to her and her gaze locked with his as it had done that morning.

The clearing of Dr. Phillips's throat reminded them they weren't alone.

"So, what brings you to Royal Memorial, Zeke?" Dr. Phillips asked, and it was evident to Sheila that Dr. Phillips had picked up on the man's interest in her.

"That baby she's holding. It was left abandoned at

the TCC today with a note claiming Brad's the father. And I intend to prove that he's not."

"In that case," Dr. Phillips said, "I think we need to go into that private examination room over there and check this baby out."

A short while later Dr. Phillips slid his stethoscope into the pocket of his lab coat as he leaned back against the table. "Well, this young lady is certainly in good health."

He chuckled and then added, "And she certainly refused to let anyone hold her other than you, Nurse Hopkins. If you hadn't been present and within her reach, it would have been almost impossible for me to examine her."

Sheila laughed as she held the baby to her while glancing down at the infant. "She's beautiful. I can't imagine anyone wanting to abandon her."

"Well, it happened," Zeke said.

A tingling sensation rode up her spine with the comment and she was reminded that Zeke Travers was in the examination room with them. It was as if he refused to let the baby out of his sight.

She turned slightly. "What makes you so sure she's not Bradford Price's child, Mr. Travers? I recall running into Mr. Price a time or two and he also has hazel eyes."

He narrowed his gaze. "So do a million other people in this country, Ms. Hopkins."

Evidently he didn't like being questioned about the possibility. So she turned to Dr. Phillips. "Did that social worker who came by while you were examining the baby say what will happen to Sunnie?" she asked.

Dr. Phillips lifted a brow. "Sunnie?"

"Yes," Sheila said, smiling. "I thought she was a

vision of sunshine the moment I looked at her. And since no one knows her name I thought Sunnie would fit. Sounds better than Jane Doe," she added.

"I agree," Dr. Phillips said, chuckling. "And the social worker, Ms. Talbert, is as baffled as everyone else, especially since Brad says the baby isn't his."

"She's not his," Zeke said, inserting himself into the conversation again. "Brad's been receiving blackmail letters for five months now, threatening to do something like this unless he paid up."

Zeke rubbed the back of his neck. "I told him to ignore the letters while I looked into it. I honestly didn't think the person would carry out their threats if Brad didn't pay up. Evidently, I was wrong."

And that's what continued to bother him the most, Zeke thought as he glanced over at the baby. He should have nipped this nasty business in the bud long ago. And what Ms. Hopkins said was true, because he'd noted it himself. The baby had hazel eyes, and not only were they hazel, they were the same shade of hazel as Brad's.

He'd asked Brad if there was any chance the baby could be his, considering the fact Brad was a known playboy. But after talking to Brad before coming over here, and now that he knew the age of the baby, Zeke was even more convinced Brad wasn't the father. Warren had confirmed the baby's age as five months and Brad had stated he hadn't slept with any woman over the past eighteen months.

"To answer your question, Nurse Hopkins," Dr. Phillips said, breaking into Zeke's thoughts, "Ms. Talbert wants to wait to see what the paternity test reveals. I agreed that we can keep the baby here until then."

"Here?"

"Yes, that would be best until the test results comes back, that is unless Brad has a problem participating in the test," Dr. Phillips said, glancing over at Zeke.

"Brad knows that it's for the best, and he will cooperate any way he can," Zeke acknowledged.

"But it doesn't seem fair for Sunnie to have to stay here at the hospital. She's in perfect health," Sheila implored. "Ms. Talbert has indicated the test results might take two weeks to come back."

She then glared over at Zeke. "Whether the baby is officially his or not, I would think your client would want the best for Sunnie until her parentage is proven or disproven."

Zeke crossed his arms over his chest. "So what do you suggest, Ms. Hopkins? I agree staying here isn't ideal for the baby, but the only other option is for her to get turned over to Social Services. If that happens she'll go into foster care and will get lost in the system when it's proven my client is *not* her father."

Sheila nibbled on her bottom lip, not having a response to give him. She glanced down at the baby she held in her arms. For whatever reason, Sunnie's mother hadn't wanted her and it didn't seem fair for her to suffer because of it. She knew how it felt not to be wanted.

"I might have an idea that might work, Nurse Hopkins, granted you agree to go along with it," Dr. Phillips said. "And I'll have to get Ms. Talbert to agree to it, as well."

"Yes?" she said, wondering what his idea was.

"A few years ago the wife of one of my colleagues, Dr. Webb, was hit with a similar incident when someone left a baby on her doorstep before they were married. Because Winona grew up in foster care herself, she hadn't wanted the baby to end up the same way. To make a long story short, Winona and Dr. Webb ended up marrying and keeping the baby to make sure it didn't get lost in the system."

Sheila nodded. "So what are you suggesting?"

Dr. Phillips smiled. "That you become Sunnie's emergency foster parent until everything is resolved. I believe I'll be able to convince Ms. Talbert to go along with it, and given the fact the Prices are huge benefactors to this hospital, as well as to a number of other nonprofit organizations, I think it would be in everyone's best interest that the baby's welfare remain a top priority."

Sheila looked shocked. "Me? A foster parent! I wouldn't know what to do with a baby."

"You couldn't convince me of that, Ms. Hopkins. The baby won't let anyone else touch her and you seem to be a natural with her," Zeke said, seeing the merits of what Dr. Phillips proposed. "Besides, you're a nurse, someone who is used to taking care of people."

Although Brad swore the baby wasn't his, he would still be concerned with the baby's health and safety until everything was resolved. And what Zeke just said was true. He thought the woman was a natural with the baby, and the baby had gotten totally attached to her. He had a feeling Ms. Hopkins was already sort of attached to the baby, as well.

"And if you're concerned as to how you'd be able to handle both your job and the baby, I propose that the hospital agrees to give you a leave of absence during the time that the child is in your care. My client will be more than happy to replace your salary," Zeke said.

"I think that would be an excellent idea," Warren said. "One I think I could push past the chief of staff.

The main thing everyone should be concerned about is Sunnie's well-being."

Sheila couldn't help agreeing. But her? A foster parent? "How long do you think I'll have to take care of her?" she asked, looking down at Sunnie, who was still smiling up at her.

"No more than a couple of weeks, if even that long," Zeke said. "The results of the paternity test should be back by then and we'll know how to proceed."

Sheila nibbled her bottom lip, when Sunnie reached and grabbed hold of a lock of her hair, seemingly forcing Sheila to look down at her—into her beautiful hazel eyes, while she made a lot of cheerful baby sounds. At that moment Sheila knew she would do it. Sunnie needed a temporary home and she would provide her with one. It was the least she could do, and deep down she knew it was something that she wanted to do. This was the first time she'd felt someone truly, really needed her.

She glanced up at both men to see they were patiently waiting for her answer. She drew in a deep breath. "Yes. I would be happy to be Sunnie's emergency foster parent."

After removing his jacket, Zeke slid into the seat of his car and leaned back as he gazed at the entrance to the hospital. He felt good about Sheila Hopkins agreeing to take on the role of foster parent. That way he would know the baby was being well cared for while he turned up the heat on the investigation to clear Brad's name.

He intended to pursue each and every lead. He would not leave a stone, no matter how small, unturned. He intended to get this potential scandal under total control before it could go any further.

Now if he could control his attraction to Sheila

Hopkins. The woman was definitely temptation with a capital T. Being in close quarters with her, even with Warren in the room, had been pure torture. She was a looker, but it was clear she didn't see herself that way, and he couldn't help wondering, why not? He hadn't seen a ring on her finger and, when he'd hung back to speak with Warren in private, the only thing his friend could tell him was that she was a model employee, caring to a fault, dependable and intelligent.

Warren had also verified she was single and had moved from Dallas last year. But still, considering everything, Zeke felt it wouldn't hurt to do a background check on her, just to be on the safe side. The last thing he wanted was for her to be someone who'd be tempted to sell this story to the tabloids. That was the last thing Brad needed. His best friend was depending on him to bring an end to this nightmare, and he would.

Zeke was about to turn the ignition in his car, when he glanced through the windshield to see Sheila Hopkins. She was walking quickly across the parking lot to the car he had seen her in that morning. She looked as if she was dashing off to fight a fire. Curious as to where she could be going in such a hurry, he got out of the car, walked swiftly to cross the parking lot and intercepted her before she could reach her vehicle.

She nearly yelled in fright when he stepped in front of her. "What do you think you're doing?" she asked, covering her heart with the palm of her hand. "You just scared me out of my wits."

"Sorry, but I saw you tearing across the parking lot. What's the hurry?"

Sheila drew a deep breath to get her heart beating back normal in her chest. She looked up at Zeke Travers and couldn't do anything about her stomach doing flips.

It had been hard enough while in the examination room to stop her gaze from roaming all over him every chance it got.

"I'm leaving Sunnie in the hospital tonight while I go pick up the things I'll need for her. I'm going to need a baby bed, diapers, clothes and all kinds of other items. I plan on shopping today and come back for her first thing in the morning once my house is ready."

She paused a moment. "I hated leaving her. She started crying. I feel like I'm abandoning her."

A part of Zeke was relieved to know she was a woman who would feel some sort of guilt in abandoning a child. His own mother had not. He drew in a deep breath as he remembered what Sheila Hopkins had said about needing to go shopping for all that baby stuff. He hadn't thought of the extra expenses taking on a baby would probably cost her.

"Let me go with you to pick up the stuff. That way I can pay for it."

She raised a brow. "Why would you want to do that?"

"Because whether or not Brad's the father—which he's not—he wants the baby taken care of and is willing to pay for anything she might need." He hadn't discussed it with Brad, but knew there wouldn't be a problem. Brad was concerned for the baby's welfare.

She seemed to be studying his features as if she was trying to decide if he was serious, Zeke thought. And then she asked, "You sure? I have to admit that I hadn't worked all the baby expenses into my weekly budget, but if I need to get money out of my savings then I—"

"No, that won't be necessary and Brad wouldn't want it any other way and like I said, I'll be glad to go with you and help."

Sheila felt a tingling sensation in the pit of her

stomach. The last thing she needed was Zeke Travers in her presence too long. "No, I'll be able to manage things, but I appreciate the offer."

"No, really, I insist. Why wouldn't you want me to help? I'll provide you with two extra hands."

That wasn't all he would be providing her with, she thought, looking at him. Besides the drop-dead gorgeous looks, at some point he had taken off his jacket to reveal the width of his shoulders beneath his white dress shirt. She also noticed the way his muscular thighs fit into a pair of dress slacks.

"We could leave your car here. I have a feeling you'll want to come back and check on the baby later. We can go in my vehicle," he added before she could respond to what he'd said.

She lifted a brow. "You have a two-seater."

He chuckled. "Yes, but I also have a truck. And that's what you're going to need to haul something as big as a box containing a baby bed. And in order to haul the kid away from here you're going to need a car seat tomorrow."

Sheila tilted her head back and drew in a deep breath. Had she bit off more than she could chew? She hadn't thought of all that. She needed to make a list and not work off the top of her head. And he was right about her needing a truck and wanting to return tonight to check on Sunnie. The sound of her crying had followed Sheila all the way to the elevator. She hated leaving her, but she had to prepare her house for Sunnie's visit.

"Ms. Hopkins?"

She looked back at Zeke Travers. "Fine, Mr. Travers, I'll accept your generosity. If you're sure it's not going out of your way."

He smiled. "I'm not going out of my way, I assure

you. Like I said, Brad would want what's best for the baby even if she isn't his."

She arched a brow. "You certainly seem so sure of that."

"I am. Now, it's going to be my job in addition to making sure the baby is safe and well cared for, to find out who's trying to nail him with this and to clear his name."

Zeke paused a moment and stared down at her. "And speaking of names, I suggest you call me Zeke, instead of Mr. Travers."

She smiled. "Why, is Mr. Travers what they call your father?"

"I wouldn't know."

Sheila's heart skipped a beat when she realized what he'd said and what he'd meant by saying it. "I'm sorry, I didn't mean anything. The last guy who told me not to call him by his last name said the reason was that's what people called his daddy."

"No harm done, and I hope you don't mind if I call you Sheila."

"No, I don't mind."

"Good. Come on, Sheila, my car is parked over here," he said.

Sheila felt her stomach twist in all kinds of knots when she heard her name flow from his lips. And as she walked beside Zeke across the parking lot, a number of misgivings flooded her mind. For one thing, she wasn't sure what role he intended to play with her becoming Sunnie's foster parent. She understood Bradford Price was his client and he intended to clear the man's name. But she had to think beyond that. If Bradford wasn't Sunnie's father then who was? Where was the mother and why had the baby been abandoned with a note claiming Bradford was the father when he said he wasn't?

There were a lot of questions and she had a feeling the man walking beside her intended to have answers for all of them soon enough. She also had a feeling he was the sort of person who got things accomplished when he set his mind to it. And she could tell he intended to investigate this case to the fullest.

His main concern might be on his friend, but hers was on Sunnie. What would happen to her if it was proven Bradford wasn't the child's father? Would the man cease caring about Sunnie's welfare? Would it matter to him that she would then become just a statistic in the system?

He might not care, but she would, and at that moment she vowed to protect Sunnie any way she could.

Three

While they were on their way to the store to pick up items for the baby, Sheila clicked off the phone and sighed deeply as she glanced over at Zeke. "I just talked to one of the nurses in Pediatrics. Sunnie cried herself to sleep," she said.

There was no need telling him that she knew just how that felt. She was reminded of how many nights as a child she had lain in bed and cried herself to sleep because her mother was too busy trying to catch the next rich husband to spend any time with her. And her father, once he'd discovered what a gold digger Cassie Hopkins was, he hadn't wasted time moving out and taking Lois with him and leaving her behind.

"That's good to hear, Sheila," Zeke responded.

There was another tingling sensation in the pit of her stomach. She couldn't help it. It did something to her each and every time he pronounced her name. He said it with a deep Texas drawl that could send shivers all through her.

"So how long have you been living in Royal?" he asked.

She glanced over at him. "A year." She knew from his conversation with Dr. Phillips that he had moved to town six months ago, so there was no need to ask him that. She also knew he'd come from Austin because he wanted to try living in a small city.

"You like it here?"

She nodded. "So far. The people are nice, but I spend a lot of my time at the hospital, so I still haven't met all my neighbors, only those next door."

She switched her gaze off him to look out the window at the homes and stores they passed. What she decided not to add was that other than working, and occasional trips to the market, she rarely left home. The people at the hospital had become her family

Now that she'd agreed to a fourteen-day leave of absence, she would have her hands full caring for Sunnie, and a part of her actually looked forward to that.

"You're smiling."

She glanced back at him. Did the man notice every single thing? "Is it a crime?"

He chuckled. "No."

The deep, husky rumble of his chuckle sent shivers sweeping through her again. And because she couldn't help herself, when the car came to a stop at the traffic light she glanced back over at him and then wished she hadn't done so. The slow smile that suddenly curved his lips warmed her all over.

"Now you're the one smiling," she pointed out.

"And is that a crime?"

Grinning, she shook her head. He'd made her see just how ridiculous her response to him had been. "No, it's not."

"Good. Because if I get arrested, Sheila, so do you. And it would be my request that we get put in the same jail cell."

She told herself not to overreact to what he'd said. Of course he would try to flirt with her. He was a man. She'd gotten hit on by a number of doctors at the hospital as well as several police officers around town. Eventually, they found out what Zeke would soon discover. It was a waste of their time. She had written men off. When it came to the opposite sex, she preferred her space. The only reason she was with him now was because of Sunnie. She considered Zeke Travers as a means to an end.

When he exited off the expressway and moments later turned into a nice gated community, she was in awe of the large and spacious ranch-style homes that sat on at least thirty acres of land. She had heard about the Cascades, the section of Royal where the wealthy lived. He evidently was doing well in the P.I. business. "You live in this community?" she asked.

"Yes. I came from Austin on an apartment-hunting trip and ended up purchasing a house instead. I always wanted a lot of land and to own horses and figured buying in here was a good investment."

She could just imagine, especially with the size of the ranch house whose driveway they were pulling into. The house had to be sitting almost six hundred or more feet back off the road. She could see a family of twelve living here and thought the place was definitely too large for just one person.

"How many acres is this?" she asked.

"Forty. I needed that much with the horses."

"How many do you own?"

"Twelve now, but I plan to expand. I've hired several ranch hands to help me take care of things. And I ride every chance I get. What about you? Do you ride?"

She thought of her mother's second and third husbands. They had owned horses and required that she know how to ride. "Yes, I know how to ride."

He glanced at his watch. "It won't take me long to switch vehicles," he said, bringing the car to a stop. "You're invited in if you like and you're welcome to look around."

"No, I'll be fine waiting out here until you return," she said.

He got out of the car and turned to her and smiled. "I don't bite, you know."

"Trust me, Zeke, if for one minute I thought you did, I wouldn't be here."

"So you think I'm harmless?" he asked, grinning.

"Not harmless but manageable. I'm sure all your focus will be on trying to figure out who wants to frame your friend. You don't have time for anything else."

He flashed a sexy smile. "Don't be so sure of that, Sheila Hopkins." He closed the door and she watched as he strolled up the walkway to his front door, thinking his walk was just as sexy as his smile.

Zeke unlocked his door and pushed it open. He had barely made it inside his house when the phone rang. Closing the door behind him, he pulled his cell phone off the clip on his belt. He checked the caller ID. "Yes, Brad?"

"You didn't call. How was the baby?"

Zeke leaned up against the wall supporting the staircase. "She's fine, but she cries a lot."

"I noticed. And no one could get her to stop. Did they check her out to make sure nothing is wrong with her?"

Zeke smiled. "She was checked out. Just so happens that Warren Phillips was on duty and he's the one who gave her a clean bill of health, although she still wanted to prove to everyone what a good set of lungs she had."

"I'm glad she's okay. I was worried about her."

Zeke nodded. "Are you sure there's nothing you want to tell me? I did happen to notice the kid does have your eyes."

"Don't get cute, Zeke. The kid isn't mine. But she's just a baby and I can't help worrying about her."

"Hey, man, I was just kidding, and I understand. I can't help worrying about her, too. But we might have found a way where we don't have to worry about her while I delve into my investigation."

"And what way is that?"

"That way happens to be a nurse who works at Royal Memorial by the name of Sheila Hopkins. She's the only one who can keep the baby quiet. It's the weirdest thing. The kid screams at everyone else, but she's putty in Sheila Hopkins's hands. She actually smiles instead of crying."

"You're kidding."

"No, I saw her smile myself. Warren suggested that Sheila keep Sunnie for the time being," Zeke explained.

"Sunnie?"

"Yes, that's the name Sheila gave the kid for now. She said it sounded better than Jane Doe and I agree."

There was a slight pause and then Brad asked, "And this Sheila Hopkins agreed to do it?"

"Yes, until the results of the paternity test come back, so the sooner you can do your part the better."

"I've made an appointment to have it done tomorrow."

"Good. And I'm going shopping with Sheila for baby stuff. She's single and doesn't have any kids of her own, so she'll need all new stuff, which I'm billing you for, by the way."

"Fine." There was a pause, and then Brad said, "I was thinking that perhaps it would be best if I hired a nanny and keep the baby instead of—"

"Hold up. Don't even consider it. We don't want anyone seeing your kindness as an admission of guilt, Brad. The next thing everyone will think is that the baby is really yours."

"Yes, but what do you know about this nurse? You said she's single. She might be pretty good at taking care of patients, but are you sure she knows how to take care of a baby?"

"I'm not sure about anything regarding Sheila Hopkins, other than what Warren told me. She's worked at the hospital about a year. But don't worry, I've already taken measures to have her checked out. Roy is doing a thorough background check on Sheila Hopkins as we speak."

Suddenly Zeke heard a noise behind him and turned around. Sheila was leaning against his door with her arms crossed over her chest. The look on her face let him know she had heard some, if not all, of his conversation with Brad and wasn't happy about it.

"Brad, I need to go. I'll call you back later." He then hung up the phone.

Before he could open his mouth, Sheila placed her hands on her hips and narrowed her eyes at him. "Please take me back to the hospital to get my car. There's no way I'm going anywhere with a man who doesn't trust me."

Then she turned and walked out the door and slammed it shut behind her.

Sheila was halfway down the walkway, when Zeke ran behind her and grabbed her arm. "Let me go," she said and angrily snatched it back.

"We need to talk and I prefer we don't do it out here," Zeke said.

She glared up at him. "And I prefer we don't do it anywhere. I have nothing to say to you. How dare you have me investigated like I'm some sort of criminal."

"I never said you were a criminal."

"Then why the background check, Zeke?"

He rubbed his hands down his face. "I'm a P.I., Sheila. I investigate people. Nothing personal, but think about it. Sunnie will be in your care for two weeks. I don't know you personally and I need to know she's not only in a safe environment but with someone both Brad and I can trust. Would you not want me to check out the person whose care she's been placed in?"

Sheila sighed deeply, knowing that she would. "But I'd never do anything to harm her."

"I believe that, but I have to make sure. All I'm doing is a basic background check to make certain you don't have any past criminal history." After a moment he said, "Come on in, let's talk inside."

She thought about his request then decided it might be best if they did talk inside after all. She had a tendency to raise her voice when she was angry about something.

"Fine." She stalked off ahead of him.

* * *

By the time Zeke followed her inside the house, she was in the middle of the living room pacing, and he could tell she was still mad. He quietly closed the door behind him and leaned against it, folding his arms across his chest, with one booted heel over the other, as he watched her. Again he was struck by just how beautiful she was.

For some reason he was more aware of it now than before. There was fire in her eyes, annoyance in her steps, and the way she was unconsciously swaying her hips was downright sensual. She had taken center stage, was holding it and he was a captive audience of one.

Then she stopped pacing and placed her hands on her hips to face him. She glared him down. The woman could not have been more than five-four at the most. Yet even with his height of six-four she was making him feel shorter. Damn. He hadn't meant for her to overhear his conversation with Brad. Hadn't she told him she hadn't wanted to come in?

"You were supposed to stay outside. You said you didn't want to come in," he blurted out for some reason.

He watched as she stiffened her spine even more. "And that gave you the right to talk about me?"

His heart thudded deeply in his chest. The last thing he had time or the inclination to do was deal with an emotional female. "Look, Sheila, like I said before, I am a private investigator. My job is to know people and I don't like surprises. Anyone who comes in contact with the baby for any long period of time will get checked out by me."

He rubbed his hand down his face and released a frustrated sigh. "Look. It's not that I was intentionally questioning your character. I was mainly assuring my client that a child that someone is claiming to be his has been placed in the best of care until the issue is resolved by way of a paternity test. There's no reason for you to take it personally. It's not about you. It's about Sunnie. Had you been the president's mother-in-law I'd still do a background check. My client is a very wealthy man and my job is to protect him at all costs, which is why I intend to find out who is behind this."

He paused for a moment. "You do want what's best for Sunnie, don't you?"

"Of course."

"So do I, and so does Brad. That baby was abandoned, and the last thing I would want is for her not to have some stability in her life over the next couple of weeks. She deserves that at least. Neither of us know what will happen after that."

His words gave Sheila pause and deflated her anger somewhat. Although she didn't want to admit it, what he said was true. It wasn't about her but about Sunnie. She should be everyone's main concern. Background checks were routine and she would have expected that one be done if they'd hired a nanny for Sunnie. She didn't know Zeke like he didn't know her, and with that suspicious mind of his—which came with the work he did—he would want to check her out regardless of the fact that Dr. Phillips had spoken highly of her. But that didn't mean she had to like the fact Zeke had done it.

"Fine," she snapped. "You've done your job. Now, take me back to the hospital so I can get my car."

"We're going shopping for the baby stuff as planned, Sheila. You still need my truck, so please put your emotions aside and agree to do what's needed to be done."

"Emotions!" Before thinking about it, she quickly crossed the room to stand in front of him.

"Yes, emotions."

His voice had lowered and he reached out and tilted her chin up. "Has anyone ever told you how sexy you look when you're angry?"

And before she could take another breath, he lowered his mouth to hers.

Why did her lips have to be so soft?
Why did she have to taste so darn good?
And why wasn't she resisting him?

Those questions rammed through Zeke's mind as his heart banged brutally in his chest at the feel of his mouth on Sheila's. He pushed those questions and others to the back of his mind as he deepened the kiss, took it to another level—although his senses were telling him that was the last thing he needed to do.

He didn't heed their advice. Instead, he wrapped his arms around Sheila's waist to bring her closer to the fit of him as he feasted on her mouth. He knew he wasn't the only one affected by the kiss when he felt her hardened nipples pressing into his chest. He could tell she hadn't gotten kissed a lot, at least not to this degree, and she seemed unsure of herself, but he remedied that by taking control. She moaned and he liked the sound of it and definitely like the feel of her plastered against him.

He could go on kissing her for hours…days…months. The very thought gave him pause and he gradually pulled his mouth from hers. Hours, days and months meant an involvement with a woman and he didn't do involvements. He did casual affairs and nothing more. And the last thing he did was mix business with pleasure.

* * *

Sheila's first coherent thought after Zeke released her lips was that she had never, not even in her wildest dreams, been kissed like that. She still felt tingling in her toes and her entire body; her every limb and muscle felt like pure jelly, which was probably the reason she was quivering like the dickens inside.

She slowly drew air into her lungs, held it a moment before slowly letting it out. She could still taste him on her tongue. How had he gotten so entrenched there? She quickly answered her own question when she remembered how his tongue had taken hold of hers, mated with it and sucked on it.

She muttered a couple colorful expletives under her breath when she gazed up at him. She should not have allowed him to kiss her like that. She'd be the first to admit she had enjoyed it, but still. The eyes staring back at her were dark and heated as if he wanted a repeat performance. She cleared her throat. "Why did you kiss me?"

Why had he kissed her? Zeke asked himself that same question as he took a step back. He needed to put distance between them or else he would be tempted to kiss her again.

"You were talking," he said, grabbing the first excuse he could think of.

"No, I wasn't."

He lifted a brow. Hadn't she been? He tried to back-track and recall just what was taking place between them before she'd stormed across the room to get in his face. When he remembered, he shrugged. "Doesn't matter. You would have said something you regretted and I decided to wipe the words off your lips."

Sheila frowned. "I suggest that you don't ever do it again."

That slow, sexy smile that she'd seen earlier returned, and instead of saying he wouldn't kiss her again, he crossed his arms over his chest and asked, "So, what brought you inside? You said you were going to wait outside."

He had changed subjects and she decided to follow his lead. "Your car began beeping loudly as if it was going to blow up or something."

His smile widened to emphasize the dimples in his cheek. "That's my fax machine. It's built into my console in a way that's not detectable."

She shook her head. "What are you, a regular James Bond?"

"No. Bond is a secret agent. I'm a private investigator. There's a big difference." He glanced at his watch. "If you're ready, we can leave. My truck is this way."

"What about the fax that was coming through?"

"I have a fax in the truck as well. It will come in on both."

"Oh."

She followed him through a spacious dining room and kitchen that was stylishly decorated. The living room was also fashionably furnished. Definitely more so than hers. "You have a nice home."

"Thanks, and if you're talking about the furniture and decorating, I can't take credit. It was a model home and I bought it as is. I saw it. I liked it. I got it."

He saw it, he liked it and he got it. She wondered if that was how he operated with everything in his life.

"Where do you want me to put these boxes?" Zeke asked, carrying two under his arms. One contained a baby car seat and the other a baby bath. He hadn't wanted to tell her, but he thought instead of purchasing just the basics that she'd gotten carried away. The kid would only be with her for two weeks at the most, not two years.

"You can set them down anywhere. I'm going to stay up late tonight putting stuff up."

After placing the boxes in a corner of the room, he glanced around. The place was small, but it suited her. Her furniture was nice and her two-story home was neat as a pin. He could imagine how it was going to look with baby stuff cluttering it up.

"I'm going to call the hospital again to check on Sunnie."

He bit down on his lips, forcing back a reminder that she had called the hospital less than an hour ago. And before that, while they had been shopping in Target for all the items on her list, she had called several times then as well. It was a good thing she knew the nurses taking care of the baby, otherwise they would probably consider her a nuisance.

While she was on the phone, he went back outside to get more boxes out of the truck. Although she didn't live in a gated community, it was in a nice section of town, and he felt good about that. And he noticed she had an alarm system, but he would check the locks on her doors anyway. Until he discovered the identity of the person who'd tried to extort money from Brad, he wasn't taking any chances. What if the blackmailer tried to kidnap the baby back?

He had made several trips back and forth into the house before Sheila had finally gotten off the phone. He glanced over at her. "Is anything wrong?"

She shook her head. "No. Sunnie awakened for a short while, but she's gone back to sleep now."

Hell, he should hope so. He glanced at his watch. It was after nine o'clock. He should know since they'd closed the store. He figured that kid should be asleep by now. Didn't she have a bedtime?

"Okay, all the boxes are in, what do you need me to do now?"

Sheila glanced over at him, tempted to tell him what he could do was leave. He was unnerving her. He'd done so while they'd been shopping for the baby items. There was something about a good-looking man that could get to a woman each and every time, and she'd gotten her share with him today. Several times while walking down the aisles of the store, they had brushed against each other, and although both had tried downplaying the connection, she'd felt it and knew he'd felt it as well. And he smelled good. Most of the men at the hospital smelled sanitized. She was reminded of a real man's scent while around him. And then there was that kiss she was trying hard to forget. However, she was finding it difficult to do so each and every time she looked at his lips. His mouth had certainly done a number on her.

She thought every woman should spend the day shopping with a man for baby items at least once in her lifetime. Sheila couldn't help remembering the number of times they'd needed assistance from a store clerk. Finally, they'd been assigned their own personal clerk, probably to get them out the store sooner. She was sure the employees wanted to go home at some point that night. And she couldn't forget how the clerk assumed they were married, although neither of them was wearing a wedding ring. Go figure.

"You can take me to get my car now," she said,

tucking a loose lock of hair behind her ear and trying not to stare at him. She shouldn't be surprised that he practically dominated her living room by standing in the middle of it. Everything else seemed to fade to black. He was definitely the main attraction with his height, muscular build and overall good looks.

"What about the baby bed?"

She quirked a brow. "What about it?"

"When are you going to put it together?"

She nibbled on her bottom lip, thinking that was a good question. It was one of the largest items she'd purchased and the clerk had turned down her offer to buy the one on display. That certainly would have made things easier for her. Instead, he'd sold her one in a box that included instructions that would probably look like Greek to her.

"Later tonight."

A smile curved his lips. "I should hope so if you plan on bringing the baby home tomorrow."

She wrapped her arms around herself. She hadn't told him yet, but she planned on bringing Sunnie home tonight. It was getting so bad with her crying that the nurses hated it when she woke up. Her crying would wake all the other babies. She had talked to the head nurse, who would be contacting Dr. Phillips to make sure Sunnie could be released into her care and custody tonight. She was just waiting for a callback.

Zeke studied Sheila. Maybe his brain was over-reacting, but he had a feeling she was keeping something from him. Maybe it was because she was giving a lot away. Like the way she had wrapped her arms around herself. Or the nervous look in her eyes. Or it could be the way she was nibbling on the lips he'd kissed earlier that day. A kiss he wished he could forget but couldn't. For some reason his mouth had felt right locked to hers.

He crossed his arms over his chest. "Is there something you want to tell me?"

She dropped her arms to her sides. "Sunnie is keeping the other babies up."

That didn't surprise him. He'd heard the kid cry. She had a good set of lungs. "She's sleeping now, right?"

"Yes, but as you know, she probably won't sleep through the night."

No, he didn't know that. "Why not?"

"Most babies don't. That's normal. The older they get the longer they will sleep through the night. In Sunnie's case, she probably sleeps a lot during the day and is probably up for at least part of the night."

"And you're prepared for that?"

"I have to be."

It occurred to him the sacrifices she would be making. His concentration had been so focused on the baby, he hadn't thought about the changes keeping Sunnie would make in her life. When she'd been on the phone and he'd been hauling in the boxes, he had taken a minute to pull his fax. It had been the background check on her. The firm he used was thorough and he'd held her life history in his hand while holding that one sheet of paper.

She was twenty-seven and every hospital she'd worked in since college had given her a glowing recommendation. She was a law-abiding citizen. Had never even received a speeding ticket. One year she had even received a medal for heroism from the Dallas Fire Department because she'd rushed inside a burning house to help save an elderly man, and then provided him with medical services until paramedics got there. That unselfish act had made national news.

On a more personal side, he knew she had a sister whom she didn't visit often. She had a mother whom she visited once or twice a year. Her mother was divorced from husband number five, a CEO of a resort in Florida. Her father had died five years ago. Her only sister, who was four years older, was from her father's first marriage. Sheila had been the product of the old man's second marriage.

"Tell me what else I can do to help," he said.

She released a deep sigh. "I want to bring Sunnie here tonight. The nurses are contacting Dr. Phillips for his approval. I hope to get a call from him any minute. Either way, whether I get Sunnie tonight or tomorrow, I'll need the bed, so if you really don't mind, I'd appreciate it if you would put it together. I'm not good at doing stuff like that."

He nodded. "No problem." He began rolling up his sleeves. "You wouldn't happen to have a beer handy, would you?"

She smiled. "Yes, I'll go grab one for you."

And then she took off and he was left standing while wondering why he couldn't stop thinking about the time he had kissed her.

"We're glad you're here," one of the nurses in Pediatrics said anxiously. "We have her packed up and ready to go," she added, smiling brightly.

"She's been expressing herself again, eh?" Zeke asked, chuckling.

Sheila glanced over at Zeke, wondering why he was there. It hadn't taken him any time to put up the baby bed, and he'd taken the time to help with the other things as well. Except for the fact Sunnie was a girl and the room was painted blue, everything else was perfect. By the time they'd left, it had looked like a genuine nursery and she couldn't wait for Sunnie to see it.

That brought her back to the question she'd wondered about earlier. Why was he here? She figured he would drop her off and keep moving. She had a baby car seat, so as far as she was concerned, she was ready to go. But she couldn't dismiss the nervous tension in her stomach.

Sunnie had clung to her earlier today when the police officers had first brought her in. What if she no longer had that attachment to her and treated her like the others and continue to cry all over the place? She drew in a deep breath, wanting to believe that that special connection between them was still there.

"Where is she?" she asked the nurse.

"Down that hall. Trust me, you'll hear her as soon as you clear the waiting area. You won't be able to miss it. All of us are wearing homemade earplugs."

Sheila knew the nurse had said it as a joke, but she didn't see anything funny. She was ready to get Sunnie and go home. Home. Already she was thinking of her place as the baby's home. Before tonight, to her it was just a place to eat and sleep. Now, taking Sunnie there had her thinking differently.

True to what the nurse had said, Sunnie could be heard the moment Sheila and Zeke passed the waiting room. He put his hand on her arm for them to stop walking. He studied her features. "What's wrong? Why are you so tense?"

How had he known? She released a nervous sigh. "I've been gone over eight hours. What if Sunnie isn't attached to me anymore? What if she sees me and continues to cry?"

Zeke stared at her. The answer seemed quite obvious to him. It didn't matter. The kid was going home with her regardless. But he could see it was important for this encounter with the baby not to constitute a rejection. He wondered why he cared. He reached out and took her hand in his and began rubbing it when it felt cold.

"Hey, she's going to remember you. She liked you too much not to. If you recall, I was here when she was clinging to you like you were her lifeline, her protector and the one person she thinks is there for her."

He saw the hopeful gleam in her eyes. "You think so?"

Hell, he wasn't sure, but he'd never tell her that. "Yes, I think so."

She smiled. "Thanks, and I hope you're right."

He hoped he was right, too. They began walking again and when they reached the door to the room where Sunnie was being kept, he watched her square her shoulders and walk in. He followed behind her.

The baby was lying in a crib on her side, screaming up a storm, but miraculously, the moment she saw Sheila, her crying turned to tiny whimpers before she stopped completely. And Zeke wasn't sure how it was possible, but he wouldn't believe it if he hadn't seen it for himself.

The abandoned baby she'd named Sunnie smiled and reached her chubby arms out for her.

Four

The alarm went off and Zeke immediately came awake. Flipping over in bed, he stared up at the ceiling as his mind recalled everything that had happened the night before. Sunnie was now with Sheila.

He had hung around long enough to help gather up the baby and get her strapped in the car seat. And the kid hadn't uttered a single whimper. Instead, she had clung to Sheila like she was her very last friend on earth. He had followed them, just to make sure they arrived back at Sheila's house safely. While sitting in his truck, he had watched her get the baby inside before he'd finally pulled off.

At one point he'd almost killed the ignition and walked up to her door to see if she needed any more help, but figured he'd worn out his welcome already that day. Hell, at least he'd gotten a kiss out of the deal. And what a kiss he'd had. Thinking about that kiss had made it very difficult to fall asleep and kept him tossing and turning all night long.

His day would be full. Although Brad was his best friend, he was also a client; a client who'd come to him for help. Zeke wanted to solve this case quickly. Doing so would definitely be a feather in his cap. It would also further improve his reputation and boost the prospects of his new partner, Darius.

He eased out of bed and was about to slide his feet into his slippers, when the phone rang.

"Hello."

"Hi, Zeke. I just want to make sure the baby is okay."

He smiled at the sound of Darius's wife, Summer's, voice. Darius was presently in D.C. doing antiterrorism consulting work. "She's fine, Summer. The nurse who's going to be taking care of her for the next two weeks took her home from the hospital last night."

"What's the nurse's name?"

"Sheila Hopkins."

"I know Sheila."

He lifted a brow. "You do?"

"Yes… She and I worked together on a domestic-abuse case six months ago. The woman made it to the hospital while Sheila was working E.R. I was called in because the woman needed a place to stay."

Summer was the director of Helping Hands Women's Shelter in Somerset, their twin city. "I hope things turned out well for the woman," he said.

"It did, thanks to Sheila. She's a real professional."

He agreed. And he thought she was also a real woman. Before they'd gone to pick up the baby and while he was putting up the crib, she had showered and changed into a pair of jeans and a top. He wasn't aware that many curves could be on a woman's body. And he

practically caught his breath each and every time he
looked at her.

Moments later, after ending his call with Summer,
Zeke drew in a deep breath and shook his head. He needed
to focus on the case at hand and not the curvaceous Sheila
Hopkins, or her sleep-stealing kisses.

The first thing he needed to do was to check the
video cameras around the TCC. According to Brad,
there were several, and Zeke was hoping that at least
one of them had picked something up.

Then he intended to question the gardeners who were
in charge of TCC's immaculate lawns to see if they'd
seen or heard anything yesterday around the time the
baby had been left on the doorstep.

And he had to meet up with Brad to make sure he'd
taken the paternity test. The sooner they could prove
that Brad wasn't Sunnie's father, the better.

As he made his way into the bathroom, he wondered
how the baby was doing. Mainly he wondered how
Sheila had fared. Last night, it had been evident after
taking several naps that Sunnie was all bright-eyed and
ready to play. At midnight. He wondered if Sheila got
any sleep.

He rubbed his hands down his face. The thought of
her in jammies beneath the covers had his gut stirring.
Perhaps she didn't sleep under the covers. She might
sleep on top of them the way he did sometimes. Then
there was the possibility that she didn't wear jammies,
but slept in the nude as he preferred doing at times, as
well.

He could imagine her in the nude. For a moment he'd
envisioned her that way last night when he'd heard the
shower going and knew she was across the hall from
where he was putting the crib together, and taking a

shower and changing clothes. Strong desire had kicked him so hard he'd almost dropped his screwdriver.

And there was the scent he'd inhaled all through her house. It was a scent he now associated with her. Jasmine. He hadn't known what the aroma was until he'd asked. It was in her candles, various baskets of potpourri that she had scattered about. But he'd especially picked it up when she'd come out of her bedroom after taking her shower. She had evidently used the fragrance while showering because its scent shrouded her when she'd entered the room she would use as the temporary nursery.

Last night it had been hard to get to sleep. To take the chill out of the air he'd lit the fireplace in his bedroom and then couldn't settle down when visions of him and Sheila, naked in front of that same fireplace, tortured his mind.

As he brushed his teeth and washed his face, he couldn't help wondering what the hell was wrong with him. He knew the score where women were concerned. The feeling of being abandoned was something he would always deal with. As a result, he would never set himself up for that sort of pain again. No woman was worth it.

A short while later he had stepped out the shower and was drying off when his cell phone rang. He reached to pick it up off the bathroom counter and saw it was Brad. "What's going on?"

"Abigail Langley is what's going on. I know she has a meeting at TCC this morning and I'm going to have it out with her once and for all."

Zeke rolled his eyes. "Lay off her, Brad. You don't have any proof she's involved in any way."

"Sure she's involved. Abigail happens to be the only person who'll benefit if my reputation is ruined."

"But you just can't go accusing her of anything without concrete proof," Zeke said in a stern tone.

"I can't? Ha! Just watch me." Brad then clicked off the phone.

"Damn!" Zeke placed the phone back on the counter as he quickly began dressing. He needed to get over to TCC before Brad had a chance to confront Abigail Langley. He had a feeling his best friend was about to make a huge mistake.

Sheila fought back sleep as she fed Sunnie breakfast. She doubted if she and the baby had gotten a good four hours' sleep. The pediatric nurse had been right. Sunnie had slept most of yesterday, and in the middle of the night while most of Royal was sleeping, she had been wide awake and wanting to play.

Of course, Sheila had given in after numerous attempts at rocking her to sleep failed. Now Sunnie looked well-rested. Sheila refused to think about how *she* looked half asleep and yawning every ten minutes. But even lack of sleep could not erase how it felt holding the baby in her arms. And when Sunnie looked up at her and smiled, she knew she would willingly spend an entire week of sleepless nights to see that smile.

And she could make the cutest sounds when she was happy. It must be nice not having any troubles. Then she quickly remembered Sunnie might have troubles after all, if Bradford Price turned out not to be her daddy. Sheila didn't want to think about could happen to her once Social Services took her away and put her into the system.

"We're not going to think about any of that right now,

cupcake," she said, wiping Sunnie's mouth after she'd finished her bottle. "Now it's time for you to burp," she said, gently hoisting the baby onto her shoulder.

Dr. Phillips had referred Dr. Greene, the head pediatrician at Royal Memorial, to the case, and he had called inquiring how Sunnie was doing. He'd also given her helpful hints as to how to help Sunnie formulate a sleeping pattern where she would stay awake during most of the day and sleep longer at night.

A short while later, she placed the baby back in the crib after Sunnie seemed to have found interest in the mobile Zeke had purchased at the last minute while in the store last night. She had almost talked him out of getting it, but now she was glad she hadn't.

Sheila had pulled up a chair to sit there and watch Sunnie for a while, when her phone rang. She immediately picked it up. "Yes?"

"I was waiting to see if you remembered that you had a mother."

Sheila rolled her eyes, fighting the urge to say that she'd also been waiting to see if her mother remembered she had a daughter, but knew it would be a waste of time. The only reason her mother was calling her now was because she was in between husbands and she had a little idle time on her hands.

"Hi, Mom," she said, deciding not to bother addressing her mother's comment. "And how are you?"

"I could be better. Did you ever get that guy's phone number?"

That *guy* her mother was referring to was Dr. Morgan. The last time her mother had come to visit they had gone out to lunch, only to run into one of the surgeons from the hospital. Dr. Morgan was ten years her mother's junior.

Did that mean her mother was considering the possibility of becoming a cougar?

"No. Like I told you then, Dr. Morgan is already in a serious relationship."

Cassie Hopkins chuckled. "Isn't everybody…except you?"

Sheila cringed. Her mother couldn't resist the opportunity to dig. Cassie felt that if she could get five husbands, her only daughter should be able to get at least one. "I don't want a serious relationship, Mom."

"And if you did want one, then what?"

"Then I'd have one." Knowing her mother was about to jump in about Crawford Newman, the last man she wanted to talk about, she quickly changed the subject. "I talked to Lois the other day."

Her mother chuckled again. "And I bet you called her and not the other way around."

"No, in fact, she called me." She didn't have to tell her mother that Lois had called to tell her not to visit her and her family in Atlanta after all. And that was after issuing her an invitation earlier in the year. There was also no need to tell her that Lois had only issued the invitation after hearing about that heroic deed Sheila had performed, which had gotten broadcast nationwide on CNN. She guessed it wasn't important any longer for Lois to let anyone know that she was her sister after all.

Her mother snorted. "Hmmph. I'm surprised. So how is the princess doing and has she said when she plans to share any of the inheritance your father left her with you?"

Sheila knew the fact that her own father had intentionally left her out of his will still bothered her mother, although it no longer bothered her. It had at first because doing such a thing had pretty much proven what she'd always known. Her father hadn't wanted her. Regardless of the fact that he ended up despising her mother, that should not have had any bearing on his relationship with his daughter. But Baron Hopkins hadn't seen things that way. He saw her as an extension of her mother, and if you hated the mother then you automatically hated the child.

Lois, on the other hand, had indeed been her father's princess. The only child from the first wife whom he had adored, he hadn't been quite ready for the likes of Cassie. Things probably wouldn't have been so bad if Baron hadn't discovered her mother was having an affair with one of his business partners—a man who later became husband number two for Cassie. Then there was the question of whether Sheila was even his child, although she looked more like him than Lois did.

She was able to get her mother off the phone when Cassie had a call come through from some man. It was the story of her mother's life and the failed fairy tale for hers. She got out of the chair and moved over to the crib. Sunnie was trying to go to sleep. Sheila would have just loved to let her, but she knew if she were to sleep now that would mean another sleepless night.

"Oh, no you don't, sweetie pie," she said, getting the baby out of bed. "You and I are going to play for a while. I plan on keeping you up as much as possible today."

Sunnie gurgled and smiled sleepy hazel eyes up at her. "I know how you feel, trust me. I want to sleep, too. Hopefully, if this works, we'll both get to sleep tonight," Sheila said softy, rubbing the baby's fingers, reveling in just how soft her skin was.

Holding the baby gently in her arms, she headed downstairs.

* * *

Zeke walked down the hall of the TCC's clubhouse to one of the meeting rooms. The Texas Cattlemen's motto, which was clearly on display on a plaque in the main room here, said, Leadership, Justice and Peace. He heard loud angry voices and recognized Brad's and knew the female one belonged to Abigail. He wondered if they'd forgotten about the peace wording of the slogan.

"And just what are you accusing me of, Brad?"

"You're too intelligent to play dumb, Abigail. I know you're the one who arranged to have that baby left with a note claiming it's mine, when you know good and well it's not."

"What! How can you accuse me of such a thing?"

"Easily. You want to be the TCC's next president."

"And you think I'll go so far as to use a baby? A precious little baby to show you up?"

Zeke cringed. He could actually hear Abigail's voice breaking. Hell, it sounded as if the woman was crying. He paused outside the door.

"Dang, Abigail, I didn't mean to make you cry, for Pete's sake."

"Well, how could you accuse me of something like that? I love babies. And that little girl was abandoned. I had nothing to do with it, Brad. You've got to believe me."

Zeke inhaled deeply. The woman was downright bawling now. Brad had really gone and done it now.

"I'm sorry, Abby. I see that I was wrong. I didn't mean to get you so upset. I'm sorry."

"You should be. And to prove I'm not behind it," she said, still crying, *"I suggest we suspend campaigning for the election until the case is solved."*

"And you'll go along with doing that?"

"Of course. We're talking about a baby, Brad, and her welfare comes first."

"I agree," Brad said. *"Thanks, Abby. And again I'm sorry for accusing you earlier."*

Zeke thought it was time for him to make his entrance before Brad made a bigger mess of things. At least he'd had the sense to apologize to the woman. He opened the door and stopped. Brad was standing in the middle of the room holding a still-weeping Abigail in his arms.

For a moment Zeke thought he should tiptoe back out and was about to do just that, when they both glanced over at him. And as if embarrassed at being caught in such an embrace, the two quickly jumped part.

Zeke placed his hands in the pockets of his jeans and smiled at the pair. "Brad. Abigail. Does this mean the two of you are no longer at war?"

A short while later Zeke was getting back in his car thinking that he hadn't needed to put out the fire after all. Brad and Abigail were a long way from being best friends, but at least it seemed as if they'd initiated a truce. If he hadn't been a victim of abandonment himself, he would think something good had at least resulted from Sunnie's appearance.

Sunnie.

He shook his head. Sheila had deemed the baby be called Sunnie for the time being, and everyone had pretty much fallen in line with her request. He had refrained from calling her earlier just in case she and the baby were sleeping in late. But now it was close to two in the afternoon. Surely they were up by now. While she had been upstairs taking a shower last night, he had opened her refrigerator to grab another beer and noticed hers was barer than his. That meant, also like him, she must eat out a lot. Chances were she wouldn't want to take the baby out, so the least he could do would be to be a good guy and stop somewhere, buy something for her to eat and take it to her.

While at the TCC he had checked and nothing had gotten caught on the video camera other than a woman's hand placing the baby on the doorstep. Whoever had done it seemed to have known just where the cameras were located, which meant the culprit was someone familiar with the grounds of the club. Could it have been an inside job? At least they knew they could erase Abigail off the list. She had been in a meeting when the baby had been dropped off.

Besides, to say Abigail Langley had gotten emotional as a result of Brad's accusation was an understatement. He couldn't help wondering why. He knew she was a widow. Had she lost a baby at some point while she'd been married? He'd been tempted to ask Brad but figured knowing his and Abigail's history, he would probably be the last to know. He'd heard from more than one source that the two of them had been butting heads since they were kids.

After buckling his seat belt he turned his car's ignition and eased out the parking lot, wondering what type of meal Sheila might have a taste for. Still not wanting to disturb her and the baby, he smiled, thinking, when in doubt, get pizza.

Sheila cocked one eye open as she gazed over at Sunnie, who was back in the crib toying with her mobile again. She sighed, not sure how long she would be able to stay awake. It had been almost eighteen hours now.

She'd done doubles at the hospital before, but at least she'd gotten a power nap in between. She didn't know babies had so much energy. She thought of closing her eyes for a second, but figured there was no way for her to do something like that. Mothers didn't sleep while their babies were awake, did they?

She had tried everything and refused to drink another cup of coffee. The only good thing was that if she continued to keep Sunnie awake, that meant when they both went to sleep, hopefully, it would be through the night. She glanced around the room, liking how it looked and hoped Sunnie liked it as well.

Zeke had been such a sweetheart to help her put the baby equipment together and hang pictures on the wall. Although he hadn't asked, he had to have been wondering why she was going overboard for a baby that would be in her care for only two weeks. She was glad he hadn't asked because she would not have known what to tell him.

She tried to ignore the growling of her stomach and the fact that other than toast, coffee and an apple, she hadn't eaten anything else that day. She didn't want to take her eyes off the baby for even a minute.

She nearly jumped when she heard the sound of the doorbell. She glanced at the Big Bird clock she'd hung on the wall. It was close to four in the afternoon. She moved over to the window and glanced down and saw the two-seater sports car in her driveway and knew who it belonged to. What was Zeke doing back? They had exchanged numbers last night, merely as a courtesy. She really hadn't expected to see him again any time soon.

She immediately thought about the kiss they'd shared...not that she hadn't thought about it several times that day already. That was the kind of kiss a girl would want to tell somebody about. Like a girlfriend. She'd thought about calling Jill then had changed her mind. On second thought, maybe it was the kind of kiss a girl should keep to herself.

The doorbell sounded again. Knowing she probably looked a mess and, at the moment, not caring since she hadn't anticipated any visitors, she walked over to the bed and picked up the baby. "Come on, Sunnie. Looks like we have company."

Zeke was just about to turn to leave, when the door opened. All it took was one look at Sheila to know she'd had a rough night and an even rougher day. Sunnie, on the other hand, looked happy and well-rested.

"Hey, you okay?" he asked Sheila when she stepped aside to let him in. And he figured the only reason she'd done that was because of the pizza boxes he was carrying.

"I'm fine." She eyed the pizza box. "And I hope you brought that to share. I've barely eaten all day."

"Yes, I brought it to share," he said, heading for the kitchen. "The kid wore you out today?"

"And last night," she said, following on his heels. "I talked to the pediatrician about her not sleeping through the night and he suggested I try to keep her awake today. That means staying awake myself."

He stopped and she almost walked into the back of him. He turned inquisitive dark eyes on her. "Sunnie hasn't taken a nap at all today?"

"No. Like I said, I'm keeping her awake so we can both sleep tonight."

He found that interesting for some reason. "When do babies usually develop a better sleep pattern?"

"It depends. Usually they would have by now. But we

don't know Sunnie's history. Her life might have been so unstable she hadn't gotten adjusted to anything." She glanced at the baby. "I hate talking about her like she isn't here."

Zeke laughed. "It's not as if she can understand anything you've said."

He shook his head. Sheila had to be pretty tired to even concern herself with anything like that. He glanced around the kitchen. It was still neat as a pin, but baby bottles lined the counter as well as a number of other baby items. It was obvious that a baby was in residence.

"Why did you stop by?" she asked.

He glanced back at her. Her eyes looked tired, almost dead on her feet. Her hair was tied back in a ponytail and she wasn't wearing any makeup. But he thought she looked good. "To check on the two of you. And I figured you probably hadn't had a chance to cook anything," he said, deciding not to mention he'd noticed last night she hadn't had anything to cook.

"So I decided I would be nice and stop and grab something for you," he said, placing the pizza boxes on the table. He opened one of them.

"Oh, that smells so good. Thank you."

He chuckled. "I've gotten pizza from this place before and it is good. And you're welcome. Do you want to lay her down while you dig in?"

She looked down at Sunnie and then back at him. "Lay her down?"

"Yes, like in that crib I put together for her last night."

"But…she'll be all alone."

He frowned. "Yes, but I hooked up that baby monitor last night so you could hear her. Haven't you tried it out?"

"Yes, but I like watching her."

He nodded slowly. "Why? I can imagine you being fascinated by her since you admitted yesterday that you've never kept a baby before, but why the obsession? You're a nurse. Haven't you worked in the nursery before?"

"Of course, but this is different. This is my home and Sunnie is in my care. I don't want anything to happen to her."

He could tell by her tone that she was getting a little defensive, so he decided to back off a bit, table it for later. And there would definitely be a later, because she wouldn't be much use to Sunnie or anybody if she wore herself out. "Fine, sit down and I'll go get that extra car seat. You can place her in it while you eat."

A short while later they were sitting at her kitchen table with Sunnie sitting in the car seat on the floor between them. She was moving her hands to and fro while making sounds. She seemed like such a happy baby. Totally different from the baby that had been screaming up a storm yesterday. Every once in a while she would raise her hazel eyes to stare at them. Mainly at him. It was as if she was trying to figure him out. Determine if he was safe.

Zeke glanced over at Sheila. She had eaten a couple slices of pizza along with the bag salad he'd bought. Every so often she would yawn, apologize and then yawn again. She needed to get some sleep; otherwise, she would fall on her face at any minute.

"Thanks for the pizza, Zeke. Not only are you nice, but you're thoughtful."

He leaned back in his chair. "You're welcome." He paused for a moment. "I got a folder with stuff out there in my car that I need to go over. I can do it here just as well as anywhere else."

Her forehead furrowed as if confused. "But why would you want to?"

He smiled. "That way I can watch Sunnie."

She still looked confused.

"Look, Sheila. It's obvious that you're tired. Probably ready to pass out. You can go upstairs and take a nap while I keep an eye on the baby."

"But why would you want to do something like that?"

He chuckled. She asked a lot of questions. Unfortunately for him they were questions he truly couldn't answer. Why had he made such an offer? He really wasn't sure. All he knew was that he liked being around her and wasn't ready to leave yet.

When he didn't give her an answer quick enough, she narrowed her gaze. "You think I can't handle things, don't you? You think I've taken on more than I can chew by agreeing to be Sunnie's temporary foster parent. You think—"

Before she could finish her next words, he was out of the chair, had eased around the baby and had pulled Sheila into his arms. "Right now I think you're talking too damn much." And then he kissed her.

For some reason he needed to do this, he thought as his mouth took possession of hers. And the instant their mouths touched, he felt energized in a way he'd never felt before. Sexually energized. His tongue slid between her parted lips and immediately began tangling with hers. What was there about kissing her that was so mind-blowing, so arousing, so threatening to his senses?

This kind of mouth interaction with her was stirring things inside him he'd tried to keep at bay with other women. How could she rouse them so effortlessly? So deeply and so thoroughly? And why did she feel so damn good in his arms? Even better today than yesterday.

Yesterday there had been that element of surprise on both their parts. It was still there today, but surprise was being smothered by heat of the most erotic kind.

And it was heat he could barely handle. Not sure that he could manage. But it was heat that he was definitely enjoying. And then there was something else trying to creep into the mix. Emotions. Emotions he wasn't accustomed to. He had thought of her all day. Why? Usually for him it had always been out of sight and out of mind. But not with Sheila. The woman was unforgettable. She was temptation he couldn't resist.

He felt a touch on his leg and reluctantly released Sheila's mouth to glance down. Hazel eyes were staring up at him. Sunnie had grabbed hold of his pant leg. He couldn't help chuckling. At five months old the kid was seeing too much. If she hadn't gotten his attention, he'd probably still be kissing Sheila.

He shifted his gaze from the baby back to the woman he was still holding in his arms. She was about to step back, so he tightened his hold around her waist. "I'm going out to my car and get my briefcase. When I come back inside you're going to go up those stairs and get some rest. I'll handle Sunnie."

"But—"

"No buts. No questions. I'll take good care of her. I promise."

"She might cry the entire time"

"If she cries I'll deal with it." He then walked out of the kitchen.

Sheila couldn't stop her smile when Zeke walked out. She glanced down at Sunnie. "He's kind of bossy, isn't he?" She touched her lips. "And he's a darn good kisser."

She sighed deeply. "Not that you needed to know that. Not that you needed to see us lock lips, either."

She then moved around the kitchen as she cleared off the table. She was standing at the sink when Zeke returned with his briefcase. "How long do you plan to be here?" she asked him.

"For as long as you need to rest."

She nodded. "I'll be fine in a couple of hours. Will you wake me?"

Zeke stared at her, fully aware she had no idea of what she was asking of him. Seeing her in bed, under the covers or on top of the covers, would not be a good idea. At least she hadn't reminded him that she'd told him not to kiss her again. But what could she say, when she had kissed him back?

"I won't wake you, Sheila. You have to wake up on your own."

She frowned. "But Sunnie will need a bath later."

"And she'll get one, with or without you. For your information I do know a little about kids."

She looked surprised. "You do?"

"Yes. I was raised by my aunt and she has a daughter with twins. They consider me their uncle and I've kept them before."

"Both?"

"Yes, and at the same time. It was a piece of cake." Okay, he had exaggerated some. There was no need to tell her that they had almost totally wrecked his place by the time their parents had returned.

"How old are they?"

"Now they're four. The first time I kept them they were barely one."

She nodded. "They live in Austin?"

"No. New Orleans."

"So you're not a Texan by birth?"

He wondered why all the questions again. He had made a mistake when he mentioned Alicia and the twins. "According to my birth certificate, I am a Texan by birth. My aunt who raised me lives in New Orleans. I returned to Texas when I attended UT in Austin."

He had told her enough and, when she opened her mouth to say something more, he placed his hand over it. Better his hand than his mouth. "No more questions. Now, off to bed."

She glanced down at the baby when he removed his hand from her mouth. "Are you sure you want to handle her?"

"Positive. Now, go."

She hesitated for a minute and then drew in a deep breath before leaving the kitchen. He glanced down at Sunnie, whose eyes had followed Sheila from the room. Then those same hazel eyes latched on to him almost in an accusatory stare. Her lips began trembling and he had an idea what was coming next. When she let out a wail, he bent down and picked up the car seat and set it on the table.

"Shh, little one. Sheila needs her rest. Come on, I'm not that bad. She likes me. I kissed her. Get over it."

When her crying suddenly slowed to a low whimper, he wondered if perhaps this kid did understand.

Five

Something—Sheila wasn't sure exactly what— woke her up, and her gaze immediately went to the clock on the nightstand: 7:00 p.m. She quickly slid out of bed and raced down the stairs then halted at the last step. There, stretched out on the sofa was Zeke with Sunnie on his chest. They were both asleep and, since the baby was wearing one of the cute pj sets they'd purchased yesterday, it was obvious he'd given her a bath. In fact, the air was filled with the fragrance of baby oil mixed with baby powder. She liked the smell.

She wished she had a camera to take a picture. This was definitely a Kodak moment. She slowly tiptoed to the chair across from the sofa and sat down. Even while sleeping, Zeke was handsome, and his long lashes almost fanned his upper cheeks. He didn't snore. Crawford snored something awful. Another comparison of the two men.

She wondered if he'd ever dumped a woman the

way Crawford had dumped her. Good old Crawford, the traveling salesman, who spent a lot of time on the road…and as she later found out while he'd been on the road, in other women's beds. She remembered the time she would anxiously await his long-distance calls and how she would feel when she didn't get them. How lonely she would be when she didn't hear from him for days.

And she would never forget that day when he did show back up, just to let her know he was marrying someone else. A woman he'd met while out peddling his medical supplies. He had wanted her to get on with her life because he had gotten on with his. She took his advice. Needing to leave Dallas, the next time an opportunity came for a transfer to another hospital, she had taken it.

She continued to stare at Zeke and wondered what his story was. He'd told her bits and pieces and she figured that was all she would get. So far he hadn't mentioned anything about a mother. His comment yesterday pretty much sealed the fact he hadn't known his father. And from what he'd told her today, his aunt in New Orleans had raised him. Had his mother died? She drew in a deep breath, thinking it really wasn't any of her business. Still, she couldn't help being curious about the hunk stretched out on her sofa. The man who had kissed her twice. The man who'd literally knocked sense right out of her brain.

And that wasn't good. That meant it was time for him to leave. Yesterday she had appreciated his help in shopping with her for baby items. Today she appreciated the pizza. There couldn't be a tomorrow.

Easing out of the chair, she crossed the room and gently shook him awake. She sucked in a deep breath when his eyes snapped open and his beautiful dark eyes stared up at her. Pinned her to the spot where she was standing. They didn't say anything but stared at each other for the longest time. She felt his stare as if his gaze was a physical caress.

And while he stared at her, she remembered things. She remembered how good his mouth felt on hers. How delicious his tongue tasted in her mouth. How his tongue would slide from side to side while driving her to the brink of madness. It made her wonder just what else that tongue was capable of doing.

She blushed and she knew he'd noticed because his gaze darkened. "What were you thinking just now?"

Did he really expect her to tell him? Fat chance! Some things he was better off not knowing and that was definitely one of them. "I was thinking that it's time for me to put Sunnie to bed."

"I doubt that would have made you blush."

She doubted it, too, but she would never admit to it. Instead of responding to what he'd said, she reached for Sunnie. "I'm taking her upstairs and putting her to bed." Once she had the baby cradled in her arms, she walked off.

When she had gone up the stairs, Zeke eased into a sitting position and rubbed his hands down his face. Surprisingly, he'd gotten a lot of work done. Sunnie had sat in her car seat and stared at him the entire time, evidently fascinated by the shifting of the papers and the sight of him working on his laptop computer. He figured the bright colors that had occasionally flashed across the screen had fascinated her.

He stood and went back into the kitchen. There was no doubt in his mind that when Sheila returned she would expect him to be packed up and ready to go. He would not disappoint her. Although he would love to hang around, he needed to haul it. There was too much attraction between them. Way too much chemistry. When they had gazed into each other's eyes, the air had become charged. She had become breathless. So had he. That wasn't good.

All there was supposed to be between them was business. Where was his hard-and-fast rule never to mix business with pleasure? It had taken a hard nosedive the first time he'd kissed her. And if that hadn't been bad enough, he'd kissed her again. What had come over him? He knew the answer without thinking—lust of the most intense kind.

By the time he clicked his briefcase closed, he heard Sheila come back downstairs, and when she walked into the kitchen he had it in his hand. "Walk me to the door," he said softly, wondering why he'd asked her to do so when he knew the way out.

"Okay."

She silently walked beside him and when they got to the door, she reached out to open it, but he took her hand, brought it to his lips and kissed it. "I left my card on the table. Call me if you need anything. Otherwise, this was my last time coming by."

She nodded and didn't ask why. He knew she understood. They were deeply attracted to each other and if they hung around each other for long, that attraction would heat up and lead to something else. Something that he knew neither of them wanted to tangle with right now.

"Thanks for everything, Zeke. I feel rested."

He smiled. "But you can always use more. She'll probably sleep through the night, but she'll be active in the morning. That little girl has a lot of energy."

Sheila chuckled. "So you noticed."

"Oh, yeah, I noticed. But she's a good kid."

"Yes, and I still can't believe someone abandoned her."

"It happens, Sheila. Even to good kids."

He brushed a kiss across her lips. "Go back to bed."

Then he opened the door and walked out.

Zeke forced himself to keep moving and not look back. He opened the car door and sat there a moment, fighting the temptation to get out of his car, walk right back up to her door and knock on it. When she answered it, he would kiss her senseless before she could say a single word. He would then sweep her off her feet and take her up to her bedroom and stretch her out on it, undress her and then make love to her.

He leaned back against the headrest and closed his eyes. How had it moved from kissing to thoughts of making love to her? *Easily, Travers,* his mind screamed. She's a beauty. She's hot. And you enjoy her mouth too damn much.

He took a deep breath and then exhaled slowly. He would be doing the right thing by staying away. Besides, it wasn't as though he didn't have anything to do. He had several people to interview tomorrow, including several TCC members who wanted to talk to him. One of them had called tonight requesting the meeting and he wondered what it would be about.

He turned the key in the ignition and backed out the driveway. He looked at the house one last time before doing so. All the lights were off downstairs. His gaze traveled to her bedroom window. The light was on there. He wondered what she was doing. Probably getting ready for bed.

A bed he wished he could join her in.

* * *

Sheila checked on Sunnie one more time before going into her bathroom to take a shower. She felt heat rush to her cheeks when she remembered waking Zeke earlier. The man had a way of looking at her that could turn her bones into mush.

A short while later after taking a shower and toweling dry her body, she slid into a pair of pajamas. She checked on Sunnie one last time and also made sure the monitor was set so she could hear her if she was to awaken. Zeke was convinced the baby would sleep through the night.

She drew in a deep breath knowing he'd told her he wouldn't be back. And she knew it was for the best. She would miss him. His appearance at her door tonight had been a surprise. But he had a way of making himself useful and she liked that. Crawford hadn't been handy with tools. He used to tell her he worked too hard to do anything other than what was required of him at his job. Not even taking out the trash.

And she had put up with it because she hadn't wanted to be alone.

Moving here was her first accomplishment. It had been a city where she hadn't known anybody. A city where she would be alone. Go figure. She had gotten used to it and now Zeke had invaded her space. So had Sunnie. The latter was a welcome invasion; the former wasn't.

As she slid into bed and drew the covers around her, she closed her eyes and ran her tongue around her mouth. Even after brushing her teeth she could still taste Zeke. It was as if his flavor was embedded in her mouth. She liked it. She would savor it because it wouldn't happen again.

* * *

The next day, Zeke leaned back on the table and studied the two men sitting before him and tried digesting their admissions.

"So the two of you are saying that you also received blackmail letters?"

Rali Tariq and Arthur Moran, well-known wealthy businessmen and longtime members of the TCC, nodded. Then Rali spoke up. "Although I was innocent of what the person was accusing me of, I was afraid to go to the authorities."

"Same here," Arthur said. "I was hoping the person would eventually go away when I didn't acknowledge the letters. It was only when I found out about the blackmailing scheme concerning Bradford that I figured I needed to come forward."

"That's the reason I'm here, as well," Rali added.

Zeke nodded. What the two men had just shared with him certainly brought a lot to light. It meant the blackmailer hadn't just targeted Brad, but had set his or her mark on other innocent, unsuspecting TCC members, as well. That made him wonder whether the individual was targeting TCC members because they were known to be wealthy or if there was a personal vendetta the authorities needed to be concerned with.

"Did you bring the letters with you?"

"Yes."

Both men handed him their letters. He placed them on the table and then pulled out one of the ones Brad had received. It was obvious they had been written by the same person.

"They looked the same," Rali said, looking over Zeke's shoulder at all three letters.

Arthur nodded in agreement.

"Yes, it appears that one person wrote them all," Zeke replied. "But the question is why did he carry out his threat against Brad but not on you two?"

He could tell by the men's expressions that they didn't have a clue. "Well, at least I'm finally getting pieces to the puzzle. I appreciate the two of you coming forward. It will help in clearing Brad's name. Now all we have to do is wait for the results of the paternity test."

An hour later he met Brad for lunch at Claire's Restaurant, an upscale establishment in downtown Royal that served delicious food. A smile curved Brad's lips after hearing about Zeke's meeting with Rali and Arthur.

"Then that should settle things," he said, cutting into the steak on his plate. "If Rali and Arthur received blackmail letters, that proves there's a conspiracy against members of the TCC. There probably are others who aren't coming forward like Rali and Arthur."

Zeke took a sip of his wine. "Possibly. But you are the only one who he or she carried out the threat with. Why you and not one of the others? Hell, Rali is the son of a sheikh. I would think they would have stuck it to him real good. So we still aren't out of the woods. There's something about the whole setup that bothers me."

He studied Brad for a moment. "Did you and Abigail Langley clear things up?"

Brad met his gaze. "If you're asking if I think she's still involved then the answer is no. Now I wished I hadn't approached her with my accusations."

A smile touched Zeke's lips. "I hate to say I told you so, but I did tell you so."

"I know. I know. But Abigail and I have been bad news for years."

"Yeah, but someone getting on your bad side is one thing, Brad. Accusing someone, especially a woman, of having anything to do with abandoning a child is another."

Brad held his gaze for the longest time. "And you of all people should know, right?"

Zeke nodded. "Yes, I should know."

Zeke took another sip of his wine. As his best friend, Brad was one of the few people who knew his history. Brad knew how Zeke's mother had abandoned him. Not on a doorstep, but in the care of his aunt. Although his aunt had been a godsend, he'd felt abandoned those early years. Alone. Discarded. Thrown away. No longer wanted.

It had taken years for him to get beyond those childhood feelings. But he would be the first to admit those childhood feelings had subsequently become adult hang-ups. That was one of the reasons he only engaged in casual affairs. He wouldn't let anyone walk out on him again. He would be the one doing the walking.

"Abigail certainly took my accusation hard," Brad said, breaking into Zeke's thoughts. "I've known her since we were kids and I've never known her to be anything but tough as nails. Seeing her break down like that really got to me."

"I could tell. You seemed to be holding her pretty tightly when I walked in."

He chuckled at the blush that appeared in Brad's features. "Well, what else was I supposed to do?" Brad asked. "Especially since I was the reason she'd gotten upset in the first place. I'm going to have to watch what I say around her."

Especially if it's about babies, Zeke thought, deciding not to say the words out loud. If Brad wasn't concerned with the reason the woman fell to pieces then he wouldn't be concerned with it, either. Besides, he had enough on his plate.

"So how's the baby?" Brad asked, breaking into his thoughts yet again.

"Sunnie?"

"Yes."

He leaned back in his chair as he thought about how she had wet him up pretty good when he'd given her a bath. He'd had to throw his shirt into Sheila's dryer. "She's fine. I checked on her yesterday."

"And the woman that's taking care of her. That nurse. She's doing a pretty good job?"

Zeke thought about Sheila. Hell, he'd thought about her a lot today, whether he had wanted to or not. "Yes, she's doing a pretty good job."

"Well, I hope the results from the paternity test come up quickly enough for her sake."

Zeke lifted a brow. "Why for her sake?"

"I would hate for your nurse to get too attached to the baby."

Zeke nodded. He would hate for "his" nurse to get too attached to Sunnie, as well.

"She is such a cutie," Summer Franklin said as she held Sunnie in her arms. Surprisingly, Sunnie hadn't cried when Summer had taken her out of Sheila's arms. She was too fascinated with Summer's dangling earrings to care.

Sheila liked Summer. She was one of the few people she felt she could let her guard down around. Because Sheila had a tendency to work all the time, this was the first time she'd seen Summer in weeks.

"Yes, she is a cutie," Sheila said. "I can't imagine anyone abandoning her like that."

"Me, neither. But you better believe Zeke's going to get to the bottom of it. I'm glad Darius brought him on as a partner. My husband was working himself to death solving cases. Now he has help."

Sheila nodded, wondering how much Summer knew about Zeke, but didn't want to ask for fear her friend would wonder why.

Although Sunnie had slept through the night, she herself, on the other hand, had not. Every time she closed her eyes she had seen Zeke, looking tall, dark, handsome and fine as any man had a right to be. Then she also saw another image of him. The one sleeping peacefully on the sofa with the baby lying on his chest. She wondered if he would marry and have children one day. She had a feeling he would make a great dad just from his interaction with Sunnie.

"Oops, I think she's ready to return to you now," Summer said, breaking her thoughts. She smiled when she saw Sunnie lift her little hands to reach out for her, making her feel special. Wanted. Needed.

"You're good with her, Sheila."

She glanced over at Summer and smiled. "Thanks."

"I wonder who her real parents are."

"I wondered that as well. But I'm sure Zeke is going to find out," Sheila said.

Summer chuckled. "I believe that, as well. Zeke comes across as a man who's good at what he does."

Sheila held the baby up to hide the blush on her face. She knew for a fact that Zeke was good at what he did, especially when it came to kissing a woman.

Zeke let himself inside his home with a bunch of papers in his hand, closing the door behind him with the heel of his shoe. He'd been busy today.

He dropped the papers on his dining room table and headed straight to the kitchen to grab a beer out of the refrigerator. He took a huge gulp and then let out a deep breath. He'd needed that. That satisfied his thirst. Now if he could satisfy his hunger for Sheila Hopkins the same way...

Twice he had thought of dropping by her place and twice he had remembered why he could not do that. He had no reason to see her again until it was time to open the paternity test results. Considering what he'd discovered with those other two TCC members, he felt confident that the test would prove there was no biological link between Brad and Sunnie. But he was just as determined to discover whose baby she was. What person would abandon their child to make them a part of some extortion scheme? It was crazy. And sick. And he intended to determine who would do such a thing and make sure the authorities threw the book at them as hard as they could.

His thoughts shifted back to Sheila as he moved from the kitchen to the dining room. He had a lot of work to do and intended to get down to business. But he couldn't get out of his mind how he had opened his eyes while stretched out on her sofa only to find her staring down at him. If he hadn't had the baby sleeping on his chest, he would have been tempted to reach out and pull her down on the sofa with him. And he would have taken her mouth the way he wanted to do. Why was he torturing himself by thinking of something he was better off not having?

He drew in a deep breath, knowing he needed to put Sheila out of his mind. He had been going through various reports when the phone rang. He grinned when he saw it was Darius.

"Homesick, Darius?" he asked into the phone, and heard a resounding chuckle.

"Of course. I'm not missing you though. It's my wife. I'm trying to talk Summer into catching a plane and joining me here—especially since there's a hurricane too close to you guys for comfort, but they're shorthanded at the shelter."

"So I heard."

"She also told me about the abandoned baby. How's that going?"

He took the next few minutes to bring Darius up to date. "I know Bradford Price and if he says the baby isn't his then it's not his," Darius said. "He has no reason to lie about it."

"I know, that's why I intend to expose the jerk who's out to ruin Brad's good name," Zeke said.

Six

Three days later Sheila sat glued to her television listening to the weather report. It was the last month of hurricane season and wouldn't you know it…Hurricane Spencer was up to no good out in the gulf. Forecasters were advising everyone to take necessary precautions by stocking up on the essentials just in case the storm changed course. Now Sheila had Sunnie to worry about, and that meant making sure she had enough of everything—especially disposable diapers, formula and purified water in case the power went out.

Sunnie had pretty much settled down and was sleeping through the night. And they were both getting into a great routine. During the day Sheila had fun entertaining the baby by taking her to the park and other kid-friendly places. She enjoyed pushing Sunnie around in the stroller. Sunnie would still cry on occasion when others held her, but once she would glance around and lock her gaze on Sheila, she was fine.

Sheila had put the baby to bed a short while ago and was ready to go herself if only she was sleepy. Over the past couple of days she'd had several visitors. In addition to Summer and Jill, Dr. Greene had stopped by to check on the baby and Ms. Talbert from Social Services had visited, as well. Ms. Talbert had praised her for volunteering to care for Sunnie and indicated that considering the baby was both healthy and happy, she was doing a great job. The woman had further indicated there was a possibility the results of the paternity test might come in earlier than the two weeks anticipated. Instead of jumping for joy at the news, Sheila had found herself hoping that would not be the case. She had been looking forward to her two weeks with Sunnie.

She heard a branch hit the window and jumped. It had been windy all day and now it seemed it was getting windier. Forecasters predicted the hurricane would make landfall sometime after midnight. They predicted that Royal would be spared the worst of it.

She glanced around the room where she had already set out candles. The lights had been blinking all day; she hoped she didn't lose power, but had to be prepared if she did.

She was halfway up the stairs when the house suddenly went black.

The winds have increased and we have reports of power outages in certain sections of Royal, including the Meadowland and LeBaron areas. Officials are working hard to restore power to these homes and hope to do so within the next few hours…

Zeke was stretched out on the sofa with his eyes

closed, but the announcement that had just blared from the television made him snap them open. He then slid into a sitting position. Sheila lived in the Meadowland area.

He knew he had no reason to be concerned. Hopefully, like everyone else, she had anticipated the possibility of a power failure and was prepared. But what if she wasn't? What if she was across town sitting on her sofa holding the baby in the dark?

Standing, he rubbed a hand down his face. It had been four days since he'd seen or talked to her. Four days, while working on clearing Brad's name, of trying hard to push thoughts of her to the back of his mind. He'd failed often, when no matter what he was working on, his thoughts drifted back to her.

What was there about a woman when a man couldn't get her out of his mind? When he would think of her during his every waking moment and wake up in the middle of the night with thoughts of her when he should be sleeping?

Zeke stretched his body before grabbing his keys off the table. Pushing aside the thought that he was making a mistake by rushing off to check on the very woman he'd sworn to stay away from, he quickly walked toward the door, grabbing a jacket and his Stetson on the way out.

Sheila glanced around the living room. Candles were lit and flashlights strategically placed where she might need them. It was just a little after ten but the wind was still howling outside. When she had looked out the window moments ago, all she could do was stare into darkness. Everything was total black.

She had checked on Sunnie earlier and the baby was

sleeping peacefully, oblivious to what was happening, and that was good. Sunnie had somehow kicked the covers off her pudgy little legs and Sheila had recovered her, gazing down at her while thinking what the future held for such a beautiful little girl.

Sheila left the nursery and walked downstairs. She had the radio on a station that played jazz while occasionally providing updates on the storm. It had stopped raining, but the sound of water dripping off the roof was stirring a feeling inside her that she was all too familiar with—loneliness.

Deciding what she needed was a glass a wine, she was headed to the kitchen when she heard the sound of her cell phone. She quickly picked it up and from caller ID saw it was Zeke.

She felt the thud in her chest at the same time she felt her pulse rate increase. "Yes?"

"I'm at the door."

Taking a deep breath and trying to keep her composure intact, she headed toward the door. The police had asked for cars not to be on the road unless it was absolutely necessary due to dangerous conditions, so why was he here? Did he think she couldn't handle things during a power failure? She was certain Sunnie was his main concern and not her.

She opened the door and her breath caught. He stood there looking both rugged and handsome, dressed in a tan rawhide jacket, Western shirt and jeans and a Stetson on his head. The reflections from the candles played across his features as he gazed at her. "I heard the reports on television. Are you and the baby okay?"

She nodded, at the moment unable to speak. Swallowing deeply, she finally said, "Yes, we're fine."

"That's good. May I come in?"

Their gazes stayed locked and she knew what her response should be. They had agreed there was no reason for him to visit her and Sunnie. But the only thing she could think about at that moment was the loneliness that had been seeping through her body for the past few hours, and that she hadn't seen him in four days. And whether she wanted to admit it or not, she had missed him.

"Please come in." She stepped aside.

Removing his hat, Zeke walked past Sheila and glanced around. Lit candles were practically everywhere, and the scent of jasmine welcomed his nostrils. A blaze was also roaring in the fireplace, which radiated a warm, cozy atmosphere.

"Do you want me to take your jacket?"

He glanced back at her. "Yes. Thanks."

He removed his jacket and handed it to her, along with his hat. He watched as she placed both on the coatrack. She was wearing a pair of gold satin pajamas that looked cute on her.

"I was about to have a glass of wine," she said. "Do you want to join me?"

He could say that he'd only come to check on her and the baby, and because they seem to be okay, he would be going. That might have worked if he hadn't asked to come in…or he hadn't taken off his jacket. "Yes, I'd love to have a glass. Thanks."

"I'll be back in a minute."

He watched her leave and slowly moved toward the fireplace. She seemed to be taking his being there well. A part of him was surprised, considering their agreement, that she hadn't asked him to leave. He was glad she hadn't. He watch the fire blazing in the fireplace while thinking that he hadn't realized just how much he had missed seeing her until she'd opened the door. She looked so damn good and it had taken everything within him not to pull her into his arms and kiss her, the way he'd done those other two times. Hell, he was counting, mainly because there was no way he could ever forget them.

And as he stood there and continued to gaze into the fire, he thought of all the reasons he should grab his jacket and hat and leave before she returned. For starters, he wanted her, which was a good enough reason in itself. And the degree to which he wanted her would be alarming to most. But he had wanted her from the beginning. He had walked into the hospital and seen her standing there holding the baby, and looking like the beautiful woman that she was. He had been stunned at the intensity of the desire that had slammed into him; it had almost toppled him. But he had been able to control it by concentrating on the baby, making Sunnie's care his top priority.

However, he hadn't been able to control himself that day at his place when she had gotten in his face. Nor had he been able to handle things the last time he was here and he'd nearly mauled her mouth off. Being around her was way too risky.

Then why was he here? And why was his heart thumping deep in his chest anticipating her return? At that moment he had little control of what he was feeling; especially because they were emotions he hadn't ever felt before for a woman. If it was just a sexual thing he would be able to handle that. But the problem was that he wasn't sure it was. He definitely wanted her, but there was something about her he didn't understand. There were reasons he couldn't fathom as to why he was so attracted to her. And there was no way he could use

Sunnie as an excuse. Sunnie might be the reason they had initially met, but the baby had nothing to do with him being here now and going through the emotions he was feeling.

"Do you think this bad weather will last long?"

He turned around to face her and wished he hadn't. She had two glasses in her hand and a bottle of wine under her arm. But what really caught his attention was the way the firelight danced across her features, combined with the glow from the candles. She looked like a woman he wanted to make love to. Damn.

She was temptation.

Zeke moved to assist her with the glasses and wine bottle, and the moment their hands touched, he was a goner. Taking both glasses, as well as the wine bottle, from her hands, he placed both on the table. And then he turned back to her, drew her into his arms and lowered his mouth to hers.

Sheila went into his arms willingly, their bodies fusing like metal to magnet. She intended to go with the flow. And boy was she rolling. All over the place.

She could feel his hand in the small of her back that gently pressed her body even closer to his. And she felt him. At the juncture of her thighs. His erection was definitely making its presence known by throbbing hard against her. It was kicking her desire into overdrive. And she could definitely say that was something that had never happened to her before. Since her breakup with Crawford she had kept to herself. Hadn't wanted to date anyone. Preferred not getting involved with any living male.

But being in Zeke's arms felt absolutely perfect. And the way he was mating his mouth with hers was stirring a yearning within her she hadn't been aware she was capable of feeling. And when he finally released her mouth, he let her know he wasn't through with her when his teeth grazed the skin right underneath her right ear, causing shivers to flow through her. And then his teeth moved lower to her collarbone and began sucking gently there.

She tilted her head back and groaned deeply in her throat. What he was doing felt so good and she didn't want him to stop. But he did. Taking her mouth once again.

He loved her taste.

And he couldn't get enough of it, which was why he was eating away at her mouth with a relentless hunger. He was driven by a need that was as primitive as time and as urgent as the desire to breathe. He could feel the rise and fall of her breasts pressed to his chest and could even feel the quivering of her thighs against his.

He hadn't had the time or inclination to get involved with a woman since moving to Royal. Brad's problems meant putting his social life on hold. He had been satisfied with that until Sheila had come along. She had kicked his hormones into gear, made him remember what it felt like to be hard up. But this was different. He'd never wanted a woman to this extreme.

And kissing her wasn't enough.

Keeping his mouth locked to hers, he walked her backward toward the sofa and when they reached it, he lowered her to it. Pulling his mouth away, he took a lick of her swollen lips before saying, "Tell me to stop now if you don't want what I'm about to give you."

She gazed up at him as if weighing his words and his eyes locked with hers. His gaze was practically drowning in the desire he saw in hers. And then he knew that she wanted him as much as he wanted her. But still, he was letting her call the shots. And if she decided in his favor, there was no turning back.

Instead of giving him an answer, she reached up and wrapped her arms around his neck and pulled his mouth back down to hers. He came willingly. Assuaging the hunger they both were feeling. At the same time, his hands were busy, unbuttoning her pajama top with deft fingers.

He pulled back from the kiss to look down at her and his breath caught in his throat. Her breasts were beautiful. Absolutely beautiful. He leaned down close to her ear and whispered, "I want to cherish you with my mouth, Sheila."

No man had ever said such a thing to her, Sheila thought, and immediately closed her eyes and drew in a deep breath when he immediately went for a breast, sucked a hardened nipple between his lips. She could feel her breasts swelling in his mouth. Her stomach clenched and she couldn't help moaning his name. She felt every part of her body stir to life with his touch.

Her response to his actions was instinctive. And when he took the tip of his tongue and began swirling around her nipple, and then grazing that same nipple with the edge of his teeth, she nearly came off the sofa.

She began shivering from the desire rushing through her body and when he moved to the next nipple, she felt every nerve ending in her breast come alive beneath his mouth. This was torture, plain and simple. And with each flick of his tongue she felt a pull, a tingling sensation between her legs.

As if he sensed the ache there, he pulled back slightly

and tugged her pj bottoms down her legs. Then he stared down at the juncture of her thighs when he saw she wasn't wearing panties. He uttered a sound that resembled a growl, and the next thing she knew he had shifted positions and lowered his mouth between her legs.

He went at her as if this had been his intent all along, using the tip of his tongue to stir a fervor within her, widening her thighs to delve deeper. What he was doing to her with his tongue should be outlawed. And he was taking his time, showing no signs that he was in a hurry. He was acting as if he had the entire night and intended to savor and get his fill. And she was helpless to do anything but rock her body against his mouth. The more she rocked, the deeper his tongue seemed to go.

And then she felt it, that first sign that her body was reaching a peak of tremendous pleasure that would seep through her pores, strip her of all conscious thought and swamp her with feelings she had never felt before. She held her breath, almost fighting what was to come, and when it happened she tried pushing his mouth away, but he only locked it onto her more. She threw her head back and moaned as sensation swept through her. She felt good. She felt alive. She felt as though her body no longer belonged to her.

And as the sensations continued to sprint through her, Zeke kept it up, pushing her more over the edge, causing a maelstrom of pleasure to engulf her; pleasure so keen it almost took her breath away. She began reveling in the feelings of contentment, although her body felt drained. It was then that he released her and slowly pulled back. With eyes laden with fulfillment, she watched as he quickly removed his own clothes and sheathed his erection in a condom. And then he returned to her. As if he wanted her body to get used to him, get to know him, he straddled her and gyrated his hips so that the tip of him made circles on her belly, before tracing an erotic path down to the area between her legs.

Sensuous pressure built once again inside her, starting at the base of her neck and escalating down. And when he eased between her womanly folds and slowly entered her, she called his name as his erection throbbed within her to the hilt. It was then that he began moving, thrusting in and out of her like as if this would be the last chance he had to do so, that she could feel her body come apart in the most sensuous way.

He stroked her for everything she was worth and then some, making her realize just what a generous lover he was. She locked her legs around him and he rocked deeper inside her. And then he touched a spot she didn't know existed and just in the nick of time, he lowered his mouth to hers to quell her scream as another orgasm hit.

Then his body bucked inside her several times, and he moaned into her mouth and she knew at that moment that both of them had gone beyond what they'd intended. But they couldn't turn back now even if they wanted to. He kept thrusting inside her, prolonging the orgasm they were sharing, and she knew at that moment this was meant to be. This night. The two of them together this way. There would be no regrets on her part. Only memories of what they were sharing now. Immense pleasure.

Entering Sheila's bedroom, Zeke's gaze touched on every single candle she had lit, bathing her bedroom in a very romantic glow. He had gotten a glimpse of her bedroom before, when he'd been in the room across the hall putting the crib together. Evidently she liked flowers, because her curtains and bedspread had a floral pattern.

He turned back the covers before placing her in the center of the bed. He joined her there and hoped Sunnie slept through the night as Sheila predicted she would. They had made a pit stop by the nursery to check on the baby and found her sleeping in spite of all the winds howling outside.

"Thanks for coming and checking on us," Sheila said, cuddling closer to him. He wrapped her into his arms, liking the feel of having her there. Her back was resting against his chest and her naked bottom nestled close to his groin.

"You don't have to thank me."

She glanced over her shoulder at him. "I don't?"

"No."

She smiled and closed her eyes, shifting her body to settle even more into his. He stayed awake and, lifting up on his elbows, he stared down at her. She was just as beautiful with her eyes closed as she was with them open. He then recalled what Brad had said about Sheila getting attached to Sunnie and could definitely see how that could happen.

He couldn't help wondering how she was going to handle it when Sunnie was taken away. And she would be taken away. Although Sunnie didn't belong to Brad, she did belong to someone. And if no one claimed her, she would eventually become a part of the system.

That was the one thing that had kept him out of trouble as a kid growing up, the fear of that very thing happening to him. Although he now knew his aunt would never have done such a thing, he hadn't known it then and had lived in constant fear that one day, if he did something wrong, his aunt would desert him in the same way his mother had.

But Clarisse Daniels had proven to be a better woman than her younger sister could ever be. A divorcée, which made her a single mother, she had raised both him and Alicia on a teacher's salary. At least child support had kicked in from Alicia's father every month. But neither his mother nor his father had ever contributed a penny to his upbringing. In fact, he'd found out later that his aunt had on several occasions actually given in to his mother's demand for money just to keep her from taking him away.

His father. He hadn't been completely honest with Sheila that day when he'd said he hadn't known his father. Mr. Travers was his father. He might not have known the man while growing up as Ezekiel "Zeke" Daniels, but he certainly knew his identity now. Matthew Travers. One of the richest men in Texas.

It seemed his mother had gotten knocked up by the man who hadn't believed her claim. In a way, considering what Zeke had heard, his father could have been one of two men. His mother hadn't known for certain which one had sired her son. She had gone after the wealthiest. Travers's attorney had talked her out of such foolishness and pretty much told her what would happen if she made her claim public. Evidently she took his threat seriously and he had grown up as Ezekiel Daniels, the son of Kristi Daniels. Father unknown. His birth certificate stated as much.

It was only while in college attending UT that there was a guy on campus who could have been his identical twin by the name of Colin Travers. When the two finally met, their resemblance was so uncanny it was unreal. Even Brad had approached the guy one day thinking it was him.

Zeke was willing to let the issue of their looks drop, but Colin wasn't. He went back to Houston, questioned his father and put together the pieces of what had happened between Matthew Travers and Kristi Daniels many years before, and a year or so before Travers had married Colin's mother.

When Zeke had been summoned to the Travers mansion, it was Brad who'd convinced him to go. It was there that he'd come face-to-face with the man who'd fathered him. The man, who after seeing him, was filled with remorse for not having believed Kristi Daniels's claim. The man who from that moment on intended to right a wrong, and make up to Zeke for all the years he hadn't been there for him. All the years he'd been denied. Abandoned.

He'd also found out that day that in addition to Colin, he had five other younger brothers and a sister. His siblings, along with their mother, Victoria, immediately accepted him as a Travers. But for some reason, Zeke had resisted becoming part of the Travers clan.

He'd always been a loner and preferred things staying that way. Although his siblings still kept in contact with him, especially Colin, who over the years had forged a close relationship with Zeke, he'd kept a distance between him and the old man. But his father was determined, regardless of Zeke's feelings on the matter, to build a relationship with him.

It was Brad and his aunt Clarisse who had been there for him during that difficult and confused time in his life. It was they who convinced him to take the last name his father wanted him to have and wear it proudly.

That's the reason why on his twenty-first birthday, he officially became Ezekiel *Travers*.

That's why he and Brad had such a strong friendship. And that was one of the main reasons his aunt meant the world to him. The first thing he'd done after being successful in his own right through lucrative investments was to buy Aunt Clarisse a house not far from the French Quarter. Alicia and her husband, both attorneys, didn't live too far away. He tried to go visit whenever he could. But now, he couldn't even consider going anywhere until he'd solved this case.

He glanced down at Sheila. And not without Sheila.

He immediately felt a tightening in his stomach. How could he even think something like that? He'd never taken a woman home to meet his family before. There had never been one he'd gotten that attached to, and he didn't plan to start doing so now.

He would be the first to say that tonight he and Sheila had enjoyed each other, but that's as far as things went. It just wasn't in his makeup to go further. Suddenly feeling as though he was suffocating and needed space, he eased away from Sheila and slid out of bed.

Tiptoeing across the hall, he went to where Sunnie was sleeping. She was lying on her stomach and sleeping peacefully. He wasn't sure what kind of future was in store for her, but he hope for her sake things worked out to her benefit.

All he knew was that the woman who'd given birth to the beautiful baby didn't deserve her.

Seven

"You want us to go to your place?" Sheila asked to make sure she'd heard Zeke correctly.

They had awakened to the forecaster's grim news that Hurricane Spencer was still hovering in the gulf. And although Royal was not directly in its path, if the storm did hit land, there would be a lot of wind and rain for the next day or so. The local news media had further indicated that although the electrical company was working around the clock, certain areas of town would remain without power for a while. Meadowland was one of them.

"Yes, I think it would be for the best for now—especially since you don't know when your power will be restored. I have a generator in case the power goes out at my house."

Sheila nibbled on her bottom lip. What he was offering made sense, but she was so used to having her own place, her own stuff. She glanced over at Sunnie, who was sitting in the middle of the kitchen table in her car seat. She had just been fed and was happy. And she hadn't seemed bothered by seeing Zeke. In fact, it seemed as if she smiled when she saw him.

"Sheila?"

"I was just thinking of all the stuff I'd have to pack up and carry with us."

"We can manage. Besides, I have my truck."

How convenient, she thought. She knew his idea made perfect sense, but going over to his place meant leaving her comfort zone. "Sunnie has gotten used to being here," she said.

"I understand, but as long as you're within her sight, she'll be fine."

Sheila nibbled on her bottom lip as she gave her attention back to the baby. Yes, Sunnie would be fine, but she wasn't sure she would be. Waking up in Zeke's arms hadn't been exactly what she'd planned to happen. But it had been so natural. Just like the lovemaking that had followed before they'd heard Sunnie through the monitor that morning.

She had just finished feeding Sunnie when Zeke had dropped what she considered a bomb. She had been thinking how, in a nice way, to suggest they rethink what had happened between them last night and give each other space to do so, when his idea had been just the opposite. Moving her and Sunnie into his house until the storm passed was not giving them space.

Deciding to come out and say what she'd been thinking, she glanced back over at Zeke. He was sitting across the kitchen, straddling a chair. "What about last night?"

He held her gaze. "What about it?"

Sheila's heart thumped hard in her chest. "W-we slept together and we should not have," she stammered, wishing she hadn't been so blunt, but not knowing what else she could have said to broach the subject and let him know her feelings on the matter.

"It was inevitable."

Her eyes widened in surprise at his comeback. "I don't think it was. Why do you?"

"Because I wanted you from the first and I picked up on the vibes that you wanted me, too."

What vibes? "I was attracted to you from the first, I admit that," she said. "But I wasn't sending off vibes."

"Yes, you were."

Had she unconsciously emitted vibes as he claimed? She tried to recall such a time and—

"Remember that day you woke me up when I'd fallen asleep on your sofa?"

She nodded, remembering. They had stared at each other for the longest time. "Yes, I remember."

"You blushed but wouldn't tell me what you were thinking, what was going through your mind to make you do so."

"So you assumed…"

"No, I knew. I think I can read you pretty well."

"You think so?"

"Yes. I can probably guess with certainty the times we've been together when your thoughts of me were sexual."

Could he really? She didn't like that and to hear him say it actually irritated her. "Look, Zeke, I'm not sure about the women you're used to getting involved with, but—"

"But you are different from them," he finished for her. "And I agree you're different in a positive way."

"We've known each other less than a week," she reminded him.

"Yes, but we've shared more in that time than a lot of people share in a lifetime. Especially last night. The connection between us was unreal."

Sheila immediately thought of her friend Emily Burroughs. If she could claim ever having a best friend it would have to be Emily. They had been roommates in college. And she believed they had a special friendship that would have gotten even stronger over the years… if Emily hadn't died. Her friend had died of ovarian cancer at the young age of twenty-three.

Sheila had been with Emily during her final days. Emily hadn't wanted to go to hospice, preferring to die at home in her own bed. And she had wanted Sheila there with her for what they'd known would be their last slumber party. It was then Emily had shared that although she wasn't a virgin, she'd never made out with a guy and felt one gigantic explosion; she'd never heard bells and whistles. Emily had never felt the need to scream. She had died not experiencing any of that. And last night Sheila had encountered everything that Emily hadn't in her lifetime.

"Do you regret last night, Sheila?"

His question intruded into her thoughts and she glanced back over at him, wondering how she could get him to understand that she was a loner. Always had been and probably always would be. She didn't take rejection well, and every time the people she loved the most rejected her, intentionally put distance between them, was a swift blow to her heart.

"No, Zeke, but I've learned over the years not to get attached to people. My mom has been married five times and my sister from my father's first marriage doesn't want to be my sister because my mother caused her father pain."

He frowned. "You didn't have anything to do with that."

She chuckled. "Try telling Lois that. She blames both me and my mother and I was only four when they split."

"Did you talk to your father about it?"

She shook her head. "When Dad left, he never wanted to see me or my mother again. I guess I would have been a reminder of what she did. She cheated on him."

"But it wasn't your fault."

"No, it wasn't," she said, wiping the baby's mouth. "And I grew up believing that one day one of them, hopefully both, would realize that. Neither did. Dad died five years ago. He was a very wealthy man and over the years he did do right by me financially—my mother saw to that. But when he died, he intended to let me know how much I didn't mean to him by leaving Lois everything. I wasn't even mentioned in his will."

She paused a moment, glanced away from him to look out the window as she relived the pain. And then back at him and said, "It's not that I wanted any of his worldly possessions, mind you. It was the principle of the thing. Just acknowledging me in some way as his daughter would have been nice."

Sheila glanced over at Sunnie, who was staring over at her, as if she understood the nature of what she'd said, of what she was sharing with Zeke. She then wondered why she had shared such a thing with him.

Maybe telling him would help him to realize that she could get attached to him, and why she couldn't let that happen.

"So, no, I don't regret last night. It was too beautiful, too earth-shattering and mind-blowing to regret. But I have to be realistic and accept that I don't do involvement very well. I get attached easily. You might want a casual affair, but a part of me would long for something more."

"Something I can't give you," he said gently. The sound of his husky voice floated across the room to her.

"Precisely," she said, nodding her head while thinking that he did understand.

"I could say I won't touch you again, even if we spend time together."

She would have taken his words to heart if at that moment a smile hadn't curved his lips. "Yes, you could say that," she agreed.

"But I'd be lying. Mainly because you are temptation."

"Temptation?" she asked, and couldn't help chuckling at that.

"Yes."

She shook her head. She had been called many things but never temptation. "You can see me in the garden with an apple?"

His eyes seemed to darken. "Yes, and very much naked."

Sensing the change in the tone of his voice—it had gone from a deep husky to a seductive timbre—she decided maybe they needed to change the subject. "How is the case coming?"

Zeke recognized her ploy to change the subject. She had reservations about sleeping with him again and he could understand that. But what she needed to understand was that there were some things a man and a woman could not ignore. Blatant sexual chemistry was one of them—it pretty much headed the list. And that was what existed between them, connecting more than just the dots.

Making love to her and waking up with her last night had affected him in a way he didn't quite comprehend, and because he didn't understand it, he wasn't ready, or willing, to walk away.

And when she'd tried explaining to him why she preferred not getting involved in a relationship for fear of getting attached, it was like hearing his own personal reservations. He had this apprehension of letting any woman get too close for fear she would do to him the very thing his mother had done. Walk away and leave him high and dry…and take his heart with her. He'd been there and done that and would never go that way again.

She was protecting her heart the way he was protecting his, so they were on the same page there. Maybe he should tell her that. Then maybe he shouldn't. Opening himself up to anyone wasn't one of his strong points. He was a private person. Few people got to know the real Ezekiel Travers. Brad and his other college friend and Royal resident, Christopher Richards, knew the real Zeke. And he felt comfortable being himself around Darius Franklin. Over the past year, while working through the terms of their partnership, he had gotten to know Darius, a man he highly respected. And he thought Summer was the perfect wife for Darius.

One night over dinner Darius and Summer had shared their story. How things had ended for them due to a friend's betrayal. They had gotten reunited seven years later and intended never to let anything or anyone come between them again. He was convinced that kind of love could only be found by a few people. He would never think about holding out for a love that sure and pure for himself.

He decided to go with Sheila's change of subject. "The case is coming along. I'm still following up possible leads."

He told her about his conversations with Rali Tariq and Arthur Moran and their admissions that they too had received blackmail letters.

"You mean they received blackmail letters claiming they fathered babies, as well?"

"Not exactly. Both are married men and they received letters threatening to expose them as having cheated on their wives, which they both deny doing. But both knew doctored pictures could have shown another story. It would have been embarrassing for their families while they tried to prove their innocence."

Sheila shook her head as she took Sunnie out of the car seat. "But knowing Bradford Price wasn't the only one who got a blackmail letter gives legitimacy to your his claim that he's not Sunnie's father, and it's all a hoax to extract money from TCC members, right?"

"In a way, yes. But you'll still have some who have their doubts. The paternity test would clear him for sure." He saw a thoughtful look in her eye. Clearing Brad also meant that Sheila would have to give Sunnie up.

Zeke stood and glanced out the window. "It's stopped raining. If we're going to my place we need to do so before it starts up again."

She frowned. "I never said I was going to your place with you."

He slowly crossed the room to her. "I know. But considering everything, even your apprehension about spending time with me, is there a reason you should subject Sunnie to another night in a house without power?"

Sheila swallowed, knowing there it was. The one person she couldn't deny. Sunnie. She looked down at the baby she held in her arms. In the end it would always be what was best for Sunnie. Right now she was all the little girl had. And she would always put her needs first. Last night hadn't been so bad, but it was November; even with fire in the fireplace, the house was beginning to feel drafty. And she couldn't risk the baby catching a cold all because she couldn't resist a tall, dark, handsome and well-built man name Zeke Travers.

She looked at Zeke, met his gaze. "Will you promise me something?"

"What?"

"That while we're at your place you won't…"

He took a step closer. "I won't what?"

She nibbled on her bottom lip. "Try seducing me into sleeping with you again."

He studied her features for a moment and then he reached out and caressed her cheek with the back of his hand while he continued to hold her gaze. "Sorry, sweetheart, that is one promise I won't make you," he said in a low, husky tone. He took a step back. "I'll start loading up Sunnie's stuff in my truck."

Sheila held her breath until he walked out of the room.

Zeke pretended not to notice how well Sheila inter-acted with Sunnie as he loaded the last of the baby items into his truck. They would probably be at his place only a day at the most. But with everything Sheila had indicated she needed to take, you would think they were moving in for a full year. He chuckled. He had no complaints. He had a huge house and lately he'd noticed how lonely it would seem at times.

He heard the baby chuckle and glanced back over at her. He couldn't tell who was giggling more, Sunnie or Sheila, and quickly decided it was a tie. He pushed his Stetson back off his head, thinking, as well as knowing, she would make a great mother. She always handled Sunnie with care, as if she was the most precious thing she'd ever touched.

She glanced over at him, caught him staring and gave him a small smile. The one he returned had a lot more depth than the one she'd given him and he understood why. She still had misgivings about spending time at his place. He didn't blame her too much. He had every intention of finishing what had gotten started between them last night. By not agreeing to her request not to get her into his bed, he'd pretty much stated what his intentions were and he wasn't backing down.

But as he'd told her, there was no way he could make her that promise. It would have died a quick death on his lips as soon as he'd made it. And the one thing his Aunt Clarisse had taught him not to do was lie. She'd always said lies could come back to haunt you. They would catch up with you at the worst possible time. And he had believed her.

He moved from around the back of the truck. "Ready to go?"

He could tell she wasn't ready. But she widened her smile a little and said, "Yes. Let me get Sunnie into her seat."

He watched as she strapped the baby in her car seat, again paying attention to every little detail of Sunnie's security and comfort. He stepped back as she closed the door, and then he opened the passenger door for her and watched how easily she slid in across the leather. Nice, he thought. Especially when he caught a glimpse of bare thigh. He'd never given a thought to how much he appreciated seeing a woman in a skirt until now.

He got into the truck, backed out her yard and was halfway down the road when she glanced over at him. "I want to use one of your guest rooms, Zeke."

"All right."

Zeke kept looking straight ahead, knowing she had glanced over at him, trying to decipher the quickness of his answer. She would discover soon enough that physical attraction was a very powerful thing. And now that they'd experienced just how things could be between them, it wouldn't be that easy to give it up. And it just so happened that his bedroom was right across the hall from the guest room he intended to put her in.

"I can make a pit stop and grab something to eat. What would you like?" he asked her.

"Oh, anything. I'm not that hungry."

He looked over at her when he brought the car to a stop at a traffic light. "Maybe not now, but you'll probably be hungry later."

And he didn't add that she should eat something to keep her strength for the plans he had for her after she put the baby to bed for the night. He felt a deep stirring inside him. There was something about her scent that made him want to mate. And mate they would again. His peace of mind and everything male within him was depending on it. He couldn't wait for night to come.

But for now he would pretend to go along with anything she thought she wanted, and making sure by the time it was over she'd be truly and thoroughly convinced what she wanted was him. Usually, when it came to women, he didn't like playing games. He liked to be honest, but he didn't consider what he was doing as playing a game. What he was doing was trying to keep his sanity. He honestly didn't think she knew just how luscious she was. Maybe he hadn't shown her enough last night. Evidently he needed to give her several more hints. And he would do so gladly. He shifted in his seat when he felt tightness in the crotch of his pants while thinking how such a thing would be accomplished.

"You don't mind if I pull into that chicken place, do you?" he asked, gesturing to a KFC.

"No, I guess you're a growing boy and have to eat sometime," she said, smiling over at him.

Growing boy was right, and there was no need to tell her what part of him seemed to be outgrowing all the others at the moment.

Sheila glanced around the bedroom she was given. Zeke had set up Sunnie's bed in a connecting room. She loved his home. It looked like the perfect place for a family.

She pulled a romance novel out of her bag before sliding into bed. When they arrived here, she had helped him get everything inside. After that was done they had both sat down to enjoy the fried-chicken lunch he'd purchased. After that was done he had gone outside to check on things. The fierce winds had knocked down several branches and Zeke and his men had taken the time to clean up the debris. While he was outside, Sheila and Sunnie had made themselves at home.

So far he had been the perfect gentleman and had even volunteered to watch the baby while she had taken a shower. Sunnie had gotten used to seeing him and didn't cry when he held her. In fact, it seemed that she was giving him as many smiles as she was giving to her.

Now Sunnie was down for the night and it had started raining again. Sheila could hear the television downstairs and knew Zeke was still up. She thought it would be better for her to remain in her room and read. She would see him in the morning and that was soon enough to suit her.

She had been reading for about an hour or so when she decided to go to the connecting room to check on Sunnie. Although the baby now slept through the night, Sheila checked on her periodically. Sunnie had a tendency to kick off her bedcovers while she slept.

Sheila tiptoed into the room. Already the scent of baby powder drenched the air and she smiled. Sunnie's presence was definitely known. When Sheila had come downstairs after taking a shower, Zeke had been holding the baby in his arms and was standing at the window. From Sunnie's giggles she could tell the baby had enjoyed seeing the huge raindrops roll down the windowpane.

It had been a spine-tilting moment to see him standing there in his bare feet, shirtless with his jeans riding low on his hips. A tall, sexy hulk of a man with a tiny baby in his arms. A baby he was holding as gently as if she was his.

She had watched them and thought that he would make a wonderful father. She wondered if he wanted kids one day. He had talked about his cousin's twins and she knew he didn't have an aversion to kids like some men did. Crawford would freeze up whenever the mention of a baby entered their conversation. That had been one topic not open for discussion between them.

Pulling the covers back over Sunnie's chubby legs, Sheila was about to exit when she felt another presence in the room. She turned quickly and saw Zeke sitting in the wingback chair with his legs stretched out in front of him. He was sitting silently and watching her, saying nothing.

The glow of the moon flowing in through the curtains highlighted his features and the look she saw in his eyes said it all. She fought not to be moved by that look, but it was more powerful than anything she'd ever encountered. It was like a magnetic force, pulling her in, weakening her, filling her with a need she had been fighting since awakening that morning.

She wished she could stop her heart from beating a mile a minute, or stop her nipples from pressing hard against her nightgown. Then there was the heat she felt between her legs; the feeling was annoying as well as arousing.

Then he stood and she had to tilt her head back to look at him. In the moonlight she saw him crook his finger for her to follow him into the hall. Knowing it was best they not speak in the room to avoid awakening Sunnie, she followed.

"I didn't know you were in there with Sunnie," she said softly.

He leaned against the wall. "I went in there to check on her…and to wait for you."

A knot formed in Sheila's throat. "Wait for me?" He seemed to have inched closer. She inhaled his masculine scent into her nostrils and her nipples stiffened even more.

"Yes. I knew you would be coming to check on Sunnie sooner or later. And I decided to sit it out until you did."

She shifted her body when she felt a tingling sensation at the juncture of her thighs. "Why would you be waiting for me?"

She was warned by the smile that tilted his lips at the same time as he slipped an arm around her waist and said, "I was waiting to give you this."

He leaned his mouth down to hers. And instinctively, she went on tiptoe to meet him halfway.

This was well worth the wait, Zeke thought as he deepened the kiss. There was nothing like being inside her mouth. Nothing like holding her in his arms. Nothing like hearing the sound of her moaning deep in his ear.

And he had waited. From the moment she had gone upstairs to put the baby to bed, he had waited for her to come back downstairs. She hadn't done so. Instead, she had called down to him from the top of the stairs to tell him good-night.

He had smiled at her ploy to put distance between them, and he put a plan into action. He figured there was no way she would settle in for the night without checking on Sunnie. So he had closed up things downstairs and gone upstairs and waited.

The wait was over.

She was where he wanted her to be. Here in his arms where he needed her to be. But he needed her someplace else, as well. His bed. Lifting his mouth from hers, he gazed down into the darkness of her eyes and whispered against her moist lips, "I need to make love to you, sweetheart. I have to get inside you."

Sheila nearly moaned at the boldness of his statement. And the desire she saw in his dark gaze was so fierce, so ferocious, that she could feel an intensity stirring within her that she'd never felt before. His need was rousing hers.

She reached up and wrapped her arms around his neck, brought her mouth close to his and whispered thickly, "And I want you inside me, too." And she meant it. Had felt each and every word she had spoken. The throbbing between her legs had intensified from the hardness of him pressing against her and she was feeling him. Boy, was she feeling him.

Before she could release her next breath, he swept her off her feet and into his arms and headed across the hall to his bedroom.

Nothing, Zeke thought, had prepared him for meeting a woman like Sheila. She hadn't come on to him like others. Had even tried keeping her distance. But the chemistry had been too great and intensified each and every time they were within a foot of each other.

The last time they'd made love had been almost too much for his mind and body to handle. And now he could only imagine the outcome of this mating. But he needed it the way he needed to breathe.

He placed her on the bed and before she could get settled, he had whipped the nightgown from her body. She looked up at him and smiled. "Hey, you're good at that."

"At what?" he asked, stepping back to remove his own clothes.

"Undressing a woman."

As he put on a condom, he glanced at her. She was the only woman he wanted to undress. The only woman he enjoyed undressing. The only woman he wanted to make love to. Suddenly, upon realizing what his mind had just proclaimed, he forced it free of such an assertion. He could and never would be permanently tied to any one woman. That was the last thing he wanted to think about now or ever.

He moved back toward the bed. The way she was gazing at every inch of his body made him aware of just what she was seeing, and just what he wanted to give her. What he wanted them to share. What he intended them to savor.

He stopped at the edge of the bed and returned her gaze with equal intensity. Moonlight pouring in through his window shone on her nakedness. There she was. Beautiful. Bare. His eyes roamed over her uplifted breasts, creamy brown skin, small waist, luscious thighs, gorgeous hips and then to the apex of her thighs.

"Zeke."

She said his name before he even touched her. She rose on the bed to meet him. The moment their lips fused, it was on. Desire burst like a piece of hot glass within him, cutting into his very core. Blazing heat rushed through his veins with every stroke of his tongue that she returned.

He lowered her to the mattress and pulled back from the kiss, needed the taste of her and proceeded to kiss her all over. He gloried in the way she trembled beneath his mouth, but he especially liked the taste of her wet center, and proved just how much he enjoyed it.

She came in an explosion that shook the bed and he cupped her bottom, locked his mouth to her while those erotic sensations slashed through her. And when his tongue found a section of her G-spot and went after it as if it would be his last meal, she shuddered uncontrollably.

It was only then that he pulled back and placed his body over hers. "I like your taste," he whispered huskily. He eased inside her, stretching her as he went deep. Her womb was still aching and he could feel it. Already she wanted more and he intended to give her what she wanted.

He began thrusting inside her, thinking he would never tire of doing so. He was convinced there would never come a time when he wouldn't want to make love to her. He slid his hands beneath her hips to lift her off the bed, needing to go even deeper. And when he had reached the depth he wanted, he continued to work her flesh. Going in and out of her relentlessly.

He threw his head back when she moaned his name and he felt her inner muscles clench him, hold him tight, trying to pull every single thing out of him. And he gave in to her demand in one guttural moan, feeling the veins in his neck almost bursting in the process. Coming inside a woman had never felt this right before. This monumental. This urgent.

He rode her hard as his body continued to burst into one hell of an explosion, his shudders combined with hers, nearly shaking the bed from the frame. This was lovemaking at its best. The kind that would leave you mindless. Yet still wanting more. When had he become so greedy?

He would try to figure out the answer to that later. Right now the only thing he wanted to dwell on were the feelings swamping him, ripping into every part of his body, taking him for all it was worth and then some. It had to be the most earth-shattering orgasm he'd ever experienced. More intense than the ones last night, and he'd thought those were off the charts.

And he knew moments later when his body finally withdrew from hers to slump beside her, weak as water, that it would always be that way with them. She would always be the one woman who would be his temptation. The one woman he would not be able to resist.

Eight

Zeke and Sheila were aware that the power had returned to her section of town. Yet neither brought up the subject of her returning home. Four days later and she was still spending her days and nights in Zeke's home and loving every moment of it.

The rain had stopped days ago and sunshine was peeking out over the clouds. Those sunny days were her favorite. That's when she would take the baby outside and push her around in the stroller. Zeke's property was enormous and she and Sunnie enjoyed exploring as much of it as they could. Sunnie was fascinated by the horses and would stare at them as if she was trying to figure out what they were.

Then there were the nights when she would fall asleep in Zeke's arms after having made love. He was the most generous lover and made her feel special each and every time he touched her. She was always encouraged by his bold sexuality, where he would take their lovemaking to the hilt. When it came to passion, Crawford had always been low-key. Zeke was just the opposite. He liked making love in or out of bed. And he especially enjoyed quickies. She smiled, thinking she was enjoying them, too.

Usually Zeke worked in his office downstairs for a few hours while she played games with Sunnie, keeping her entertained. Then when he came out of his office, he would spend time with them. One day he had driven them to a nearby park, and on another day he took them to the zoo.

On this particular day Zeke had gone into his office in town to work on a few files when his house phone rang. Usually he received calls on his cell phone, and Sheila decided not to answer it. The message went to his voice mail, which she heard.

"Hi, Ezekiel. This is Aunt Clarisse. I'm just calling to see how you're doing. I had a doctor's appointment today and he says I'm doing fine. And how is that baby someone left on the doorstep and claiming it's Brad's? I know you said you were going to keep an eye on the baby real close, so how is that going? Knowing you, you're probably not letting that baby out of your sight until you find out the truth one way or another..."

A knot twisted in Sheila's stomach. Was that why she was still here? Is that why Zeke hadn't mentioned anything about taking her home? Why he was making love to her each night? Was his main purpose for showing interest in her to keep his eye on Sunnie?

She fought back the tears that threatened to fall from her eyes. What other reason could there be? Had she really thought—had she hoped—that there could be another reason? Hadn't she learned her lesson yet?

Hadn't her father, mother and sister taught her that in this life she had no one? When all was said and done, she would be left high and dry. Alone.

Her only excuse for letting her guard down was that usually to achieve their goal of alienating her the ones she loved would try putting distance between them. That's why her father never came to visit, why Lois preferred keeping her from Atlanta and why her mother never invited her to visit her and her husbands.

But Zeke had been the exception. He had wanted to keep her close. Now she knew the reason why.

She drew in a deep breath. When Zeke returned she would tell him she wanted to go home. He would wonder why, but frankly she didn't care. Nor would she tell him. It was embarrassing and humiliating enough for her to know the reason.

One day she would learn her lesson.

Zeke glanced over at Sheila, surprised. "You want to go home?"

She continued packing up the baby's items. "Yes. The only reason Sunnie and I are here is because of your generosity in letting us stay due to the power being out at my place. It's back on now and there's no reason for us to remain here any longer."

He bit back the retort that she'd known the power was back on days ago, yet she hadn't been in a hurry to leave…just as he hadn't been in a hurry for her to go. What happened to make her want to take off? He rubbed the back of his neck. "Is something going on that I need to know about, Sheila?"

She glanced up. "No. I just want to go home."

He continued to stare at her. He'd known she'd eventually want to return home. Hell, he had to be realistic here. "Fine, we can take some of Sunnie's things now and you can come back for the rest later on in the week."

"I prefer taking all Sunnie's items now. There's no reason for me to come back. "

That sounded much like a clean break to him. Why? "Okay, then I'd better start loading stuff up." He walked out of the room.

Sheila glanced at the door Zeke had just walked out of, suddenly feeling alone. She might as well get used to it again. Sunnie's days were numbered with her either way. And now that she knew what Zeke was about, it would be best if she cut the cord now.

In the other room Zeke was taking down the baby bed he'd gotten used to seeing. Why was he beginning to feel as if he was losing his best friend? Why was the feeling of abandonment beginning to rear its ugly head again?

Waking up with her beside him each morning had meant more to him than it had to her evidently. Having both Sheila and Sunnie in his home had been the highlight of his life for the past four days. He had gotten used to them being around and had enjoyed the time they'd spent together. A part of him had assumed the feelings were mutual. Apparently he'd assumed wrong.

A short while later he had just finished taking the bed down, when his cell phone rang. He pulled it out of his back pocket. "Yes?"

"I just got a call from my attorney," Brad said. "There's a possibility I might get the results of the paternity test as early as tomorrow. Hell, I hope so. I need to get on with my life. Get on with the election."

"That's good to hear." At least it would be good for

Brad, but not so good for Sheila. Either way, she would be turning the baby over to someone, whether it was Brad or the system. And the way he saw it, there was a one-hundred-percent chance it would be the system.

"Let me know when you get the results," he said to Brad.

His best friend chuckled. "Trust me. You'll be the first to know."

A few hours later back at her place Sheila stood at the window and watched Zeke pull off. He had stayed just long enough to put up the crib. No doubt he'd picked up on her rather cold attitude, but he hadn't questioned her about it. Nor had he indicated he would be returning.

However, since his sole purpose in seeing her was to spy on her, she figured he would return eventually. When he did, it would be on her terms and not his. She had no problem with him wanting to make sure Sunnie was well taken care of, but he would not be using her to do so.

She turned from the window, deciding it was time to take Sunnie upstairs for her bath, when she heard the phone ringing. She crossed the room to pick it up. "Hello?"

"Ms. Hopkins?"

"Yes?"

"This is Ms. Talbert from Social Services."

Sheila felt an immediate knot in her stomach. "Yes?"

"We received notification from the lab that the results of Bradford Price's paternity test might be available earlier than we expected. I thought we'd let you know that."

Sheila swallowed as she glanced across the room at Sunnie. She was sitting in her swing, laughing as she played with the toys attached to it.

"Does Mr. Price know?"

"I would think so. His attorney was contacted earlier today."

She drew in a deep breath. It would be safe to assume that if Bradford Price knew then Zeke knew. Why hadn't he mentioned this to her? Prepared her?

"Ms. Hopkins?"

The woman reclaimed her attention. "Yes?"

"Do you have any questions for us?"

"No."

"Okay, then. How is the baby doing?"

Sheila glanced over at Sunnie. "She's fine."

"That's good. I'll call you sometime this week to let you know when to bring the baby in."

"All right." Sheila hung up the phone and forced the tears back.

Zeke entered his house convinced something in Sheila's attitude toward him had changed. But what and why?

He went straight into the kitchen to grab a beer, immediately feeling how lonely his house was. It had taken Sheila and the baby being here for him to realize there was a difference between a house and a home. This place was a house.

He had drunk his beer and was about to go upstairs when he noticed a blinking light on his phone. He crossed the room to retrieve his messages and smiled upon hearing his aunt's voice. Moments later a frown touched his lips. When had his aunt called? He played back the message to extract the time. She had called around noon when Sheila had been here. Had she heard it?

He rubbed his hands down his face, knowing the assumptions that would probably come into her mind if she had. Sunnie was not the reason he'd been spending time with her. But after hearing his aunt's message, she might think that it was.

He moved to the sofa to recall everything between them since returning home that day. Even on the car ride back to her place she hadn't said more than a few words. Although the words had been polite, and he hadn't detected anger or irritation in them, he'd known something was bothering her. At first he'd figured since this was the beginning of the second week, she was getting antsy over Sunnie's fate. He had tried engaging her in conversation, but to no avail.

He drew in a deep breath. Did she know that she had come to mean something to him? He chuckled. *Hell, man, how could she know when you're just realizing such a thing yourself?* Zeke knew at that moment that he had done with Sheila the very thing he hadn't wanted to do with any woman. He had fallen in love with her.

He didn't have to wonder how such a thing happened. Spending time with her had made him see what he was missing in his life. He had enjoyed leaving and coming home knowing she was here waiting for him. And at night when they retired, it was as if his bed was where she belonged.

He had thought about bringing up the subject of them trying their luck dating seriously. But he had figured they would have the opportunity to do that after everything with Sunnie was over. He envisioned them taking things slow and building a solid relationship. But now it looked as if that wouldn't be happening.

He then thought about the call he'd gotten from Brad, indicating the test results might be arriving sooner than later. He probably should have mentioned it to her, but after seeing her melancholy mood, he'd decided to keep the information to himself. The last thing he wanted her to start doing was worry about having to give up the baby she'd gotten attached to.

A part of him wanted to get in his car and go over to her place and tell her she had made wrong assumptions about his reason for wanting to be with her. But he figured he would give her space tonight. At some point tomorrow he would be seeing her, and hopefully they would be able to sit down and do some serious talking.

He stood from the sofa, when his cell phone rang. He quickly pulled it off his belt hoping it was Sheila, and then grimaced when he saw the caller was his father. Matthew Travers was determined not to let his oldest son put distance between them as Zeke often tried to do.

The old man made a point of calling often, and if Zeke got the notion not to accept the call, Matthew Travers wasn't opposed to sending one of his offspring to check on their oldest sibling. Hell, the old man had shown up on his doorstep a time or two himself. Zeke had learned the hard way his father was a man who refused to be denied anything he wanted.

Zeke shook his head thinking that must be a Travers trait, because he felt the same way about certain things. He was definitely feeling that way about Sheila. "Hello?"

"How are you doing, son?"

Zeke drew in a deep relaxing breath. That was always the way the old man began the conversation with him, referring to him as his son. Letting Zeke know he considered him as such.

Zeke sat back down on the sofa and stretched his legs out in front of him. "I'm doing fine, Dad."

At times it still sounded strange referring to Matthew

Travers as "Dad," even after twelve years. They hadn't talked in a while and he had a feeling that today his father was in a talkative mood.

The next day Zeke got to the office early, intending to follow up a few leads. Regardless of whether Brad was cleared of being Sunnie's father, there was still someone out there who'd set up an extortion scheme and had made several members of the TCC his or her victims.

He hoped he would be able to call it a day at Global Securities by five and hightail it over to Sheila's place. He hadn't been able to sleep for thinking about her last night. And he hadn't liked sleeping in his bed alone. Those days she'd spent with him had definitely changed his life.

He sat down at his desk remembering the conversation he'd had with his father. His father still wasn't overjoyed that Zeke had turned down the position of chief of security of Travers Enterprises to come work here with Darius. As he'd tried explaining to the old man, he preferred living in a small town, and moving from Austin to Houston would not have given him that.

And had he not moved to Royal, he thought further, *he would not have met Sheila.*

A few hours later while sitting at his desk with his sleeves rolled up and mulling over a file, his intercom buzzed with a call from his secretary. "Yes, Mavis?"

"Mr. Price and his attorney are here and want to see you."

Zeke glanced at the clock on his desk, a sterling-silver exclusive from his cousin. He frowned, not believing it was almost four in the afternoon. He couldn't help wondering why Brad and his attorney would be dropping by. "Please send them in."

Seconds later the door flew open and an angry Brad walked in followed by Alan Nelson, Brad's attorney. Zeke took one look at a furious Brad and a flustered Alan and knew something was wrong. "What the hell is going on?" he asked.

"This!" Brad said, tossing a document in the middle of Zeke's desk. "Alan just got it. It's a copy of the results of the paternity test and it's claiming that I'm that baby's father."

Sheila hung up the phone. It was Ms. Talbert again. She had called to say the results of the paternity test were in. Although the woman couldn't share the results with her, she told her that she would call back later that day or early tomorrow with details about when and where Sheila was to drop off the baby.

Sheila felt her body trembling inside. She was a nurse, so she should have known not to get attached to a patient. Initially, she had treated Sunnie as someone who'd been placed in her care. But that theory had died the moment that precious little girl had gazed up at her with those beautiful hazel eyes.

The baby hadn't wanted much. She just wanted to be loved and belong to someone. Sheila had certainly understood that, since those were the very things she wanted for herself. She hoped that Sunnie had a better chance at it than she'd had.

But not if she ends up in the system. And that thought bothered Sheila most of all. A part of her wanted to call Zeke, but she knew she couldn't do that. He hadn't gotten attached to her the way she had to him. Oh, he had gotten attached to her all right, but for all the wrong reasons.

She moved over toward the baby. Their time was

limited and she intended to spend as much quality time as she could with Sunnie. Although the baby was only five months old, she wanted her to feel loved and cherished. Because deep in Sheila's heart, she was.

"Calm down, Brad." Zeke then glanced over at Alan. "Will you please tell me what's going on?" he asked Brad's attorney.

Brad dropped down in the chair opposite Zeke's desk, and Zeke could tell the older man seemed relieved. There was no doubt in Zeke's mind that once Alan had delivered the news to Brad he'd wished he hadn't.

The man took out a handkerchief and wiped sweat off his brow before saying, "The paternity report shows a genetic link between Mr. Price and the baby."

Zeke lifted a brow. "Meaning?"

"It means that although there's a link, it's inconclusive as to whether he is Jane Doe's father."

Zeke cringed at Alan's use of the name Jane Doe for Sunnie. "Her name is Sunnie, Alan."

The man looked confused. "What?"

"The baby's name is Sunnie. And as far as what you're saying, we still don't know one way or the other?"

"No, but again, there is that genetic link," Alan reiterated.

Zeke released a frustrated sigh. He then turned his attention to Brad. "Brad, I know you recall not having been sexually involved with a woman during the time Sunnie would have been conceived, but did you at any time donate your sperm to a bank or anyplace like that?"

"Of course not!"

"Just asking. I knew a few guys who did so when we were in college," Zeke said.

"Well, I wasn't one of them." Brad stood up. "What am I going to do? If word of this gets out I might as well kiss the TCC presidency goodbye."

Zeke knew the word would probably get out. He'd found out soon enough that in Royal, like a number of small towns, people had a tendency to thrive on gossip, especially when it involved the upper crust of the city.

"Who contacted you about the results?" Zeke asked Alan.

"That woman at Social Services," Alan replied. "She's the one who called yesterday afternoon as well, letting me know there was a chance the results would be arriving sooner than expected. I called Brad and informed him of such."

Zeke nodded. And Brad had called him. "Did she mention she would be telling anyone else?"

"No, other than the woman who has custody of Jane Doe." Upon seeing Zeke's frown, he quickly said, "I mean Sunnie."

Zeke was immediately out of his chair. "She called Sheila Hopkins?"

"Yes, if that's the name of the woman keeping the baby. I'm sure she's not going to tell her the results of the test, only that the results are in," Alan replied. "Is there a problem?"

Yes, Zeke saw a problem but didn't have time to explain anything to the two men. "I need to go," he said, grabbing his Stetson and jacket and heading for the door.

"What's wrong?" Brad asked, getting to his feet and watching him dash off in a mad rush.

"I'll call you," Zeke said over his shoulder, and then he was out the door.

* * *

Sheila heard a commotion outside her window and, shifting Sunnie to her hip, she moved in that direction. Pushing the curtain aside, she watched as Summer tried corralling a group of pink flamingos down the street.

She had heard about the Helping Hands Shelter's most recent fundraiser. Someone had come up with the idea of the pink flamingos. The plan was that the recipient of the flamingos had to pay money to the charity for the opportunity to pass them on to the next unsuspecting victim, and then the cycle would start all over again.

Sunnie was making all kinds of excited noises seeing the flamingos, and the sound almost brought more tears to Sheila's eyes, knowing the day would come when she wouldn't hear that sound again. She knew she had to get out of her state of funk. But it was hard doing so.

She moved from the window when Summer continued to herd the flamingos down the street. Sheila was glad her friend hadn't ditched the flamingos on her. She had enough to deal with and passing on pink flamingos was the last thing she had time for.

She glanced down at Sunnie. "Okay, precious, it's dinnertime for you."

A short while later, after Sunnie had eaten, Sheila had given her a bath and put her to bed. The baby was usually worn-out by six and now slept through the night, waking to be fed around seven in the morning. Sheila couldn't help wondering if the baby's next caretaker would keep her on that same schedule.

She heard the doorbell ring as she moved down the stairs. She figured it was Summer dropping by to say hello, now that she'd dumped the flamingos off on someone's lawn. Quickly moving to the door so the sound of the bell wouldn't wake Sunnie, she glanced out the peephole and her heart thumped hard in her chest. It wasn't Summer. It was Zeke.

She didn't have to wonder why he'd dropped by. To spy on her and to make sure she was taking care of Sunnie properly. Drawing in a deep breath, she slowly opened the door.

Nine

She'd been crying. Zeke took note of that fact immediately. Her eyes were red and slightly puffy, and when he looked closer, he saw her chin was trembling as if she was fighting even now to keep tears at bay. He wasn't sure if the tears she was holding back were for Sunnie or what she assumed was his misuse of her.

He wanted more than anything to take her into his arms, pull her close and tell her how wrong she was and to explain how much she had come to mean to him. But he knew that he couldn't do that. Like him, his distrust of people's motives didn't start overnight. Therefore, he would have to back up anything he said. Prove it to her. Show her in deeds instead of just words. Eventually he'd have to prove every claim he would make here tonight.

He may have been the one abandoned as a child, but she, too, had been abandoned. Those who should have loved her, been there for her and supported her had not. In his book, that was the worse type of abandonment.

"Zeke, I know why you're here," she finally said, after they had stood there and stared at each other for a long moment.

"Do you?" he asked.

She lifted that trembling chin. "Yes. Sunnie's asleep. You're going to have to take my word for it, and we had a fun day. Now, goodbye."

She made an attempt to close the door, but he put his foot in the way. "Thanks for the information, but that's not why I'm here."

"Then why are you here?"

"To see the woman I made love to several times. The woman I had gotten used to waking up beside in the mornings. The woman I want even now."

She lifted her gaze from the booted foot blocking her door to him. "You shouldn't say things you don't mean."

"Sheila, we need to talk. I think I know what brought this on. I listened to the message my aunt left on my answering machine. You jumped to the wrong conclusion."

"Did I?"

"Yes, you did."

She crossed her arms over her chest. "I don't think so."

"But what if you did? Think of the huge mistake you're making. Invite me in and let's talk about it."

He watched as she began nibbling on her bottom lip, a lip he had sucked into his mouth, kissed and devoured many times since meeting her. Had it been less than two weeks? How had he fallen in love with her so quickly and know for sure it was the real thing?

He drew in a huge breath. Oh, it was definitely the real thing. Somehow, Sheila Hopkins had seeped into his bloodstream and was now making a huge statement within his heart.

"Okay, come in."

She stood back and he didn't waste any time entering in case she changed her mind. Once inside he glanced around the room and noticed how different things looked. All the baby stuff was gone. At least it had been collected and placed in a huge cardboard box that sat in the corner.

Not waiting for him to say anything when she saw the way his gaze had scanned the room, she said, "And please don't pretend that you don't know that I'll be turning Sunnie over to someone, as early as tomorrow."

He lifted a brow. "And someone told you that?"

She shrugged. "No, not really. But Ms. Talbert did call to say the results of the paternity test had come in. And since you were so certain Sunnie doesn't belong to your friend, then I can only assume that means she's going into the system."

He moved away from the door to walk over to stand in front of her. "You shouldn't assume anything. My investigation isn't over. And do you know what your problem is, Sheila?"

She stiffened her spine at his question. "What?"

"You assume too much and usually you assume wrong."

She glared at him before moving away to sit down on the sofa. "Okay, then you tell me, Zeke. How are my assumptions wrong?"

He dropped into the chair across from the sofa. "First of all, my aunt's phone call. She knew about the case I'm handling for Brad. And she knows Brad is my best friend and that I intend to clear his name or die trying. She was right. I intend to keep an eye on Sunnie and that might be the reason I hung around you at first. But that's not what brought me back here. If you recall, four days went by when I didn't see you or the baby."

"Then what brought you back?"

"You. I couldn't stay away from you."

He saw doubt in her eyes and knew he had his work cut out for him. But he would eventually make her believe him. He had to. Even now it was hard not to cross the room and touch her. Dressed in a pair of jeans and a pullover sweater and in bare feet, she looked good. Ravishing. Stunning. Even the puffiness beneath her eyes didn't take away her allure. And where she was sitting, the light from the fading sun made her skin glow, cast a radiant shine on her hair.

"Why didn't you tell me there was a chance the test results would come back early, to prepare me?"

"Because I know how attached you've gotten to Sunnie and I didn't want to deliver bad news any sooner than I had to. And what you assumed regarding that is wrong as well. The test results were not conclusive that Brad isn't Sunnie's father."

She leaned forward and narrowed her gaze accusingly. "But you were so convinced Bradford Price is not Sunnie's father."

"And I'm still convinced. The test reveals there is a genetic link. Now I'm going to find out how. It's not Brad's sister's child, but he did have a brother who died last year. I'd only met Michael once and that was when Brad and I were in college and he showed up asking Brad for money."

Zeke drew in a deep breath as he remembered that time. "Michael was his younger brother and, according to Brad, he got mixed up with the wrong crowd in high school, dropped out and became addicted to hard drugs. That's when Mr. Price disinherited him."

She nodded. "What happened to him?"

"Michael died in a drunk driving accident last year but foul play was never ruled out. There were some suspicious factors involved, including the amount of drugs they found in his system."

"That's horrible. But it would mean there was no way he could have fathered Sunnie."

"I thought about that possibility on the way here. He would have died a couple of months after she was conceived. It might be a long shot, but I am going to check it out. And Brad also has a few male cousins living in Waco. Like Brad, they enjoy their bachelor lifestyles, so I'll be checking with them as well."

She leaned back on the sofa. "So what will happen with Sunnie in the meantime?"

"That decision will be up to Social Services. However, I plan to have Brad recommend that she remain with you until this matter is resolved."

He saw the way her eyes brightened. "You think they'll go for it?"

"I don't know why they wouldn't. This is a delicate matter, and unfortunately it puts Brad in an awkward position. Even if Sunnie isn't directly his, there might be a family link. And knowing Brad the way I do, he will not turn his back on her, regardless. So either way, he might be filing for custody. She's doing fine right here with you, and the fewer changes we make with her the better."

He stood and crossed the room to sit beside her on the sofa. Surprised, she quickly scooted over. "Now that we got the issue of Sunnie taken care of, I think there is another matter we need to talk about," he said.

She nervously licked her lips. "And what issue is that?"

He stretched his arm across the back of the sofa. "Why you were so quick to assume the worst of me. Why you don't think I can care for you and refuse to believe that I'd want to develop a serious relationship with you."

"Why should I think you care and would want to develop something serious with me? No one else has before."

"I can't speak for those others, Sheila. I can only speak for myself."

"So you want me to believe it was more than just sex between us?" she asked stiffly.

"Yes, that's what I want you to believe."

It's a good thing he understood her not wanting to believe. How many times had he wanted to believe that if he got involved with someone seriously, they wouldn't just eventually disappear? And he knew deep down that's why he couldn't fully wrap his arms around the Travers family. A part of him was so afraid he would wake up one day and they would no longer want to include him in their lives. Although they had shown him more than once that was not the case, he still had those fears.

He stood and walked to the window and looked out. It was getting dark outside. He scrunched up his brow wondering why all those pink flamingos were across the street in Sheila's neighbor's yard and then remembered the TCC's fundraiser.

Drawing in a deep breath, he turned around to glance over at Sheila. She was watching him, probably wondering what he was about. What he had on his mind. "You know you aren't the only one who has reasons to want to be cautious about getting involved with someone. The main reason I shy away from any type of serious relationship is thinking the person will be here one day and gone the next."

At her confused expression he returned to sit beside her on the sofa. "My mother left me, literally gave me up to my aunt when I was only five. In other words, I was abandoned just like Sunnie. I didn't see her again until I turned nineteen. And that was only because she thought with my skills as a football player in college that I'd make the pros and would be her meal ticket."

He saw the pity that shone in Sheila's eyes. He didn't want her pity, just her understanding. "Since Mom left me, for a long time I thought if I did anything wrong my aunt would desert me as well."

"So you never did anything wrong."

"I tried not to. So you see, Sheila, I have my doubts about things just like you."

She didn't say anything for a moment and then asked, "What about your father?"

He leaned back on the sofa. "I never knew my father growing up. My aunt didn't have a clue as to his identity. My mother never told her. Then when I was in college, the craziest thing happened."

"What?" she asked, sitting up as if she was intrigued by what he was telling her.

"There was a guy on campus that everyone said looked just like me. I finally ran into him and I swear it was like looking in the mirror. He was younger than me by a year. And his name was Colin Travers."

"Your brother?"

"Yes, but we didn't know we were brothers because I was named Ezekiel Daniels at birth. Colin found our likeness so uncanny he immediately called his father. When he told his father my name, his old man remembered having a brief, meaningless affair with my mother years ago, before he married. He also remembered my mother's claim of getting pregnant when the affair ended. But she'd also made that claim to another man. So he assumed she was lying and had his attorney handle the situation. My mother wasn't absolutely sure Travers was my father, so she let it go."

"When your father finally discovered your existence, how did he treat you?" she asked.

"With open arms. All of his family welcomed me. His wife and my five brothers and one sister. At his request, on my twenty-first birthday, I changed my last name from Daniels to Travers and to this day that's all I've taken from him. And trust me he's offered plenty. But I don't take and I don't ask. Since acknowledging him as my father twelve years ago, I've never asked him for a single thing and I don't intend to."

"And who is your father, Zeke?"

"Matthew Travers."

Her mouth dropped open. "The self-made millionaire in Houston?"

He couldn't help chuckling at the shock he heard in her voice. "Yes. That's him."

"Do you blame him for not being a part of your life while growing up?"

"I did, but once I heard the whole story, and knowing my mother like I did, what he told me didn't surprise me. He felt badly about it and has tried making it up to me in various ways, although I've told him countless times that he doesn't owe me anything.

"So you see, Sheila, you aren't the only one with issues. I have them and I admit it. But I want to work on them with you. I want to take a chance and I want you to take a chance, too. What I feel with you feels right, and it has nothing to do with Sunnie."

He shook his head. "Hell, Sunnie's a whole other issue that I intend to solve. But I need to know that you're willing to step out on faith and give us a chance."

Sheila could feel a stirring deep in her heart. He was asking for them to have a relationship, something more than a tumble between the sheets. It was something she thought she'd had with Crawford, only to get hurt. Could she take a chance again?

"My last boyfriend was a medical-supply salesman. He traveled a lot, left me alone most of the time. I thought I'd be satisfied with his calls and always looked forward to his return. Then one day he came back just to let me know I'd gotten replaced."

"You don't need to worry about that happening," Zeke said quietly.

She glanced over at him. "And why wouldn't I?"

He leaned closer to her and said in a low husky tone, "Because I am so into you that I can't think straight. I go to sleep dreaming of you and I wake up wanting you. When I make love to you, I feel like I'm grabbing a piece of heaven."

"Oh, Zeke." She drew in a deep breath, thinking that if this was a game he was playing with her then he was playing it well. Stringing her as high and as tight as it could go. She wanted to believe it wasn't a game and that he was sincere. She so much wanted to believe.

"I will always be there for you, Sheila. Whenever you need me. I won't let you down. You're going to have to trust me. Believe in me."

She fought back the tears. "Please don't tell me those

things if you don't mean them," she said softly. "Please don't."

"I mean them and I will prove it," he said, reaching out and gently pulling her toward him.

"Just trust me," he whispered close to her lips. And then he leaned in closer and captured her mouth with his.

Sheila thought being in Zeke's arms felt right, so very right. And she wanted to believe everything he'd said, because as much as she had tried fighting it, she knew at that moment that she loved him. And his words had pretty much sealed her fate. Although he hadn't said he loved her, he wanted to be a part of her life and for them to take things one day at a time. That was more than anyone before had given her.

And she didn't have to worry about him being gone for long periods of time and not being there for her if she needed him.

But she didn't want to think about anything right now but the way he was kissing her. With a hunger she felt all the way to her bones.

And she was returning the kiss as heat was building inside her. Heat mixed with the love she felt for him. It was thrumming through her, stirring up emotions and feelings she'd tried to hold at bay for so long. But Zeke was pulling them out effortlessly, garnering her trust, making her believe and beckoning her to fall in love with him even more.

She felt herself being lifted into his arms and carried up the stairs. They didn't break mouth contact until he had lowered her onto the bed. "Mmm," she murmured in protest, missing the feel of his lips on hers, regretting the loss of tongue play in her mouth.

"I'm not going far, baby. We just need to remove our clothes," he whispered hotly against her moist lips.

Through desire-laden eyes she watched as he quickly removed his clothes and put on protection before returning to her. He reached out and took her hand and drew her closer to him. "Do you know how much I missed waking up beside you? Making love to you? Being inside you?"

She shook her head. "No."

"Then let me show you."

Zeke wanted to take things slow, refused to be rushed. He needed to make love to her the way he needed to breathe. After removing every stitch of her clothing, he breathed in her scent that he'd missed. "You smell good, baby."

"I smell like baby powder," she said, smiling. "One of the pitfalls of having a baby around."

His chuckle came out in a deep rumble. "You do smell like a baby. *My* baby." And then he kissed her again.

Moments later he released her mouth and began touching her all over as his hands became reacquainted with every part of her. He continued to stroke her and then his hands dipped to the area between her legs and found her wet and ready. Now another scent was replacing the baby powder fragrance and he was drawn into it. His erection thickened even more in response to it. He began stroking her there, fondling her, fingering the swollen bud of her womanhood.

"Zeke…"

"That's right, speak my name. Say it. I intend for it to be the only name you'll ever need to say when you feel this way."

And then he lowered himself to the bed, needing to

be inside her now. His body straddled hers and he met her gaze, held it, while slowly entering her. He couldn't help shuddering at the feel of the head of his shaft slowly easing through her feminine core.

She wrapped her legs around him and he began moving to a beat that had been instilled inside his head from the first time he'd made love to her. And he knew he would enjoy connecting with her this way until the day he took his last breath. He'd never desired a woman the way he desired her.

And then he began moving in and out of her. Thrusting deep, stroking long and making each one count. Shivers of ecstasy began running up his spine and he could feel his hardness swell even more inside her. He reached down, lifted her hips to go deeper still and it was then that she screamed his name.

His name.

And something exploded inside him, made him tremble while wrapped in tremendous pleasure. Made him utter her name in a guttural breath. And he knew at that moment, whatever it took, he was determined that one day she would love him back. He would prove to her she had become more than just temptation to him. She had become his life.

Sheila snuggled deeper into Zeke's arms and glanced over at the clock on her nightstand. It was almost midnight. They had gotten up earlier to check on Sunnie and to grab a light dinner—a snack was more like it. He had scrambled eggs and she had made hash browns. While they ate he told her more about his relationship with the Travers family. And she shared with him how awful things had been for her with Crawford, and how strained her relationships were with her mother and sister.

He had listened and then got up from the table to come around and wipe tears from her eyes before picking her up in his arms and taking her back upstairs where they had made love again. Now he was sleeping and she was awake, still basking in the afterglow of more orgasms tonight than she cared to count, but would always remember.

She gently traced the curve of his face with the tip of her finger. It was hard to believe this ultrahandsome man wanted her. He had a way of making her feel so special and so needed. Earlier tonight in this very bed she had felt so cold. But now she wasn't cold. Far from it. Zeke was certainly keeping her warm. She couldn't help smiling.

"Hmm, I hate to interrupt whatever it is you're thinking about that's making you smile, but…"

And then he reached up, hooked a hand behind her neck to bring her mouth down to his. And then he took possession of it in that leisurely but thorough way of his. And it was a way that had her toes tingling. Oh, Lord, the man could kiss. Boy, could he kiss. And to think she was the recipient of such a drugging connection.

He finally released her mouth and pulled her up to straddle him. He then gazed up at her as he planted his hands firmly on her hips. "Let's make love this way."

They had never made love using this position before, and she hesitated and just stared at him, not sure what he wanted her to do. He smiled and asked, "You can ride a horse, right?"

She nodded slowly. "Yes, of course."

"Then ride me."

She smiled as she lifted the lower part of her body and then came down on him. He entered her with accurate precision. She stifled a groan as he lifted his hips off the bed to go deeper inside her. She in turned pressed down as hard as she could, grinding her body against his.

And then she did what he told her to do. She rode him.

Brad glanced across the desk at Zeke. "Is there a reason you ran off yesterday like something was on fire?"

Zeke leaned back in his chair. He had left Sheila's house this morning later than he'd planned, knowing he had to go home first to change before heading into the office. He wasn't surprised to find Brad waiting on him. He'd seen the newspaper that morning. Brad's genetic connection to Sunnie made headline news, front page and center, for all to read.

When Zeke had stopped by the Royal Diner to grab a cup of coffee, the place where all the town gossips hung out, it seemed the place was all abuzz. There must have been a leak of information either at the lab where the test was processed or at the hospital. In any case, news of the results of the paternity test was all over town.

Everyone was shocked at the outcome of the test. Those who thought the baby wasn't Brad's due to the blackmailers hitting on other TCC members—even that news had somehow leaked—were going around scratching their heads, trying to figure out how the baby could be connected to Brad.

"It had to do with Sheila," he finally said.

Brad lifted a brow. "The woman taking care of the baby?"

"Yes."

Brad didn't say anything as he studied him, and Zeke knew exactly what he was doing. He was reading him like a book, and Zeke knew his best friend had the ability to do that. "And why do I get the feeling this Sheila Hopkins means something more to you than just a case you're working on?" Brad finally asked.

"Probably because you know me too well, and you're right. I met her less than two weeks ago and she has gotten to me, Brad. I think…I've fallen in love with her."

Zeke was certain Brad would have toppled over in his chair if it had not been firmly planted on the floor. "Love?"

"Yes, and I know what you're thinking. And it's not that. I care for her deeply." He leaned forward. "And she is even more cautious than I am about taking a chance. I'm the one who has to prove how much she means to me. Hell, I can't tell her how I feel yet. I'm going to have to show her."

A smile touched Brad's lips. "Well, this is certainly a surprise. I wish you the best."

"Thanks, man. And you might as well know one of her concerns right now is what's going to happen to Sunnie. She's gotten attached to her."

He paused a moment and then said, "Since you're here I have a video I want you to watch."

"A video?"

"Yes. I want you to look at that video I pulled that shows a woman placing the car seat containing the baby on the TCC doorstep. All we got is a good shot of her hands."

"And you think I might be able to recognize some woman's hands?" Brad asked.

Zeke shrugged. "Hey, it's worth a try." He picked up the remote to start rolling the videotape on the wide screen in his office.

Moments later they looked up when there was a tap

on the door. He then remembered his secretary had taken part of the morning off. "Come in."

Summer entered. "Hi, guys, sorry to interrupt. But you know it's fundraiser time for the shelter and I——"

She stopped talking when she glanced at the wide screen where Zeke had pressed Pause and the image had frozen on a pair of hands. "Why are you watching a video of Diane Worth's hands?"

Both men stared at her. Zeke asked in astonishment, "You recognize those hands?"

Summer smiled. "Yes, but only because of that tiny scar across the back of her right hand, which would have been a bigger scar if Dr. Harris hadn't sutured it the way he did. And then there's that little mole between the third and fourth finger that resembles a star."

Her smile widened when she added, "And before you ask, the reason I noticed so much about her hand is because I'm the one who bandaged the wound after Dr. Harris examined her."

Zeke got out of his chair to sit on the edge of his desk. "This woman came through the shelter recently?"

Summer shook her head. "Yes, around seven months ago. She was eight months pregnant and her boyfriend had gotten violent and cut her on her hand with a bowie knife. She wouldn't give the authorities his name, and stayed at the shelter one week before leaving without a trace in the middle of the night."

Zeke nodded slowly, not believing he might finally have a break in the case. "Do you have any information you can give us on her?"

"No, and by law our records are sealed to protect the women who come to the shelter for our protection. I can tell you, however, that the information she gave us wasn't correct. When she disappeared I tried to find her to make sure she was okay and ran into a dead end. I'm not even sure Diane Worth is her real name."

Zeke rubbed his chin. "And you said she was pregnant and vanished without a trace?"

"Yes, but Abigail might be able to help you further."

Brad lifted a brow. "Abigail Langley?"

Summer nodded. "Yes. It just so happened the night Diane disappeared, we thought she might have met with foul play. But Abigail had volunteered to man our suicide phone line that night, and according to Abigail, when she went out to put something in her car, she saw Diane getting into a car with some man of her own free will."

"That was a while back. I wonder if Abigail would be able to identify the guy she saw?" Brad mused.

"We can pay Abigail a visit and find out," Zeke said. He looked over at Summer. "We need a description of Diane Worth for the authorities. Can we get it from you?"

Summer smiled. "With a judge's order I can do better than that. I can pull our security camera's tape of the inside of the building. There were several in the lounge area where Diane used to hang out. I bet we got some pretty clear shots of her."

Adrenaline was flowing fast and furious through Zeke's veins. "Where's Judge Meadows?" he asked Brad.

Brad smiled. "About to go hunting somewhere with Dad. Getting that court order from him shouldn't be a problem."

"Good," Zeke said, glancing down at his watch. "First I want to pay Abigail Langley a visit. And then I want to check out those videotapes from the shelter's security camera."

"I'm coming with you when you question Abigail," Brad said, getting to his feet.

Zeke raised a brow. "Why?"

Brad shrugged. "Because I want to."

Zeke rolled his eyes as he moved toward the door. "Fine, but don't you dare make her cry again."

"You made Abigail cry?" Summer asked, frowning over at him.

"It wasn't intentional and I apologized," a remorseful-sounding Brad said, and he quickly followed Zeke out the door.

Ten

"You need a husband."

Sheila groaned inwardly. Her mother was definitely on a roll today. "No, I don't."

"Yes, you do, and with that kind of attitude you'll never get one. You need to return to Dallas and meet one of Charles's nephews."

Sheila shook her head. Her mother had called to brag about a new man she'd met. Some wealthy oilman and his two nephews. Cassie had warned her that they were short for Texans, less than six feet tall, but what they lacked in height, they made up for in greenbacks.

"So, will you fly up this weekend and—"

"No, Mom. I don't want to return to Dallas."

Her mother paused a moment and then said, "I wasn't going to mention it, but I ran into Crawford today."

Sheila drew in a deep breath. Hearing his name no longer caused her pain. "That's nice."

"He asked about you."

"I don't know why," she said, glancing across the room to where Sunnie was reaching for one of her toys.

"He's no longer with that woman and I think he wants you back," her mother said.

"I wouldn't take him back if he was the last man on earth."

"And you think you can be choosy?"

Sheila smiled, remembering that morning with Zeke. "Yes, I think I can."

"Well, I don't know who would put such foolishness into your head. I know men. They are what they are. Liars, cheaters, manipulators, all of them. The only way to stay ahead of them is to beat them at their own game. But don't waste your time on a poor one. Go after the ones with money. Make it worth your while."

A short time later as she gave Sunnie her bath, Sheila couldn't help thinking of what her mother said. That had always been her mother's problem. She thought life was a game. Get them before they get me first. There was no excuse for her cheating on her first husband. But then she had cheated on her second and fourth husbands, as well.

Her phone rang and she crossed the room to pick it up, hoping it wasn't her mother calling back with any more maternal advice. "Yes?"

"Hi, beautiful."

She smiled upon recognizing Zeke's voice. "Howdy, handsome."

She and Zeke had made love before he'd left that morning and she had felt tingly sensations running through her body all day. They had been a reminder of what the two of them had shared through the night.

And to think she had ridden him. Boy, had she ridden him. She blushed all over just thinking about it.

"I think we have a new lead," he said excitedly.

"You do? How?"

He told her how Summer had dropped by when he was showing the videotape in his office to Brad, and that she had identified the hands of the woman who had left Sunnie on the TCC's doorstep. He and Brad were now on their way to talk to Abigail Langley. There was a chance she could identify the man who the pregnant woman had left with that night. Then they would drop by the shelter to pull tapes for the authorities. There was a possibility Sunnie's mother was about to be identified.

By the time she'd hung up the phone from talking to Zeke, she knew he was closer to exposing the truth once and for all. Was Diane Worth Sunnie's biological mother? If she was, why did she leave her baby on the TCC's doorstep claiming she was Bradford Price's child?

Abigail led Zeke and Brad into the study of her home. "Yes, I can give you a description of the guy," she said, sitting down on a love seat. "I didn't know who he was then, but I do now from seeing a picture of him flash on television one night on CNN when they did an episode on drug rings in this country. His name is Miguel Rivera and he's reputed to be a drug lord with an organization in Denver."

"Denver?" Zeke asked, looking at Brad. "Why would a drug lord from Denver be in Royal seven months ago?"

Brad shrugged. "I wouldn't know unless he's connected to Paulo Rodriguez." Brad then brought Zeke up to date on what had gone on in Royal a few years ago when the local drug trafficker had entangled prominent TCC members in an embezzlement and arson scandal.

"I think I need to fly to Denver to see what I can find out," Zeke said. He glanced over at Abigail. "I appreciate you making time to see us today."

"I don't mind. No baby should have been abandoned like that."

Knowing that the subject of the baby was a teary subject with her for some reason, Zeke said, "Well, we'll be going. We need to stop by the shelter to see what we can find out there."

They were about to walk out the study, when Brad noticed something on the table and stopped. "You still have this?" he asked Abigail.

Zeke saw the trophy sitting on the table that had caught Brad's eye.

"Yes. I was cleaning out the attic at my parents' house and came across it," she said.

Intrigued, Zeke asked. "What is it for?"

"This," Brad said, chuckling as he picked up the trophy and held it up for Zeke to see, "should have been mine. Abigail and I were in a spelling bee. It was a contest that I should have won."

"But you didn't," she said, laughing. "I can't believe you haven't gotten over that. You didn't even know how to spell the word *occupation*."

"Hell, I tried," Brad said, joining her in laughter.

"Trying wasn't good enough that day, Brad. Get over it."

Zeke watched the two. It was evident they shared history. It was also evident they had always been rivals. He wondered if they could continue to take their boxing gloves off and share a laugh or two the way they were doing now more often.

After a few moments, the pair remembered he was there. Brad cleared his throat. "I guess we better get going to make it to the shelter. Goodbye, Abby."

"Bye, Brad, and I'll see you around, Zeke."

"Sure thing," Zeke responded, not missing the fact this was the second occasion that he'd heard Brad refer to her as Abby. The first time occurred when he'd been holding her in his arms, comforting her. Um, interesting.

"So what do you think?" Brad asked moments later while snapping on their seat belts in Zeke's car.

Zeke chuckled. "I think it's a damn shame you couldn't spell the word *occupation* and lost the spelling bee to a girl."

Brad threw his head back and laughed. "Hey, you didn't know Abigail back then. She was quite a pistol. She could do just about anything better than anyone."

Zeke wondered if Brad realized he'd just given the woman a compliment. "Evidently. Now to answer your question about Miguel Rivera, I think I'm going to have to fly to Denver. If Diane Worth is Sunnie's mother, I want to know what part Miguel Rivera is playing in her disappearance. I think all the answers lie in Denver."

Brad nodded. "And you think there's a possible connection to my brother, Michael?"

"I'm not sure. But I know that baby isn't yours and she has to belong to someone. And you and I know Michael was heavy into alcohol and drugs."

"Yes, but as a user, not a pusher," Brad said.

"As far as we know," Zeke countered. "When you went to collect his belongings, was there anything in them to suggest he might have been involved with a woman?"

"I wasn't checking for that. Besides, there wasn't much of anything in that rat hole he called an apartment.

I boxed up what he had, if you want to go through it. I put it in storage on my parents' property."

"I do. We can check that out after we leave the shelter." Zeke backed out of Abigail's driveway.

"You're leaving for Denver tomorrow?" Sheila asked hours later, glancing across the kitchen table at Zeke. He was holding Sunnie, making funny faces to get her to laugh. Sheila tried to downplay the feeling escalating inside her that he was leaving her.

This is work, you ninny, a voice inside her said. *This is not personal. He is not Crawford.* But then she couldn't help remembering Crawford's reason for leaving was all work-related, too.

"Yes, I need to check out this guy named Miguel Rivera. He might be the guy who picked Diane Worth up from the shelter that night. Thanks to security cameras inside the shelter, we were able to get such good shots of the woman that we've passed them on to law enforcement."

The woman who might be Sunnie's mother, she thought. "How long do you think you'll be gone?" she asked.

"Not sure. I don't intend to come back until I find out a few things. I have a lot of questions that need to be answered."

Sheila nodded. She knew his purpose in going to Denver would help close the case on Sunnie and bring closure. It was time, she knew that. But still… "Well, I hope you find out something conclusive. For Sunnie's sake," she said.

· *And for yours,* Zeke thought, studying her features. He knew that with each day that passed, she was getting attached to Sunnie even more. The first thing

152 TEMPTATION

he'd noticed when he arrived at her place was Sunnie's things were once again all over the place.

"So what are you going to be doing while I'm gone?" he asked her, standing to place the baby back in her seat.

"You can ask me that with Sunnie here? Trust me, there's never a dull moment." She paused and then asked quietly, "You won't forget I'm here, will you?"

He glanced up after snapping Sunnie into the seat. Although Sheila had tried making light of the question, he could tell from the look on her face she was dead serious. Did she honestly think when he left for Denver that he wouldn't think of her often, probably every single day? And although he would need to stay focused on solving the case, there was no doubt in his mind that she would still manage to creep into his thoughts. Mainly because she had his heart. Maybe it was time for him to tell her that.

He crossed the room to where she sat at the table and took her hands into his and eased her up. He then wrapped his arms around her waist. "There's no way I can forget about the woman I've fallen in love with."

He saw immediate disbelief flash across her features and said, "I know it's crazy considering we've only known each other for just two weeks but it's true. I do love you, Sheila, and no matter what you think, I won't forget you, and I am coming back. I will be here whenever you need me, just say the word."

He saw the tears that formed in her eyes and heard her broken words when she said, "And I love you, too. But I'm scared."

"And you think I'm not scared, too, baby? I've never given a woman my heart before. But you have it—lock, stock and barrel. And I don't make promises I don't keep, sweetheart. I will always be here for you. I will be a man you can count on."

And then he lowered his mouth and sealed his promise with a kiss, communicating with her this way and letting her know what he'd just said was true. He wanted her, but he loved her, too.

She returned his kiss with just as much fervor as he was putting into it. He knew if they didn't stop he would be tempted to haul her upstairs, which couldn't happen since Sunnie was wide awake. But there would be later and he was going to start counting the minutes.

Sheila woke when the sunlight streaming through the window hit her in the face. She jerked up in bed and saw the side next to her was empty. Had Zeke left for Denver already without telling her goodbye?

Trying to ignore the pain settling around her heart, she wrapped the top sheet around her naked body and eased out of bed to stare out the window. Was he somewhere in the skies on a plane? He hadn't said when he was returning, but he said he would and that he loved her. He *loved* her. She wanted so much to believe him and—

"Is there any reason you're standing there staring out the window?"

She whipped around with surprise all over her face. "You're here."

He chuckled. "Yes, I'm here. Where did you think I'd be?"

She shrugged. "I assumed you had left for Denver already."

"Without telling you goodbye?"

She fought back telling him that's how Crawford would do things, and that he had a habit of not returning when he'd told her he would. Something would always come up. There was always that one last sale he just had to make. Instead, she said, "What you have to do in Denver is important."

He leaned in the doorway with a cup of coffee in his hand. "And so are you."

He entered the room and placed the cup on the nightstand. "Come here, sweetheart."

She moved around the bed, tugging the sheet with her. When she came to a stop in front of him, he said, "Last night I told you that I had fallen in love with you, didn't I?"

"Yes."

"Then I need for you to believe in me. Trust me. I know, given your history with the people you care about, trusting might not be easy, but you're going to have to give me a chance."

She drew in a deep breath. "I know, but—"

"No buts, Sheila. We're in this thing together, you and me. We're going to leave all our garbage at the back door and not bring it inside. All right?"

She smiled and nodded. "All right."

He was about to pull her into his arms, when they heard the sound of Sunnie waking up on the monitor in the room. "I guess we'll have to postpone this for later. And later sometime, I need to look through some boxes Brad put in storage that belonged to his brother. His cousins in Waco swear they are not Sunnie's daddy, and since Michael is not here to speak for himself, I need to do some digging. But I am flying out for Denver tomorrow sometime."

He took a step back. "You go get dressed. Take your time. I'll handle the baby. And please don't ask if I know how to dress and feed her. If you recall, I've done it before."

She chuckled. "I know you have. And you will make a great father."

His smile widened. "You think so?"

"Yes."

"I take that as a compliment," he said. "And like I said, take your time coming downstairs. Sunnie and I will be in the kitchen waiting whenever you come down."

Zeke decided to do more than just dress and feed Sunnie. By the time Sheila walked into the kitchen, looking as beautiful as ever in black slacks and a pretty pink blouse, he had a suggestion for her. "The weather is nice outside. How about if we do something?"

She raised a brow. "Do something like what?"

"Um, like taking Sunnie to that carnival over in Somerset."

"But I thought you had to go through Brad's brother's boxes," she said.

"I do, but I thought we could go to the carnival first and I can look through the boxes later. I just called the airlines. I'll be flying out first thing in the morning, and I want to spend as much time as I can today with my two favorite ladies."

"Really?"

He could tell by her expression that she was excited by his suggestion. "Yes, really. What do you say?"

She practically beamed. "Sunnie and I would love to go to the carnival with you."

Considering how many items they had to get together for Sunnie, it didn't take long for them to be on their way. He had passed the carnival a few days ago and had known he wanted to take Sheila and Sunnie there. It had been only a couple of weeks, but Sunnie had become just as much a part of his life as Sheila's.

Although he'd told her how he felt about her, he could see Sheila was still handling him with caution, as if she was afraid to give her heart to him no matter how much she wanted to. He would be patient and continue to show her how much she meant to him. As he'd told her, considering her mother, sister and ex-boyfriend's treatment of her, he could definitely understand her lack of trust.

"And you're sure Brad is okay with you putting the investigation on hold to spend time with me and Sunnie?"

He glanced over at her as he turned toward the interstate. "Positive. A few hours won't hurt anything. Besides, I'll probably be gone most of next week and I'm missing you already."

It didn't take them long to reach the carnival grounds. After putting Sunnie in her stroller, they began walking around. It was Saturday and a number of people were out and about. He recognized a number of them he knew and Sheila ran into people she knew, as well. They ran into Brad's sister, Sadie, her husband, Ron, and the couple's twin daughters.

"She is a beautiful baby," Sadie said, hunching down to be eye level with Sunnie.

And as usual when strangers got close, Sunnie glanced around to make sure Sheila was near. "Yes, she is," Sheila said, smiling. She waited to see if the woman would make a comment about Sunnie favoring her brother or anyone in the Price family, but Sadie Price Pruitt didn't do so. But it was plain to see she was just as taken with Sunnie as Sheila was with Sadie's twins.

They also ran into Mitch Hayward and the former Jenny Watson. Mitch was the interim president of the TCC, and Jenny, one of his employees, when the two had fallen in love. And they had a baby on the way.

But the person Zeke was really surprised to see was Darius. He hadn't known his partner had returned to town. "Darius, when did you get back?" he asked, shaking his business partner's hand.

"Last night. We finished up a few days early and I caught the first plane coming this way."

Zeke didn't have to ask why when Darius drew Summer closer to him and smiled down at her.

"I would have called when I got in, but it was late and…"

Zeke chuckled. "Hey, man, you don't have to explain. I understand." He was about to introduce Darius and Sheila, but realized when Darius reached out and gave Sheila a hug that they already knew each other.

"And this is the little lady I've heard so much about," Darius said, smiling at Sunnie. "She's a beautiful baby."

They all chatted for few minutes longer before parting ways, but not before agreeing to get together when Zeke returned from Denver.

"I like Darius and Summer," Sheila said. "That time when Summer and I worked together on that abuse case, Darius was so supportive and it's evident that he loves her very much."

Zeke nodded and thought that one day he and Sheila might share the kind of bond that Darius and Summer enjoyed.

Eleven

Zeke was grateful for the friendships he'd made while at UT on the football team. The man he needed to talk to who headed Denver's Drug Enforcement Unit, Harold Mathis, just so happened to be the brother of one of Zeke's former teammates.

Mathis wasted no time in telling Zeke about Miguel Rivera. Although the notorious drug lord had been keeping a low profile lately, in no way did the authorities believe he had turned over a new leaf. And when they were shown photographs of Diane Worth, they identified her as a woman who'd been seen with Rivera once or twice.

Zeke knew he had his work cut out in trying to make a connection between Diane Worth and Michael Price. Michael's last place of residence was in New Orleans. At least that's where Brad had gone to claim his brother's body.

His belongings hadn't given a clue as to who he might have associated with, especially a woman by the name of Diane Worth. But Zeke was determined to find out if Diane Worth was Sunnie's mother.

The Denver Drug Enforcement Unit was ready to lend their services to do anything they could to get the likes of Miguel Rivera off the streets. So far he had been wily where the authorities were concerned and had been able to elude all undercover operations to nab him.

Since Zeke knew he would probably be in Denver awhile, he had decided to take residence in one of those short-term executive apartments. It wasn't home, but it had all the amenities. He had stopped by a grocery store to buy a few things and was reminded of the time when he had gone grocery shopping with Sheila and the baby when they'd stayed over at his place. He had been comfortable walking beside her and hadn't minded when a few people saw them and probably thought they were an item. As far as he was concerned, they were.

He glanced out a window that had a beautiful view of downtown Denver. He was missing his *ladies* already. Sunnie had started to grow on him as well, which was easy for her because she was such a sweet baby. She no longer screamed around strangers, although you could tell she was most comfortable when he or Sheila was around.

Sheila.

God, he loved her something awful and was determined that distance didn't put any foolishness in her mind, like her thinking he was falling out of love with her just because he didn't see her every day. Already he'd patronized the florist shop next door. They would make sure a bouquet of flowers was delivered to

Sheila every few days. And he intended to ply her with "thinking of you" gifts often.

He chuckled. Hell, that could get expensive because he thought of her all the time. The only time he would force thoughts of her from his mind was when he was trying to concentrate on the case. And even then it was hard.

He picked up the documents he had tossed on the table that included photographs of both Rivera and Worth. A contact was working with hospitals in both New Orleans and Denver to determine if a child was born to Diane Worth five months ago. And if so, where was the baby now?

He was about to go take a shower, when his phone rang. "Hello."

"I got another blackmail letter today, Zeke."

He nodded. Zeke figured another one would be coming sooner or later. The extortionist had made good his threat. But that didn't mean he was letting Brad off the hook. It was done mainly to let him know he meant business. "He still wants money, right?"

"Yes, and unless I pay up, Sunnie's birth records will be made public to show I had a relationship with a prostitute."

Of course, that was a lie, but the blackmailer's aim was to get money out of Brad to keep a scandal from erupting. It would have a far-reaching effect not only for Brad's reputation but that of his family.

"I know it's going to be hard for you to do, but just ignore it for now. Whoever is behind the extortion attempt evidently thinks he has you where he wants you to be, and we're going to prove him wrong."

By the time Zeke ended his call with Brad, he was more determined than ever to find a link between Rivera and Worth.

* * *

"You're thinking about getting married?" *Again?* Sheila really should not be surprised. Her mother hated being single and had a knack for getting a husband whenever she wanted one…

"Um, I'm thinking about it. I really like Charles."

You only met him last week. And wasn't it just a couple of weeks ago she'd asked her about Dr. Morgan? Sheila decided not to remind her mother of all those other men she'd liked, as well. "I wish you the best, Mom." And she did. She wanted her mother to be happy. Married or not.

"Thanks. And what's that I hear in the background? Sounds like a kid."

Sheila had no intention of telling her mother the entire story about Sunnie. "It is a baby. I'm taking care of her for a little while." That wasn't totally untrue since she was considered Sunnie's caretaker for the time being.

"That's nice, dear, since chances are you won't have any of your own. Your biological clock is ticking and you have no prospects."

Sheila smiled, deciding to let her mother think whatever she wanted. "You don't have to have a man to get pregnant, Mom. Just sperm."

"Please don't do anything foolish. I hope you aren't thinking of going that route. Besides, being pregnant can mess up a woman's figure for life."

Sheila rolled her eyes. Her mother thought nothing of blaming her for the one stretch mark she still had on her tummy. She was about to open her mouth and say something—to change the subject—when her doorbell sounded.

"Mom, I have to go. There's someone at the door."

"Be careful. There are lunatics living in small towns."

"Okay, Mom, I'll be careful." At times it was best not to argue.

After hanging up the phone, she glanced over at Sunnie, who was busy laughing while reaching for a toy that let out a squeal each time Sunnie touched it. She was such a happy baby.

Sheila glanced through the peephole. There was a woman standing there holding an arrangement of beautiful flowers. Sheila immediately figured the delivery was for her neighbor, who probably wasn't at home. She opened the door. "Yes, may I help you?"

The woman smiled. "Yes, I have a delivery for Sheila Hopkins."

Sheila stared at the woman, shocked. "I'm Sheila Hopkins. Those are for me?"

"Yes." The woman handed her a huge arrangement in a beautiful vase. "Enjoy them."

The woman then left, leaving Sheila standing there, holding the flowers with the shocked look still in place. It took the woman driving off before Sheila pulled herself together to take a step back into the house and close the door behind her as she gazed at the flowers. It was a beautiful bouquet. She quickly placed the vase in what she considered the perfect spot before pulling off the card.

I am thinking of you. Zeke.

Sheila's heart began to swell. He was away but still had her in his thoughts. A feeling of happiness spread through her. Zeke, who claimed he loved her, was too real to be true. She wanted to believe he was real…but…

She turned to Sunnie. "Look what Zeke sent. I feel special…and loved."

Sunnie didn't pay her any attention as she continued

to play with the toy Zeke had won for her at the carnival. Sheila was satisfied that even if Sunnie wasn't listening, her heart was. Now, if she could just shrug off her inner fear that regardless of what he did or said, for her Zeke was a heartbreak waiting to happen.

A few days later, during a telephone conversation with a Denver detective, Zeke's hand tightened on the phone. "Are you sure?" he asked.

"Yes," the man replied. "I verified with a hospital in New Orleans that Diane Worth gave birth to a baby girl there five months ago. We could pick her up for questioning since abandoning a baby is a punishable crime."

Zeke inhaled a deep breath. "She could say the baby is living somewhere with relatives or friends, literally having us going around in circles. We need proof she's Sunnie's mother and have that proof when she's brought in. Otherwise, she'll give Miguel Rivera time to cover his tracks."

Zeke paused a moment and then added, "We need a DNA sample from Worth. How can we get it without her knowing about it?"

"I might have an idea." The agent then shared his idea with Zeke.

Zeke smiled. "That might work. We need to run it by Mathis."

"It's worth a try if it will link her to Rivera. We want him off the streets and behind bars as soon as possible. He's bad news."

Later that night, as he did every night, Zeke called Sheila. Another bouquet of flowers as well as a basket of candy had been delivered that day. He had been plying her with "thinking of you" gifts since he'd been gone, trying to keep her thoughts on him and to let her know how much he was missing her.

After thanking him for her gifts, she mentioned that Brad had stopped by to see how Sunnie was doing. Sheila had been surprised to see him, but was glad he had cared enough about the baby's welfare to make an unexpected visit. She even told Zeke how Sunnie had gone straight to the man without even a sniffle. And that she seemed as fascinated with him as he had been with her.

Zeke then brought her up to date on what they'd found out about Diane Worth. "It seems she has this weekly appointment at a hair salon. One of the detectives will get hair samples for DNA testing. Once they have a positive link to Sunnie, they will bring her in for questioning."

"What do you think her connection is to Michael Price?" Sheila asked.

"Don't know for sure, but I have a feeling things will begin to unravel in a few more days."

They talked a little while longer. He enjoyed her sharing Sunnie's activities for that day, especially how attached she had gotten to that toy he'd won for her at the carnival.

"I miss you," he said, meaning it. He hadn't seen her in over a week.

"And I miss you, too, Zeke."

He smiled. That's what he wanted to hear. And since they were on a roll… "And I love you," he added.

"And I love you back. Hurry home."

Home. His chest swelled with even more love for her at that moment. "I will, just as soon as I get this case solved." And he meant it.

* * *

A few days later things began falling into place. As usual, Worth had her hair appointment. It took a couple of days for the DNA to be matched with the sample taken from Sunnie. The results showed Diane was definitely Sunnie's biological mother.

Although Zeke wasn't in the interrogation room when Worth was brought in, she did what they assumed she would do—denying the abandoned child could be hers. She claimed her baby was on a long trip with her father. However, once proof was presented showing Sunnie was her child and had been used in a blackmail scheme, and that her hand had been caught on tape, which could be proven, the woman broke down and blurted out what she knew of the sordid scheme.

She admitted that Rivera had planned for her to meet Michael Price for the sole purpose of having him get her pregnant. Once Rivera found out Michael was from a wealthy family, he set up his plan of extortion. She was given a huge sum of money to seduce Michael, and once her pregnancy was confirmed, Rivera had shown up one night and joined the party. Throughout the evening at Diane's, he'd spiked Michael's drinks with a near-lethal dose of narcotics and made sure he got behind the wheel to drive home. What had been made to look like a drunk-driving accident was anything but—Michael had been murdered. She also said that up until that night, Michael had been drug-free for almost six months and had intended to reunite with his family and try to live a decent life. With Worth's confession linking Rivera to Michael's death, a warrant was issued and Rivera was arrested.

Zeke had kept Brad informed of what was going on. The Price family was devastated to learn the truth behind Michael's death and looked forward to making Sunnie part of their family. Brad, who had never given up hope that Michael would have eventually gotten his life together if he'd survived, had decided to be Sunnie's legal guardian. He felt Michael would have wanted things that way.

That night when he called Sheila and heard the excitement in her voice about receiving candy and more flowers he'd sent, he hated to be the deliverer of what he had to tell her. Although it was good news for Sunnie, because she would he raised by Brad and kept out of the system, it would be a sad time for Sheila.

"The flowers are beautiful, Zeke, and the candy was delicious. If I gain any weight it will be your fault."

He smiled briefly and then he said in a serious tone, "We wrapped things up today, Sheila. Diane Worth confessed and implicated Miguel Rivera in the process. He then told her how things went down and how in the end the authorities had booked both Worth and Rivera. Since Worth worked with the authorities, she would get a lighter sentence, and Rivera was booked for the murder of Michael Price.

"That is so sad, but at least we know what happened and why Brad had a genetic link to Sunnie," she said softly.

"Yes, and Brad is stepping up to the plate to become Sunnie's legal guardian. He's going to do right by her. Already his attorneys have filed custody papers and there is no doubt in my mind he will get it. That's another thing Worth agreed to do to get a lighter sentence. She will give up full rights to Sunnie. She didn't deserve her anyway. She deliberately got pregnant to use her baby to get money."

Zeke paused and then added, "She claims she didn't

know of Rivera's plans to kill Michael until it was too late."

"I guess that means I need to begin packing up Sunnie's stuff. He'll come and get her any day," Sheila said somberly.

"According to Brad, Social Services told him the exchange needs to take place at the end of the week. I'll be back by then. I won't let you be alone."

He thought he heard her sniffing before she said, "Thanks, Zeke. It would mean a lot to me if you were here."

They talked for a little while longer before saying good-night and hanging up the phone. Zeke could tell Sheila was sad at the thought of having to give up Sunnie and wished he was there right now to hold her in his arms, make love to her and assure her everything would be all right. They would have babies of their own one day. All the babies she could ever want, and that was a promise he intended to make to her when he saw her again.

A couple of days later, after putting Sunnie down after her breakfast feeding, Sheila's phone rang. "Hello?"

"Sheila, this is Lois. Are you okay?"

Sheila almost dropped the phone. The last time her sister called her was to cancel her visit to see her and her family. "Yes, why wouldn't I be?"

"You were mentioned on the national news again. The Denver police and some hotshot private investigator solved this murder case about a drug lord. According to the news, he'd been using women to seduce rich men, get pregnant by them and then use the resulting babies as leverage for extortion. I understand such a thing happened in Royal and you are the one taking care of the abandoned baby while the case was being solved."

Sheila released a disappointed sigh. Ever since the story had broken, several members of the media had contacted her for a story and she'd refused to give them one. Why did her sister only want to connect with her when she appeared in the news or something? "Yes, that's true."

"That's wonderful. Well, Ted was wondering if perhaps you could get in touch with the private investigator who helped to solve the case."

"Why?"

"To have him on his television talk show, of course. Ted's ratings have been down recently and he thinks the man's appearance will boost them back up."

Sheila shook her head. Not surprising that Lois wanted something of her. Why couldn't she call just because?

"So, do you have a way to help Ted get in touch with his guy?" Lois asked, interrupting Sheila's thoughts.

"Yes, in fact I know him very well. But if you or Ted want to contact him you need to do it without my help," she said. "I'm your sister and the only time you seem to remember that is when you need a favor. That's not the kind of relationship I want with you, Lois, and if that's the only kind you're willing to give then I'm going to pass. Goodbye."

She hung up the phone and wasn't surprised when Lois didn't call back. And she wasn't surprised when she received a call an hour later from her mother.

"Really, Sheila, why do you continue to get yourself in these kinds of predicaments? You know nothing about caring for a baby. How did you let yourself be talked into being any child's foster parent?"

Sheila rolled her eyes. "I'm a nurse, Mom. I'm used to taking care of people."

"But a kid? Better you than me."

"How well I know that," she almost snapped

Her mother's comments reminded her that in two days she would hand Sunnie over to Bradford Price. He had called last night and they had agreed the exchange would take place at the TCC. It seemed fitting since that was the place Diane Worth had left her daughter—although for all the wrong reasons—that she would begin her new life there again.

Sheila wasn't looking forward to giving up Sunnie. The only good thing was that Zeke would be flying in tonight and she wouldn't be alone. He would give her his support. No one had ever done that for her before. And she couldn't wait to see him again after almost two weeks.

Zeke paused in the middle of packing for his return home and met DEA Agent Mathis's intense gaze. "What do you mean Rivera's attorney is trying to get him off on a technicality? We have a confession from Diane Worth."

"I know," Mathis said in a frustrated tone, "but Rivera has one of the slickest lawyers around. They are trying to paint Worth as a crackhead and an unfit mother who'd desert her child for more drugs, and that she thought up the entire thing—the murder scheme—on her own. The attorney is claiming his client is a model citizen who is being set up."

"That's bull and you and I know it."

"Yes, and since he drove from Denver to New Orleans instead of taking a flight, we can't trace the car he used." Mathis let out a frustrated sigh and added,

"This is what we've been dealing with when it comes to Rivera. He has unscrupulous people on his payroll. He claims he was nowhere near New Orleans during the time Michael Price was killed. We have less than twenty-four hours to prove otherwise or he walks."

"Damn." Zeke rubbed his hand down his face. "I refuse to let him get away with this. I want to talk to Worth again. There might be something we missed that can prove that now she's the one being set up."

A few hours later Zeke and Mathis were sitting at a table across from Diane Worth. "I don't care what Miguel is saying," she said almost in tears. "He is the one who came up with the plan, not me."

"Is there any way you can prove that?" Zeke asked her. He glanced at his watch. He should be on a plane right this minute heading for Royal. Now he would have to call Sheila to let her know he wouldn't be arriving in Royal tonight as planned. He refused to leave Denver knowing there was a chance Miguel Rivera would get away with murder.

She shook her head. "No, there's no way I can prove it." And then she blinked as if she remembered something. "Wait a minute. When we got to New Orleans we stopped for gas and Miguel went inside to purchase a pack of cigarettes. The store clerk was out of his brand and he pitched a fit. Several people were inside the store and I bet one of them remembers him. He got pretty ugly."

Zeke looked over at Mathis. "And even if they don't remember him, chances are, the store had a security camera."

Both men quickly stood. They had less than twenty-four hours to prove Miguel was in New Orleans when he claimed that he wasn't.

* * *

Sheila shifted in bed and glanced over at the clock as excitement flowed down her spine. Zeke's plane should have landed by now. He would likely come straight to her place from the airport. At least he had given her the impression that he would when she'd talked to him that morning. And she couldn't wait to see him.

She had talked to Brad and she would deliver Sunnie to him at the TCC at three the day after tomorrow. It was as if Sunnie had detected something was bothering her and had been clingy today. Sheila hadn't minded. She had wanted to cling to the baby as much as Sunnie had wanted to cling to her.

She smiled when her cell phone rang. She picked it up and checked caller ID. It was Zeke. She sat up in bed as she answered it. "Are you calling to tell me you're outside?" she asked, unable to downplay the anticipation as well as the excitement in her voice.

"No, baby. I'm still in Denver. Something came up with the case and I won't be returning for possibly three days."

Three days? That meant he wouldn't be there when she handed Sunnie over to Bradford Price. "But I thought you were going to return tonight so you could be here on Thursday. For me."

"I want to and will try to make it, but—"

"Yes, I know. Something came up. I understand," she said, trying to keep the disappointment out of her voice. Why had she thought he was going to be different?

"I've got to go, Zeke."

"No, you don't. You're shutting me out, Sheila. You act as if I'd rather be here than there, and that's not true and you know it."

"Do I?"

"You should. I need to be here or else Miguel Rivera gets to walk away scot-free."

A part of her knew she was being unreasonable. He had a job to do. But still, another part just couldn't accept he wasn't doing a snow job on her. "And of course you can't let him do that," she said snippily.

He didn't say anything for a minute and then, "You know what your problem is, Sheila? You can't take hold of the future because you refuse to let go of the past. Think about that and I'll see you soon. Goodbye."

Instead of saying goodbye, she hung up the phone. How dare he insinuate she was the one with the problem? What made him think that he didn't have issues? She didn't know a single person who didn't.

She shifted back down in bed, refusing to let Zeke's comments get to her. But she knew it was too late. They already had.

Twelve

Two days later, it was a tired Zeke who made it to the Denver airport to return to Royal. He and Mathis had caught a flight from Denver to New Orleans and interviewed the owner of the convenience store. The man's eyewitness testimony, as well as the store's security camera, had pinned Rivera in New Orleans when he said he hadn't been there. With evidence in hand, they had left New Orleans to return to Denver late last night.

After reviewing the evidence this morning, a judge had ruled in their favor and had denied bail to Rivera and had refused to drop the charges. And if that wasn't bad enough, the lab had delivered the results of their findings. DNA of hair found on Michael's jacket belonged to Rivera. Zeke was satisfied that Rivera would be getting just what he deserved.

He glanced at his watch. The good thing was that he was returning to Royal in two days instead of three. It wasn't noon yet and if his flight left on time, he would arrive back in Royal around two, just in time to be with Sheila when she handed Sunnie over to Brad. He had called her that morning from the courthouse in Denver and wasn't sure if she had missed his call or deliberately not answered it. He figured she was upset, but at some point she had to begin believing in him. If for one minute she thought she was getting rid of him she had another thought coming. She was his life and he intended to be hers.

A few moments later he checked his watch again thinking they should be boarding his plane any minute. He couldn't wait to get to Royal and see Sheila to hold her in his arms, make love to her all night. He hadn't meant to fall in love with her.

An announcement was made on the nearby intercom system, interrupting his thoughts. *"For those waiting on Flight 2221, we regret to inform you there are mechanical problems. Our take-off time has been pushed back three hours."*

"Damn." Zeke said, drawing in a frustrated breath. He didn't have three hours. He had told Sheila he was going to try to be there, and he intended to do just that. She needed him today and he wanted to be there for her. He could not and would not let her down.

He knew the only way he could make that happen. He pulled his phone out of his pocket and punched in a few numbers.

"Hello?"

He swallowed deeply before saying, "Dad, this is Zeke."

There was a pause and then, "Yes, son?"

Zeke drew in another deep breath. He'd never asked his father for anything, but he was doing so now. "I have a favor to ask of you."

* * *

"Thank you for taking care of her, Ms. Hopkins," Bradford Price said as Sheila handed Sunnie over to him the next day at the TCC headquarters.

"You don't have to thank me, Mr. Price. It's been a joy taking care of Sunnie these past few weeks," Sheila said, fighting back her tears. "And I have all her belongings packed and ready to be picked up. You paid for all of it and you'll need every last item." Sunnie was looking at her, and Sheila refused to make eye contact with the baby for fear she would lose it.

"All right. I'm make arrangements to drop by your place sometime later, if that's all right," Brad said.

"Yes, that will be fine." She then went down a list of dos and don'ts for the baby, almost choking on every word. "She'll be fussy if she doesn't eat breakfast by eight, and she sleeps all through the night after being given a nice bath. Seven o'clock is her usual bedtime. She takes a short nap during the day right after her lunch. She has a favorite toy. It's the one Zeke won for her at the carnival. She likes playing with it and will do so for hours."

"Thanks for telling me all that, and if it makes you feel better to know although I'm a bachelor, I plan to take very good care of my niece. And I know a little about babies myself. My sister has twin girls and I was around them a lot when they were babies."

"Sorry, Mr. Price, I wasn't trying to insinuate you wouldn't take good care of her."

Bradford Price smiled. "I know. You love her. I could see it in your eyes when you look at her. And please call me Brad. Mr. Price is my father."

A pain settled around Sheila's heart when she remembered Zeke's similar comment. Then later, he had explained why he'd said it. She was missing him so much and knew she hadn't been fair to him when he'd called last night to explain his delay in returning to Royal.

"Yes, I love her, Brad. She's an easy baby to love. You'll see." She studied him a minute. He was Zeke's best friend. She wondered how much he knew about their relationship. At the moment it didn't matter what he knew or didn't know. He was going to be Sunnie's guardian and she believed in her heart he would do right by his niece.

"I'm looking forward to making her an integral part of my family. Michael would have wanted it that way. I loved my brother and all of us tried reaching out to help him. It was good to hear he was trying to turn his life around, and a part of me believes that eventually he would have. It wasn't fair the way Miguel Rivera ended his life that way."

"No, it wasn't," she agreed.

"That's why Zeke remained in Denver a couple more days," Brad said. "Rivera's shifty attorney tried to have the charges dropped, claiming Rivera wasn't in New Orleans when Michael died. Zeke and the DEA agent had to fly to New Orleans yesterday to get evidence to the contrary. Now Rivera will pay for what he did. And I got a call from Zeke an hour ago. His flight home has been delayed due to mechanical problems."

Sheila nodded. Now she knew why Zeke wasn't there. She understood. She should have understood two nights ago, but she hadn't given him the chance to explain. Now, not only was she losing Sunnie, she had lost Zeke, as well.

She'd pushed him away because she couldn't let go of the past. She was so afraid of being abandoned;

she couldn't truly open her heart to him. And now she feared she was truly alone.

She continued to fight back her tears. "I call her Sunnie," she said, fighting to keep her voice from breaking. "But I'm sure you're going to name her something else."

Brad smiled as he looked at the baby he held. "No, Sunnie is her name and it won't get changed. I think Sunnie Price fits her." He then glanced over at her. "What's your middle name?"

She was surprised by his question. "Nicole."

"Nice name. How does Sunnie Nicole Price sound?"

Sheila could barely find her voice to ask. "You'll name her after me?"

Brad chuckled. "Yes, you took very good care of her and I appreciate it. Besides, you're her godmother."

That came as another surprise. "I am?"

"I'd like you to be. I want you to always be a part of my niece's life, Sheila."

Joy beamed up inside Sheila. "Yes, yes, I'd love to. I would be honored."

"Good. I'll let you know when the ceremony at the church will be held."

"All right."

"Now I better get her home."

Sheila leaned up and kissed Sunnie on the cheek. The baby had taken to Brad as easily as she had taken to her and that was a good sign. "You better behave, my sunshine." And before she could break down then and there, she turned and quickly walked away.

Sheila made it to the nearest ladies' room and it was there that the tears she couldn't hold back any longer came flooding through and she began crying in earnest. She cried for the baby she'd just given up and for the man she had lost. She was alone, but being alone was the story of her life, and it shouldn't have to be this way. She wanted her own baby one day, just like Sunnie, but she knew that would never happen. She would never find a man to love her again. A man who'd want to give her his babies. She'd had such a man and now he probably didn't want to see her again. He was right. She couldn't take hold of the future because she refused to let go of the past.

She saw that now. Zeke was right. It was her problem. But he wasn't here for her to tell that to. He had no reason to want to come back to her. She was a woman with issues and problems.

"Excuse me. I don't want to intrude, but are you all right?"

Sheila turned at the sound of the feminine voice and looked at the woman with the long, wavy red hair and kind blue eyes. She was a stranger, but for some reason the woman's question opened the floodgates even more and Sheila found herself crying out her pain, telling the woman about Sunnie, about the man she loved and had lost, and how she'd also lost the chance to ever have a child of her own.

The stranger gave her a shoulder to cry on and provided her with comfort when she needed it. "I understand how you feel. More than anything I'd love to have a child, but I can't have one of my own," the woman said, fighting back her own tears.

"My problem is physical," she continued as a slow trickle of tears flowed down her cheeks. "Every time I think I've accepted the doctor's prognosis, I discover I truly haven't, so I know just how you feel. I want a child so badly and knowing I can't ever have one is something I've yet to accept, although I know I must."

Sheila began comforting the woman who just a moment ago had comforted her.

"By the way, I don't think I've introduced myself. I'm Abigail Langley," the woman said once she'd calmed down.

"I'm Sheila Hopkins." She felt an affinity for the woman, a special bond. Although they had just met, she had a feeling this would be the start of an extraordinary friendship. She was convinced she and Abigail would be friends for life.

A short while later they managed to pull themselves together and with red eyes and swollen noses they walked out of the ladies' room, making plans to get together for lunch one day soon.

The sun was shining bright when Sheila and Abigail stepped outside. Sheila glanced up into the sky. Although it was a little on the chilly side, it was a beautiful day in November. The sun was shining and it made her think of Sunnie. Thanksgiving would be next week and she had a feeling Brad would have a big feast to introduce the baby to his entire family.

Abigail nudged her in the side. "I think someone is waiting for you."

Sheila glanced across the parking lot. It was Zeke. He was standing beside her car and holding a bouquet of flowers in his hand. At that moment she was so glad to see him. Her heart filled with so much love. He had come back to her, with her problems and all. He had come back.

As fast as her legs could carry her, she raced across the parking lot to him and he caught her in his arms and kissed her hard. And she knew at that moment he was also her sunshine and that her heart would always shine bright for him.

* * *

God, he'd missed her, Zeke thought as he continued to deepen the kiss. Two weeks had been too long. And the more she flattened her body to his, the more he wanted to take her then and there. But he knew some things came first. He pulled back to tell her how much he loved her. But before he could, she began talking, nearly nonstop.

"I'm sorry, Zeke. I should have been more supportive of you like I wanted you to be supportive of me. And you were right, I do have a problem, but I promise to work on it and—"

He leaned down and kissed her again to shut her up. When he pulled his mouth away, this time he handed her the flowers. "These are for you."

She looked at them when he placed them in her hands and for a moment he thought she was going to start crying. When she glanced up at him, he saw tears sparkling in her eyes. "You brought me more flowers after how mean I was to you on the phone?"

"I know you were upset, but your being upset was not going to keep me away, Sheila."

She swiped at a tear. "I'm glad you think that way. I thought your plane had gotten delayed. How did you get here so fast?"

"I called my dad and asked a favor. I needed to get here for you, so I swallowed my pride and asked my father if I could borrow his jet and its crew to get me here ASAP."

He knew the moment the magnitude of what he'd said registered within Sheila's brain. The man who had never asked his father for anything had asked him for a favor because of her.

"Oh, Zeke. I love you so much," she said as fresh tears appeared in her eyes.

He held her gaze. "Do you love me enough to wear my last name, have my babies and spend the rest of your life with me?"

She nodded as she swiped at her tears. "Yes."

It was then and there, in the parking lot of the TCC, he dropped down on his knee and proposed. "In that case, Sheila Hopkins, will you marry me?"

"Yes. Yes!"

"Good." He then slid a beautiful ring on her finger.

Sheila's mouth almost dropped. It was such a gorgeous ring. She stared at it and then at him. "But... how?"

He chuckled. "Another favor of my dad. He had his personal jeweler bring samples on the plane he sent for me."

Sheila blinked. "You father did all that?"

"Yep. The plane, the jeweler and a travel agent on board."

She lifted a brow. "A travel agent?"

Zeke smiled as he stood and reached into his pocket and pulled out an envelope. "Yes, I have plane tickets inside. We'll marry within a week and then take off for a two-week honeymoon in Aspen over the Thanksgiving holidays. I refuse to spend another holiday single. Since neither of us knows how to ski, Aspen will be great—we'll want to spend more time inside our cabin instead of out of it. I think it's time we start working on that baby we both want."

Sheila's heart began to swell with even more love. He'd said she was his temptation, but for her, he would always be her hero. Her joy.

"Come on," he said, tucking her hand firmly in his. "Let's go home and plan our wedding...among other things. And before you ask, we're taking my car. We'll come back for yours later."

Clutching her flowers in her other hand, she walked beside him as she smiled at him. "You think of everything."

He chuckled as he tightened her hand in his. "For you I will always try, sweetheart."

And as he led her toward his car, she knew within her heart that he would. He was living proof that dreams did come true.

Epilogue

Just as Zeke had wanted, they had gotten married in a week. With Summer's help she was able to pull it off and had used the TCC's clubhouse. It was a small wedding with just family and friends. Brad had been Zeke's best man and Summer had been her maid of honor. And her new friend, Abigail Langley, had helped her pick out her dress. It was a beautiful above-the-knee eggshell-colored lace dress. And from the way Zeke had looked at her when she'd walked down the aisle, she could tell he had liked how she looked in it.

As nothing in Royal could ever be kept quiet, there had been mention of the wedding and small reception to be held at the TCC in the local papers. The story had been picked up by the national news wires as a follow-up to the stories about Zeke's heroics in the Miguel Rivera arrest.

Apparently, news of the wedding had reached as far as Houston and Atlanta.

Cassie had arrived with her short Texan in tow, and Sheila could tell she was trying real hard to hook him in as husband number six. Even Lois had surprised her by showing up with her family. It seemed Ted intended to take advantage of the fact Zeke was now his brother-in-law.

Then there were the Traverses. Lois's mouth dropped when she found out Zeke was one of "those" Travers. But she was smart enough not to ask Sheila for any favors. Sunnie was there dressed in a pretty, pink ruffled dress and it was quite obvious that Brad was quite taken with his niece. Sheila was Sunnie's godmother and Zeke was her godfather.

"I can't get over how much you and your siblings look alike," she whispered to Zeke, glancing around. "And your father is a handsome man, as well."

Zeke threw his head back and laughed. "I'll make sure to tell him you think so."

He glanced across the room and saw Brad talking to Abigail. They sure seem a lot friendlier these days, and he wondered if the truce would last when the election for president of the TCC started back up again. But for now they seemed seen to have forgotten they were opponents.

He glanced back at his wife, knowing he was a very lucky man. And they had decided to start working on a family right away. And he was looking forward to making it happen. "We'll be leaving in a little while. You ready?"

"Yes." Sheila smiled as she glanced over at Sunnie, who was getting a lot of attention from everyone. She appreciated the time she had spent with the baby.

"What are you smiling about?" Zeke leaned down to ask her.

Sheila glanced back at her husband. "You, this whole day, our honeymoon, the rest of our lives together...the list is endless, need I go on?"

Zeke shook his head. "No need. I know how you feel because I feel the same way."

And he meant it. She was everything he'd ever wanted in a woman. She would be his lover, his best friend and his confidante. The woman who was and always would be his temptation was now his wife. And he would love and cherish her forever.

* * * * *

"That was the first place I kissed you. Do you remember that?"

"How could I forget?" she asked.

"That was the summer we were getting ready to go into the first grade," he said. "Do you think that was what started our little game of one-upmanship?"

"Maybe." She tried to remember when their rivalry began, but the feel of him stroking her hair distracted her. "I—it's been so long, I'm not really certain when it began or why."

"Me either. But one thing's for sure. You've been driving me nuts for most of my life, Abigail Langley."

Her heart sped up as she met his piercing hazel gaze. "I'm sorry, but you've done your fair share of driving me to the brink, too."

"Don't be sorry." He cupped the back of her head with his hand to gently pull her forward. "There are different kinds of crazy, darlin'." His lips lightly brushed hers. "Right now, I'm thinking that it's the good kind."

Dear Reader,

One of my favorite things about being an author is when I'm asked to collaborate with other authors on a miniseries like the THE MILLIONAIRE'S CLUB. I not only get to work with some of the most talented authors in romance, I get to help refine the details that make the stories compelling and remembered long after the series ends.

By now, I'm sure you've met Bradford Price and Abigail Langley. Life-long competitors, they have been playing a game of one-upmanship since they were six years old. But finding themselves in a close race for the presidency of the club, the stakes have never been higher.

I really enjoyed the journey Brad and Abby take as they learn that sometimes just below the surface of a fierce rivalry, there's a burning attraction that once surfaced can't be denied—no matter how hard they try. It is my fervent hope that you enjoy reading *In Bed with the Opposition* as much as I enjoyed writing it.

All the best,

Kathie DeNosky

IN BED WITH THE OPPOSITION

BY
KATHIE DeNOSKY

MILLS &
BOON

Published in Great Britain 2012
by Mills & Boon, an imprint of Harlequin (UK) Limited,
Eton House, 18-24 Paradise Road, Richmond, Surrey TW9 1SR

© Harlequin Books S.A. 2011

Special thanks and acknowledgement to Kathie DeNosky for her contribution to the MILLIONAIRE'S CLUB series.

ISBN: 978 0 263 89169 0
ebook ISBN: 978 1 408 97765 1

951-0512

Kathie DeNosky lives in her native southern Illinois with her big, lovable Bernese Mountain Dog, Nemo. Writing highly sensual stories with a generous amount of humor, Kathie's books have appeared on the Waldenbooks bestseller list and received the Write Touch Readers Award and the National Readers' Choice Award. Kathie enjoys going to rodeos, traveling to research settings for her books and listening to country music. Readers may contact Kathie at PO Box 2064, Herrin, Illinois 62948-5264, USA, or e-mail her at kathie@kathiedenosky.com. They can also visit her website at www.kathiedenosky.com.

This book is dedicated to the wonderful authors I worked with on this miniseries. You all are amazing!

And to Charles Griemsman. It's been a real treat and I look forward to working on many more projects together.

One

Brad Price stared at the object in his hand, then at the tiny baby girl grinning up at him as she grabbed her foot and tried to stuff her tiny toes into her mouth. When had Sunnie lost her little pink sock?

Scratching his head, he scanned the floor. She had it on when they arrived at the Texas Cattleman's Club not two minutes ago. How could a baby barely six months old be so quick?

He once again glanced at the disposable diaper he held. What in the name of all that was holy had he gotten himself into, taking on the responsibility of raising his late brother's child? He knew about as much when it came to taking care of a baby as he did about piloting a spacecraft to the moon.

When he had made the decision to adopt Sunnie, he had even gone so far as to give serious consideration to dropping out of the race for the TCC presidency. But only briefly. He had made a commitment to seek the office, and he never went back on his word. Besides, he believed in the club and everything it stood for, and he intended to raise Sunnie to believe in those values, too.

The organization needed someone with a level head and a solid plan, and he was the man with both. He had several ideas on ways to bridge the ever-widening gap between the old guard and the younger members in order to unite the club and renew the solidarity that had always been an integral part of the TCC. It was something that had to be done to ensure its future and to continue the valuable services it had always provided for the residents of Royal, Texas.

But if he didn't figure out how to change Sunnie's diaper, and damned quick, it would all be a moot point. He would miss outlining his vision for the TCC at the annual general meeting, and for the first time in the club's history, a woman—the only woman ever to be allowed to join the organization—would be voted into office by default. He'd be damned if he'd let that happen.

Closing his eyes, Brad counted to ten. He could do this. He had a master's degree in financial planning, had graduated from the University of Texas summa cum laude and in the years since had built a thriving career as a certified financial planner, amassing a sizable fortune of his own. Surely he could figure out something as simple as changing a baby's disposable diaper.

But where did he start? And once he figured out

how to get the one she was wearing off and the new one in position, how the hell was he supposed to fasten it around her waist?

As he studied the sides of the diaper Sunnie was wearing, he tried to remember what his housekeeper, Juanita, had told him when she gave him a detailed lecture on diaper changing before she left him high and dry to rush off to Dallas for the birth of her third grandchild. Unfortunately, he had been preoccupied with putting the final touches on the campaign wrap-up speech he was supposed to give at today's meeting and barely heard the woman. In hindsight, he should have taken extensive notes or at the very least given the matter his undivided attention.

Just when he decided he was going to have to find one of the club's female employees and ask her to do the honors of changing his niece, he heard the door of the coat room open. "Thank God," he muttered, hoping it was someone who knew more about the intricacies of a disposable diaper than he did. "Would you mind giving me a hand here?"

"Having a bit of a problem, Mr. Price?" a familiar female voice asked. Relieved that help had arrived, Brad couldn't work up the slightest bit of irritation at the obvious humor in Abigail Langley's tone.

Turning to find his lifelong nemesis standing just inside the door, a knowing smile curving her full coral lips, Brad released a frustrated breath. They had been rivals for as long as he could remember and for the past several months bitter opponents for the coveted office of president of the TCC. At any other time her perceptive expression would have no doubt had him grinding his teeth. At the moment, he couldn't feel anything but gratitude.

"How are you at putting these things on a baby?" he asked, holding up the offending object.

Laughing, Abby hung up her coat. "Don't tell me the mighty Bradford Price has run into a problem he can't solve with his superior logic."

Not at all surprised that she took the opportunity to make fun of him, he gave her a sarcastic smile. "Cute, Langley. Now will you get over here and help me out?"

She walked over to stand beside the plush sofa, where his niece lay nibbling on her toes as she stared happily up at them. "You don't have the slightest clue what you're doing, do you, Bradford?"

Her use of his given name never failed to cause a slow burn deep in his gut. He knew she was using it to taunt him, much as she had done when they were in school. But he couldn't afford to retaliate. If he did she might not help him, and there was no point in denying the obvious anyway. They both knew he was in way over his head. Besides, arguing with her wouldn't get him any closer to getting the damned diaper changed.

"Isn't it apparent?" The familiar irritation he always felt when they were together had replaced his earlier relief at seeing her. "Now, are you going to help me or am I going to have to go in search of someone who will?"

"Of course I'll change Sunnie," she said, as she set down her purse and seated herself on the couch beside the baby. "But I'm not doing it to help you." She tickled the baby's rounded little tummy. "I'm doing it for this little angel."

"Fine. Whatever."

He didn't care who Abby was doing it for, as long as his niece was changed and dry in time for him to make arrangements for someone to watch her while he gave his closing campaign speech to the TCC general membership. Then, when all of the candidates had finished speaking and were asked to leave the room for final comments from the members, he fully intended to take Sunnie home for a much-needed nap for both of them.

The day had barely begun and he was already exhausted. Taking care of a baby was proving to be a lot more work than he had anticipated. Aside from the feedings at the most god-awful hours of the day and night, there was so much to take along when they left the house, it was like moving.

"Why didn't you leave the baby with your housekeeper?" Abby asked as she tucked her long, dark red hair behind her ears and reached for the diaper bag Juanita had packed before leaving on her trip.

"She got a call early this morning that her youngest daughter has been scheduled to have a Caesarian delivery tomorrow. She's on her way up to Dallas to be there for the birth," he answered, absently. "She won't be back for a couple of weeks."

Fascinated by Abby's efficiency, he watched her line up baby wipes and powder, then lift Sunnie to place a white pad with pink bunnies on it beneath her. How did women automatically know what to do? Were women born with an extra gene that men didn't have?

That had to be the reason, he decided. He and Abby were the same age, and up until Sunnie came into his life they had both been childless. Yet taking care of a baby seemed to come as naturally to Abby as drawing her next breath, while he was at a loss as to what he should do about everything.

In what Brad would judge to be record time, Abby had the old diaper off of Sunnie and the new one in place. "These are what you use to fasten the diaper around her." She pointed to the tabs on the sides he hadn't noticed before. "They are a softer version of Velcro so as not to scratch her tender skin. All you have to do is make sure it's snug, but not too tight, then—"

Fascinated by the sound of her melodic voice and wondering why he suddenly found it so enchanting, it took a moment for Brad to realize Abby had stopped speaking. "What?"

"Pay attention, Price. You can't be assured that someone will always be around to come to your rescue whenever Sunnie needs changing."

"I am paying attention." He had been listening—just not to the crash course on diapering a baby that Abby had been delivering. He wisely kept that bit of information to himself.

Looking doubtful, she asked, "What did I just tell you?"

Abby had to have the bluest eyes in Texas, he decided as she stared up at him expectantly. They were the color of the blue bonnets that grew wild in the spring, and Brad couldn't help but wonder why he'd never before noticed how vibrant and expressive they were.

"Well, Mr. Price?" The diaper successfully changed,

she picked up Sunnie and stood to face him. "Your niece and I are waiting."

He cleared his throat as he tried to remember what she had said. But the sight of her holding Sunnie, tenderly pressing her lips to the baby's soft cheek, was one Brad didn't think he would ever forget, and he couldn't for the life of him think of one single reason why he found it so compelling.

"Uh...well...let's see."

What the hell was wrong with him? Why all of a sudden was he having trouble concentrating? And why did his lapse of attention have to happen in front of *her?*

He never had problems focusing on a conversation. Why then, couldn't he think of anything but how perfectly shaped Abby's lips were and how soft they would feel on his skin?

"Get it snug. Fasten with Velcro. Avoid pinching tender skin," he finally managed with no small effort. "Got it." He gave himself a mental pat on the back for at least remembering that much.

"It took you that long to remember something this simple?" she asked, giving him an accusatory look. "Lucky guess."

"Yup." He shrugged. "But it doesn't matter. The important thing is that I got it right."

She shook her head. "You have to do better than that, Bradford. You can't just guess. You have to learn how to do these things for her." Abby slowly swayed side to side the way he'd seen many women do when they held a baby. "You're her daddy now. You've got to step up to the plate and hit a home run on this. Sunnie is depending on you to know exactly what you're doing and to do it when it needs to be done."

Abby was right. At times he found the responsibility of adopting his late brother's child and raising her as his own to be overwhelming. "Let me assure you, I'll do whatever it takes to see that Sunnie has the best of everything, including the care she needs," he said, irritated that she thought he would do anything less. "I think you know me well enough to realize that I never do anything halfway. When I commit to something, I'll see it through or die trying."

Staring at him a moment, she finally nodded. "Be sure that you do."

They both fell silent when Sunnie laid her little head on Abby's shoulder. It was obvious she was about to go to sleep.

As he watched, Abby closed her eyes and cuddled the baby close. "Don't ever lose sight of how blessed you are to have her in your life, Brad."

"Never." Something about her heartfelt statement and the fact that she had used the preferred variation of his name caught him off guard and without thinking he reached up to lightly run the back of his knuckles along her smooth cheek. "You're going to be a great mom someday, Abigail Langley."

When she opened her eyes, he wasn't prepared for the haunted look that clouded Abby's crystalline gaze. "I'm so sorry, Abby." He could have kicked himself for being so insensitive. It had barely been a year since her husband, Richard, passed away and Brad knew for a fact that they had being trying to start a family when the man died. "I'm sure that one day you'll have a family of your own."

She shook her head. "I wish that were true, but um…" She paused to take a deep breath. "…I'm afraid children aren't in my future."

The resigned tone in her voice had him nodding. "Of course they are. There will be plenty of time for you to have kids. You're only thirty-two, the same as me, and even if you don't meet another man you want to spend the rest of your life with, there are a lot of women choosing single motherhood these days."

She was silent a moment before she spoke again. "It's more complicated than meeting someone or choosing to be a single mother."

"Maybe it seems that way now, but I'm sure later on you'll feel differently," he insisted.

When she looked up at him, a single tear slowly slid down her smooth cheek. "It won't make a difference no matter how much time passes."

He couldn't understand her abject resignation. "What's wrong, Abby?"

She stared at him for several long seconds before she answered. "I'm…not able to have…children."

It was the last thing he expected her to say, and it made him feel like a complete jerk for pressing the issue. "I'm really sorry, Abby. I wasn't aware…" His voice trailed off. What could he say that wouldn't make matters worse?

She shrugged one slender shoulder. "It's not like I haven't known about it for a while. The test results came back the week after Richard's funeral."

That had been a little over a year ago, and Brad

could tell she still struggled with the gravity of it all. Why wouldn't she? To lose your husband and within days learn that you could never have a child? That had to be devastating.

Not wanting to cause her further emotional pain by saying the wrong thing, he decided it would be best not to lend his support with words. He had already put his foot in his mouth once and wanted to avoid doing so again. Putting his arms around her and his sleeping niece, he simply stood there and held her.

But the comforting gesture quickly reminded him of another time when he would have given anything to have her slender body pressed to his. They had just started high school, and over the summer between middle school and freshman year, he had developed more hormones than good sense. At fifteen, he had been more than ready to abandon their rivalry in favor of being able to call her his girlfriend.

Unfortunately, Richard Langley had caught her attention about that time, and from then on it had been obvious that Abby and Richard were destined to be together. And it was just as well, Brad decided. She could push his buttons faster than any female he had ever met and have him grinding his teeth in two seconds flat. It had been that way back then and it was still, after all these years, that way now.

"It would probably be a good idea if we head toward the assembly room," she said, effectively ending his trip down memory lane. "It's almost time for the meeting to be called to order." Her tone was soft, but her voice was steadier than it had been earlier, and he knew she had regained the majority of her composure.

Nodding, Brad released her and took a step back. He wasn't sure what to say that wouldn't make the moment more awkward than it already was. "I should have just enough time to get one of the staff to watch Sunnie before the speeches begin," he finally said, checking his watch.

"How long do you think she'll nap?" Abby asked, walking over to carefully place the infant in the car-seat carrier. "If you think she'll sleep through the speeches, I'll watch her while you address the general membership."

Since Sunnie had come into his life, they had established a truce of sorts, but old habits died hard. He didn't believe for a minute Abby was willingly helping him to win the office they both sought. But neither did he believe she would do something underhanded like wake the baby in the middle of his speech. In all of their years of competing against each other, neither of them had ever resorted to sabotage to come out on top.

"You don't mind?"

"Not at all." She put the baby wipes and powder back into the diaper bag. "But don't think I'm doing it to help you with this election or that I won't take great pleasure in beating the socks off of you when the results are announced at the Christmas Ball."

More comfortable with the return of the rivalry they'd shared for as long as he could remember, he smiled. "Of course not. You're doing it for—"

"Sunnie," she said, picking up her purse and the diaper bag.

Grinning, Brad took hold of the baby carrier's

handle, then put his hand to the small of Abby's back to guide her toward the coat room door. "Ready to go in there and listen to the best wrap-up speech you've ever heard?"

"In your dreams, Price," she said, preceding him out the door and into the hall. "I know you've always been a windbag, but you would have to produce a Texas tornado to impress me."

Walking toward the assembly room, he laughed. "Then you had better prepare yourself, Ms. Langley, because you're about to be blown away."

Seated at the table with all of the candidates running for the various club offices, Abby checked on Sunnie napping peacefully in the baby carrier on the chair between her and Brad. Satisfied the infant would sleep through at least the majority of the speeches, Abby looked around the assembly of Texas Cattleman's Club members.

Up until seven months ago, the TCC had been an exclusively male organization with no thoughts to making it open to women. But she had broken through the glass ceiling and become the first female member in the club's long history.

Unfortunately, the invitation to join had not been because of what she could bring to the club, but due to her last name. Founded by her late husband's great-great-great grandfather, Tex Langley, over a hundred years ago, the TCC had always boasted a member of the Langley family in its ranks. But with Richard's death a year ago, it had been the first time since the organization's inception that a Langley had not been listed on the club's membership roster. She had a little known bylaw requiring Langley representation within the club to thank for her admittance.

She sighed, then squared her shoulders and sat up a little straighter. It didn't matter what the reason was that had gained her membership in the TCC; she'd blazed a trail. Now she fully intended to see that other women were considered for entry into the prestigious ranks just as soon as she became the new club president. She couldn't think of a more fitting way to open the new clubhouse she was sure the members were going to vote to build than to have a membership roster with the names of many of the women who had supported the Texas Cattleman's Club throughout the years.

When her name was announced as the next speaker, she checked on Sunnie one last time before walking up to the podium to outline her agenda. Looking out over the room, she could tell that the older members were less than pleased to have her in their ranks, let alone see her running for the high office. But that was just too bad. It was time they joined the twenty-first century and realized that a woman was just as capable of getting things accomplished as any man.

After going over each point in her plan for the future of the TCC, she ended her speech with a mention of her pet project. "The building committee has hired an architect and presented his plans for a new clubhouse. It is my sincere hope that you vote to move forward with this project to build a new home for our club and the exciting new era we are entering into. In closing, I ask that you all consider what I've said here today and base your vote on what I can bring to the Texas Cattleman's Club presidency, not on my gender or my last name. Thank you, and I look forward to serving as the next president of the Texas Cattleman's Club." As she walked back to the table to take her seat, she received a rousing ovation from some of the club's newer members and a grudging nod of respect from a couple of the older ones.

She was confident that she had done all she could do and represented the Langleys, as well as her gender, to the best of her ability. Now it would be up to the members to decide what direction they wanted the TCC to take when the actual voting took place tomorrow.

"Top that, Price," she said, throwing down a challenge to her lifelong rival.

His hazel eyes twinkled as he rose to his feet and prepared to walk up to the front of the room. "Piece of cake, darlin'."

She wasn't fooled by his use of the endearment. Like most Texas men, Bradford Price called all women "darlin'." What she couldn't understand was why it sent a tiny little shiver coursing throughout her body.

Deciding it was best to ignore her reaction, she concentrated on Brad delivering his speech. She had to admit he was an engaging speaker and had a lot of good ideas—some of them paralleling her own. But that didn't mean she was ready to concede.

For as long as she could remember she and Brad Price had been pitted against each other in one competition or another. Sometimes he won, other times she came out on top. But the rivalry was ever present and at times quite fierce.

Abby couldn't help but smile as she remembered some of the contests they'd found themselves embroiled in. Their game of one-upsmanship had started in the first grade, when they worked to see who would be ranked higher on the honor roll at the end of each term. In middle school, they had competed to represent their class on the student council. By the time they reached high school, they were in an all-out race to see which one of them would be at the top of their graduating class. That particular competition had turned out to be a draw, and they ended up sharing the honor of being co-valedictorians.

Through it all, they had goaded, teased and thrown out challenges, and although their rivalry had never become a cutthroat battle, they hadn't been friends, either. That was why, earlier in the coat room when Brad had shown such genuine concern and compassion, he had thrown her off guard. Maybe that was the reason she had felt compelled to tell him about her infertility.

She took a deep breath. Her inability to bear a child wasn't something she discussed freely, and she couldn't believe that she had opened up to him about it. She hadn't even been able to bring herself to tell some of her close friends. Why had she shared one of her most painful secrets with him?

As she pondered her uncharacteristic behavior, Sunnie began to squirm within the confines of the baby carrier, and Abby knew she was about to wake up. If the infant's whimpering was any indication, she was working up a lusty cry. Before they disrupted the rest of Brad's speech, Abby grabbed the diaper bag and her purse, then picked up the baby from the carrier and walked to the double doors at the back of the room.

They hadn't been out in the main hall more than a few minutes when Brad—baby carrier in hand—and the other men running for the board joined them. "After the vote tomorrow, all we have to do is wait until the Christmas Ball to see who wins," he said, setting the carrier on the floor beside them.

"We're done for the day?" she asked, placing a pacifier to Sunnie's eager lips.

Brad nodded. "It's a good thing, too. I think I need to take this little lady home and give her a bottle before we both crash for the afternoon."

"Have you considered hiring a nanny?" Abby asked, patting the baby's back as she swayed from side to side in an effort to keep Sunnie calm.

"I don't intend to hire anyone to take care of Sunnie," he said, stubbornly shaking his head. "I took on the responsibility of raising her and that's what I fully intend to do. I'm not handing her care over to someone else, other than an occasional night out or a business meeting."

When he didn't elaborate, she felt compelled to ask, "How on earth are you going to manage taking care of her for the next couple of weeks without your housekeeper being around to advise you?" She hoped he was better at feeding a baby than he was at changing diapers.

Abby watched him run his hand through his thick, dark brown hair. She could tell he was a bit uneasy about being solely responsible for Sunnie's care. "I'll do my best, and if I run into something I can't handle,

I'll call my best friend Zeke Travers' wife, Sheila, or my sister, Sadie, for advice," he said decisively. "Sheila's a nurse and took care of Sunnie until I got custody. I'm sure if needed, one of them would be willing to come over and show me what to do." He smiled. "By the way, thank you for watching her while I finished my speech. I really appreciate it."

"I didn't mind at all." Setting the diaper bag on the floor, Abby knelt to place Sunnie in the carrier, then secured the straps and tucked a blanket in around her. "My ranch isn't far from your house. If you can't get hold of Sheila or Sadie, you can always give me a call and I'll try to answer whatever questions you might have."

"I'll keep that in mind," he said seriously.

When she stood up, they stared at each other for several long moments as they both realized the other candidates had left and they were alone.

He suddenly gave her a lopsided grin. "Have you looked up?"

"No," she answered slowly. "Should I?"

He pointed to something hanging from one of the heavy beams on the ceiling. "You're standing under the mistletoe."

"I hadn't…" her breath caught when he stepped forward and put his arms around her waist "…noticed." Surely he wasn't going to kiss her?

"I have to," he said, as if reading her thoughts. "It's a tradition."

Before she had the chance to remind him that they were opponents and that she wasn't interested in observing that particular custom with him or anyone else, his mouth settled over hers in a kiss so gentle it left her speechless. Firm and warm, his lips caressed hers with a mastery that confirmed all the rumors she had heard about him being a ladies' man. No man kissed that way without having one of two things—either a natural sense of what pleased a woman or a wealth of experience. Abby suspected that Bradford Price had an abundance of both.

Feeling as if her legs were about to fold beneath her, she reached up to put her hands on his wide shoulders. The solid strength she felt beneath the fabric of his black Armani jacket sent her heart racing and did nothing to help steady her wobbly knees. But when he wrapped his arms around her and pulled her more fully against him, her legs failed her completely and she sagged against him.

Thankfully Sunnie chose that moment to spit out her pacifier and wail at the top of her little lungs, effectively bringing Abby out of the spell Brad had put her under. Leaning back, she quickly looked around to see if anyone had been watching them. She was relieved to find that the hall was empty.

"I…need to…get my coat," she said, feeling as if the oxygen had been sucked from the room. "Sheila and I have…some shopping to do for the party…at the women's shelter."

"Yeah, I should get Sunnie home for a bottle and a nap." To her extreme displeasure, Brad didn't act as if he had been affected one darned bit by the kiss.

He stuck his hand out and without thinking, Abby reached out to shake it. The moment their palms touched, a warm tingling sensation streaked up her arm. She quickly drew back.

"May the best man—"

"Or woman," she automatically corrected him.

Shaking his head, he gave her that knowing grin of his—the one that never failed to make her want to bop him. "I suppose it won't hurt for you to hang on to that little dream until it's announced that I've won."

"Oh, don't worry, Price. I most certainly will," she said, with renewed determination. "I can't wait to see the look on your face when I win."

"We'll see about that, Langley." He picked up the baby carrier and diaper bag, then turned toward the exit. "If I were you I wouldn't start polishing your gavel just yet."

"I could say the same thing about you and your presidential gavel," she shot back.

His deep laughter as he walked down the hall and out of sight sent a wave of anger coursing through her. What on earth had gotten into her? Why had she let him kiss her? And why was she standing there like a complete ninny, watching him leave?

Unable to understand her atypical behavior, Abby started toward the coatroom. She wished she had the answers to why she'd acted so out of character, but at the moment nothing came to mind—other than she might have temporarily lost her mind.

Shaking her head, she pulled on her coat and walked to her car. She wasn't certain who she was more angry with, him for being so blasted arrogant or herself for letting him get away with it.

But one thing was crystal clear. Nothing like that

was going to happen again. Aside from the fact that she wasn't interested in being kissed by any man, she was far more comfortable dealing with Bradford Price her lifelong opponent than she would ever be with Brad Price—arguably the best kisser in southwest Texas.

Two

"Zeke, is Sheila at home?" Brad asked, as soon as his best friend answered the phone.

"Hey man, how are things going?" Zeke Travers asked cheerfully.

Brad tried to rub away the tension building at the back of his neck. "At the moment, not good."

"I can tell." Zeke laughed. "It sounds like Sunnie is throwing one grand and glorious fit. Where's Juanita?"

"Out of town and—"

"Uh-oh, you're on your own with the baby," Zeke finished for him.

"Yeah and she won't stop crying," Brad said, wondering how something as small as a baby could make so much noise. He was pretty sure her wailing had the dogs barking in downtown Royal. "I was hoping Sheila might have an idea of what could be wrong with her."

"Sorry, man. Sheila went with Abby Langley to do some shopping for the Christmas party they're throwing next week for the kids at the women's shelter over in Somerset." His friend paused. "Do you think Sunnie might be hungry? When Sheila took care of her, I noticed that Sunnie was pretty short on patience when she wanted a bottle."

"It hasn't been that long since I fed her, and everything was fine up until about ten minutes ago," Brad said miserably. "That's when she started crying, and she won't stop."

"Maybe she needs her diaper changed," Zeke suggested, sounding as mystified as Brad felt.

"I just put a new one on her." Brad walked over to the baby swing, where his niece sat screaming at the top of her lungs. "I've tried rocking her, holding her to my shoulder and walking the floor with her. Nothing seems to help. She normally likes her swing, but that isn't cutting it with her this evening, either."

"Man, I don't know what to tell you." Zeke paused. "Hang on a minute. Abby's car just pulled into the driveway. Let me fill Sheila in on what's going on and then have her call you back."

"Thanks, Zeke. I owe you one," Brad said, ending the call. He tossed the phone on the couch and picked up Sunnie to pace the floor with her again.

He hated having to bother Zeke and Sheila. They were newlyweds, and he was pretty sure they had more pleasurable things to do in the evenings than give him advice on how to care for a baby. But he was at his wit's end and man enough to admit that he needed help.

"It's okay, baby girl," he crooned as he patted her

back and walked from one room to another. "We'll get through this."

If anything Sunnie's screaming got louder and made him feel like a complete failure for the first time in his life. He had thought he was doing the right thing when he made the decision to adopt his late brother Michael's daughter. But if today was any indication of his parenting skills, he might have been wrong. Although he had gotten the hang of diapering and feeding Sunnie, it appeared he was a complete washout at knowing what was wrong and how to calm her.

What was taking Zeke and Sheila so long to return his call? he wondered, checking his watch. It had been a good ten minutes since Zeke assured him that Sheila would call him back.

With Sunnie wailing in his ear like a banshee gone berserk, it took a moment for Brad to realize that someone was ringing the doorbell. "Thank God," he muttered, as he rushed over to open the door. He fully expected to see Zeke and Sheila Travers standing on the other side. "I really appreciate—"

Instead of Sheila, Abigail Langley stood on the front porch with her hand raised to ring the doorbell again. Great. The last thing he needed was her witnessing yet another of his inadequacies in child care.

"I don't want to be here any more than you want me here," she said, as she hurried into the foyer. "But Sheila became ill while we were out shopping and asked me to stop by to check on you and Sunnie."

Apparently he hadn't been very good at hiding his displeasure at seeing her again. But Abby's help was better than no help at all, he quickly decided when the baby's screaming reached a crescendo. Explaining everything he'd tried to get Sunnie to stop crying, Brad shook his head. "Nothing works. She'll start to wind down and look like she's going to nod off, then she'll open her eyes and start screaming again. If she keeps this up much longer, I'm afraid she'll hurt herself."

Quickly removing her coat, Abby handed it and her purse to him as she reached to take the baby. "It's all right, angel. Help has arrived. Where's her pacifier?"

He handed Abby the one he had been trying to get Sunnie to take. "I don't think it will do any good. She keeps spitting it out."

As soon as Abby placed the pacifier in the baby's mouth and cradled her close, Sunnie's crying began to lessen. "Do you have a rocking chair?" Abby asked.

All she had to do was walk in the door and take the baby from him and Sunnie reduced the racket she was making by a good ten decibels. "What the hell does she have that I don't?" he muttered under his breath, as he laid Abby's coat and purse on a bench in the hall, then led the way to the family room.

Motioning toward the new rocking chair he'd bought the day before bringing Sunnie home from Sheila and Zeke's, Brad stuffed his hands into the front pockets of his jeans and watched as Abby seated herself and began to gently rock the baby. In no time at all Sunnie's cries had settled to occasional whimpers and he could tell she was about to go to sleep.

"When I tried rocking her, she just screamed louder," he said, unable to keep from feeling a bit resentful. The immediate change in the baby when Abby took her made him feel completely inept, and it annoyed him beyond words that she had been witness to it.

"I think the problem is that you're nervous about taking care of her without help." Abby shifted Sunnie from her shoulder to the crook of her arm. "She senses that."

"I don't get nervous," he said flatly. Frowning, he stubbornly shook his head. "I might feel a little apprehensive about being solely responsible for her care, but I'm not the nervous type."

Abby laughed softly. "Apprehension, nervousness, whatever you want to call it, I think she's picking up on it and she's letting you know the only way she can that it upsets her."

Feeling a little insulted, he glared at the woman calmly rocking his niece. "So you're saying it's my fault she wouldn't stop crying?"

Her indulgent smile as she shook her head had him clenching his teeth. "Not entirely. I think a big part of her problem is that she's fighting to stay awake."

Brad grunted. "I'd rather fight *for* sleep than against it."

She nodded. "Me, too. But with each day Sunnie is becoming more alert and aware of what's going on around her. I think she's probably afraid she'll miss something."

While Abby rocked the baby, Brad went into the kitchen to start a pot of coffee and see if there was some of Juanita's apple cake left. The least he could do was offer Abby cake and coffee for bringing the noise level down. When he returned to the family room, Sunnie was sound asleep.

"I don't think we should risk waking her when you pick her up," Abby said, her tone low.

"Good God, no." Just the thought of another crying marathon like the one that had just ended made him cringe.

Rising from the chair, she smiled. "If you'll tell me where the nursery is, I'll put her to bed for you."

He led the way up the stairs to the bedroom he'd turned into a nursery and couldn't help but notice how natural Abby looked with a baby in her arms. If any woman was meant to mother a child, it was Abigail Langley. It bothered him to think she wasn't going to give herself that chance.

He had come to fatherhood through adoption. She could reach motherhood that way, too. All she had to do was open herself to the possibility. But she apparently wasn't ready to consider her options and it wasn't his place to point out what they were.

While she put Sunnie to bed in the crib, he turned on the camera and picked up the video baby monitor to take with them. "Thank you for stopping by," he said once they'd left the nursery and were descending the stairs. "It seems like you've had to come to my rescue twice today."

She gave him a questioning look. "Since Sunnie is wearing a dry diaper, I assume you mastered that challenge?"

Nodding, he grinned. "It turned out to be a lot easier than getting her to bed for the night." When they reached the bottom of the stairs, he asked, "Would you like to stay for a cup of coffee and a piece of cake?"

"I...should go and let you enjoy the quiet," she said,

walking over to the bench where he had laid her coat and purse earlier. "If you have any more problems you can always call me."

Before she had a chance to pick up her things, he placed his hand to the small of her back and ushered Abby toward the family room. "To tell you the truth, I could use the company of another adult for a little while. As you've seen this evening, Sunnie isn't exactly a witty conversationalist just yet."

"No, but you have to admit, she gets her point across," Abby said, smiling.

"No kidding." He rubbed the side of his head. "I'm still experiencing some ringing in my left ear."

When they went into the family room, she sat down on the edge of the couch. "If you don't mind, I think I'll pass on the cake and coffee. If I drink caffeine now, I'll be up all night."

"Would you like something else?" He walked over to turn on the gas log in the fireplace. "I think there are some soft drinks in the fridge."

Abby shook her head. "I'm fine. Thank you."

"I'd offer you something stronger, but since I don't drink, I don't keep it around the house."

Brad's sister, Sadie, had told her that he never drank anything stronger than coffee or iced tea, due to the fact that their older brother, Michael, had been an alcoholic, as well as a drug addict. It had ultimately led to the man's death when, in a drug and alcohol induced haze, he'd crashed through a guardrail and driven over the side of a cliff.

"I'm not much of a drinker, either," she admitted.

"I might have an occasional glass of wine with dinner, but that's about it."

Brad sank into the big, overstuffed armchair flanking the couch. "Don't get me wrong. I have nothing against drinking in moderation. It's when a person doesn't know when to quit that it becomes a problem."

"Like it did for your brother?" she asked.

He nodded. "Mike had a rebellious streak a mile wide and would do anything he could think of to humiliate our dad. What better way to do it than to become the town drunk?"

She could tell Brad resented the fact that his brother had gone out of his way to humiliate the Price family. She could sympathize. In her senior year in high school she had suffered through her own family's scandal, and knowing they were the subject of intense gossip and speculation had been one of the worst times in her life.

"A lot of kids go through a reckless stage," she offered gently. "I'm sure Michael never meant for it to become the huge problem that it did for him."

"You're probably right. Unfortunately, Mike never seemed to be able to come out of that phase and it just got worse when Dad disowned him."

Two years older than she and Brad, all she could remember about Michael Price was that he had a reputation for partying hard and raising hell. "Was your dad disowning him the reason he left Royal?"

"Dad had reached the end of his rope," Brad said, nodding. "He ordered Mike out of the house and rather than stick around to see how Dad felt once he had cooled down, Mike took off. The first news we had of him was eight months ago when we were notified that he'd been killed."

"Michael's death must have broken your father's heart," she said, unable to imagine the degree of desperation Brad's father had to have reached to take such a drastic stand. To lose his son without making amends had to have been crushing.

"I'm sure it affected him more than he let show." Raising one dark eyebrow, Brad gave her a pointed look. "But don't get the idea that Robert Price would have handled it any other way. You know how he is about appearances. Sadie wouldn't have made the decision to move to Houston when she got pregnant with the twins if she hadn't been worried about our father's disapproval."

Abby had been in Seattle at the time, working at the web development company she and one of her college friends had started right after graduation. It wasn't until she sold her interest in the highly successful venture and moved back to Royal to marry Richard that she learned the story behind Sadie's move.

"I'm glad she decided to return to Royal," Abby said sincerely. "If she hadn't, she and Rick might not have run into each other."

Brad's sister had become pregnant after one night with Rick Pruitt, just before the dashing Marine had been deployed to the Middle East. Losing touch, it wasn't until some three years later that they were reunited when they ran into each other at the TCC clubhouse. Now they were happily married, raising their adorable two-year-old twin daughters and looking forward to a bright future together.

"Dad mellowed over the years and was pleased about her and the girls moving back, so it all worked out for the best." Brad glanced at the video monitor he still held. "Do you think Sunnie will be all right? She cried awfully hard there for a while."

"Babies do that." Abby couldn't help but be a bit amused. She had never seen Brad Price look more unsure of himself, and she found it oddly fascinating. "I think she'll be fine, Brad. Really."

"I hope that's the case," he said, placing the monitor on the end table beside his chair.

"This afternoon you mentioned that you don't intend to hire a nanny," she said, when he glanced at the monitor again as if needing to reassure himself that the baby was all right. "Having help might give you a bit more peace of mind about caring for her."

"I'm not entirely certain that handing Sunnie's care over to someone else would be in her best interest," he said, surprising her. His expression told her that he had given the matter a considerable amount of thought.

"You're going to try to do this on your own?" She hadn't meant to sound so incredulous, but men with the kind of fortune Bradford Price had amassed hired help to take care of their children, even if they were married.

"Yes, I am," he answered decisively. He sat forward, propping his forearms on his knees, and stared down at his hands as if trying to put his reasoning into words. "This isn't about me or my comfort. This is about Sunnie. In her short little life, she's been abandoned by her mother, used as a pawn in a blackmail scheme and passed from one stranger to another. She hasn't really had the chance to bond with anyone." His tone took on a hard edge. "She deserves a hell of a lot better than that."

Abby couldn't have agreed more. Sunnie had been the result of Michael Price's only night with an unscrupulous woman who, after giving birth, had tried using her infant daughter at the request of a dangerous drug lord to extort money from the Price family. They had sent blackmail notes to Brad, as well as a few other TCC members, telling each of them they were the father in an effort to get as much money as they could. He had correctly assumed they'd be too embarrassed to reveal to each other that they were being blackmailed. But when Brad and the other men who had received notes refused to pay, the career criminal had given up on his scheme and the mother abandoned the baby on the doorstep of the club with a note pinned to her blanket, declaring Brad was Sunnie's father. A DNA test proved that there was indeed a genetic link, but when Zeke Travers tracked down the baby's mother, she admitted that it was Michael Price and not Brad who had fathered Sunnie. Whether it was due to a sense of obligation to his late brother or the fact that Sunnie had captured his heart, Brad had taken responsibility for her and started the adoption process.

"I applaud your dedication," she said, choosing her words carefully. He was trying so hard to do the right thing for Sunnie, she certainly didn't want to discourage him. "But don't you think it would be wise to have a little help? At least until you become more accustomed to caring for her by yourself?"

"She's had so many people come and go in her life,

I want her to know that I'm not just another person taking care of her until the next one comes along." He shrugged. "I want her to know early on that I'm always going to be here for her. That's why I'm working from home for the next six months."

"You're serious," she said softly, in total awe of the lengths he was willing to go to for the baby girl.

"Very. My assistant is running the day to day operation at the firm and forwarding anything she can't handle through email and faxes. After Sunnie's first birthday, I'll see how things are going and make my decision whether to continue working from home or go back into the office."

Abby had gained a newfound respect for Brad when she heard he was taking on the responsibility of raising Sunnie as his own, but that admiration had just gone up a good ten notches. She knew a lot of men with his wealth and position in the business community who wouldn't even consider going to such lengths for their own children, let alone a niece or nephew they were adopting.

The contrast between Bradford Price, the playboy financial genius, and Brad Price, the dedicated new daddy, was disconcerting and Abby needed time to assimilate and understand the two sides of his personality. It had been much easier to view him as her lifelong rival and fierce opponent in the race for the TCC presidency than it was to see him as the down-to-earth, caring man she had seen over the course of the day.

Needing to put distance between them, she made a show of checking her watch as she rose from the couch.

"I should go. I have to get up early tomorrow to help Summer Franklin with the charity drive."

"In other words, you're going to put those god-awful pink flamingos in some poor unsuspecting soul's front yard, so he'll have to donate money to the Helping Hands Women's Shelter to get rid of them," Brad said, getting up to walk her to the door.

"It's for a good cause," Abby defended.

"I'm not saying it isn't." Brad laughed. "But pink flamingos? Seriously, couldn't they come up with something a lot more attractive and a little less tasteless?"

She picked up her coat and purse as they passed the bench in the hall. "If they were attractive, people might not be as eager to get rid of them and donate less."

"I guess you have a point," he conceded. "But do me a favor."

"What's that?" she asked as he took her coat from her and held it while she put it on.

Placing his hands on her shoulders, he turned her to face him. "When you drive by my place, keep on going," he said, grinning. "I'll send in a donation just to keep from having to look at them." Before she realized what was happening, he wrapped his arms around her and pulled her close for a hug. "Thank you again for helping me out with Sunnie this morning and then again this evening. I really appreciate it, darlin'."

For some reason, the endearment most Texas men used freely when talking to a woman sent a shiver straight up her spine and the awareness she had experienced when Brad kissed her under the mistletoe came rushing back tenfold. When had the skinny kid she had always competed against developed so many muscles? And why did they feel so darned good pressed against her?

Hastily backing away from him, she walked to the door, hoping he hadn't noticed the fact that she had clung to him a little longer than was required for an embrace of appreciation. "If it gives you any measure of comfort, I can guarantee the pink flamingos won't be on your lawn tomorrow morning when you get up."

Grinning, he slipped his hands up to his thumbs into the front pockets of his jeans and rocked back on his heels. "That's good to know."

Stepping out onto the porch, she couldn't resist turning back for one parting shot. "But don't get too complacent, Price. Your day will come when you least expect it."

What was wrong with her? she wondered, as she walked to her car. Why after all these years was she suddenly noticing Brad's impressive muscles? How could it be that she felt more secure with his arms around her than she had in very long time? Had it been so long since she had been held by a man that even Bradford Price could make her feel breathless and cause her pulse to speed up?

"You've lost your mind, girlfriend," she muttered to herself as she steered her luxury SUV around the circular drive and out onto the street.

She wasn't looking to be held by any man, let alone a playboy like Bradford Price. With his piercing hazel eyes and dark good looks, he represented trouble with a great big capital T and she wanted no part of it.

Besides, after experiencing the pain of losing her

husband, she wasn't about to give her heart to another man and put herself in the position to go through something like that again. She was a survivor and it was only through working for various charities that she had kept herself going after the many disappointments of the past year. And although she did get lonely at times, community service would have to be enough for her. It was far less dangerous to her peace of mind than the almost irresistible combination of Bradford Price, with his rock-hard biceps and movie star good looks, and the most adorable baby girl Abby had ever seen.

"How much longer do you think we need to stay before it's socially acceptable to leave?" Brad asked Zeke, as he checked his watch.

If the informal cocktail party he was attending hadn't been in honor of the candidates for the various club offices, he would have declined the invitation. Instead, he had sipped on his club soda, engaged in the obligatory mingling with all of the other guests and counted the minutes until he could politely thank the election committee chairman, Travis Whelan, and his wife, Natalie, for hosting the party and leave.

"What's the rush?" Zeke asked, looking puzzled. "I thought you'd be glad to have an evening off from your child-care duties. After all, you've been on your own with Sunnie now for the past week."

Brad shrugged. "Sunnie isn't the easiest baby to get to sleep, and I'm pretty sure my sister will be ready to throw me to the coyotes by the time I get back."

"What happened to Bad Brad, the heartthrob of every sorority sister on the UT campus?" Zeke laughed.

"If you're not careful, you're going to ruin your reputation as a world-class player."

"The reports of my past conquests are greatly exaggerated," Brad said, grinning. "If you'll remember, I was the one sitting in our dorm room studying while you and Chris Richards were out on the town."

"Yeah, maybe once," Zeke shot back, his smile wide. "If you'll remember, Chris Richards and I were usually with you in those days and doing anything but studying."

As he and his best friend stood there reminiscing about their college days and their friend, Chris, another member of the TCC, Brad noticed Abby walk through the Whelans' front door. Wearing a pair of black slacks, a matching jacket and a pink silk blouse, she was utterly stunning. To his amazement, the sight of her robbed him of breath.

Maybe Zeke was right about his needing a night out, Brad decided, forcing himself not to stare. If the sight of his lifelong nemesis peaked his interest like this, then he was in definite need of some female companionship.

"Looks like Sheila's trying to get my attention," Zeke said, nodding toward his wife. "I'll bet she's not feeling well again and wants to go home."

"Has she seen a doctor?" Brad asked, concerned for the woman who would soon be Sunnie's godmother. He couldn't think of anyone else he'd rather have for the baby's godparents than the Traverses. Brad knew for certain that if anything happened to him, they would see that Sunnie was loved and cared for.

"Not yet," Zeke said, looking worried. "She has an

appointment tomorrow." He placed his champagne glass on a passing waiter's tray. "I'll see you the day after tomorrow at our meeting with the commissioner."

"Tell Sheila I hope she's feeling better soon," Brad said, as his friend started across the room toward his wife.

"I'm worried about Sheila," Abby said, walking over to him.

"So is Zeke, but I'm sure she'll be all right," Brad said, turning his attention to the woman beside him. "You look very nice this evening."

She gave him a suspicious look. "Really?"

Her question surprised him. "I wouldn't have said it if I hadn't meant it."

"In that case, thank you," she said, taking a sip of the drink she held.

"Why would you think I'm not sincere?" he asked, frowning.

"You have to ask?" Her laughter caused an unfamiliar warmth in his chest. "I'm not used to something like that from you, Price. Veiled insults and jokes at my expense—yes. Compliments—no."

Brad started to deny her claim, but with sudden clarity, he realized she was right. When she had joined the TCC, he had made comments and jokes about her that, looking back, he wasn't overly proud of. It was no wonder she didn't believe him when he made a favorable remark.

"I believe an apology is in order," he said, clearing his throat.

"You're out of your mind if you think I owe you an

apology, Price," she said incredulously. "Of all the arrogant—"

"Hush." Setting his drink on a nearby table, Brad took her by the elbow and led her out into the Whelans' enclosed courtyard before she drew too much attention to them. If he was going to have to eat crow, he didn't particularly want witnesses.

"What are you up to now, Price?" she demanded.

When they were safely out of earshot of anyone eavesdropping, he placed his hands on her shoulders to keep her from walking away. "If you'll stop jumping to conclusions and let me finish, I would like to tell you that my behavior the past several months has been out of line and uncalled for." He could tell by the widening of her vibrant blue eyes that it was the last thing she expected from him. "I'm sorry for that, Abby."

She shook her head. "I…um…don't know what to say."

"You could start by telling me you accept my apology." He shrugged. "But that's up to you."

"Y-yes…" She cleared her throat. "I accept."

"Good." He smiled. "Now that we have that out of the way, I want you to know that I meant what I said." He slowly slid his palms down her arms until he caught her hands in his, then stepped back and took in the sight of her. "You really do look incredible, Abby."

"Thank you," she said, her voice soft.

From the muted landscape lighting, he wasn't certain, but it looked as if she blushed. Fascinating. For reasons he didn't fully understand, Brad pulled her into his arms and held her close.

"What on earth do you think you're doing?" she asked, starting to pull away from him.

"I'm giving you a friendly hug to go along with my apology," he said, enjoying the feel of her lithe body pressed to his a little more than he anticipated. He felt a tiny shiver course through her and instinctively knew it had nothing to do with her being cold.

"When have we ever been friends?" she asked.

Releasing her, Brad stepped back. "Maybe it's about time to put this rivalry behind us and declare a truce."

She looked suspicious. "Why now after all these years?"

He shrugged. "Once I become the president of the TCC it would be nice to see unity restored to the club."

"Oh, really? *You're* going to win the presidency?" She laughed as she turned to walk back into the house. "I knew there had to be an underlying motive to your sudden generosity."

After watching her go inside, Brad stuffed his hands into his trouser pockets and stared up at the clear night sky. What the hell had gotten into him?

Lately, it seemed that he seized every opportunity to touch Abby, to hold her to him. It had started the other day at the clubhouse when she had helped him change Sunnie's diaper. He'd hugged her to offer his comfort when she told him about her inability to have children. But that didn't explain his kissing her under the mistletoe. And later that evening when she stopped by to help him get Sunnie to stop crying, he had told himself he hugged her out of gratitude. But the truth was, a simple thank-you would have sufficed.

Brad shook his head as he rejoined the party.

There was a simple explanation for his actions and it didn't take a genius to figure out what it was. He was a healthy male with a healthy appetite for the ladies. Since taking on the responsibility of his niece, he had curtailed his pursuit of female companionship, and it was only natural that he would gravitate toward Abby, since she was the only single female he'd had contact with in the past few weeks.

Satisfied that he had determined the reason for his uncharacteristic actions, Brad found the host and hostess, thanked them for the party and headed for the door. He would have to ask his sister to babysit again some evening in the near future in order for him to have a night out. Until then, he'd just have to make sure he steered clear of Abigail Langley.

Three

Brad smiled down at his niece as he placed the baby carrier in the shopping cart. "So far, so good, baby girl. You got a clean bill of health from the pediatrician and slept through the meeting with the commissioners from the football league. Now all we have to do is pick up more formula and diapers for you, a couple of frozen pizzas for me, as well as some stain remover for the clothing you've christened when you burp. Then we should be good to go home and crash."

After confirmation from the doctor today that Sunnie was perfectly healthy, Brad was doing his best to take whatever came along in stride and not worry so much about the things he couldn't change. It was a fact of life—babies cried. A lot. Sometimes there were tears, sometimes not. He had a strong suspicion that most times, Sunnie screamed at the top of her lungs just to keep him on his toes. But she had been an absolute angel this afternoon when he, Zeke and Chris Richards met with the minor-league football commissioner to work out the final details for the semipro team they were going to buy.

Just the thought of bringing the team to Royal made him smile. Like every other town in Texas, football was like a religion for the residents of Royal, and it had been a huge part of his life throughout high school and college. Playing quarterback, he, along with his two best friends, Chris and Zeke, had been a force to reckon with on the playing field, and he was happy to be partnering with them to bring the team to town. But they were going to wait until the night of the TCC Christmas Ball to make the official announcement. By that time, they hoped to have former pro player Mitch Hayward locked in as the team's general manager and Daniel Warren, the architect with the winning plans for the proposed new TCC building, working on designs for the new stadium they planned to have built.

As he pushed the cart down the grocery store aisle, he couldn't help but chuckle to himself. If someone had told him six months ago that he would trade going into the office for working from home in order to be available for diaper changes, or that he would be pushing a baby around the grocery store in a cart, he would have laughed his head off.

Looking up, Brad spotted Abby coming down the aisle toward him. Wearing boots, jeans, a pink T-shirt and a jeans jacket, her appearance was every bit the ranchwoman, and he couldn't stop himself from thinking about how good she looked.

He frowned. That was twice in the past few days that he'd found himself thinking of Abby as being attractive. Now he knew for certain he was in need of an evening out with a warm, willing female. As soon as he got home, he fully intend to call Sadie and arrange for her to babysit Sunnie one evening at her earliest convenience.

Satisfied with his plan of action, he couldn't help but smile.

"You seem to be quite pleased with yourself about something, Mr. Price." Abby tilted her head slightly. "Still anticipating that big win you're so sure of?"

"Of course." Feeling that he had regained his perspective, he nodded. "I'm as sure of winning the presidency as you are of beating me out of it."

"As a matter of fact, I'm going to do just that." She walked over to smile down at the baby. "How's the little angel?"

"Sunnie got a clean bill of health from the doctor this afternoon and didn't cry too much when he gave her an immunization shot." He grinned. "We're going to celebrate with a bottle for her and a frozen pizza for me, and veg out tonight in front of the TV."

"I assume the pediatrician told you there might be a reaction and what to watch for?" she asked, as she tickled Sunnie's chin.

The baby gave Abby a toothless grin and a gurgling laugh.

He glanced at his happy niece. "The doctor covered everything. Sunnie didn't like the shot much, but she's doing great. Rest assured, I'm getting the hang of taking care of her, and I don't anticipate that we'll have any more problems."

Abby raised her gaze to meet his. "I hope not."

Her doubtful expression rubbed him the wrong way. "We'll be just fine. I even figured out that getting her to go to sleep at night is a lot easier if she doesn't know that's what I'm doing."

To his immense irritation, Abby laughed out loud. "Oh, this should be good. Do tell what your secret is, Mr. Price."

"Why don't you stop by this evening to see for yourself?" he found himself asking. He could tell she didn't believe him, and it suddenly became a challenge to prove her wrong.

Some habits were hard to break, he decided, as he stared at the woman in front of him. For as long as he could remember, whenever Abby threw down a gauntlet he hadn't been able to resist picking it up—the same as she couldn't pass up answering his challenges.

She shook her head, and her long auburn ponytail swayed from side to side. "As much as I'd like to see this great feat of parenting you seem so proud of, I'm going to have to pass. I've been working around the ranch all day and I'm pretty tired."

"Afraid to see that I'm right and that I have it all worked out, are you?" he goaded.

Her vivid blue eyes narrowed. "Maybe I just don't want to witness your embarrassment when you fall flat on your face."

"I don't believe that for a minute," he said, shaking his head. "You'd like nothing better than to see me fail at something and we both know it."

"I do admit it's tempting," she said, glancing down at the baby. "But I—"

"Great. Do you like pepperoni, sausage or just plain cheese?"

She frowned. "I didn't say I would be—"

"It doesn't matter. I'll just pick up a variety of frozen pizzas, and you can choose when you get to my place." He quickly started pushing the cart toward the end of the aisle. "Sunnie and I will see you around six-thirty."

Before she had a chance to call out a refusal, he turned the corner and headed straight for the freezer section of the store. Abby might have gotten away with declining, had he not seen her resistance as a contest of wills.

Brad smiled down at Sunnie happily playing with her fingers. "I came out on top in this round, but you have to help me out with the next one. Abby doesn't believe I can get you to go to sleep without you screaming like a cat with its tail caught in the door. We're going to prove her wrong, aren't we?"

Sunnie's high-pitched squeal of laughter encouraged him.

"Great," he said, heading for the checkout counter. "Keep up your end of the bargain, and I'll buy you a new car when you turn sixteen."

After parking her SUV in the circular drive in front of Brad's house, Abby shook her head as she prepared to get out of the car. She had to have lost what little mind she had left or else she would be home curled up on the couch reading a book instead of walking up to knock on Brad's door.

She had spent the past couple of hours at war with herself. As much as she wanted to be around Sunnie, Abby wasn't at all comfortable with being around the baby's uncle. She had even gotten as far as picking up the phone to call and tell him that something had come up and she wouldn't be over after all.

But the lure of holding and playing with the beautiful baby girl had won out. Sunnie had remained happy and extraordinarily well-adjusted despite being handed from one person to another for the first few months of her life, and Abby was finding it impossible to pass up an opportunity to be with the precious little bundle of joy. Unfortunately, the baby came along with six feet two inches of pure trouble, and to her displeasure she was suddenly finding Brad to be the best-looking, most intriguing trouble she'd seen in a very long time.

Sadie had jokingly told her on more than one occasion that Brad had made it his mission in life to date every available woman in Royal, earning him the reputation of being a player. But it appeared that he had given up his playboy lifestyle in favor of caring for the tiny six-month-old little girl, and without the benefit of a nanny. Very few men she knew would even consider something like that, let alone actually do it. Brad seemed to be trying so hard to be a good parent to Sunnie, and Abby couldn't help but find that endearing and, much to her bewilderment, quite sexy. If that wasn't proof enough that she had lost what little sense she had left, she didn't know what was.

Promising herself that she would stay only a few minutes, then find an excuse to leave, Abby took a deep breath and knocked on the door. When Brad opened it a moment later, her breath caught and her heart skipped several beats. He held Sunnie in one arm and had a black T-shirt draped over the other arm.

"Y-you aren't wearing a shirt."

"Really? I hadn't noticed," he said, his voice filled with laughter.

She hadn't meant to blurt out the obvious, but she had never seen so many impressive ripples and ridges on a chest and abdomen in her entire life. Gulping, she couldn't seem to avert her eyes. Had he always had shoulders that wide and a waist that trim? She couldn't stop her gaze from following the narrow line of dark hair that ran from his navel down his flat lower belly to disappear beneath the waistband of his jeans. Jeans that rode low on narrow hips and emphasized his well-defined flank muscles.

Good Lord, the man had been hiding a fabulous body beneath those Armani suits all this time, and she hadn't had a clue. Her cheeks heated and she averted her gaze as she forced herself to walk past him and into the foyer.

"Would you mind holding Sunnie while I put on my shirt?" he asked, closing the door behind her. "She's been fussy since we got home and wants to be held all of the time."

Brad was apparently oblivious to her shocked re-action at the sight of his magnificent body, and Abby was just as glad that he hadn't noticed. She was having enough trouble coming to terms with the effect he was having on her, she didn't need to deal with him com-menting on it.

Taking the baby from him, she watched as he pulled

on the black T-shirt. "I think babies are nauseated by the smell of clean shirts," he said, shaking his head as he tucked the tail of the garment into his jeans. "Every shirt I own has a stain on it."

"Don't you drape a burp cloth over your shoulder when you give her a bottle?" Abby asked, concentrating on the little girl in her arms. It was much safer to give Sunnie her undivided attention than it was to watch Brad.

Putting his hand to her back, he nodded as he guided her toward the family room. She did her best to ignore the warmth that radiated throughout her body from his touch.

"I try using one of those whenever I feed her," he said, chuckling. "But there are times when the cloth slips or she grabs it with her fist and it gets pulled out of the way. The result is me having to change shirts a lot."

"If it's any consolation, she should be coming out of the worst of it within another month or so," Abby assured him, continuing to stare down at the baby in her arms. It was far less dangerous than looking at Sunnie's uncle. "Normally, having to be burped tapers off around the age of six months for an infant—about the time she starts sitting by herself."

"You know a lot about babies." His smile caused her to catch her breath. How could she have gone all these years without realizing, until just recently, how good-looking he was?

"There for a while, I read everything I could about babies and all the stages of their development," she said, concentrating on how she was going to make a graceful but hasty exit. "That was—"

"When you and Richard first started trying to have a baby?" he asked, his tone gentle.

She hesitated a moment, then nodded. "Yes."

It was easier to let him think that the only time she had studied the stages of an infant's development was when she and her husband first started trying to get pregnant. Explaining the last time she had thought there would be a baby in her future was still too painful to share with anyone.

They fell silent until Sunnie laid her head on Abby's shoulder and she noticed the baby felt warmer than normal. "Uh-oh. Brad, do you have a thermometer?"

"There was one of those digital kind that you stick in the baby's ear in Sunnie's things when I brought her home from Sheila's," he said, nodding. "Why?"

Abby placed her cheek to Sunnie's. "I think she's running a little bit of a fever."

"Should I call the pediatrician?" he asked, a worried frown suddenly creasing his forehead.

She shook her head. "Not yet. Go get the thermometer. We need to check what her temperature is first."

"Be right back," he said, taking off down the hall at a jog. When he returned, he handed her the electronic device as he reached for the baby. "I'm not exactly sure how this works. Why don't I hold her while you take the reading?"

Gently placing the thermometer in Sunnie's ear, she pushed the button. The reading appeared on the digital screen almost instantly. "She is running a low-grade fever."

"How high is it?" he asked, clearly alarmed.

"It's only slightly elevated," she assured him. "Did the doctor tell you what kind of fever reducer to use in case she had a reaction to the shot he gave her this afternoon?"

Brad nodded as he placed the baby back in her arms. "He had me pick up some drops from the pharmacy. Do you think that could be what's happening?"

"I think that's probably it." She gave him a reassuring smile as she lowered herself and the baby into the rocking chair. "It's not at all uncommon for a baby to be fussy and run a bit of a temperature after a vaccination."

While Brad went to get the medication, she held Sunnie close and rubbed her back to soothe her. "It's all right, little one. You'll feel better soon." Abby had no sooner gotten the words out than she felt something wet against her shoulder. "Hmm, looks like I should have practiced what I preached about those burp cloths, doesn't it?"

"It says we can give this to her every four to six hours," Brad said, reading the directions on the small box he held as he walked back into the room.

"I can help you with the first dose," Abby said, when he walked over to stand beside the rocking chair. "But I have to leave after that."

"Why?" he asked, looking alarmed.

She pointed to the wet spot on her shoulder. "You might have been right about the smell of clean clothes nauseating babies."

"So she got you too, huh?" He chuckled as he filed the dropper with the recommended dosage of fever re-

ducer and gave it to Sunnie. "There's no need for you
to go. You can wear one of my shirts."

That sounded way more cozy than she was comfortable with. "Thank you, but—"

He squatted down in front of her and placing his
hands on the arms of the rocking chair, effectively
trapped her. "I hate to admit this, Abby, but since this is
the first time Sunnie has been sick, I'd feel more comfortable if you stayed for a while." When he reached
up to touch the baby's cheek, the backs of his fingers brushed Abby's breast. "At least until her fever is
gone."

Abby could understand Brad's apprehension. He was
just getting comfortable with caring for Sunnie, and it
had to be intimidating now that he was faced with her
first illness, even if it was a minor reaction to an immunization. But the feel of his hand against her sensi-
tive skin even through her clothing sent an awareness
coursing through her that set off alarm bells deep in her
soul. She needed to make her excuses and leave. Now.

"I'm sure Sheila or Sadie would be more than willing to come over and help you with Sunnie," Abby said,
intrigued by his uncertainty. It was a side of Brad she
had never seen before, and she found it to be in direct
contrast to the self-assured, independent man she had
known all of her life and, to her complete disconcer-
tion, oddly endearing.

He shook his head. "Zeke and Sheila have gone out
of town for the weekend, and Sadie, Rick and the girls
have gone over to Somerset for the annual Christmas
Lights Festival."

Abby might have been able to refuse him, but she

made the mistake of looking into his piercing hazel eyes. She had never seen him look more worried and as unwise as it was, she rationalized that he didn't have anyone else to help him. "Well, maybe for just a little while."

His relief was evident in the easing of the tension lines bracketing his mouth. "I'll get you one of my shirts to change into," he said, rising to his feet.

It crossed her mind to tell him not to bother. Wearing someone's shirt seemed a little too intimate for two people who had spent the majority of their lives in competition with each other. But the spot on her blouse was rather large, and the damp silk against her skin was pretty uncomfortable.

"Here you go," he said, returning to the family room to hand her a soft cotton T-shirt. "The guest bathroom is just off the hall to your right." He reached for the baby. "Besides giving her the drops for her fever, is there anything else we should do?"

Abby tried to think of what else she had read about infants running temperatures. "I don't think giving her water or formula would be a good idea. Do you have a bottle of liquid electrolyte replacement? That would be the best to give to her while she has a fever."

"If I don't, I'll go into town and get some."

"Where did you put all of the things Sheila sent over?" She started down the hall. "As soon as I change, I'll check to see if you have some."

"I put everything in the pantry," he answered.

Quickly finding the guest powder room, Abby eyed the shirt Brad had given her to put on as she unbuttoned her blouse. Thankfully it was heather gray and a little thicker than the average T-shirt. At least her bra wouldn't show through as much as it would have if the shirt had been white.

As she pulled it over her head, it was as if the man waiting for her just down the hall surrounded her. She closed her eyes as she savored his clean, masculine scent. There was only one word to describe the smell and that was…sexy.

Her eyes snapped open and she shook her head at her own foolishness. Brad might smell good—maybe even downright delicious—but she couldn't let herself be interested in anyone, especially the man who had been a thorn in her side all of her life.

Besides, caring for anyone was just too dangerous to her peace of mind. She and her mother had both suffered broken hearts when Abby's father had abandoned them for a life with his young secretary. Then, just when she had decided to take a chance on love, she had been devastated when her husband, Richard, suffered the aneurysm that took his life a little over a year ago. But the most recent heartbreak had been just a few months ago, when the mother of the baby she was supposed to adopt changed her mind. Abby had vowed afterward that there wouldn't be another chance of her losing someone she loved.

Taking a deep breath, she squared her shoulders and reached for the doorknob. She would help Brad with his adorable baby niece, then remove herself from the situation as soon as possible.

"I think she's finally gone to sleep," Brad said, careful to keep his voice low. He and Abby had taken turns all evening, rocking and walking the floor with Sunnie. "Do we dare try to take her temperature again?"

Nodding, she hid a yawn behind one delicate hand. "It was almost normal the last time we took it, and I'd really like to know that the fever has run its course before I leave."

As he picked up the thermometer and walked over to the rocking chair where she sat holding Sunnie, he glanced down at Abby. When they had run into each other in the grocery store that afternoon, she mentioned working all day around her ranch and she had just spent the entire evening helping him take care of a sick infant. She had to be dead on her feet, and he didn't think it was a good idea for her to drive home as tired as she was. But knowing Abby, if he insisted that she stay the rest of the night, she would leave just to spite him.

When he checked the digital screen on the thermometer, the numbers were normal. Breathing a sigh of relief he started to tell Abby, but her eyes were heavy lidded, and he could tell she was having to fight to stay awake.

"What's the verdict?" she asked, sounding as tired as she looked.

"Still slightly elevated," he lied. He hated not telling the truth, but he wasn't willing to take the risk of her falling asleep behind the steering wheel and having a car accident on the drive back to her ranch. He couldn't have that on his conscience. "Why don't you let me take Sunnie, while you stretch out on the couch and rest? If you go to sleep, I'll wake you when it's your turn to be up with her."

Before she had a chance to protest, he took Sunnie from her and, cradling the baby in one arm, helped Abby to her feet and guided her to the couch. "I think Sunnie is going to be fine," she said, sounding exhausted. "I'll just go on home and if you have any further problems, you can always call me."

"You know so much more about taking care of babies than I do. I'd really feel more at ease if you stay," he said, thinking quickly.

He purposely didn't tell her that at the moment it was her welfare and not Sunnie's that concerned him. Even if he told her, she probably wouldn't believe it.

Abby hesitated. Then just when he thought she was going to refuse, she sat down on the couch and removed her shoes. "I'll just lean my head back against the cushion and rest my eyes. Let me know when you need me to take over."

"Will do," he said, smiling.

Abby hadn't much more than rested her head against the back of the couch, and he could tell by her even breathing that she had already fallen asleep. He glanced down at the sleeping baby girl in his arms and hoped that she wouldn't wake up when he put her in the portable crib he had set up earlier. Once he had Sunnie down and he was assured she was resting peacefully, he turned his attention to the woman across the room. He wasn't about to wake her, but if he didn't try to get her into a more comfortable position, her back and neck were going to be stiff as hell by morning.

Sitting on the end of the couch, Brad reached to take Abby into his arms and pull her over against his shoulder. For a moment, he thought he'd awakened her, but instead of sitting up and demanding to know what he was doing, she placed her hand on his chest and snuggled closer. Her soft breath on the side of his neck immediately sent a wave of awareness to every cell in his body and had him cursing himself as a fool for making the noble gesture.

He closed his eyes and tried to think about something—anything—that would get his mind off of the woman lying against him. Starting out with his stats as quarterback in high school and college, by the time he had run through every football play he had called in every game, he gave up.

All he could think about was how good her body felt cuddled against his and how much he had enjoyed her unexpected reaction to seeing him with his shirt off when she first arrived for the evening. Abby might have thought she hid it, but her eyes were so expressive there was no way he could have missed her perusal of his body. He hadn't planned to answer the door bare chested, but he sure wasn't sorry it worked out that way.

His heart stalled, then pounded against his ribs. Why was it that lately every time he was around Abby, his libido went on full alert and he started thinking of her as an attractive, desirable woman?

For years, Abigail Langley was his nemesis and he was quite comfortable with that. Oh, there had been a time in high school that he had been attracted to her—even contemplated asking her to one of the homecoming dances. But Abby had eyes only for Richard Langley, and Brad had quickly reverted back to thinking of her as his rival and moved on to pursuing the girls on the cheerleading squad—all eight of them.

Back then, he had been looking at her with the innocent eyes of a youthful crush and would have been happy with a good-luck kiss and hug behind the bleachers before a game. But now? He was a man with a man's needs. A man who hadn't been with a woman in a while, and what he was thinking—feeling—at the moment, was anything but innocent.

When her hand slipped from his chest to his stomach, he gritted his teeth and shifted to relieve the rapidly building pressure against his fly. He had only thought to make her more comfortable, but in doing so he had succeeded in causing himself a great deal of discomfort.

Brad took a deep breath and concentrated on getting his body to relax. He wasn't sure why, but it appeared that he had come full circle. He was once again looking at Abby as more than his competitor. The only difference between now and their high school days was that this time she was looking back.

Four

When Abby opened her eyes, any traces of sleep that might have been lingering were instantly chased away as several things became apparent all at once. It was morning, she wasn't at home in her bed and her head was pillowed on…Brad's thigh.

Turning her head, she looked up to find him smiling down at her. "Good morning, Ms. Langley. Did you sleep well?"

"I…uh, yes." Good lord, how had she ended up with her head on his lap? The last thing she remembered was agreeing to stretch out for a few minutes until it was her turn to take care of the baby again.

She sat up and pushed her hair back away from her face. "How is Sunnie? Is her temperature down?"

He nodded. "She's doing just fine. Her fever broke around midnight."

"I wanted to go home." She wasn't the least bit happy with the situation. "Why didn't you wake me?"

He reached out to brush a wayward strand of her unruly hair from her cheek, sending a shiver of awareness straight up her spine. "The reason I let you sleep was because you were dead tired and I wasn't about to let you drive home and run the risk of you falling asleep at the wheel."

"You weren't about to *let me drive* home?" She could appreciate his concern, but the implication that she was incapable of making the decision herself was, in her estimation, out of line. "Let me tell you something, Mr. Price. I don't need your approval or permission to—"

Before she could finish telling him what she thought of his high-handedness, he pulled her into his arms. When his mouth came down on hers, Abby's first thought was to free herself, then bop him a good one. But the feel of his firm lips on hers, of his arms closing around her to pull her to his wide, solid chest, sent a shock wave straight through her, and she couldn't seem to work up even a token protest.

When he deepened the kiss and explored her with a thoroughness that stole her breath, her heart beat double time and a delightfully lazy warmth began to spread through every cell in her body. If she'd thought the kiss he gave her under the mistletoe at the TCC clubhouse had been moving, it had only been a glimpse of the skill and mastery Brad was showing her now.

Lightly stroking her tongue with his, he coaxed and teased until she felt herself responding in kind. With her hands trapped between them, she felt the steady beating of his heart beneath his padded pectoral muscles and she couldn't resist testing the strength of his chest with her palms. Bringing her arms up to encircle his shoulders, she gave in to the temptation of exploring the width and corded sinew there as well.

He brought his hand up to cup her breast, sending tingles of excitement racing up her spine and a jolt of longing through every part of her. It had been over a year since Abby had experienced the stirrings of passion and desire. The fact that she felt them in Brad Price's arms was not only unbelievable, it scared her as little else could. Because in Brad's arm, the feelings were stronger than she would have thought possible with any man.

Gathering the shreds of what was left of her good sense, she tried to put space between them, but he continued to hold her in a loose embrace. "Th-that shouldn't…have happened," she said, struggling to catch her breath.

"Probably not." His hazel eyes seemed to see right through her as they stared at each other. "But I'll be damned if I'm sorry it did, darlin'."

What was he trying to do to her and why? Was this some kind of ploy to get her to drop out of the race for the TCC presidency before the ballots were counted, giving him the office by default?

"What are you up to, Brad?" She hadn't meant to sound quite so accusatory, but she refused to apologize for asking the uppermost question running through her mind.

Before he could reply, the distinct sound of someone clearing their throat drew both of their attention. "I knocked, but when there was no answer, I used the key you gave me. I just stopped by to see how you're faring alone with the baby," Sadie said, grinning like a Cheshire cat. She was standing in the doorway leading to the kitchen and couldn't have looked more smug. "But I see that everything is under control here." She took a step backward. "Feel free to continue what you were doing. I let myself in. I can see my way out."

"No, don't go," Abby said, glaring at an unrepentant Brad. It appeared that he was going to just sit there grinning like his sister, leaving it up to her to make excuses. "I was just getting ready to leave myself."

"Go ahead and continue…talking," Sadie said, taking another step backward. "I really need to get over to the women's center to help sort through the toys that have been donated for the children's party."

"I was supposed to help with that," Abby said, wondering where her shoes were.

"I'll tell everyone that something came up and you won't be able to make it today," Sadie said, as she turned to leave.

"Well, she's right about one thing." Abby knew from his wicked grin what Brad was thinking. "Something did—"

"Don't even think about saying it," she warned.

Abby's cheeks felt as if they were suddenly on fire and she couldn't think of a solitary thing to say that wouldn't make things worse. She closed her eyes and tried to will away the entire situation. Unfortunately, when she opened them again, she was still in Brad's house, on his couch with his arms loosely wrapped around her.

"I've got to get out of here," she muttered, breaking free of his embrace to look for her shoes.

When she rose to her feet, he got up to stand beside her. "Thank you for spending the night with me."

"I was here because Sunnie needed me."

His knowing grin told her that he wasn't going to let it go. "You woke up with your head in my lap this morning. I think that means you were here with me all night. And if you want to get technical, we were both asleep—together."

"Don't even go down that road, Price." She shook her head. "I did not sleep with you."

"Well, there's sleeping and then there's *sleeping*," he said, laughing.

She refused to play his silly little word game as she looked around for the blouse he had laundered for her earlier. "Where's my shirt?"

"It isn't dry yet." His grin widened. "Since it was silk, I didn't think putting it in the dryer would be a good idea. You'll have to come back this evening to pick it up."

Turning to glare at him, she shook her head. "You can keep it."

"I appreciate the offer, but it's not my color." His rich laughter sent a tingle skipping over every nerve in her body. "Besides, you look a lot better in my shirt than I would in yours."

If she could have found her handbag, she would have bopped him for sure. "Where are my purse and shoes?"

"I hung your coat and purse in the guest closet just off the foyer," he said, bending down to reach for something under the coffee table. "Your shoes are right here."

"Thank you," she said, taking the cross-trainers from him. Seating herself on the armchair farthest from him, she put them on and stood up. "I'll have my ranch foreman drop your shirt off when he goes into Royal for supplies later on this week."

Brad shook his head. "No need. I'll get it from you the next time I see you."

Deciding it would be better to leave than to stand there and debate the point with quite possibly the most infuriating man she had ever met, Abby walked down the hall to the foyer closet. Not at all surprised that he followed, she put on her coat, then turned to face him.

"I think it would be a good idea for you to make sure Sheila or Sadie is around the next time there's a problem with the baby," she said, regretfully.

Not seeing Sunnie or being able to hold the baby would be difficult, but it was a matter of self-preservation. The more she was around the sweet baby girl and her exasperating uncle, the more it reminded Abby of what she wanted most in the world, but couldn't have—a family of her own.

Instead of arguing, as she thought he would, Brad simply stared at her for several long moments before he finally shrugged. "We'll see."

It wasn't the answer she expected, but it was apparently the best she was going to get from him. At least for now. "I'll see you at the Christmas Ball," she said, walking across the foyer to open the door.

"Oh, I'm sure we'll see each other before then." The

sound of the baby awaking drew their attention. "That's my call," he said, smiling. "See you later."

After watching him turn to go attend to the baby, Abby quietly closed the door behind her and walked to her SUV. Why did she feel as if she was taking the "morning after" walk of shame?

Nothing had happened last night and other than that steamy kiss this morning it wasn't going to. Ever.

She had stayed the night, to help Sunnie get through the reaction to her immunization shot. Period. The fact that Brad had taken it upon himself not to awaken her for the drive home wasn't her fault, and she refused to take the blame for it. He was also responsible for the kiss this morning. She certainly hadn't initiated it, and the fact that she hadn't discouraged it was immaterial. He'd simply taken her by surprise, and she had ended it as soon as she had been able to gather her wits about her.

Satisfied that she had things back in perspective, she got into the SUV and started the engine. As she steered it down the long drive toward the main road, she went over her plans for the day. She intended to take a shower, call Sadie for an impromptu lunch after they finished sorting toys at the women's center and do a little damage control.

Once Sadie heard the explanation for why she had seen them kissing, Abby was certain her best friend would understand. After all, Sadie was Brad's sister and knew how incorrigible the man could be.

Abby sighed heavily as she turned the Escalade onto the private road leading up to the big sprawling ranch house she had shared with Richard. Maybe if she kept telling herself how easily her actions could be explained and how innocent she had been in the whole matter, she might even start to believe it herself.

Seated in a booth at the Royal Diner, Abby anxiously awaited the right moment in her conversation with Sadie. She had gone over what she wanted to say at least a dozen times before she settled on just the right words to explain her atypical behavior with Brad. She didn't have long to wait.

"Okay, I assume you wanted to have lunch for the post-mortem of that kiss," Sadie said, smiling.

Abby was so preoccupied that she'd failed to notice Sadie had stopped talking about the cultural center she wanted to build. "There's a simple explanation for what you saw," Abby said, unable to keep the defensiveness from her tone.

Sadie grinned. "There always is."

"It was your brother's fault," Abby heard herself saying.

Her talk with Brad's sister wasn't going the way Abby had planned. She was supposed to remain calm and collected, not feel as if she had been caught making out with the high school football captain.

The woman across the chipped Formica table nodded. "Oh, I don't doubt Brad was the instigator. But what I want to know is why you let him get away with it?"

"We were arguing and—"

"He kissed you to shut you up," Sadie finished for her. Shaking her head, she laughed. "But that doesn't explain your reaction."

Before Abby could respond, a young waitress walked over to take their order. "What can I get for you ladies? The cook just made a new pot of his world famous chili, if you'd care to try that," she suggested, snapping the gum she was chewing.

"Hi, Suzy. Chili would be fine," both women said in unison.

"Bring us a couple of sweet teas with lemon, too," Sadie added.

Nodding, Suzy smiled. "Be right back with your order."

As if by unspoken agreement, Abby and Sadie both waited for their lunch to be served before they got back to the topic of the kiss.

"So tell me why you didn't stop my charming brother from giving you one of the steamiest kisses I've ever seen," Sadie said, picking up a cracker to dip into her bowl. "And why you were kissing him right back."

"He took me by surprise," Abby said, hoping her explanation didn't sound as lame to Sadie as it did to her.

"Abigail Langley, this is me you're talking to." Sadie shook her head. "I know you as well as anyone, and if you hadn't wanted Brad's kiss, you would have stopped it before it ever got started."

Abby opened her mouth to refute what her friend said, but quickly snapped it shut. Sadie was right. She could have called a halt to the embrace way before she had. Why hadn't she?

To her relief Sadie was on a roll and saved her from having to make a comment. "What were you doing at his house to begin with? You and Brad have been sworn enemies since grade school. I was under the impression that hadn't changed, and especially with the two of you running for TCC president."

"I…that is…" She stopped to take a deep breath. "It's complicated."

With her spoon halfway to her mouth, Sadie stopped, then placed it back into the bowl. "You wanted to see Sunnie again, didn't you?" she asked gently.

Seizing on the explanation provided by her friend, Abby nodded. They both knew how much Abby had wanted a child and how concerned she had been for the baby girl from the moment Sunnie had been left on the TCC's doorstep. But seeing the baby meant spending time with her infuriating, sexy-as-sin uncle. How could she put into words her conflicted feelings for the man when she didn't fully understand them herself? How could she possibly explain that as angry as he made her, she felt more alive when she was around him than she had in a very long time?

"Am I that transparent?" she asked, more comfortable with Sadie's explanation than she was her own.

"I understand." Placing her hand over Abby's, Sadie gave it a gentle squeeze. "I know how much it must hurt to want a baby and not be able to have one. But when you're ready, there are alternatives, Abby. You could always adopt a child."

Knowing that Sadie was only trying to help, Abby nodded. Sadie had no way of knowing that Abby's dream of becoming a mother had ended on that front as well.

She took a deep breath. "Maybe one day I'll consider it."

They were silent for a time before Sadie asked, "So how are you planning on getting even with my brother for taking advantage of the situation?"

"Hopefully, I'll win the TCC office and prove to him once and for all that I'm quite serious about my membership in the club." Abby took a sip of her iced tea. "I might have been accepted into the fold because of an obscure bylaw, but that doesn't mean that I don't intend to get involved."

"Well, you know I'm pulling for you," Sadie said, sitting back against the red vinyl upholstery. "Brad is so set in his ways, it's past time that someone turned his carefully crafted world upside down."

Abby laughed. "I think taking responsibility for Sunnie has been a good start. When Juanita left to go to Dallas the other day, he didn't even know how to fasten a disposable diaper."

Sadie nodded. "That's true. He loves my twins and he's a fantastic uncle. But I lived in Houston when the girls were babies. He wasn't around to help or witness the sleepless nights and hectic pace I had to keep in order to care for them."

"I'd say he's learning," Abby said, grinning. Deciding it was time to change the subject, she asked, "Have you had any more luck with finding a building for the Family Cultural Center?"

"I'm hoping the TCC will decide to build a new clubhouse and donate the current building to my foundation," Sadie said, looking hopeful. "Do you have any idea how that vote is going to go? With the economy the way it is, there's a real need for a place families in crisis can turn to for help."

Shaking her head, Abby picked up the check that Suzy had brought to them. "The last I heard, the membership was split right down the middle. The old guard wants to stick with tradition and stay in the original clubhouse and the new members want to build the design Daniel Warren presented."

As they slid from the booth and walked to the cash register at the end of the lunch counter, Sadie looked at the clock on the wall above the door. "I have to run." She gave Abby a hug. "Let me know if you hear anything about it one way or the other. I'd like to get started as soon as possible."

"I will," Abby said, as she paid the bill.

When she walked out of the diner and headed for her car, a note on the windshield drew her attention, and an immediate sense of apprehension surrounded her. It was all too reminiscent of the notes Brad and other members of the TCC had received in months past, claiming Sunnie was their child.

She took a deep breath and reached for the piece of paper. There wasn't any reason to be concerned. Zeke Travers had solved the mystery of the blackmail notes when he investigated who Sunnie's father was. The career criminal who had written them would be spending the rest of his life in jail for a variety of crimes.

Opening the folded paper, her eyes widened. It was from Brad, telling her that he and Sunnie would be visiting her ranch that evening. Abby looked around to see if he was anywhere in sight. The parking lot and street in front of the diner were deserted.

Hadn't she made it clear that she wanted him to look to others for help when he had problems with the baby?

Fit to be tied, she stuffed the note in her coat pocket and got into her SUV for the drive back to her ranch. It appeared Brad Price was deliberately tormenting her, and she had every intention of putting a stop to it.

If he showed up at her place later that evening, she would just have to impress upon him that she wanted to be left alone. She liked her nice, quiet, uneventful life. She had her charity work, her involvement with the TCC and the responsibility of running one of the largest horse ranches in Texas. The fulfillment of helping others and the enjoyment of raising her horses was enough for her. She didn't want or need the drama and tension that accompanied having a man around like Bradford Price.

Brad parked his newly purchased minivan in front of Abby's ranch house that evening, then got out and opened the sliding side door to unbuckle Sunnie's car seat. He still couldn't believe that he had bought the vehicle, let alone started driving it more than he did his Corvette. But now that he had a baby in his life, he found himself thinking of Sunnie's safety first. Trying to impress the ladies took a backseat to her welfare. Funny how someone so small could change his priorities so drastically, he thought as he smiled down at his sleeping niece.

Hanging the diaper bag on his shoulder, he took the carrier's handle in one hand, then picked up a bouquet of roses in the other. He owed Abby for all the help she had given him the past few days and although flowers didn't seem nearly enough to express how grateful he was to have her help last night, they would have to do for now. Once Juanita returned from Dallas, he would get her to watch Sunnie for an afternoon while he took Abby out for lunch.

Pleased with himself for thinking ahead, he climbed the porch steps and knocked on the front door. While he waited for Abby, he looked around. Although he and Richard Langley hadn't been especially good friends, Brad had been invited over for a few poker games with the guys throughout the years, and he could tell a big difference in the place since Abby moved in and put her stamp on it. Instead of the rustic wooden rocking chairs that Richard had preferred, a white wicker table and two matching chairs had been put in their place, and wind chimes hung on either end of the long, wide porch.

"What are you doing here, Brad?" Abby asked, opening the door.

"Didn't you find my note?" He knew for a fact that she had. Otherwise, he wouldn't have received the voice mail from her, telling him not to bother stopping by. "I left it under your windshield wiper."

"I found it." She folded her arms beneath her breasts as she stood, blocking the doorway. "Apparently you failed to get the message I left, telling you that I had made plans for the evening."

Smiling, he handed her the bouquet of roses. "Oh, I got it. But I promised Sunnie we would come over to thank you for all of your help the past few days, and I didn't want to disappoint her."

Brad knew he wasn't playing fair, considering Abby's fascination with the baby. But for reasons he didn't care to dwell on, he was the one who found himself disappointed at the prospect of not seeing Abby again. That alone should have been enough to send him running so far in the opposite direction that he crossed the border into Mexico before he stopped. But the truth was, he found that he enjoyed being with Abby. No other woman had ever challenged him the way she did. She kept him on his toes, and although he hadn't realized it, he had missed that when she was living in Seattle.

She stared at the peach-colored roses for a moment before she sighed and stepped back for him to enter the house. "I suppose I can put up my Christmas decorations tomorrow evening."

"There's no need to put it off." He waited for her to close the door behind him before setting the carrier down to remove his coat. Then, bending down, he pulled back the blanket he had draped over the baby. "Sunnie and I will be more than happy to help you put up the tree, string lights and do whatever else you want in the way of decorating."

She knelt down on the other side of the baby carrier and began unbuckling the safety straps. "That's all right. I can take care of it tomorrow."

"Actually, I'd really appreciate it if you'd let me help. It might give me some ideas about what I'm going to do for the holidays," he said truthfully.

"Haven't you decorated in the past?" she asked, frowning.

Shaking his head, Brad straightened to his full height. "Beyond buying a few gifts for my family, I really haven't taken the time to pay much attention to Christmas."

"And I'll bet your secretary did your shopping." Abby had guessed correctly. Her knowing look made him feel a bit guilty about his lack of attention to his gift giving.

"I gave her a price range and she took care of it for me," he admitted.

In hindsight, the least he could have done was to put a little thought into it and told his secretary what to buy. Hell, most of the time he hadn't even known what the woman had chosen until the recipient opened his gift.

"Now that you have Sunnie, you're going to have to start doing more to make the holidays special," Abby said, picking up the baby.

As they stood there eyeing each other, an idea began to form. He knew next to nothing about making Christmas a magical experience for a child, but he would bet every dime he had that Abby had thought about it—a lot.

"Will you help me?" he asked.

She frowned. "I'm sure Sadie would be more than happy to give you a few suggestions. After all, she has experience with what she's done for the twins."

He shook his head. "I want to start my own traditions with Sunnie, not copy what my sister does for her kids. Besides, now that she and Rick are married, it's their first Christmas together as a family. I don't want to intrude on that."

Abby was silent for several seconds as she seemed to think over what he had said. "I suppose that makes sense," she finally said, nodding. "But I'm not sure I'm the one you want to be giving you pointers on this."

"I am." Without a thought, he stepped closer. "Come

on, darlin'. Tell me you'll help me learn how to make Christmas all it should be for Sunnie."

Brad watched Abby close her eyes as if she struggled with her decision. When she opened them, she shook her head. "I wouldn't be doing this to help you. I'd be doing it for Sunnie."

"Of course," he said, careful to keep his tone from sounding triumphant. Whether it was for his or Sunnie's benefit, Abby was doing what he wanted, and he had the good sense not to draw attention to that fact.

He took a deep breath, then another. It was past time that he admitted what he'd been avoiding since kissing her under the mistletoe that day at the clubhouse. There was more than rivalry and teasing going on between them, and he was pretty sure she was as aware of it as he was. So what did he want to do about it? Was he ready to acknowledge that they had a chemistry between them that had quite possibly been there for most of their lives?

He wasn't sure. It could open up a whole can of worms that he would just as soon not deal with. He normally preferred women who weren't interested in anything more than a good time. But Abby never had been, nor would she ever be, that type. Abigail Langley was the type of woman who committed to a relationship, the type a man settled down with and raised a family.

Swallowing hard, he told himself to slow down. All he was asking for and all he wanted at the moment was her advice and help with his niece's first Christmas.

He leaned down to kiss Sunnie's cheek, then smiled at Abby. "So where do we start?"

"Start what?" she asked, looking distracted.

"Focus, Langley. You said you would help me with Christmas for Sunnie," he said, laughing. "I want to know where we should start."

Her cheeks colored a pretty pink. "For the record, I said if I helped it would be for Sunnie—not that I *would* help."

"But you will," he said. It wasn't a question, and he had no doubt that she was going to do it. He suspected her reticence had more to do with exercising a bit of the independence that was so much a part of her than any kind of reluctance to help him out.

She stared at him a moment longer, then sighing, she nodded. "Yes, I'll help you get ready for Sunnie's Christmas."

"Good." He picked up the empty baby carrier. "Now let's get this place decorated so we can start on mine. Where do you want the tree?"

"In front of the picture window in the living room," she said, heading in that direction.

As he followed her into the room, Brad couldn't wait to get her house finished so they could start on his place. He already had an idea of what he wanted to do, and if he was successful, it might very well prove to be one of the most enjoyable holiday seasons he'd had in a very long time.

Five

While Brad put the finishing touches on stringing the white twinkle lights around the front porch, Abby heated milk for two mugs of hot cocoa. She hadn't planned on doing much more than putting up a tree and maybe a wreath on the door, but as she opened each box of the decorations she had been collecting since childhood, her enthusiasm for the holidays grew.

It was amazing how much different this holiday season was from last year, she thought as she poured the milk into their cups. Newly widowed and dealing with the news that she would never have a family of her own, she hadn't had the heart to celebrate. But the passage of time had dulled the emotional pain of losing Richard, and although she still mourned her infertility, she was learning to deal with it.

"You can check 'lights around the outside of the

front windows' off your list," Brad said, walking into the kitchen. "What do you want me to put up next?"

"I think that's it." She dropped a spoonful of marsh-mallow cream into each mug, and turned to hand him his. "Is the baby still asleep?"

He nodded. "She seems to like sleeping in that car-rier, but I'll be damned if I can figure out why." He took a sip of his cocoa. "It looks cramped to me."

"Why is it that as soon as some men sit in a reclin-ing chair and put their feet up, they fall asleep?" she asked, smiling.

A frown creased his forehead. "I don't own one, but I guess most guys go to sleep in them because they're comfortable."

Laughing, she nodded as she walked back into the living room. "Just think of her carrier as a recliner for babies."

"I suppose that makes sense," he said, following her.

She sat down on the couch in front of the fireplace and looked around at their handiwork. "It's as pretty as I imagined it would be."

"You didn't decorate like this last year?" he asked, sitting down beside her.

Shaking her head, she shifted to face him. "Richard had just passed away a few weeks before the holidays, and I didn't want to be here alone for what should have been our first Christmas together as a married couple."

"I can understand that," Brad said, nodding. "Where did you go?"

"Back to Seattle." She shrugged one shoulder. "I still have my house on Lake Washington."

"How much shoreline do you have?" he asked, setting his mug on the end table.

"None." She grinned. "My house is *on* the lake."

He rested his arm along the back of the couch behind her. "Oh, you mean a houseboat like the one Tom Hanks lived in with his son in that movie several years ago?"

"They're called floating homes," she explained. "But my place isn't in as crowded of an area as the one in *Sleepless in Seattle.* I actually have a view that reminds me a lot of the lake where we used to go fishing when we were children."

A smile curved the corners of his mouth. "That was the first place I kissed you. Do you remember that?"

"How could I forget?" she asked, shuddering. "Right after that little peck on the lips you tried to put a grasshopper down the back of my shirt."

"If I remember correctly, you threatened to make me eat the damned thing if I did," he laughed.

She laughed with him. "And I would have, too." Taking a sip of her cocoa, she shook her head. "I'm surprised you remember that little incident."

They fell silent for a moment before she felt him lightly touch her hair. "That was the summer we were six years old and getting ready to go into the first grade," he said, his tone thoughtful. "Do you think that was what started our little game of one-upsmanship?"

"Maybe." She tried to recall when their rivalry began, but the sound of his rich voice and the feel of him stroking her hair distracted her. "I-it's so long ago, I'm not really certain when it began or why."

"Me, either." He threaded his fingers through her long curls. "But one thing's for sure—you've been driving me nuts for most of my life, Abigail Langley."

Her heart sped up as she met his piercing hazel gaze. "I'm sorry, but you've done your fair share of driving me to the brink, too."

"Don't be sorry." He cupped the back of her head with his hand to gently pull her forward. "There are different kinds of crazy, darlin'." His lips lightly brushed hers. "Right now, I'm thinking that it's the good kind."

Brad's mouth settled over hers, and Abby's eyes drifted shut. She wasn't so sure he was right about whether what was happening between them was good, but he was correct about one thing. It was definitely making her question her sanity. This was Brad Price, her lifelong nemesis and, most recently, her opponent for the presidency of the Texas Cattleman's Club. He was the very last man she should be kissing. But heaven help her, she couldn't seem to find the will to stop him.

When he pulled her against him and deepened the kiss, her heart skipped several beats and she abandoned all thought. The feel of his wide chest pressed against her breasts, and the tingling excitement of his tongue stroking her inner recesses, sent a wave of heat spiraling through every part of her. She had missed the intimacy of having a man's strong arms around her, of tasting the desire in his kiss. Without a thought to the consequences, she brought her arms up to wrap them around his shoulders as she gave in to the temptation of once again feeling cherished by a man.

Moving his hand, Brad cupped her breast and worried the hardened tip with the pad of his thumb. Even through her clothing, the sensations he created caused a spiraling surge of need that stole her breath.

She suddenly felt weightless, and it took a moment for her to realize that Brad had lifted her to sit on his lap. Melting against him, she could have easily lost herself in the moment had it not been for the feel of his rapidly changing body against the side of her hip and the answering ache of emptiness settling deep within her.

He wanted her and she wanted him. The realization was enough to send panic sweeping through her and immediately helped to clear her head.

"I—I think…I'll go make us another cup of… cocoa," she said breathlessly, pulling away from him.

His smile meaningful, he shook his head. "Cocoa isn't what I want."

Abby's heart fluttered wildly at his low, intimate tone. "That's all I'm offering, Brad."

"For now," he said, nodding. "But that doesn't mean the door is permanently closed on the subject." Before she could tell him differently, he gave her a quick kiss and set her on the couch beside him, then stood up. "I think it's time for Sunnie and I to call it a night. What time do you want to go shopping tomorrow?"

The speed at which he switched topics made her head spin. "What are you talking about? I didn't mention anything about going shopping with you."

"I told you I've never bothered to decorate before and I don't have anything," he said, pulling her up from the couch. Placing his hands on her shoulders, he smiled. "We have to pick out a tree, get ornaments and lights and whatever else you think I need."

"I could give you a list," she offered, desperately trying to think of an excuse not to help him.

"Nope." He smiled as he turned to arrange blankets over his sleeping niece in the baby carrier. "It would be best for you to go with me."

"I'd rather not," she said, shaking her head.

He stopped getting the baby ready to leave and turned to face her. "Why?"

How could she explain that the more time she spent with him and the baby, the more time she wanted to spend? How it reminded her of all the things she wanted but would never have?

When she hesitated a little too long, he smiled. "I'll be by around noon to pick you up." He gave her a kiss that curled her toes inside her fuzzy slippers, then picked up the baby and walked to the door. "We'll grab a bite of lunch and then hit the mall. See you tomorrow, darlin'."

Rendered speechless by his kiss, Abby simply watched the door close behind him. What on earth was wrong with her? Why was it that all Brad had to do was kiss her and she lost control of her thought processes and did what he wanted? And why was she letting him kiss her in the first place?

She had never been a pushover in her entire life. In fact, she had been accused of being the exact opposite on numerous occasions. Her mother had always told her she was a little too self-reliant for her own good, and even Richard had complained that at times he didn't think she needed him as much as he needed her.

Sinking back down on the couch, she stared at her

Christmas tree. What was it about Bradford Price that caused her to act so out of character?

From the time they were children just the thought of being around him caused her to feel edgy and anxious, as if she were waiting for…something. But what? A gesture? A move to let her know how he felt about her?

Her heart slammed into her ribs and she had to struggle to draw her next breath. Had what she thought was a spirited rivalry all these years actually been a mask for the attraction that was only now boiling to the surface?

Ridiculous. She took a deep, steadying breath. There had to be a perfectly good explanation for what was happening between her and Brad.

Most likely it was the combination of her wanting a baby but not being able to have one and him having just gained custody of his niece. Couple that with the fact that they were the only two single members of their circle of friends, and it was only natural that they would gravitate toward each other.

Satisfied that she had discovered the reason for what was happening between them, she rose to her feet and started toward the stairs leading up to her bedroom. Now that she had solved the mystery, she felt ready to deal with the situation. The first thing tomorrow morning, she would call and cancel their excursion to the mall, then she fully intended to throw herself into helping Sadie with plans for her family cultural center, as well as doubling her volunteer work at the women's shelter.

Changing into her night shirt, Abby pulled back the

comforter and climbed into bed. As long as she stayed busy and kept her distance from Brad and his adorable little niece, she would be just fine.

"Good morning," Brad said as soon as Sadie answered the phone. "How is my favorite little sister?"

"Suspicious," she answered without the least bit of hesitation. "What do you want, Brad?"

"I didn't mention wanting anything," he said, grinning as he spooned a bit of cereal into Sunnie's eager little mouth.

"You didn't have to," Sadie said, laughing. "Your choice of greetings tells me that you're up to something. What do you need?"

He wasn't the least bit surprised that his sister had figured out there had to be a motive behind his early-morning call. She knew him better than anyone else, and at times he suspected she might know him better than he knew himself.

"Could you watch Sunnie this afternoon for a couple of hours?" he asked, anticipating her affirmative answer.

"Of course," she said, just as he thought she would. "The twins will love spending time with their baby cousin."

"Great." He wiped a smear of cereal from Sunnie's chin. "I'll bring her over a little before noon."

"Are you having lunch with one of your clients?" Sadie asked conversationally.

"No, I'm taking Abby to lunch before we go shopping for Christmas decorations." He tucked the phone between his ear and shoulder as he lifted the baby from the high chair. "Abby is helping me get ready for Sunnie's first Christmas." Dead silence followed his announcement. "Sadie, are you still there?"

"Yes."

"Okay, what do you have against Abby and I spending time together?" He knew Sadie wouldn't comment unless asked.

"Actually, I don't have anything against it," she said, sounding as if she weighed each word carefully. She hesitated a moment before she continued, "I just don't want to see Abby get hurt."

"I'm not about to hurt Abby," he said, frowning. "What gives you the idea that I would?"

He heard her sigh. "I know you wouldn't mean to do it, but let's face it, you have a 'love 'em and leave 'em' reputation. And whether deserved or not, you'll have to admit you've dated a lot of women with absolutely no thought of commitment."

There was no way he could refute what his sister said. He had seen his share of the ladies over the past ten years, but it wasn't as if he had led them on. They had all known right up front that he wasn't interested in anything more than the pleasure of their company for an evening or two.

"Abby and I are friends." He walked into the family room to put Sunnie in her swing. "She's been helping me figure out things with the baby."

"Bradford Price, don't feed me a line," Sadie said, her tone stern. "For one thing, you and Abby have never been friends."

"We're both competitive and have been for as long

as either one of us can remember, but we've never been sworn enemies, either," he said in his own defense.

"I suppose that's true," Sadie said, sounding thoughtful. "But if you'll remember, I witnessed that kiss you gave her the other morning. That wasn't a gesture of friendship. It was more like the prelude to seduction."

He wasn't about to insult his sister's intelligence by denying that the kiss had been passionate. But he didn't want to discuss the motive behind it, when he wasn't exactly certain what it was.

"Sadie, I give you my word that I would never intentionally do anything to upset Abby or cause her any kind of emotional pain," he assured her.

"Thank you, Brad." They were both silent for a moment before Sadie spoke again. "Just be extremely careful not to hurt her, even unintentionally. I know I'm being overly protective, but she's my best friend, and the past year has been terribly rough for her. I just think it's time she experienced some happiness in her life."

Brad couldn't fault his sister for being loyal to a friend. It was one of the traits he admired most about her.

"Abby is lucky to have you on her side," he said, meaning it.

For some time after their call ended, Brad stood in the middle of the family room staring at the phone he still held. The last thing in the world he wanted to do was cause Abby any kind of distress. Maybe it would be in both of their best interests if he backed off and let her go her way while he went his.

But he rejected that train of thought almost as soon as it came to mind. He had no idea why he felt so compelled to spend time with Abby, why he wanted to hold her in his arms, kiss her until they both gasped for breath and more, but he did. And although she was doing her best to fight it, he suspected that she was experiencing the same magnetic pull he was.

Considering it was the first time in his life he felt that way about any woman, he owed it to both of them to take the time to find out what was going on. He had always believed that life was full of possibilities, and passing one up might very well mean a missed opportunity. And for reasons he couldn't quite put his finger on, he sensed that this was one chance that was important enough not to miss.

Abby couldn't believe she was standing in the Royal Diner with Brad, waiting to be seated. She had tried calling him several times throughout the morning to cancel their shopping trip, and even left a message on his voice mail telling him to count her out. Unfortunately he either failed to check his messages or simply ignored them. She suspected the latter, but when he showed up on her doorstep at noon, he denied knowing anything about it.

"Would you rather sit at a table or in one of the booths?" he asked, leaning close.

A shiver streaked straight up her spine at the feel of his warm breath feathering over her ear. "A...booth," she answered, cursing the breathless tone of her voice.

"There's an empty booth in the corner," he said,

placing his hand to the small of her back to guide her to the far side of the diner.

Thankful the table would be between them, Abby quickly slid into one side of the booth. When she noticed a couple of TCC members sitting across the room, their curious gazes fixed on her and Brad, it was all she could do not to groan aloud.

"I don't think this was a good idea," she said, picking up one of the menus left by a passing waitress.

"Why do you say that?" he asked, frowning. "I thought everyone in town liked the food here."

"It's not that I don't like the food." Apparently he hadn't noticed the attention they were getting. "I think Travis Whelan and David Sorensen are going to choke on their chili at the sight of the two of us together."

Instead of being subtle about looking over at the two men, Brad turned to call out a greeting. "Hey, Trav. Dave. How are things going?"

"Can't complain," Travis said, smiling.

"Are you two ready for the Christmas Ball and the announcement of the new TCC officers?" David asked.

"About as ready as we'll ever be," Brad said, smiling.

Travis nodded. "Good luck to both of you."

"Thank you," Abby said, wanly.

Great. Just what she needed. By the end of the day, the entire membership of the Texas Cattleman's Club would be speculating about the fact that she and Brad were seen having lunch together.

"What's wrong?" Brad asked, frowning.

She sighed. There were times men could be so clueless. "In case you hadn't noticed, we just supplied the rumor mill with enough grist to last until the ball next week."

"Is that all?" He laughed. "I doubt that our having lunch together will be cause for any kind of gossip."

"You're kidding, right?" She stared at him in disbelief. "It's been a well-known fact for the past several months that you didn't even want me to gain membership to the club, let alone run for president."

His easy expression faded. "I'm not denying that I wanted the club to remain the way it's been since its inception. But that doesn't mean I haven't accepted that the majority of the membership saw it differently when they voted to honor the bylaws and let you in." He reached across the table to cover her hand with his. "Relax, darlin'. If anyone asks, we're just two club members having lunch together. Hell, they might even speculate that we're trying to bridge the gap between the old guard and the newer TCC members."

What Brad said made sense, but it was hard to concentrate with his hand engulfing hers. "I suppose you're right," she finally managed. "I just hate being the hot topic for all of the gossips in town until the next scandal comes along for them to dissect. I've been there before and once was enough to last me a lifetime."

His frown told her that he had no idea what she was talking about. "I don't recall you ever doing anything that would cause the gossips' tongues to start wagging."

"I didn't. But I can't say the same about my father." It had been sixteen years ago but Abby still cringed when she thought about dealing with the aftermath he had left behind.

"You mean when your dad left you and your mom?" Brad asked gently.

She nodded. "I hated having people suddenly stop talking when I walked into a room or catching them stare at me while they whispered to each other."

"I can understand that." He lightly squeezed her hand. "But the best way to combat that is to act as if nothing is going on." He looked thoughtful a moment before he spoke again. "I think as a show of solidarity, we should plan on attending the Christmas Ball together."

She stared at him, then laughed out loud. "You've lost your mind, haven't you?"

"Probably, but I think it would send a message to the membership that we have nothing to hide and that no matter who wins the presidency, we're willing to work together." Grinning, he shrugged. "People are going to talk no matter what we do, and that's just a fact of life, darlin'. But if we act as if nothing out of the ordinary is going on, they quickly lose interest."

"You're serious," she said incredulously.

"Yup." He released her hand and picked up his menu as if she had already agreed to his harebrained idea. "I'm going to have the chili. What would you like?"

"I, um, guess I'll have the chef salad," Abby said, unable to get her mind off of his plan for them to attend the ball together.

As Brad gave the waitress their order, Abby had to admit that she could understand his reasoning. If they went together to the annual event, it would definitely send a clear message to the general membership that no matter which one of them took over leadership of the prestigious club, they intended to put the past behind them and work to heal the rift that had threatened the club in the past several months. But the way he said it made it sound too much like a date for her peace of mind.

"I suppose I could meet you there and then we could sit at the same table," she said, after the waitress walked toward the kitchen to turn in their order.

"Not acceptable," he said, shaking his head. "I'll pick you up and we'll go together."

"I don't think that would be—"

"You're overthinking this, Abby," he interrupted her. "It doesn't send a strong enough message if we just sit together. Hell, they'll probably seat us at the same table anyway. All you have to do is tell me what time I should pick you up."

She couldn't argue with what he said. All of the candidates for the various offices and their guests would most likely be sitting at a handful of tables in the front of the room. But how on earth did she manage to get into situations like this? More important, how was she going to get out of it?

"I'll give it some thought," she said, avoiding a definite answer. She had a week or so before the ball. Surely she could come up with a plausible reason why they should drive to the ball separately.

When the waitress returned with their food, then moved to the next table, Brad smiled. "Now that we have that settled, I think we had better eat and get this shopping trip underway. I promised Sadie that we wouldn't be gone long." He chuckled. "By the time we get back there, she'll probably be tearing her hair from taking care of three kids under the age of three."

Having so many little ones to take care of sounded like heaven to Abby. "You'll have to give your sister a break and babysit for her sometime," she said, smiling.

She couldn't help but laugh at his horrified expression. "That sounds like a recipe for disaster. There are times I'm still not entirely certain of what to do for Sunnie. I can't imagine adding a couple of toddlers to the mix." He frowned. "I would definitely need help."

Abby took a bite of her salad and chewed thoughtfully. "Maybe when your housekeeper returns from Dallas, you can get her to volunteer."

He shook his head. "Number one, Juanita doesn't volunteer for anything. I'd have to pay her. And number two, I doubt there's enough money in the state of Texas to tempt her into agreeing to watch three babies at once." He took a sip of his iced tea. "You're good with kids. You could help."

"I didn't say anything about—"

"Don't think you can handle it, Langley?" he asked, his hazel gaze capturing hers.

There was just enough challenge in his tone to put her on the defensive. "I'm sure I could handle it better than you."

"Then let's put it to a test," he suggested. "When we pick up Sunnie, I'll tell Sadie that we'll babysit while she and Rick go out tomorrow evening."

Abby opened her mouth to decline, but the combination of Brad's challenge and the temptation of spending time with the adorable twin girls and the sweet baby who had captured her heart were more than she could resist. Besides, weekends seemed to drag on interminably for her, and taking care of children would be a welcomed relief from the most boring part of the week.

"All right." She smiled. "Challenge accepted. We'll see just who loses a handful of their hair first."

A mischievous look crossed his handsome face. "Let's make this interesting."

"What do you…have in mind?" she asked hesitantly. What was he up to this time?

"At the end of the evening, whoever complains first about being tired or even yawns has to make dinner for the other." He looked so self-assured she almost laughed.

"You do realize you're going to lose, don't you?"

"Oh, I'm not so sure about that, Langley," he said, sounding quite confident. "We'll just see who's left standing when the dust settles."

"Yes, we most certainly will," she agreed, relishing the challenge.

Her competitive nature had come to full alert and it was game on. She was really going to enjoy watching the indomitable Mr. Price eat crow when he learned that taking care of children was the one thing she would never get tired of.

Three hours after driving Abby home and picking Sunnie up from his sister's place, Brad found himself pulling every Christmas decoration known to God and man from the mountain of shopping bags on his family room floor. He was searching for the one filled with mistletoe.

"I know it's here," he muttered.

When he finally found the plastic bag with enough mistletoe to decorate half the town of Royal, he grinned. By the time Abby showed up tonight, he fully intended to have the most important part of his decorating complete.

Checking on the baby to make sure she was still napping, he grabbed the small box of pushpins from the desk in his study and started to work. Twenty minutes later, just as he finished hanging the last sprig of the greenery, the doorbell rang.

"Right on time," he said, opening the door.

"Time for what?" Abby asked, frowning.

"Come in and I'll show you." He took her by the arm and led her into the middle of the foyer. "Look up, darlin'."

When she glanced up at the chandelier, she shook her head. "Of all the things you could have decorated, you chose to start with hanging mistletoe over putting up the tree?"

Taking her into his arms, he kissed her chin. "It's the most important decoration of all."

"Oh, really? By whose definition?" she asked, putting a bit of space between them.

"Mine," he said, brushing her lips with his. She wasn't pushing away from him, and as long as he kept her off guard, there was a chance she wouldn't. "It's one of the oldest of holiday traditions. For something to be around for a couple of hundred years or more, it has to be significant."

"When did you decide this?" she asked, sounding a little breathless.

"I think the first time I realized mistletoe's importance was over a week ago at the TCC clubhouse," he said, pulling her a little closer. "When I kissed you."

He watched her nervously moisten her lips. "This isn't wise, Brad."

"Why?" he asked, enjoying the feel of her slender form within the circle of his arms. "I like kissing you and you like being kissed. Where's the harm in that?"

"I…" She caught her lower lip with her teeth as if she were trying to find the right words. "I can't be what you want me to be."

Noticing that she hadn't denied she liked having him kiss her, Brad brought his hand up to brush her dark auburn hair from her soft cheek. "What do you think that is, Abby?"

"I'm not…entirely sure." She took a deep breath. "But I know what I can't be. I can't be one of your casual affairs. That's just not me. That's not who I am."

"I know that, darlin'." Threading his fingers through her silky waves, he gently pulled her closer. "All I want is for you to be who you've always been—Abby Langley, the woman who has challenged me to be the best I can be all of my life and recently became a good friend."

Before she could speculate further on what she thought he wanted from her, Brad lowered his mouth to hers. He didn't want to think about where their friendship was going or why kissing her was quickly becoming an obsession for him. He had a feeling he wouldn't be overly comfortable with what might be one of the most meaningful realizations of his life.

The moment their lips met, heat spread throughout

his body. Without a second thought, he deepened the kiss to once again lose himself in the sweetness that was uniquely Abby. He moved to take her hands in his and raise them to his shoulders, giving him free access to her full breasts. Covering the soft mounds with his palms, he felt the tips bead in eager anticipation, and his body answered with an urgent tightening of its own.

He would have liked nothing more than to feel Abby's much softer skin pressed to his, to hear her sigh of pleasure as he sank himself deep inside of her. But aside from the fact that the barrier of their clothing prevented that from happening, she wasn't yet ready to take that step, and he had never been a man to push for more than a woman was willing to give. Hell, he wasn't entirely certain he was ready for that step himself.

As if on cue, the sound of Sunnie's awakening for a bottle came through the speaker on the baby monitor, adding one more reason for him to break the kiss.

Brad regretfully raised his head to stare down into Abby's dazed blue eyes. "While I get the baby's bottle ready, why don't you go up to the nursery before she really gets wound up?"

Abby stared at him for several seconds before she nodded and turned to go upstairs. But he felt rooted to the spot. The sight of her blue-jeans-clad bottom swaying enticingly as she ascended the steps was driving him crazy, and it wasn't until she had disappeared down the hall at the top of the stairs that he forced himself to move.

There was no doubt about it. He and Abby would

eventually take that next step and become lovers. He just hoped he didn't end up going completely crazy before they did.

Six

Cradling Sunnie in one arm, Abby pointed to the lights Brad had just wound around the Christmas tree. "If you leave those there, you're going to have a bare spot with no lights at all on the other side."

"I probably should have bought another string of them," he said, moving the lights around to cover the area she had pointed out.

When he finished, she eyed the rearrangement. "For all of your grumbling, it looks good," she said, smiling. "Now you need to start hanging the ornaments."

"Aren't you going to help with that?" he asked, reaching for a box of silver balls. "It was your idea that I get a tree this big. The least you could do is get in on some of the fun."

Abby ignored his sarcastic tone. She was perfectly content to direct the project while holding Sunnie. "I've been having fun taking care of this little angel," she said, staring down at the sweet baby girl in her arms. "She's fascinated with all of this activity."

Brad stepped over a pile of garland to come over and tickle Sunnie's tummy. "We're doing all of this for you, munchkin. I hope you appreciate it."

The baby squealed with delight as she reached for Brad's hand.

Abby could tell the baby adored him, and her chest tightened from the knowledge that she would never experience that kind of love from a child. "I think I'll put Sunnie in her swing and make a couple of mugs of cocoa while you finish putting the ornaments on the tree," she said, suddenly needing a few minutes to herself.

"That sounds good." He glanced at his watch. "I'd like to get this done so we can relax for a few minutes before I have to get Sunnie in bed for the night."

Nodding, Abby put the baby in her swing, then went into Brad's kitchen. Leaning against the counter, she closed her eyes as she fought to keep the emotions building inside of her at bay.

The life she wanted, had always dreamed about having for as long as she could remember, was just in the other room. But it wasn't hers. She was just a guest Brad had asked to help him get ready for his first Christmas with the baby—the outsider looking in at what she wanted with all of her heart, but could never have.

She took a deep breath, swiped at the lone tear slowly making its way down her cheek and forced herself to move. Throwing herself a pity party was counterproductive and a waste of time and energy. A family of her own was never going to be hers, and she might as well get used to it.

Composing herself while she prepared the cocoa, she decided to make her excuses and leave as soon as possible. It made absolutely no sense to stay around and torture herself. Sunnie was not her child to love and care for, and Brad, with his killer kisses and sexy charm, could quickly become an addiction for which she strongly suspected there wasn't a cure. And that was something she wanted to avoid at all costs.

It was definitely in her best interest to back away from the situation and let Brad and his niece form their little family unit without her. If she didn't, she could very well become too attached to both of them and end up getting her heart broken. That was something she couldn't let happen. Her survival depended on it.

By the time she walked back into the family room with the steaming mugs, Abby felt a little more in control and ready to distance herself from temptation. "Where's Sunnie?" she asked, immediately noticing the baby wasn't in her swing.

"I put her in her crib upstairs," Brad said, taking the mug Abby handed him. "I guess the combination of the swing's motion and watching me wrestle with that damned garland was boring enough to put her to sleep."

"Well, bah humbug to you, too, Mr. Scrooge," Abby said, gazing at his handiwork. "Whether you liked doing it or not, you did a good job. Everything looks very nice."

"Thanks." He took her mug from her, then placing

both cups on the end table, gathered her into his arms. "I couldn't have done it without your help, darlin'."

Her heart beat double time, and every one of her good intentions evaporated like mist in the morning sun. She might have been able to cling to her resolve had he not touched her. But the feel of his strength surrounding her and the lull of his deep baritone caused her to forget the importance of putting distance between them.

"I'm sure you could have managed," she said, trying to find the will to pull away from him.

"Probably, but it wouldn't have been nearly as much fun," he whispered close to her ear.

Tingles of excitement skipped over every nerve in her body and she had to remind herself to breathe. "You had fun grumbling about the lights and the garland?"

His deep chuckle vibrated against her breasts. "I'll let you in on a secret. I grumble about a lot things that I really don't mind doing."

Feeling as if the tendons in her legs had been replaced with rubber bands, Abby wrapped her arms around his waist to support herself. "W-why?"

"It's a guy thing." He nuzzled his cheek against hers. "It's expected of us."

Closing her eyes, Abby couldn't stop herself from leaning into his touch. "What else is expected of you?"

"This," he said as his mouth brushed over hers.

He nibbled at her lips without really kissing her, and she couldn't believe the level of tension building inside of her. More than anything, she wanted him to deepen the caress and allow her to once again experience his passion.

"Do you want me to kiss you, Abby?" he asked, as he continued his tender teasing.

She knew she shouldn't, but that was exactly what she wanted. "Y-yes."

When he finally settled his mouth over hers, then parted her lips with his tongue to deepen the kiss, Abby felt as if the earth moved. The level of anticipation, the desperate need that Brad created, was unlike anything she had ever experienced.

Lights flashed behind her closed eyes as his tongue grazed hers, then engaged her in a game of advance and retreat. If she had thought his kisses were intoxicating before, they were but a mere glimpse of the erotic expertise he was showing her now.

Forgetting all of the reasons she should pull out of his arms and run back to the sanctuary of her ranch, she shamelessly pressed herself more fully against his lower body at the same time she tugged his T-shirt from the waistband of his jeans. There would be plenty of time later to regret her recklessness. At the moment, all she could do—all she wanted to do—was feel. She wanted to once again feel cherished. Needed to feel desired. And she craved the feel of his hard body inside of hers.

"I can't believe…I'm going to say this…darlin'," Brad said, sounding completely out of breath. He reached down to catch her hands in his. "But we need… to slow this…down."

It took a moment for Abby to realize what he had said. When she did, it was as effective as taking a plunge into a pool of icy water.

What on earth had she done? Why had she let go of the tight control that was so much a part of her?

Humiliated and unable to think of anything to say that would even come close to explaining her wanton actions, she remained silent. Pulling away from Brad, she refused to look at him as she rushed down the hall to the foyer closet. She needed to go home, crawl into bed and pray that when she awoke in the morning, she would find that she hadn't let her guard down and made a fool of herself with Brad, that it had all been a bad dream.

"Abby, where the hell do you think you're going?" Brad called, following close behind.

When his large hands came down on her shoulders, he turned her to face him and Abby made a point of fixing her gaze on the ribbed collar of his T-shirt. "H-home," she stammered. "I…need to get home."

"Why?"

She tried to back away from him. "I…just do."

"No, you don't." He applied just enough pressure to keep her firmly in place without hurting her. "You need to stay right here and talk to me. Do you have any idea why I called a halt to that kiss?"

Why wouldn't he let it go? Couldn't he at least let her keep a small scrap of her dignity?

"I don't think you have to put it into words," she said, shaking her head.

She still hadn't looked him directly in the eye and she wasn't sure she could. The well-respected, extremely independent Abigail Langley had never in her life let go and lost control of herself with any man—not even with her late husband.

"Look at me, Abby," he commanded. When she continued to stare at his chest, he placed his forefinger beneath her chin and raised her head to meet his gaze. "The reason I stopped you wasn't because I don't want you. Right now, I'm hard as hell and would like nothing more than to carry you up the stairs and spend the entire night loving you the way you were meant to be loved. But you're not ready for that." He gave her a kiss so tender she had to blink back tears. "When we make love, it's going to be long and slow, and the next morning there won't be any regrets."

Abby's heart skipped a beat at the determination in his piercing hazel eyes. What was she supposed to say to that? What could she say?

Thanking him for keeping her from making a fool of herself or for telling her that he intended to make love to her the way she'd never been made love to before was inappropriate and would be humiliating beyond words.

"I, um…really should go, Brad," she finally managed to say.

He kissed her forehead, then hugged her close. "I'll see you tomorrow evening, darlin'."

"I don't think—"

"Hush, Abby," he said, placing one finger to her lips. He gave her a smile that left her insides feeling like warm pudding. "We'll have three kids to chaperone us."

She had forgotten about babysitting for Rick and Sadie and didn't feel that she could back out of helping Brad. Her conscience wouldn't allow her to leave him to care for three children by himself when he was adjusting to taking care of one, nor did she want to keep her best friend from spending some much-needed alone time with her husband.

Resigned, she nodded. "I'll see you tomorrow."

"I'll be looking forward to it," he said, giving her a smile that could melt the polar ice caps.

Shrugging into her jacket, she simply walked to the door and left. There was no point in trying to argue with him that the more time they spent together, the more dangerous the situation became for her. He wouldn't listen anyway. Besides, she needed to analyze her uncharacteristic behavior. She needed to figure out why she had so easily let herself go with Brad when she hadn't even been able to be that free with Richard.

Once she had the answer, she had every intention of shoring up her defenses to prevent it from happening again. If she didn't, there was a very real possibility she would end up falling for Brad.

And make an even bigger fool of herself than she had tonight.

"I took the liberty of ordering for both of us," Sadie said when Abby hurried over to where she sat in a booth at the Royal Diner.

"Sorry I'm late." Abby slid across the red and white vinyl seat on the other side of the booth. "After you called this morning about meeting for lunch, my foreman sent for me to go down to the barn because one of my mares went into labor sometime during the night. She didn't give birth until about an hour ago."

"I hope everything went well." Sadie smiled. She waited for the waitress to set their plates in front of them and move on to another table before she asked, "Did the mare have a little stud or a filly?"

"Filly," Abby said, happily. "I had a special name picked out and it wouldn't have sounded right if the foal had been a stud."

Her friend laughed. "Well, don't keep me in suspense. What are you going to name her?"

"Sunnie's Moonlight Dancer is the name she'll be registered under with the American Quarter Horse Association," Abby explained. "But around the ranch we'll call her Dancer."

"You named her after the baby?" Her glass of iced tea half-way to her mouth, Sadie stopped to give her a questioning look.

"I thought it sounded pretty," Abby said, placing her paper napkin in her lap. "Besides, when Sunnie's old enough, I plan on giving Dancer to her."

There wasn't a question of whether the baby would grow up riding horses. Everyone in and around Royal either had a horse or knew how to ride one.

"It's very pretty." Looking thoughtful, Sadie set her glass back on the table. "You've fallen in love with my brother and niece, haven't you?"

Abby's heart stopped for several beats as a jolting panic coursed through her. She couldn't dispute caring deeply for the baby. But Brad? Was that why she always gave in to his insistence that he needed her help with this or that? Could that be the reason she lost all will to resist whenever he held her, kissed her?

No, definitely not. She couldn't—wouldn't—allow herself to love anyone else. It was too risky, would be too painful if she lost them the way she had lost Richard—or the baby she had tried to adopt, only to have the mother change her mind.

"N-no. I mean, of course I think the world of Sunnie. Who doesn't? But Brad? No, definitely not." She knew she was babbling, but couldn't seem to stop herself. "He's nice enough, but...well, no, I don't love him. We're just friends."

"Of course you don't," Sadie said smugly.

Abby could tell by the look on her best friend's face that she didn't believe a word Abby had just said. "No, really. I like Brad, but we're just friends."

Sadie nodded. "That's why the two of you have been almost inseparable for the past week."

"I'm just helping him get ready for Sunnie's first Christmas," Abby heard herself saying defensively. She knew she was beginning to sound like a broken record, but she couldn't think of any other plausible excuse.

"You don't have to explain yourself to me, Abby." Sadie's smile was filled with understanding. "I'm not condemning you. Heaven knows, I was a complete wreck when Rick and I were trying to sort out everything."

"I'm so very glad it worked out for the two of you," Abby said, meaning it. "But there's nothing going on between—"

"Save it." Sadie laughed. "I've heard that song before. I don't need to hear it again." Her expression turned serious. "I didn't invite you to lunch to quiz you on your feelings for my brother."

"Why did you want to meet with me?" Abby asked curiously. Normally when they had lunch together it was planned well in advance due to Sadie's need to find a sitter.

"Actually there are a couple of things." Sadie took a sip of her tea. "I've made a couple of decisions about the family cultural and community center I want to run by you."

Much more comfortable with the topic of conversation, Abby picked up her fork. "What have you decided?"

"I want it to be a place where families can not only expose their children to the arts, but also receive the help they need in times of crisis." Her friend looked thoughtful. "Times are tough for a lot of people right now, and I want them to have a place to go when they have a shortfall and find that they need assistance with things like utility bills or a month's rent."

"I think that's a wonderful idea. Let me know when and where to volunteer." Abby took a bite of her salad. "Where do you plan on putting it? Are you still hoping the TCC will donate their clubhouse if they vote to build a new one, or are you going to try to find some land and start fresh?"

"I'm still hoping for the clubhouse," Sadie said, staring into space as if imagining the possibilities the building afforded. "It really has everything I need—office space, a ballroom that could easily be turned into an auditorium for concerts and art exhibits, as well as the gym for physical activities. But if that doesn't happen, I'll explore building."

Abby nodded enthusiastically. "I'm hoping you get the clubhouse. I think it would be ideal." They fell silent a moment before she asked, "What was the other thing you wanted to discuss with me?"

Sadie looked a bit hesitant. "Some of the TCC members have been talking," she said slowly. "Rick told me that several of them have asked him what's going on with you and Brad spending so much time together."

Abby's heart sank. She had warned Brad it would happen when they were seen having lunch together just the day before.

"What did Rick tell them?" she asked, rubbing at the tension headache suddenly building at her temples.

"You know how Rick is. He politely but firmly told them that if they worried more about what was going on in their own lives, they wouldn't have time to wonder about others." Sadie smiled. "Actually, I think he was a little more graphic when he talked to them, but that's the gist of what he said."

Groaning, Abby pushed her plate away from her. Ravenous when she had arrived, she suddenly found that her appetite had deserted her. "I appreciate that he put them in their places, but I hate being gossiped about."

"I know what that's like," Sadie said, nodding. "If you'll remember back about five months ago, Rick and I were the talk of the town."

"That's the one thing about living in Seattle that I miss more than anything else." She sighed wistfully. "It's big enough that no one knows or cares who your friends are or what you're doing."

"Gossip is one of the hazards of living in a small town, that's for sure," Sadie agreed. "But I thought you should be aware of it."

"Thanks." Truthfully, she wasn't sure if she wouldn't have been better off being blissfully unaware. At least, she wouldn't have felt like everyone was whispering about her when she walked into a room.

"There's one other thing I wanted to ask you about," Sadie said, placing her paper napkin on the table. "Are you and Brad sure you want to babysit this evening?"

"Of course." Even though being with Brad was going to be a bit awkward after last night, she couldn't disappoint her friend. "I'm looking forward to it. You know how much I love your girls."

Sadie looked relieved. "Thanks. I would really like to spend some quality time with my husband. Alone."

"I don't blame you," Abby said. "Brad and I actually have a little wager on who will tire out first—me or him."

"Oh, sweetie, you've seen the girls in action. I think you and Brad will both be wiped out by the end of the evening." Sadie grinned. "By the way, what's the prize?"

"Whoever loses has to make dinner for the other one." Abby laughed for the first time since learning she and Brad were the hot topic in Royal. "I have every intention of being the winner on this one."

"You go, girlfriend," Sadie said, checking her watch. She tossed a few dollars on the table for the waitress, then gathered her purse and jacket. "I've got to run. One of the neighbors down the way from us woke up with the pink flamingos in his yard this morning. He was on his way to Houston on business and asked me to take his donation to the women's shelter to get rid of them."

"Don't blame me for that one," Abby said, laughing. "I've helped put them in people's yards a few times, but I have no idea who all is on the list."

Sadie shrugged one shoulder. "I really don't mind. It's for a good cause. But the sooner that I make Mr. Higgins's donation, the sooner they can be put in someone else's yard and make more money for the shelter."

"I expect to see them in my yard any day," Abby said, sliding out of the booth.

"Rick and I will bring the girls over to Brad's place around seven this evening," Sadie said, as they walked toward the cashier at the end of the lunch counter.

"That sounds good." After paying for their lunch, Abby followed Sadie outside. "But I thought we would be watching them at your house."

Her friend shook her head as they walked across the parking lot. "The twins will probably still be awake when we get back, but I'm sure Sunnie will be asleep. I thought it would be easier for you to go ahead and put her to bed for the night, instead of having to get her up to bring her home."

"You're probably right," Abby said, giving her friend a hug. "I'll see you tonight at Brad's."

On the drive back to her ranch, Abby couldn't help but think about what Sadie had told her. The last thing she had wanted was to once again be the talk of the TCC membership. Some of the older members had been downright outraged when she decided to run for the office of president and still grumbled about her admittance into the prestigious club. Now that the actual voting had taken place, things seemed to have died down a bit as they awaited the election results. That was just the way she wanted it to stay, too.

She was going to have to discuss the matter with Brad and tell him that attending the ball together was definitely off the table. She had been looking for an excuse not to go with him, anyway, and this was as good as any. There was no way she wanted to attend the event with him and cause the rumors to escalate. Now all she had to do was get that point across to him.

Abby sighed. She most definitely had her work cut out for her. If there was one thing she had learned in the past couple of weeks, it was that Brad Price was about as determined to have his way as anyone she had ever met.

Abby smiled as she sat in the rocking chair, giving Sunnie a bottle while she observed Brad interacting with his nieces, Wendy and Gail. After pretending he was a pony and crawling around on the floor giving them rides, helping them build towers of blocks to knock over and holding a stuffed bunny for the girls to feed pretend food to, he was seated on the couch with one snuggled close on either side of him. They were watching a classic Disney cartoon on a DVD that Sadie had brought over with them and he seemed just as focused on the television as the girls were.

She could tell Wendy and Gail adored their uncle and he returned their feelings. Every time one of them pointed out something that happened on the television, Brad gave her his full attention and acted as if what she told him was of the utmost importance. He was going to be a wonderful father to Sunnie and any other children he would eventually have.

Abby's chest tightened with emotion at the thought that she wouldn't be a part of it all. There were no nights spent watching classic children's shows with toddlers in her future, no rocking babies to sleep and...no Brad.

Her breath caught. Where had that come from?

"Abby, darlin', are you all right?" Brad asked, interrupting her disturbing thoughts.

Glancing over at him, she nodded. "Of course. Why do you ask?"

"You seem like you're a million miles away," he said, smiling. "You aren't about to concede our wager are you?"

She laughed. "Not on your life."

"I asked if you thought it was about time for us to get the twins changed into their pajamas and give them their snack," he said, smiling. He nodded at the yawning little girls at his sides. "Any more of watching the singing teapot and the French candelabra and these two are going to be out like a couple of lights."

"Do you want me to get them ready or can you handle it?" she asked.

Abby smiled when she realized they were both avoiding mentioning the words *sleep* or *bed*. Having seen Sadie get the girls ready for bed before, she had firsthand knowledge of the fuss they raised when key words were mentioned.

Brad shrugged. "It doesn't matter to me who gets them changed. Is Sunnie asleep?"

Nodding, Abby rose to her feet. "I'll take her upstairs

and put her in her crib. When I come back down, I'll get Wendy and Gail into their pajamas while you get the snacks Sadie left for them."

He stretched his arms along the back of the couch. "Sounds like we have a plan."

"You sound a little tired," she said, grinning.

"Just wait and see, darlin'," he said, laughing. "I'm going to come out the winner on that bet."

"Hang on to that little dream, Mr. Price," she said, walking down the hall.

Twenty minutes later, the twins had been dressed in their matching pink-footed pajamas and were just finishing their cheese flavored crackers shaped like goldfish and their milk when the doorbell rang.

"I didn't expect them back this soon," Abby said, picking up a handful of plastic blocks to place into a mesh bag.

"Sadie told me they were only going out for dinner." Brad chuckled. "I think they wanted to enjoy a meal for a change without a toddler food fight."

"Just think, you have that to look forward to with Sunnie," Abby said, grinning.

"And here I thought those days were over when I graduated college." He started down the hall to open the door. "I'll have to give Zeke and Chris a call to come over and join the fun. They used to like a good food fight."

"Unless you want your housekeeper to quit, I wouldn't if I were you," she advised.

A half hour later, after bidding good-night to Sadie, Rick and the twins, Abby found herself alone with Brad for the first time since the humiliating incident the night before. Fortunately, he hadn't brought up the subject and she was grateful for that. But it was time to discuss another uncomfortable matter.

"There's something we need to talk over," she said, making sure she wasn't standing under the mistletoe. Knowing his newfound fondness for the holiday tradition, he would probably insist on kissing her again, and she needed her wits about her.

He stared at her for several seconds as if trying to determine what she wanted to tell him. "If it's about what happened when I kissed you—"

"It's not," she interrupted. "Well, not exactly."

"Okay," he said, placing his hand to her back to guide her toward the kitchen. "I'll make us some coffee."

Shaking her head, she stopped in the middle of the foyer. "Thank you, but I won't be here that long." She took a deep breath. "I won't be going with you to the Christmas Ball."

His frown was filled with displeasure. "Why not?"

"There's been some talk among several of the TCC members about our spending so much time together," she stated flatly. "I don't like it and I want it to stop. Our attending the ball together will only increase the gossip, not put a halt to it."

"I don't give a damn what people say and you shouldn't, either." A muscle worked along his lean jaw, and she could tell that Brad wasn't in the least bit happy. "First of all, it's none of their business. And second, if we don't go together now, the rumors will only increase."

"How do you figure that?" she asked. Sometimes his logic was hard to follow.

"Think about it. If there's talk about our seeing each other and we aren't together, then they'll start speculating about that," he explained. He cupped her face with his hands. "Don't you see, Abby? No matter what we do, people are going to talk. We can't control that."

"Unfortunately," she said, feeling trapped.

"But there is a way for us to take charge of the situation." He held her questioning gaze with his. "We don't have anything to hide. We can go together with our heads held high and show them that we don't care what's said, that we'll do whatever we damned well please."

She supposed it made sense when put that way. By ignoring the gossipmongers, she and Brad took the power away from them. But that wasn't going to keep her from feeling uncomfortable with the entire situation.

She nodded. "I suppose you're right."

"I know I am, darlin'."

He lowered his head to fuse his lips with hers and just as she feared, her will to resist was nonexistent. She had told herself she wouldn't allow him to kiss her, wouldn't take the chance on making a fool of herself again. But the truth of the matter was, she wanted his kiss, wanted to feel his body pressed close to hers, and whether it was wise or not, she wanted him.

That fact alone should have been enough to send her running as far and fast as her legs could carry her. Instead, she raised her arms to his shoulders and threaded her fingers in the hair at the nape of his neck as she surrendered herself to the mind-altering feelings she had come to expect from his kiss.

When he slipped his hand beneath her blouse, the feel of his large, warm palm caressing her waist, then sliding up along her ribs, caused a delicious warmth to flow through her from the top of her head all the way to her toes. But when he deepened the kiss at the same time his hand covered her breast, the heat within her settled low in the pit of her stomach and caused her knees to give way. Sagging against him, she felt the evidence of his desire and an answering ache formed in the most feminine part of her.

His thumb teasing her through the fabric of her bra, and the ridge of his hard arousal pressed to her lower belly quickly had her aching for him to touch her without the encumbrance of their clothing. She wanted to feel his hard flesh against her much softer skin, needed to touch and explore his body as she wanted him to explore hers.

Lost in the passionate sensations Brad had created, she whimpered when he eased away from the kiss and removed his hand from beneath her shirt. Resting his forehead against hers, he took a deep breath, then another.

"I know I'm going to regret this, but I think it's time for you to go home and get a good night's sleep," he said, his voice hoarse as he released her to get her coat from the closet. "You look as tired as I feel."

She slipped her arms into the jacket he held for her, and a bit of the tension that still gripped her began to ease as she realized what he had said a few moments earlier. Walking to the door, she turned back to smile at him. "You're tired?"

Frowning, he nodded. "Aren't you?"

"A little," she said, stepping out onto the porch. Turning back, she added, "But you mentioned it first, Mr. Price. Now you owe me dinner."

Smiling as he watched the door close behind Abby, Brad stuffed his hands in the front pockets of his jeans and rocked back on his heels. He hadn't forgotten about the wager. He had made it a point to see that she won. It had been well worth conceding just to see the triumphant look on her pretty face.

But as he stood there thinking about how special he intended to make the evening for her when he paid up on the bet, the thought of her being upset over the gossip among some of the TCC members began to burn at his gut. He had a feeling that the majority of those talking behind their backs were from the faction that clung to tradition—those who had wanted to keep the prestigious club an all-male organization and resented that Abby had joined the ranks.

He drew in a deep breath. It wasn't something he was overly proud of, but until recently he had been in complete agreement with them. But now?

Times had changed, and in order to make sure the club remained relevant and an institution of high regard in the Royal community, the membership had to be more progressive in their thinking. Abby had been a member for most of the past year, and he could honestly say that in that length of time nothing had changed about the club's mission. The entire membership, including Abby devoted themselves to upholding the values set forth by Tex Langley over a hundred years ago.

That's why the gossip had to stop. Besides the fact that it was upsetting Abby, if it kept up, the club would end up destroying itself from within. The honor they had all pledged to uphold was already in jeopardy. Fortunately, he was pretty sure he had a way to put a stop to all the backbiting, and that was exactly what he intended to do.

The next afternoon, Brad sat at the head of the heavy mahogany conference table in one of the private meeting rooms in the TCC clubhouse, waiting to brief his two friends on his plan. Provided for members to strategize the various secret missions of goodwill they had carried out over the years, the meeting rooms were available to any member with an objective to right a wrong.

"What's up, Brad?" Chris asked as he and Zeke entered the room.

"Some of the members have been pretty vocal about the time I've been spending with Abby Langley and I intend to put a stop to it," he said bluntly.

Zeke nodded as he pulled out the chair to one side of Brad and sat down. "I overheard a couple of them gossiping about it the other day at the diner, but as soon as I walked by, they had the good sense to shut up."

Brad didn't ask what was said. He didn't care to know. That he and Abby were the topic of conversation was enough to upset Abby, and that, in turn, didn't set well with him.

"Yeah, my father-in-law mentioned that the two of

you were getting pretty tight," Chris said, taking the seat on the other side of Brad. "Harrison asked if I knew anything about it, and I told him I wouldn't discuss it with him if I did."

"Thanks." Brad appreciated his friends' loyalty. "I have an idea how to pretty much put a stop to it, but I'm going to need your help."

"You know you can count us in," Zeke said emphatically.

"You bet," Chris agreed. "What did you have in mind?"

"I'd like to get the word out that Abby and I are working on restoring unity to the club," Brad said.

Chris nodded. "That sounds reasonable. No matter which of you wins the presidency, the members backing the loser are going to have their nose out of joint."

"Do you have a plan on how to go about letting people know?" Zeke asked.

"If the two of you could mention it to a few of the biggest windbags in the club, I think the word would spread pretty quick," Brad explained. "By the time the election results are announced at the Christmas Ball, the members will hopefully be thinking along the lines of maintaining the club's integrity and make the transition easier for whichever one of us is elected."

"Sounds like a solid plan to me," Chris said.

Zeke grinned. "Nothing against Abby, but this is the very reason you need to win the office. If there's a chance in hell to get the TCC back on track, you're it."

A look of anticipation crossed Chris's face. "I'll tell Harrison Reynolds. It'll be all over town by the end of the day. It's my bet he's one of the windbags that's been speculating on what's going on."

"You're calling your father-in-law a windbag? I thought you and he had buried the hatchet and called a truce," Brad said, referring to the animosity the older man had displayed for Chris in years past. A self-made man, Chris came from a modest background and his father-in-law had never thought Chris was good enough for his daughter, Macy.

"We have made peace," Chris admitted. "But only to a point. He still forgets himself from time to time and gets in his digs about me being born on the other side of the tracks."

Zeke uttered a graphic curse that had them all nodding their heads. "He'd be lucky if he was half the man you are, Chris."

Chris shrugged. "We'll never be best friends, that's for damned sure. But we both love Macy, and we've worked out our differences enough to tolerate each other for her sake."

"Anything else?" Zeke asked.

"I got a call from Mitch Hayward this morning, asking for a few more details about managing the football team," Brad said, grinning. "It looks like he's about to commit."

"Man, that's awesome," Zeke said, grinning.

"Do you think he'll make his decision before the Christmas Ball?" Chris asked, sounding hopeful.

"It looks like he might," Brad said. "It would be nice to make the announcements about the team at the Ball. By that time, we should have commitments from a couple of Mitch's former pro teammates for the other management positions we'll have open."

Checking his watch, Zeke rose to his feet. "There should be several of the TCC members at the diner right now having coffee. I think I'll drop in and set your plan into motion. The sooner we get the word out, the better."

"And I'll stop by Reynolds Construction to set things straight on that front," Chris assured, standing to leave.

As Brad followed his best friends out of the club-house, he felt confident that by evening there wouldn't be any more speculation about why he and Abby had been spending so much time together. Or if there was, it would have a more positive spin.

Seven

In the few days that followed their babysitting Sadie and Rick's twins, Abby hadn't seen Brad and Sunnie at all, and she had spoken to Brad on the phone only a few times. She had been busy with the party she volunteered to help with for the children at the women's shelter, as well as getting up in the wee hours of the morning several days in a row to place the pink flamingos on the lawns of the unsuspecting wealthier residents of Royal.

As she parked the SUV in front of his house, her heart sped up in anticipation. She took pride in the fact that hers and others' efforts had raised several hundred thousand dollars in donations for the worthwhile charity. But as fulfilling as it was to be of service to the community, she had missed seeing Sunnie and her devastatingly handsome uncle. It wasn't wise and would probably end up causing her immense emotional upset, but she hadn't been able to stop it. Brad and his precious niece were becoming an extremely important part of her life.

Before she could knock, Brad swung the door open and pulled her into his arms. "Are you ready for the culinary event of the year?" he asked, giving her a kiss that made her head spin.

"I—I...suppose so," she said, feeling delightfully breathless.

"Good." He took her by the hand. "Close your eyes."

"What are you up to this time?" she asked, laughing.

His smile caused her pulse to flutter. "Our bet was for the loser to make a nice dinner for the winner. Now, close your eyes."

When she did as he commanded, he led her through the house to the formal dining room. "Okay, you can open them now," he whispered close to her ear.

She opened her eyes and looked at the table. "Oh, my! Brad, this is gorgeous!"

The red place mats and green napkins contrasted beautifully with the pristine white tablecloth. An elegant silver vase filled with at least two dozen dark red roses served as a centerpiece, with silver candlesticks holding lit red tapers standing on either side.

She hadn't expected him to go to such lengths. Thinking he would prepare something simple for dinner like spaghetti, possibly served at the kitchen table, she was touched by the thought and effort he had obviously put into the meal.

Standing behind her, he wrapped his arms around

her waist to pull her back against him. "Only the best for you, darlin'."

His warm breath on the side of her neck and the feel of him pressed against her back side sent tiny electric charges streaking through every part of her. She might have fought what was happening between them at first, but over the course of the past couple of weeks, he had worn her down and she had come to look forward to their time together, to his gestures of affection. It seemed that Brad used every excuse imaginable to touch her cheek or her hair, or kiss her until they both gasped for breath. And God help her, she loved every single minute of it.

She realized she was playing a dangerous game and that frightened her. But as long as she kept things in perspective and didn't allow herself to start caring too much, she should be able to maintain their newfound friendship and still protect herself from being hurt.

In theory it all sounded good, but putting it into practice might prove difficult. With Brad holding her, nibbling tiny kisses along the column of her neck, it was becoming harder to remember why it was so important to keep from giving him her heart.

"Where's the baby?" she asked, trying to distract herself from her disturbing thoughts.

"She's spending the night with Sadie and Rick," he whispered against her skin. "I thought it would be nice for you and I to have an evening to ourselves for a change."

The idea of spending the entire evening alone with Brad, without the buffer of having to take care of the baby, should have sent her running for the door. That it didn't bothered her even more.

"Are you sure that's…wise?" she asked. It was more a question for herself than it was for him.

He turned her to face him, then cupping her face with his hands, met her questioning gaze. "I give you my word that nothing is going to happen unless you want it to, darlin'."

She wasn't about to tell him that was what worried her. She didn't have to. They both knew that the chemistry between them was stronger than either had ever imagined was possible.

"Why don't we have the wonderful dinner you promised me?" she asked, avoiding the subject of what might happen later.

Brad stared at her a moment longer, then smiling, pulled out one of the dining room chairs. "Let's get you seated for the best Bourbon Street steak you've ever had."

She wasn't surprised they were having steak. Most Texas men preferred a good steak to any other kind of meal.

"Which restaurant did the catering?" she asked when he brought two plates in from the kitchen.

"Chez Price," he said, setting her plate down in front of her.

"You did the marinade, as well as grilled the steaks?" she asked.

"Why are you so surprised?" he asked, sitting down at the head of the table. "The bet was that the loser had to make dinner."

"I know, but most men I know think that throwing

steaks on the grill is good enough," she said, placing her napkin in her lap. "They don't even consider marinating them."

He gave her a teasing smile as he reached for his knife and fork. "Darlin', haven't you figured out by now that I'm not like most men?"

As she took a bite of the succulent-looking steak, Abby had to admit that over the past couple of months, Brad had been full of surprises. First he had stepped forward to take on the responsibility of raising his brother's child as his own. That was completely out of character for a self-confessed playboy. Then, when he told her that he had taken a leave of absence from his financial planning firm to stay home with Sunnie because he didn't think it would be in her best interest to turn her over to a nanny, she had really been taken aback. Abby knew for a fact that was unheard of among men of his caliber in the business world. But the biggest surprise of all had come the night that Sunnie had the reaction to the immunization shot. Brad had not only been extremely worried about the baby, he had extended that concern to her as well when, knowing how tired she was, he had refused to wake her for the drive home.

"How do you like your steak?" he asked, interrupting her introspection.

"It's delicious," she said, meaning it.

"Good." He picked up his glass of iced tea. "Do they have any good steak houses in Seattle?"

Smiling, she nodded. "There's a place in Redmond called the Stone House that has excellent steaks."

"Is that the suburb where you lived when you were out there?"

"No, Redmond was where my partners and I started our software company." She smiled fondly as she thought of the billion-dollar business they had built from the ground up. "We used to eat dinner there when we had to work late."

"I've heard your computer program is the gold standard for the insurance industry." He set his glass back on the table. "Do you think you'll ever go back to work in software development?"

"I gave it some thought right after Richard died, and my former partners have recently approached me about starting a new company," she admitted. "But I would have to move back to the Seattle area and I'm not sure I want to do that. I have the ranch to take care of and…" Pausing, she grinned. "…when I win the TCC presidency, I think the membership would prefer that I live a little closer to Royal."

Brad laughed as he rose to take their plates into the kitchen. "You're pretty sure of yourself there, aren't you, Langley?"

"No more so than you are," she said, enjoying their good-natured banter.

When he returned to the dining room, he held out his hand. "I thought we would have dessert in front of the fireplace."

"That sounds nice," she said, placing her hand in his.

Rising from the chair, she let him lead her into the family room where he had set a silver tray with two champagne flutes and a bowl of chocolate-dipped strawberries on the coffee table. A bucket of ice sat to the side chilling a bottle of champagne. The fireplace and the twinkling lights from the Christmas tree in the corner were the only illumination in the otherwise dark room.

Before she could comment on the scene obviously set for seduction, Brad put his arms around her. "I want you to know that I'm not planning anything but a nice relaxing evening. Anything that progresses beyond that is going to be your call, darlin'."

Abby appreciated his candidness, as well as his willingness to give her control of the situation. But considering the way she melted into a wanton puddle of need whenever he kissed her, she wasn't certain that leaving how the evening would go up to her was the best of ideas.

"I didn't think you drank anything alcoholic," she said, deciding not to address the subject until she had to.

"I normally don't," he said, slowly rubbing his cheek against her hair. "But I made an exception for tonight."

"W-why?" she asked, distracted by his warm breath whispering over her skin and the feel of his muscular frame pressed against her much softer one.

"There's something we need to do," he said, releasing her to remove the bottle from the ice bucket. He popped the cork and poured the sparkling pink liquid into the flutes. "One of us is going to become the new president of the Texas Cattleman's Club tomorrow evening, and as soon as the announcement is made, whoever wins will be asked to give a little speech. After that we'll be surrounded by members congratulating whoever wins." He handed her one of the glasses. "I'd rather have a quiet moment to celebrate with you, and tonight is about the only time that's going to happen."

His thoughtfulness touched her. Raising her glass, she lightly touched his. "Congratulations to whoever wins."

"To us," he said, taking a sip of the champagne. He reached down to pick up one of the strawberries, then held it to her lips. "In the event that you win, I can't think of anyone I'd rather lose to, Abby."

"Nor I, you," she said, taking a bite of the strawberry.

Her breath caught when he leaned forward to kiss away a drop of the berry juice from her lips. "You taste good."

"Champagne and chocolate-covered strawberries always taste good together," she agreed.

His smoldering gaze made her heart flutter wildly. "I wasn't talking about the berries or the champagne, darlin'."

When he took their flutes to set them on the coffee table, the look in his eyes reflected his intent, and she automatically swayed toward him as he wrapped his arms around her.

The moment his mouth covered hers, Abby knew the decision had been made. She wanted Brad's kiss, wanted to feel his body tight with desire, wanted to taste his passion. And heaven help her, she wanted him to experience the same things from her as well.

Pulling Abby to him, Brad savored the taste of champagne, strawberries and chocolate on her perfect coral lips. He didn't think he had ever tasted anything as erotic or as sensual in all of his thirty-two years.

But when he deepened the kiss to tease and coax, her passion, the desire he detected in her eager response, was everything he had hoped for and more. In the beginning, she might have fought against the attraction that drew them together, but he knew as sure as the sun came up in the mornings that Abby had been as powerless to resist it as he had been.

When she wrapped her arms around his waist and took the initiative to excite him as he had been doing to her, his heart thumped against his ribs like a jackhammer, and it felt as if every drop of blood in his body rushed to the area south of his belt buckle. His arousal was almost instantaneous and made him feel slightly dizzy from its intensity.

Without so much as a second thought, he slid his hands down her back to her shapely bottom and drew her forward to rest more fully against him. He wanted her to feel what she did to him, how much she made him want her.

He felt a shiver course through her a moment before she tightened her arms around him, and he could tell she was as turned on as he was. "You're driving me crazy, darlin'," he said, his voice sounding rusty.

"I think…it's mutual." She sounded as winded as he felt.

Bringing his hand up to thread his fingers through her long wavy hair, he leaned back to look into her vibrant blue eyes. "I'm not going to lie to you, Abby. I want you more than I want my next breath. But I swear I didn't intentionally set out to seduce you this evening.

If you would rather we sit down and just talk, I'm okay with that." He knew he would suffer something awful if she chose the latter, but he could live with that as long as she was comfortable with whatever decision she made.

She sent his blood pressure soaring when she put her index finger to his lips and shook her head. "I don't have the will to fight this any longer and I don't want to talk. I want you, Brad."

"Are you sure?" he found himself asking. If she changed her mind, he had a feeling he would go stark raving mad. But he wasn't going to push for more if she wasn't ready to take things to the next level.

"There are a lot of things I'm not sure of, but this isn't one of them, Brad," she said seriously. "Yes, I want you."

Cradling her face with his palms, he gazed down at her. "Once we go upstairs to my bedroom, there won't be any turning back, darlin'. We'll cross a line and things will never be the same between us again."

"I know."

"And I don't want there to be any regrets," he added.

She closed her eyes a moment, then opening them, stared up at him. "The only possibility of my regretting anything is if we don't make love," she said softly.

The strength in her tone and the truth in her expressive eyes were all the answer he needed. Stepping away from her, he walked over to switch off the gas log in the fireplace, then turn the lights off on the Christmas tree.

Neither spoke when he returned to take her hand in his and lead her down the hall to climb the stairs.

Words were unnecessary. They both knew the risk they were taking and that they could never go back to the way things had been between them.

Walking into the master suite, he closed the door behind them. He switched on the lamp in the sitting room and turned to take her into his arms. He had every intention of going slow, of savoring every second of his first night making love to her. That there would be many more nights wasn't in question. He wasn't sure how he knew that. He just did. And he never doubted his instincts.

He kissed her slowly, thoroughly, then, raising his head to capture her gaze with his, he slowly tugged her teal blouse from the waistband of her black slacks. "You don't know how many times in the past couple of weeks I've thought about doing this," he said, as he reached up to release the small pearl button at the top of the garment.

"Probably as many times as I've thought about this," she said, unbuttoning the top of his shirt. Her fingertips brushed the skin along his collarbone and sent fire streaking through his veins.

By the time they released the last buttons on her blouse and his shirt, Brad felt as if he had run a race. As he slid his hands beneath each side of the silk fabric and along her ribs, Abby pressed her palms against his chest. He could have sworn that he had been branded.

"I've also wanted to do this since seeing you without your shirt the other night," she said, tracing the ridges of his abdomen and testing the strength of his pectoral muscles.

Feeling as if the air had been sucked from the room,

he struggled to draw in some much-needed oxygen. "Why don't we get this out of the way?" he asked, sliding the teal silk over her slender shoulders and down her arms.

When he tossed her blouse to the side, he closed his eyes and enjoyed the feel of her hands skimming across his shoulders as she pushed his shirt off as well. "I never realized how beautiful your body is," she said, tracing her finger down the thin line of hair below his navel.

He sucked in a sharp breath and forced himself to stand still as her finger followed it to the waistband of his dress trousers. "I wouldn't say my body…is all that great." He concentrated on what she had said in an effort to slow down the flood of desire pumping through his veins. Running his finger along the lace edge of her bra, he released the front clasp on the scrap of lace and silk with a flick of his fingers. "I'm all hard angles and ridges," he said, sliding it from her body to toss it on top of her blouse and his shirt lying on the carpet beside them. "You're the one with the perfect body," he said, cupping her with his hands. "You're soft, curvy and…" He lowered his head to kiss the puckered tip of each full breast. "…so sweet."

Rewarded by her soft moan, he wrapped his arms around her to pull her to him. He groaned at the contact of his hair-roughened flesh meeting her softer, feminine skin. "You feel good, darlin'."

"So…do you." Her sigh of contentment feathering over his bare chest sent a shaft of heat straight to his groin.

Wanting to feel all of her against him, he took a

step back, then after kneeling to remove their shoes, he straightened and reached for the button and zipper at her waist. "Look at me, Abby," he commanded, as he slid his fingers beneath the waistband of her slacks and panties. When the black linen and silk fell to the floor, she stepped out of them, then used her foot to push them toward the growing pile of their clothes.

"You're breathtaking, Abby," he said, forcing himself to breathe as he drank in the sight of her. Beautiful in every way, her confidence and pride sent his pulse racing, and the only word he could think to describe the moment was *perfection.*

"Don't you think you're a little overdressed for the occasion?" she asked, her velvet voice sending a shaft of heat right through him.

"That can be remedied right now," he said, making short work of removing his tailored slacks and boxer briefs.

Tossing them on the pile at their feet, he didn't immediately step forward and pull her to him. He was determined not to rush. He was going to make the night the most magical experience of both their lives or die trying. But it was damned difficult, considering the most exciting woman he had ever known stood before him, caressing every inch of his body with her eyes. She wanted him as badly as he wanted her, and the knowledge that she would soon be his robbed him of breath.

Without a word, he held out his arms, and to his immense satisfaction she stepped forward to melt against him. Their bodies touching from shoulders to knees fanned the flames building in his lower body and made his knees feel as if they were about to buckle.

He leaned back, and their gazes met. Without a word, he swung her up into his arms and carried her into the bedroom. He paused at the side of the bed long enough for Abby to pull the comforter and sheet back, then gently lowered her to the mattress.

Giving him a smile that lit the darkest corners of his soul, Abby raised her arms in invitation. "Make love to me, Brad."

His heart hammered inside his chest as he stretched out beside her and took her back into his arms. "I want to take this slow," he said, clenching his teeth against the wave of need coursing through him. "But I'm not sure that's going to be possible, darlin'."

She shook her head. "I don't think so, either. It's been so long."

He kissed the fluttering pulse at the base of her throat at the same time he ran his hand from her back, along her side and up to cover her full breast. "There's been no one since—"

"No," she whispered, cutting him off his question as if not wanting to mention her late husband's name.

Brad could respect that. He didn't particularly want her reminded of the man. Richard Langley would always be a part of her past. There was no getting around that. But he wanted her to think of Brad Price as her future.

The thought should have scared the hell out of him. It didn't. Deciding there would be plenty of time later to figure out why it didn't, he lowered his head and fused their lips.

He reacquainted himself with her sweetness at the same time he moved his hand back down her side to the curve of her hip, then down her leg. Her flawless skin beneath his palm felt like satin and he didn't think he could ever get enough of touching her. When she restlessly moved her legs, he knew the sensations within her were building. Easing his hand down to her inner thigh, he stopped just short of his goal.

"Do you want me to bring you pleasure, Abby?"

"Y-yes."

Nibbling tiny kisses along her collarbone, he parted her to tease and stroke, to make sure she was ready for him. Her tiny moan of need, the fact that she wanted him as badly as he wanted her, sent fire streaking through his veins. But when she moved her hand from his chest down his abdomen to do a little exploring of her own, Brad felt as if his head might fly right off his shoulders.

"Darlin', I love the way your hands feel on my body," he said, capturing her hand with his. "But if you keep that up, you're going to be disappointed and I'm going to be mighty embarrassed."

"I want you, Brad."

"Now?"

"Y-yes!"

The level of desire he detected in her voice was all the encouragement he needed, and parting her legs with his knee, he eased himself over her. His heart stalled when she reached down to guide him to her, and he had to struggle to hold onto what little control he had left.

Slowly, carefully, he pushed his hips forward, and he felt her body accept him with an eagerness that threatened to rob him of every good intention he had of taking things slow. He clenched his teeth and fought the need to thrust into her. It had been over a year since Abby had made love, and she needed time to adjust.

As he watched for any trace of discomfort, she closed her eyes and a slight smile curved her lips. "You feel wonderful," she said, wrapping her arms around his shoulders.

Gathering her close, he sank himself deep inside of her and, holding himself perfectly still, covered her mouth with his. He wanted to draw out the pleasure, to make it last as long as possible. But his need for her was greater than anything he could have imagined, and apparently she felt the same way about him. When she wrapped her legs around him and arched her back, he sank even deeper and there was no way he could stop himself from rocking against her.

The combination of his need for her and her ready acceptance of his body joining with hers was mind-blowing and quickly had the pleasure spiraling out of control. He felt her tighten around him and knew she was close to reaching the pinnacle they both sought.

Several moments later, he heard her soft gasp as the building pressure overtook her. Tiny feminine muscles caressed him and quickly had him joining her as together they got caught up in the spiraling sensations of their release.

As they slowly drifted back to reality, Brad held Abby close. What they had just shared was more powerful, more meaningful, than he could have ever imagined.

"Are you all right?" he asked, raising his head from her shoulder.

Nodding, she smiled. "That was amazing."

"You're amazing," he said, kissing the tip of her nose. He eased to her side and pulled her to him. "Spend the night with me."

"I'm not sure that's—"

He placed his finger to her lips. He knew it had to be difficult for her to cast aside years of caring what others thought of her, but it was time she realized people were going to talk no matter what choices she made.

"I don't give a damn what anyone thinks and you shouldn't either, Abby. We're adults." He gave her a smile to soften his words. "We don't need permission or approval to spend time together."

"I know you're right," she said slowly.

He gave her a wicked grin as he moved his hips to press himself against her. "Now, let's concentrate more on what I'm thinking and less about what anyone else thinks."

Eight

As Abby put the finishing touches on her makeup, she looked at the woman in the mirror staring back at her. Less than twenty-four hours ago, she had stood in front of the same mirror, getting ready to go to Brad's for a nice dinner, some stimulating conversation and, as she had come to expect from him, a couple of steamy kisses. Nothing more. But instead of leaving at the end of the evening as she had planned on doing, all he had to do was kiss her and she had ended up spending the entire night with him.

She sighed as she walked into her bedroom to take off her robe and pick up the long, black evening gown she had laid out on the bed before her shower. After they had made love for the second time, he had teased and cajoled her into doing as he asked, and that was what she couldn't understand. No one had ever been able to talk her into doing something she didn't want to do. Yet Brad seemed to be able to talk her into doing whatever he wanted.

Closing her eyes for a moment, Abby took a deep breath and shook her head. She had to stop lying to herself. No matter how unwise, no matter how complicated it made things for her, the truth was she hadn't wanted to leave. She had wanted every one of his kisses, wanted to experience the degree of passion that he created within her and wanted him to make love to her.

When she stepped into the dress, the clingy fabric sliding over her skin reminded her of the way Brad's hands had felt as he explored and teased to heighten the exquisite pleasure that had all but consumed her. A shiver of longing streaked up her spine—just the thought of their lovemaking left her breathless.

As she stepped into her black high heels and walked over to get her earrings from the jewelry box, she wished she could tell herself that what she had shared with Brad was nothing more than two lonely people coming together for the physical intimacy missing in their lives. But in all honesty, she couldn't.

Glancing at the rings Richard had given her on their wedding day, which were tucked into one corner of the jewelry chest, Abby knew that her lovemaking with Brad had been far more than just the need to once again be desired by a man. And that confused her more than anything else.

She had loved her late husband for as long as she could remember. They had been together since her freshman year in high school, but in all those years, both before and after they were married, the passion and desire in their relationship had never been as intense as what she had shared with Brad. What she had with Richard had been more sedate, more… comfortable.

Abby frowned. "What an odd way to describe a marriage," she said aloud. Surely she and Richard had more going for them than…

The sound of the doorbell interrupted her disturbing thoughts and, quickly fastening her earrings, she picked up her sequined clutch and left the bedroom. She fully intended to give the state of her marriage more thought, but it would have to wait until later when she was alone and not getting ready to go out for the evening.

On her way down the hall to answer the door, she couldn't help but notice that her pulse sped up and her step was a bit quicker than usual from the anticipation of seeing Brad again. That gave her a bit of an uneasy feeling, but she didn't have time to dwell on it as she opened the front door.

The look in Brad's eyes when he saw her caused her heart to skip a beat. Without a word he stepped forward to wrap her in his arms. He gave her a kiss that left her breathless, then stepped back to look at her again.

"You're absolutely breathtaking, Abby."

"I could say the same about you," she said honestly. Dressed in a black tuxedo, white pleated shirt and black bow tie, he could have easily been a cover model for *GQ*.

Opening a small florist's box that she hadn't noticed before, he removed a beautiful white orchid. "Let's get this pinned into place before we leave."

His fingers brushed her breast as he positioned the

delicate corsage, sending excitement skipping over every nerve in her body. "Thank you, Brad. It's beautiful."

He shook his head as he worked the pin through the fabric of her evening gown. "It pales in comparison to you, darlin'." He smiled. "Are you ready for the biggest night of the year in Royal, Texas?"

"As ready as I'll ever be," she said, nodding as he helped her with her shawl. As he guided her down the porch steps and out to the waiting limo, she asked, "Who's watching Sunnie for the evening?"

"Juanita got back from Dallas after you left this morning and agreed to watch the baby and the twins for the evening." Helping her into the back seat, he chuckled. "This time last year, I never dreamed that I'd be arranging for a babysitter and leaving phone numbers where I could be reached in case of an emergency."

"Having a baby in the house changes everything," Abby said, wishing she had a baby to give her life meaning.

As the chauffeur drove them to the Christmas Ball, neither mentioned that in just a few short hours one of them would become the new president of the Texas Cattleman's Club, while the other would go home the loser.

"Do you know how much I missed you after you left this morning?" he asked, his voice taking on a low, intimate tone.

"I...uh, no," she said, feeling as if the temperature in the car rose several degrees.

"All I could think about was how good you felt last

night and how much I wanted you again," he said, his hazel eyes darkening with desire.

Thankful the window between the driver and the backseat was closed, Abby smiled. "Last night was wonderful."

The smoldering look he gave her curled her toes. "I give you my word, darlin', tonight's going to be even better."

Just the thought of spending another night in Brad's arms caused her already fluttering pulse to race. "But Sunnie—"

"—will be sound asleep," he said, as the driver steered the car up the drive to the TCC clubhouse.

Before she could respond, the chauffeur opened the back door of the limo and Brad got out of the car, then turned to help her to her feet. "We'll have to talk about that later," she warned, as they passed the uniformed doorman.

"I'll look forward to it," Brad said, his tone suggestive.

Two or three times a year the normally relaxed atmosphere of the clubhouse was transformed into formal social events, with the Christmas Ball being the biggest and most elaborate. Already decorated for Christmas, a canopy of white twinkle lights had been added to give the entrance to the establishment a magical feel.

Abby marveled at the staff's obvious hard work. "This is stunning," she said, looking around at the multitude of potted poinsettias and hanging pine boughs. "I've never seen it look quite like this."

"I know you said you didn't attend last year, but

haven't you been here for the Ball before?" Brad asked, as they walked toward the ballroom.

Abby, nodded. "It's been years, and I really don't remember the old building looking quite this charming."

"That's why it will be a shame if the vote goes in favor of the new building," he said, shaking his head. "I'm all for progress, but there has to be a way to preserve this tradition and still move forward."

It hadn't been a secret that Brad had been among the ranks of members in favor of keeping the old clubhouse instead of building a new one. "Has Sadie talked to you about what she would like to do with the clubhouse if the members vote for a new building?" Abby asked.

He looked puzzled. "No. Does she have something in mind?"

Looking up, Abby noticed Sadie and Rick Pruitt walking toward them. "Why don't you ask her yourself? I'm sure she could explain her ideas much better than I could.

"Sadie, you look gorgeous." Abby hugged her friend. "I love your dress."

Brad's sister smiled. "And I love yours. Rick and I were just commenting on what a nice couple the two of you make when you got out of the limo."

Before Abby could correct Sadie and tell her that they were just attending the ball together, Brad asked, "So I hear you have plans for the old clubhouse?"

Sadie glanced at Abby, who nodded. "I was telling him that you might be interested in the building."

While Sadie outlined her ideas for turning the clubhouse into a family cultural center, Zeke and Sheila Travers joined them. "Are you ready to become the

first female president of the Texas Cattleman's Club?"
Sheila whispered.

Abby smiled. "I haven't been elected yet, but yes,
I think I'm up for the challenge." Concerned that the
last time she had seen Sheila, the woman hadn't been
feeling well, Abby asked, "You must be over the flu.
You're positively glowing tonight."

Zeke's grin could have lit a small town. "There's a
reason for that." Leaning down to kiss his wife's cheek,
he asked, "Would you like to tell them or should I?"

"You go ahead," Sheila said, gazing lovingly at her
husband.

"It turns out that Sheila hasn't had the flu for the
past couple of weeks after all." Zeke put his arm around
his wife's shoulders and hugged her to his side. "We
just found out we're pregnant."

"I'm so happy for you," Abby said, hugging the
beautiful mocha-skinned woman.

Sheila was one of the kindest, sweetest women Abby
had ever known, and she knew how much Sheila had
wanted a child. It was something they had both had
in common. Now it looked as if Sheila's hopes had
come true, and Abby was truly happy for her. She only
wished that by some miracle, hers would, too.

"Are you okay?" Brad whispered close to her ear, as
he put his arm around her.

"O-of course," she said, touched by his consideration. He knew how much she wanted a baby, and he
must have sensed how heart-wrenching it was to see
others realize their dreams, all the while knowing that
she never would.

"Honey, I think Summer Franklin is trying to get

your attention," Rick said, motioning toward a gathering of other members and their wives standing across the way. Zeke's business partner, Darius Franklin, stood at its center.

"I'll be right back," Sadie said, hurrying over to see what the coordinator of the Helping Hands Women's Shelter needed.

While they waited for Sadie to return to the group, Mitch Taylor and his wife, Jennifer, walked over to say hello. "Are you two ready for the big announcement?" Mitch asked. He was the interim president of the TCC, and Abby thought he looked extremely happy to be stepping down and letting someone else take over the job.

"I've been looking forward to this for months," Brad said happily.

"Abby, how many more days will the flamingos be showing up in people's yards?" Jennifer asked, laughing. "I thought our neighbor, Mr. Hargraves, was going to suffer a stroke the other morning when he got up to find them on his lawn."

The man in question was legendary for his thrifty ways, and it must have come as quite a shock to think that he was actually going to have to part with some of his money to get rid of the plastic birds. "I think New Year's Eve is scheduled to be the end of this year's campaign," Abby said, laughing with the woman. "Apparently, Mr. Hargraves made a donation to get rid of them, because I saw them on someone else's lawn this morning."

Abby noticed Brad and Mitch exchange a look. "Is something going on?" she asked.

Brad shook his head, as Mitch and Jennifer walked away to mingle with some of the other attendees. "We've been working on a little project together, and we intend to make an announcement about it sometime during the evening."

She had a good idea she knew what they were going to tell everyone. During the campaign he had taken great pains to let it be known that he was thinking about buying a semipro football team and moving it to Royal. Some had thought it was a ploy to gain more votes for the presidency, since he had waited to tell everyone after the campaigning was in full swing. Apparently that hadn't been the case, although she suspected that it hadn't hurt his run for office.

"You bought the football team?" she guessed.

Placing his index finger to her lips, he nodded. "Zeke, Chris and I are co-owners, and Mitch has agreed to be the general manager," he said close to her ear. "But we want to wait to tell everyone until after the new officers are announced."

"That's wonderful. The town has needed something like this for a long time," she said, meaning it.

For the majority of the townspeople, Houston and Dallas were too far away to attend a professional football game more than once or twice during the season. Having a semiprofessional team in town would allow them to enjoy going to games more often.

"Well, the list of lucky recipients for the last week of the flamingo campaign has been finalized," Sadie said, walking back to join the group.

"I hope my name's not on there," Brad said, a mock-disgusted expression crossing his handsome face. "It's a worthy cause and I support it one hundred percent. But I swear that I'll donate twice if you'll just pass by my place."

Smiling, Abby patted his lean cheek. "Please feel free to donate as much as you wish, but we're making no promises that you won't find the flamingos on your lawn some morning."

Everyone laughed as the group moved into the ballroom, where tables with elegant settings surrounded the hardwood dance floor. A long table had been set up at the front of the room for the current board of officers, and a popular band from Austin had just finished setting up on the bandstand.

When they found their place cards at a table close to the dance floor, Abby was delighted to see that along with the Traverses, she and Brad were seated at the same table with Chris and Macy Richards and Daniel and Elizabeth Warren. All were good friends, and she looked forward to hearing how they planned to spend the holidays.

An hour later, after enjoying a scrumptious prime rib dinner, Abby and the other women excused themselves to go to the powder room to freshen their makeup. When they returned, the band had just started to play a very popular tune, and several couples were making their way to the dance floor.

Draping her shawl over the back of her chair, Abby sat down beside Brad to enjoy watching couples two-step around the dance floor. Dancing in Texas was almost mandatory for every social event, and the fact that there would be dancing before and after the election announcements came as no surprise to Abby.

When the song ended and the band started playing a slow love song, Brad stood and took her hand. "I like the slow ones," he said, leaning close so she could hear him above the band. "I get to hold you."

"Are you sure that's a good idea?" she asked, even as she rose to follow him.

Thus far she hadn't noticed them drawing any undue attention from the ball attendees. But that didn't mean people weren't taking note of the fact that they were together or that they appeared to be a lot more friendly with each other than they had ever been in the past.

"I think it's an excellent idea," he said, pulling her close. "I've been wanting to do this all evening."

She automatically raised her arms to his shoulders as they began to sway in time with the music. "I didn't realize you liked dancing so much."

"I wasn't talking about dancing, darlin'." He gave her a grin that left no doubt what he meant. "I've wanted to hold your body against mine ever since you opened your door when I came to pick you up."

The feel of his hands on her bare skin made her wonder if the backless gown had been the best choice. It reminded her of the night before and having his hands touch her in places she would love for him to be touching her now.

"I can't wait to get you back to my place," he said huskily. "As much as I like seeing you in this slinky black dress, I can't wait to take it off of you."

His impassioned words sent a tingle of excitement straight up her spine. "I don't remember saying I would go home with you."

"But you will," he said. It wasn't a question, and she

was certain Brad believed that she would go along with what he wanted.

Truth to tell, that was exactly what she wanted, too, and that frightened her. Falling asleep in his arms after the most incredible lovemaking she had ever experienced, then waking up with him, had been wonderful. It made her want to do it again and again. For the rest of her life.

Abby bit her lip and forced herself to breathe. What had she done? How could she have let it happen?

She had fought against it, tried to hide from it and denied it was happening. But there was no sense in lying to herself any longer. She had done the unthinkable. She had fallen in love with Brad Price, and it scared her to death. How ironic that she could hold her own in a corporate boardroom, but love terrified her.

What if, like her husband and the baby she was supposed to adopt, Brad was lost to her? It seemed in the past those she loved were taken away from her.

Panic like nothing she had ever known coursed through her. She needed time to think, time to analyze what had happened and why her feelings for Brad were so much more intense than what she had felt for Richard.

As the song ended and Brad led Abby off the dance floor, he noticed that she looked a little shaken. "Are you feeling all right?" he asked.

She stared at him a moment before she finally nodded. "Y-yes. I'm…um, fine."

The sheer panic he saw in the depths of her vibrant

blue eyes had him shaking his head. "I'm not buying it. What's wrong?"

She tried smiling, but it just made her look more unnerved. "I'm just a little…tired," she said, her eyes darting around as if looking for an escape. "That's all."

He had seen her when she was dead on her feet and the expression she wore now wasn't one of fatigue. She looked…desperate?

Frowning, he held her chair as she sat back down at their table, then took his seat beside her. He had no idea what happened to suddenly make her look as if she were trapped, but he was sure as hell going to get to the bottom of whatever was wrong. If she had witnessed anyone at the ball pointing or staring longer than was polite, or if she'd heard a whisper of gossip about them, he personally intended to make whoever it was rue the day they were born.

Unfortunately, Mitch Taylor chose that exact moment to step up to the microphone to address the crowd, preventing Brad from questioning her about who or what had upset her.

"Good evening," Mitch said cheerfully. "I think it's time to announce who will be leading the Texas Cattleman's Club for the next couple of years." He waited for the applause to die down. "Let me start off by saying the vote was a sixty-forty split. That's a lot closer than we've had in several years."

Brad tuned out the rest of what the man was saying as he concentrated on the woman beside him. Abby had to be the most beautiful, alluring woman he had ever known. With her long, dark auburn hair swept up into some kind of twisted knot at the back of her head and the diamond earrings dangling down from her delicate ears, she looked regal, sophisticated and so damned sexy, he had been fighting with himself the entire evening to keep everyone at the ball from learning just how much she made him want her.

Unable to stop himself, Brad reached over to touch the shoulder of her long, black evening dress. Soft and slinky, it hugged her upper body like a second skin, then flared out at her hips to sway with every move she made. That had been enough to drive him half out of his mind. But when he had taken her into his arms to dance, the feel of her bare back beneath his palms had all but sent him over the edge. It brought back the erotic memory of having her in his bed, of touching her satiny skin and feeling her warm from the sizzling heat that he built inside of her.

"...Bradford Price," he heard Mitch say a moment before the room broke out into applause.

Concentrating solely on Abby, it took a moment for Brad to realize that he had won the presidency of the Texas Cattleman's Club. When the news began to sink in, he couldn't help but feel that it was a hollow victory. He had won, but that meant Abby had lost.

"Congratulations," she said, sticking out her hand to shake his.

He ignored the gesture and pulled her into his arms to hold her close. "I'm sorry, darlin'. I know how much you wanted to be the first female president of the TCC."

"Believe me, I'm going to be just fine." Leaning back, she shook her head. "You won fair and square. Now I think you had better get up there and thank everyone for their vote."

He knew she was right. It was expected of the winner to give a victory speech. But at the moment, the last thing he wanted to do was stand up in front of the crowd to thank them for entrusting the club's future to him. He would much rather stay at her side and find out what was bothering her.

As he rose to his feet, he gave her what he hoped was an encouraging smile. "As soon as it's socially acceptable, we're leaving."

"We'll see," she said, as he started toward the podium.

When Mitch presented him with the carved gavel that had called the club to order for over a hundred years, Brad couldn't help but feel humbled as well was honored. "Thank you all for being here tonight and for trusting me to uphold the Leadership, Justice and Peace that this prestigious organization stands for."

As he stared out at the crowd, he realized it was time for the healing to begin—to bridge the gap between the old guard and the new generation of the TCC. "As my first order of business, I'm going to break protocol for a few moments and ask that we take a vote on a handful of issues that I believe will ensure a successful future for the Texas Cattleman's Club and that our esteemed founder would support without hesitation."

He could tell the crowd was intrigued and felt confident in proceeding. "I would like to propose that instead of a new building, we ask Daniel Warren to design an addition that will encompass this clubhouse, merging tradition with modernization. By doing it this way, the existing structure Tex Langley built all those years ago will truly become the heart of our organization."

There was a moment of silence as everyone digested what he was proposing, then to his immense satisfaction the entire room rose to their feet to applaud. Someone shouted that they seconded the motion, enabling the members to vote.

"Will members of the club, please vote by a show of hands?" Brad instructed. "All in favor." There wasn't a single member who didn't have his hand high in the air. Even though Brad knew there were no objections, he had to ask as a rule of order to make the vote official. "Opposed?" When no one responded, he brought the gavel down for the first time as TCC president. "The motion carries by unanimous vote."

"What about the plans for the new building?" someone in the back called out.

"What do you propose we do with them?" another chimed in.

"That's my next order of business," Brad said, smiling. "It has recently been brought to my attention that my sister, Sadie, has plans underway to start a new family center—one that will not only bring cultural exhibits and activities to Royal for families to enjoy together, but also provide assistance and aid for families in crisis. Her plan is for the foundation to work in conjunction with the Helping Hands Women's Shelter over in Somerset. I would like to propose that the design for the new building be donated to the Pruitt Foundation for the purpose of constructing the Tex Langley Cultural Family Center. And to alleviate the problem of where it will be built, I'm donating land that I own at the edge of town, as well as pledging a million dollars toward the construction of the Center."

Before he could even bring it to an official vote, TCC members began calling out pledges for the project. He then went through the procedure to make things official, and by the time he glanced over at the table where Sadie was seated, tears of happiness were streaming down his sister's cheeks.

"Now for my last order of business before I make an official announcement and we get back to celebrating the season, I want to acknowledge the many contributions made over the past year by the women of Royal," he said, knowing he was quite possibly wading into the proverbial swamp filled with alligators. "Without their help and support we wouldn't have found Daniel Warren, the architect whose brilliant designs are going to carry our organization as well as the good town of Royal into the future. I would also like to personally add my heartfelt gratitude to the women—especially Sheila Travers—for the support and caring shown my niece when she was abandoned on the club's doorstep."

To the men's credit, they all rose to their feet to give the women a standing ovation.

"I think we all have to agree that these women have met the standards set forth by our founder, Tex Langley," Brad stated firmly.

He noticed that many of the old guard—the ones most staunchly opposed to admitting female members to the club—were glancing nervously at their wives. Brad almost laughed out loud. Apparently the rumors he had heard of the women withholding certain marital privileges as a way of protesting their husbands' stalwart stand on the issue were true.

"I would therefore like to propose that after the first of the year, we take a vote to admit women with all rights and privileges into the Texas Cattleman's Club," he finished.

The thunderous applause that followed was almost deafening, and by the time they died down, Brad wondered how long it would take for his ears to stop ringing.

Looking over at the table where he and Abby had been seated, he frowned when he noticed her chair was empty. Where was she?

Announcing his news about semipro football coming to Royal and the plans to use the stadium he, Chris and Zeke were having built for entertainment events as well as games, Brad ended by wishing everyone happy holidays. When he stepped away from the podium, it seemed as if it took forever to make his way through the crowd of well-wishers over to the table where Sadie and Rick had been seated.

"Where's Abby?" he demanded, as soon as he reached them.

Sadie looked worried as she handed him a folded piece of paper. "She had one of the waiters bring this for me to give to you." His sister caught her trembling lower lip between her teeth for a moment before adding, "I think Abby's gone, Brad."

He hadn't looked at the piece of paper and a nagging suspicion deep in his gut told him that he wasn't going to like the message inside. The last time he had received a note someone had been trying to blackmail him, and he had come to think of missives like the one in his hand as bearing nothing but bad news. He stuffed the paper into his pocket without so much as glancing at it.

The word Brad uttered was graphic and one he normally reserved for the guys in the locker room. "I have a feeling I know where she's headed."

His sister's hand on his arm stopped him in his tracks. "Don't follow her if you don't mean it, Brad. Right now she's running from herself more than she is running from you."

"I have to talk to her," he said, feeling desperation begin to claw at his insides. "This could take some time. Will you—"

"Rick and I will go back to your house and relieve Juanita from watching the kids," Sadie said, gathering her evening bag and satin capelet. "We'll stay with Sunnie until you get back."

Rick nodded as he reached into the front pocket of his tuxedo. "Take my Navigator," he said, handing a set of keys to Brad. "She probably had the limo driver take her home. We'll catch a ride with Zeke and Sheila. Good luck, man."

"Thanks, Rick. I owe you one," Brad called over his shoulder, already starting toward the ballroom's emergency exit. The side door was closer to the parking lot, and the way he saw it every second counted.

Quickly finding his brother-in-law's luxury SUV, Brad jumped in behind the steering wheel and, gunning the engine, shot from the parking space. When he reached the street, the tires squealed and left a good amount of rubber on the asphalt as he pressed down on the gas pedal. He had to stop Abby and find out why she was leaving Royal, leaving him.

When he reached the city limits, Brad pushed the accelerator all the way to the floor as he sped down the highway toward her ranch outside of town. He remembered her mentioning the offer from her former associates, but she had told him she wasn't going to accept due to her run for the TCC presidency. Could winning the office have meant more to her than she let on?

He didn't think that was the case. With the announcement that he was the winner, she had almost seemed relieved. Could the loss have made it convenient for her to run from him and what had developed between them?

A sinking feeling began to spread through his chest as he turned the vehicle onto the drive leading up to the Langley ranch. The house was completely dark, and Abby's SUV was gone from where she usually kept it parked. Knowing in his heart it was futile, Brad got out of the truck and walked up onto the porch to try the door anyway. It was locked up tight. Even her housekeeper had left for the evening

Feeling a mixture of anger and pain begin to settle in his chest, he walked back to Rick's SUV and climbed in. She must have left as soon as he got up to give his speech. That meant she had a good half hour's head start on him and most likely had taken the Langley jet back to Seattle. There was no way he could catch her tonight. But if she thought that leaving was the end of things between them, she had another think coming.

For as long as he could remember there had been a tension between them that, up until recently, he hadn't been able to figure out. But in the past several weeks, the feelings had reached a fevered pitch, and now he recognized them for what they were. He had fallen in love with Abby. Hell, he had probably loved her all of his life and had just been too stubborn to realize it.

So what was he going to do about it? What could he do about it with her running away to hide out in Seattle?

Reaching into the inside pocket of his tuxedo jacket, he pulled out his cell phone and called his house. When his sister answered, he didn't mince words.

"Sadie, ask Rick to start calling airlines to get me on the first available nonstop flight to Seattle tomorrow morning while you start packing Sunnie's clothes and whatever else you think I'll need for her."

"How long do you think you'll be gone?" she asked.

"I don't know," he admitted, shaking his head. "But I can tell you this much. We won't be coming back until we bring Abby with us."

Nine

Standing at the floor-to-ceiling window, Abby pulled her bulky sweater close around her as she watched a bald eagle swoop down to scoop up a fish from the waters of Lake Washington. Her jet had landed sometime around dawn and although she had gone to bed as soon as the taxi had dropped her off at her home, sleep had eluded her. She had a feeling that was going to be the case for some time to come.

When she finally gave up trying, she had spent the rest of the day laundering the clothes she had stored at the house and removing the sheets draped over the furniture to keep them from being coated with dust. Once the agency opened, she arranged for a rental car to use until she could have her SUV transported from the Dallas airport. She had managed to keep herself busy enough not to think for the majority of the day, but now that evening was rapidly approaching, Abby found herself with too much time on her hands and nothing to do but think.

Sighing heavily, she turned to walk back into the kitchen for another cup of coffee. She had always loved her house on the water, loved the view that reminded her of the lake just outside of Royal. But now it reminded her only of Brad, of the first time he had kissed her. They had been only six years old at the time, but there had been something in that innocent kiss—some kind of magic—that she feared may very well have branded her for life.

For years, she had attributed the uneasiness, the feeling of being on edge, whenever she was anywhere near Brad to the game of one-upsmanship they had played throughout their lives. He kept her sharp, kept her waiting for a move so that she could make a countermove. Now she knew that all of that had been a veneer, a concealment of the attraction and sexual tension that lay just beneath the surface of their rivalry.

What had taken her so long to figure it out? Why hadn't she been able to see it before now?

Curling up on the couch with her cup of coffee, she closed her eyes as she tried to sort through her tangled emotions. She had loved Richard, and if he hadn't passed away, she had no doubt they would have spent the rest of their lives together. He had been her best friend and confidant, her safe haven. The comfortable companionship they shared more than made up for the lack of passion in their marriage. Abby now recognized that she had married him because he was safe and reliable—a man who she was certain wouldn't have a roving eye and leave her for someone else the way her father had left her mother.

But her relationship with Brad was at the opposite end of the spectrum. They had never been friends in the traditional sense and she doubted they ever would be, doubted it was even possible. He challenged her to go further and achieve more, and there was way too much explosive chemistry between them for their relationship to ever be sedate. The degree of passion and smoldering desire that she had experienced with Brad was unlike anything she had ever known. And God help her, she loved it that way, loved that he made her feel vital and alive. Simply put, she loved him.

But loving him scared her as little else could. What if she lost him the way she'd lost everyone else she cared about?

Looking back, she could see now that it had started with the loss of her father when he abandoned his family. She had been a daddy's girl and was devastated by his betrayal and total lack of contact with her. Then, Richard had been taken from her barely six months after their wedding. She had even lost the baby she had hoped to adopt when the birth mother changed her mind at the last minute.

Shaking her head, she put her cup down. She got up from the couch, went over to open the sliding door and walked out onto the deck. The moon had just begun to rise over the Cascade Mountains in the distance. Its reflection on the dark waters of the lake normally fascinated her, but tonight she barely noticed it.

No matter how much she loved Brad and his adorable baby niece, she couldn't subject herself to that kind of pain again. What would she do when he decided to move on to the next woman he found intriguing? Then where would she be? Or God forbid, what if something happened to one of them?

As difficult as it had been to leave Royal again, she knew in her heart that she had made the right decision. She was much better off in Seattle where she couldn't see them almost daily and wouldn't be reminded of what she could never have. In time, she might even be able to reduce the amount of time she spent wondering about them to once or twice a day.

As she tried to convince herself that was even possible, she heard someone walking along the side deck. Sighing, she waited for them to make their way around to the back. She should have known the solitude she so desperately wanted wouldn't last for very long. Mrs. Norris down the way had been out walking her poodle, Max, when Abby walked back from the market earlier in the evening, and she wasn't at all surprised that the elderly woman had decided to stop by to welcome her back to the neighborhood.

"Mrs. Norris, I'm sorry but I just got back into town and this really isn't a good time," she called out. Hopefully, the woman would take the hint that Abby didn't want to be bothered and give her at least one day to regain what little composure she had left. "Could you please come back in the morning? We'll have coffee and catch up."

"I'm not Mrs. Norris, and no, I'm not going to wait until tomorrow morning," she heard Brad say, as he came around the corner of the house. "You and I are going to have a long talk. Now."

When she turned to face him, Abby's breath caught on a sob. Standing just a few feet away with a baby carrier in one hand, a large duffel bag in the other and a diaper bag slung over his shoulder he had never looked more appealing or more angry.

"W-what are you…" Her voice trembled, and she paused to try to get it back under control. "…doing here, Brad?" She didn't question how he'd found her. He had obviously gotten her address from Sadie.

"Sunnie and I decided to find out why the hell you took off like a thief in the night," he said, setting the duffel bag at his feet. "That was rude of you, darlin'."

A stiff breeze whipped her hair around and she brushed it out of her eyes to point to the house. "Let's go inside. Sunnie doesn't need to be out in this night air." She started to take the baby carrier from him, but his body language held her back.

Walking to the sliding door, her hand shook as she opened it. She stood aside for him to pick up his bag and carry it and the baby inside. When she followed him into her living room, she found the spacious area seemed to have shrunk in size, and she suspected that Brad's presence was the reason.

She had always heard the phrase *larger than life,* but she had never fully understood it until that moment. At the best of times, Brad Price could be imposing. Angry, he was downright intimidating.

As she stood there, wondering what she could say that would get him to leave and let her get back to trying to rebuild her life—a life without him and Sunnie—Brad set the duffel and the diaper bag on the

floor with a thump. The sound seemed to echo throughout the room and emphasized the strained silence.

"Imagine my surprise last night when I stepped
down from the podium to discover that my date for
the evening had ditched me." He set the baby carrier
on the couch, pulled the blanket back and unbuckled
the straps holding the baby safely in the seat. "The least
you could have done was stick around long enough to
say goodbye," he said, lifting Sunnie to his shoulder.
Turning to face her, his hazel gaze seemed to bore all
the way to her soul. "You owed me that much, Abby."

"I-I'm sorry," she said, unable to think of anything
else to say.

The man she loved more than she could have ever
believed possible was standing there holding the baby
she adored and it was breaking her heart. Whatever she
finally settled on saying to him would send them back
to Texas and out of her life for good.

He shook his head. "*Sorry* doesn't cut it with me. I
didn't travel two thousand miles with a baby in tow to
leave here without some damned good answers. You
owe me an explanation for what happened last night
and what sent you running back here."

Sunnie began to whimper and squirm, saving Abby
from having to think of something to say that would
appease him. She knew it was only prolonging the inevitable, but maybe it would give her a little time to
think of what she could say that would convince him
that her leaving Royal was for the best.

"Let me take her," Abby said, reaching for the baby.
"I'll change her diaper while you get a bottle ready."

He stared at her a moment before he nodded and

reached for the diaper bag. "We'll wait until we have her down for the night before we resume this conversation. But rest assured, darlin'. We will be having a heart-to-heart talk."

Ten minutes later, Abby sat on the couch, giving Sunnie a bottle while Brad sat in the armchair across from her. Neither had a lot to say, and the tension was almost more than she could bear.

"I'm sure everyone was excited to hear about the football team," she said, unable to stand the silence a moment longer.

"It generated a fair amount of excitement," he said, nodding.

When he didn't say more, she tried again. "What did the membership decide about the clubhouse?"

"They voted to donate Daniel Warren's plans to Sadie's foundation for the purpose of building her cultural center and put on an addition that will encompass the entire existing clubhouse," he answered, his expression as stoic as his voice.

She lifted Sunnie to her shoulder for a burp. "Who made that proposal?"

"I did."

"It's an excellent idea," she said.

He shrugged, but didn't comment further.

As she gave Sunnie the rest of her bottle, Abby felt as if her nerves were going to snap in two. In all of the years she had known him, she had never seen Brad so emotionless, so completely detached. It was as if he was sizing up an adversary, learning her weaknesses in order to use them to his advantage. Knowing she was the opponent he focused on only increased her anxiety.

"Do you think the men will eventually vote to allow more women into the club?" she asked, grasping at anything to keep him talking. If she could get him to open up a bit, then maybe their conversation later would be a little less intense.

"You should have stuck around," he said, his tone lacking even a trace of inflection. "After the first of the year, there will be a vote to admit women to the club. I fully expect it to pass."

"That's wonderful." She was happy to hear that women would finally be admitted to the TCC, but due to the state of her nerves and the fact that Sunnie had gone to sleep, Abby found it hard to work up a lot of enthusiasm.

The time she had dreaded since seeing Brad walk around the corner of her house had come. They were finished with small talk. There was nothing stopping them from the confrontation he was determined they were going to have.

"I'll put Sunnie in her carrier," he said, reaching down to pick up the baby.

Abby jumped. She had been so distracted by the thought of their upcoming conversation, she failed to notice that Brad left the chair and walked over to where she sat.

When he lifted Sunnie from her arms his fingers brushed her breast, sending a bittersweet longing throughout her body. "I—I think I'll make a pot of coffee," she said, suddenly needing to put space between them in order to regain her equilibrium. "If you would like, you can put the baby in my bedroom down the hall."

He nodded. "That's probably a good idea. I don't want our talking to wake her."

Rising to her feet, she showed him the way to the master bedroom. While he set up the baby monitor he had removed from the diaper bag, she went into the kitchen to make coffee. She really didn't think caffeine was a good idea, considering the state of her nerves and his level of tension, but Brad didn't drink anything alcoholic, so offering him wine was out of the question. She reached into the wine rack hanging beneath the cabinet to remove a bottle of chardonnay. He might not need anything stronger than coffee, but she did.

Brad quickly set up the baby monitor, checked to see that Sunnie was sleeping peacefully and walked back into the living room and over to the sliding glass door. Staring out at the lake, he stuffed his hands into the front pockets of his jeans. When his fingers came into contact with the item he had carried with him all the way from Texas, he narrowed his eyes with renewed determination.

"Why did you run, Abby?" he asked, when she walked up behind him. He could tell by her soft gasp that his question startled her.

"I—I don't know what you mean." There was a slight tremor in her voice and he knew she was lying.

"Don't you think it's about time you stop playing your little game and start being honest with both of us?" he asked, turning to face her.

Dear God, she had to be the most beautiful woman he had ever seen. Even with her hair escaping her loose ponytail and wearing baggy sweatpants and a sweater that practically swallowed her, she made him ache to hold her close and love her with every fiber of his being. It was all he could do to keep from walking over to her, taking her in his arms and kissing her until she admitted the reason she fled: because she was scared to death of what they had between them.

"Brad, I think that…my moving back here is…for the best," she said hesitantly.

"What makes you think that?" he asked, pressing for the answer he knew she was trying to avoid.

"I don't belong in Texas anymore," she said, her gaze not quite meeting his.

"Why not?" All he had to do was keep asking the right questions and he knew it was just a matter of time before she broke down and told him the truth. "With the exception of the years between graduating college and getting married, you've always lived in Royal. Don't you like it there?"

"Yes…I mean no…I—"

"Which is it, darlin'?" He took a step toward her. "No, you don't like it there? Or yes, you do?"

She stared at him for a moment before she gave him a jerky nod. "Y-yes, I love Royal. It's home. But it's not where I…belong."

The abject misery he saw clouding her vivid blue eyes almost tore him apart, but he couldn't give up now. He was too close to getting her to admit the real reason she came running back here, and until she did that, she would never be free of the fear that kept her from embracing the future.

"Where *do* you belong, Abby?"

She wore that trapped look again—the one he'd seen

cross her pretty face last night at the Christmas Ball. "I…here. I belong here."

"Liar." He took another step toward her. "You want to know where I think you belong?"

She shook her head until her ponytail swung back and forth. "No."

"I'm going to tell you anyway, darlin'." He took the last step separating them. "You belong right here in my arms," he said, putting them loosely around her.

"No, Brad," she insisted, still shaking her head emphatically.

"Yes, you do, Abby." He brushed a strand of dark auburn hair from her creamy cheek. "Now, don't you think it's time to stop running and admit why you left me at the ball to come back here?"

"Please…don't do this to me, Brad," she pleaded.

The tears welling up in her eyes caused him to feel like the biggest jerk ever to walk on two legs. Placing his finger beneath her chin, he raised her gaze to his and pressed on. "Why, Abby?"

She closed her eyes tight. "B-because I love you and I don't want to take the chance of losing you, too," she said, tears running down her cheeks. "I lose everyone I love. My dad…Richard…the baby. I can't lose anyone else. I just…can't."

"That's all I needed to hear, darlin'," he said, pulling her tightly against him.

He kissed the top of her head and smoothed her hair away from her face as she sobbed against his chest. He hated himself for causing her so much emotional pain, but there hadn't been any other way around it. In order for them to move forward, she had to share the fear with him that was holding her back. He knew that would have never happened without him pushing her for the truth.

When her sobbing ran its course, he cradled her face in his hands. "Darlin', there are no guarantees in life and no promises that there will be a tomorrow. That goes for all of us. But I can assure you of this. There isn't one single minute of one day for as long as I have breath in my body that I won't love you."

"I can't lose anyone else," she said stubbornly. "It hurts too much."

He should have known Abby wouldn't give up until there wasn't any fight left in her. It was one of the things about her that irritated him the most and at the same time made him love her.

"Darlin', I don't think you have any choice in the matter," he said gently. "You love me, don't you?"

To his immense relief there was no hesitation in her response. "Yes. I didn't want to, but I do."

He laughed. That was his Abby—stalwart until the end. "Then you owe it to the three of us to take a chance. Come back home with me, darlin'. Be my wife and Sunnie's mother."

"You want us to get married?"

Nodding, he walked over to take a small velvet box from Sunnie's diaper bag, then removing the diamond solitaire inside, dropped to one knee in front of her. "Will you marry me, Abigail Langley? Will you help me raise Sunnie and any more children we choose to adopt?" He hoped the tears streaming down her face this time were tears of joy.

As he watched her glance at the ring, then turn her

attention back to him, she slowly began to nod her head. "I can't say no. Yes, I'll marry you, Brad. But where did you get this ring?"

"Sunnie and I did a little shopping in downtown Seattle before we came here," he said, loving her more with each passing second.

He slid the ring on the third finger of her left hand, then rose to take her into his arms and give her a kiss that sealed what he knew would be the union of a lifetime. "I've loved you since that day at the lake when we were six years old," he said seriously. "You stole my heart then and never gave it back." Reaching into the front pocket of his jeans, he pulled out the note she had left with Sadie to give to him the night before and pressed it into her hand. "I traveled over two thousand miles to give this back to you, darlin'. I haven't read it and I don't ever intend to."

"Why?" she asked. Her gaze was filled with so much love that it made him feel weak.

"Because I knew it wasn't over for us," he said, kissing her forehead. "You're my soul mate—my other half. Words on a piece of paper could never end that."

Content just to be in each other's arms once again, they remained silent for some time before she leaned back to look up at him. "Are you sure you want me, Brad? I can't have children and won't be able to give you a child of your own."

He used his index finger to smooth away her worried frown. "I want us to adopt Sunnie together," he said, loving her more than he ever thought was humanly possible. "We'll have Sunnie and adopt as many more kids as you want. But I'm not one of those men who thinks that he can't be a dad unless his blood flows through a child's veins."

"I tried to adopt a baby this past summer," she said quietly. "I didn't tell anyone because I was afraid something might happen to stop it."

Her reluctance to talk about her options to become a mother when she first told him about her infertility suddenly made sense. She had tried another way to have the baby she wanted so desperately and it obviously hadn't worked out.

"What prevented the adoption from going through?" he asked, knowing she was ready to talk about it. Otherwise, she wouldn't have brought up the subject.

"When the baby was born, the birth mother changed her mind," she said, her voice filled with sadness. "I went to the hospital to bring my son home and had to leave without him."

So in less than a year Abby had suffered two devastating losses. She had lost a husband as well as the baby she planned to adopt, and there hadn't been a damned thing she could do but stand back and let it happen.

"You don't have to worry about that happening with Sunnie," he said, hoping to find the right words that would reassure her. "Hell, you're already her mother. You've been with her as much as I have. You've changed, fed and put her to bed. You were there to worry over her and help me walk the floor with her when she had the reaction to the immunization. If that doesn't make you her mother, I don't know what does, darlin'."

"I do love her with all my heart," she admitted, smiling.

"Oh, and I guess your loving me is just an after-thought because she and I are a package deal?" he teased.

Her smile warmed him all the way to his soul. "Let's just say I want to keep both of you and leave it at that." Something outside suddenly caught her attention. "Oh, look. It's snowing."

Brad frowned. "Is that unusual?"

She stepped back to take him by the hand. "We don't normally get a lot of snow, but I have something I want you to see."

He willingly followed her out onto the wide deck at the back of the floating home, not sure of what she wanted to show him. When she pointed to the shore across the way, he understood why she liked living on the lake and why it reminded her of the one just outside of Royal.

A dusting of snow covered the hillside and pine trees on the opposite side of Lake Washington, and the lights from the houses made the water look as if diamonds danced on the waves. "It's almost as beautiful as you, darlin'."

"You're only saying that because you love me," she said, wrapping her arms around his waist.

He held her close. "And I'm never going to let you forget it. I'm going to sleep with you in my arms every night and wake up still holding you every morning."

"I love you, Brad."

"And I love you, darlin'. For the rest of our lives."

Epilogue

"Brad, have you seen Sunnie's pacifier?" Abby asked, as they started walking back to the SUV after attending the groundbreaking ceremony for the new Tex Langley Cultural Family Center on New Year's Eve. "She had it in her mouth just a minute ago."

Shaking his head, he reached into the pocket of his suit jacket. "Here's another one." His good-natured laughter made her love him even more. "If our daughter is typical of how often a baby loses these things, then I think I'll buy a few thousand shares of stock in the company that makes them. We'll make a fortune in no time."

Abby smiled at Brad's reference to being Sunnie's daddy. On the return flight from Seattle, they had discussed how they should handle the relationship with the little girl and decided that it would be less confusing for the baby if they referred to her as their daughter. They were going to be raising her as their own and fully intended for her to know that they loved her and wanted to be her parents. Every child needed a mommy and a daddy, and that was exactly what they intended to be for Sunnie.

When he lifted the baby from her arms to secure her in the car seat, Brad's fingers grazed Abby's breast, and even through her coat the sensation sent an exciting thrill skipping up her spine. Their gazes met, and the smoldering promise in his hazel eyes made her feel as if she were the most cherished woman in the world.

"Are you ready to head on over to the clubhouse?" he asked, giving her a quick kiss.

"I've never been more ready for anything in my entire life," she said, meaning every word. "But what about you? You'll be giving up a lot. Are you sure you want to do that?"

He helped her into the passenger seat, then walked around to get in on the driver's side. "You know, I've thought a lot about all the women I dated over the years, and I've come to the conclusion that I was trying to see if one of them could make me feel even a fraction of what I've always felt for you." He lifted her hand and kissed the engagement ring he gave her two weeks earlier. "I can honestly say none of them even came close, darlin'."

"Good answer, Price," she said, grinning.

"It's the truth," he said, starting the truck. Steering her Escalade out onto the road leading across town, he asked, "Did my sister tell you she and Rick are keeping the baby tonight?"

Abby nodded. "Sadie said to bring the baby's things to the ceremony so she and Rick can take Sunnie home with them. That's the extra bag you put in the back before we left the house."

"You do realize we won't be staying long at the reception, don't you?" he asked, the suggestive look in his eyes leaving no doubt what he had planned for later.

As they passed his home on the way to the TCC clubhouse, Abby couldn't help but laugh out loud. "Look, Brad. Your name must have been the last one on the list."

She laughed even harder when he pulled the SUV to a halt in the middle of the road to stare open-mouthed at the hot pink flamingos scattered all over his front lawn. The rare dusting of snow the area had got the night before made the hot pink seem more bright and gaudy than ever.

Restarting the truck, Brad shook his head as he drove on toward the TCC clubhouse. "I don't want to think about a herd of—"

"I think you mean flock," she corrected. "And it could be worse. They could be pink elephants."

"Whatever. We have other things to concentrate on today." Taking her hand in his, he smiled. "Nothing is more important to me than meeting you under the Leadership, Justice and Peace sign in the main ballroom at two o'clock."

Her heart was filled with more love than she could have ever imagined. "I love you more than life itself, Brad Price. I'll be there."

An hour later, as Zeke Travers walked Abby across the ballroom toward the sign that for generations had been a reminder of what the Texas Cattleman's Club stood for, her eyes never left Brad's. He looked so handsome waiting for her in his black tuxedo, a red rosebud pinned to the lapel.

He was the man she loved with all her heart, the man who had made her realize that love was worth more than the risk of losing, and the man who was going to make her dream of having a family of her own come true.

"Are you ready to start the New Year as Mrs. Price?" Brad asked, when she stood facing him beneath the sign.

"I think I've been ready for this all of my life," she said sincerely as they turned to face the minister.

* * * * *

A sneaky peek at next month...

Desire™

PASSIONATE AND DRAMATIC LOVE STORIES

2 stories in each book - only £5.49!

My wish list for next month's titles...

In stores from 18th May 2012:

☐ Wanted by Her Lost Love – Maya Banks

& Nothing Short of Perfect – Day Leclaire

☐ Terms of Engagement – Ann Major

& Lessons in Seduction – Sandra Hyatt

☐ Improperly Wed – Anna DePalo

& An Innocent in Paradise – Kate Carlisle

☐ A Cowboy Comes Home & A Cowboy in Manhattan
   – Barbara Dunlop

Available at WHSmith, Tesco, Asda, Eason, Amazon and Apple

Just can't wait?

Special Offers

Every month we put together collections and longer reads written by your favourite authors.

Here are some of next month's highlights— and don't miss our fabulous discount online!

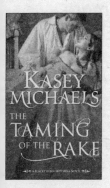

On sale 18th May

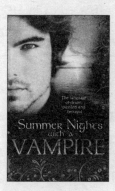

On sale 1st June

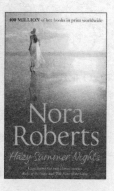

On sale 1st June

Save 20% *on all Special Releases*

Find out more at
www.millsandboon.co.uk/specialreleases

Visit us Online

0512/ST/MB375

MILLS & BOON® Book Club — 2 Free Stories!

Get your free stories now at
www.millsandboon.co.uk/freebookoffer

Or fill in the form below and post it back to us

THE MILLS & BOON® BOOK CLUB™—HERE'S HOW IT WORKS: Accepting your free stories places you under no obligation to buy anything. You may keep the stories and return the despatch note marked 'Cancel'. If we do not hear from you, about a month later we'll send you 2 Desire™ 2-in-1 books priced at £5.49* each. There is no extra charge for post and packaging. You may cancel at any time, otherwise we will send you 4 stories a month which you may purchase or return to us—the choice is yours. *Terms and prices subject to change without notice. Offer valid in UK only. Applicants must be 18 or over. Offer expires 31st July 2012. **For full terms and conditions, please go to www.millsandboon.co.uk/freebookoffer**

Mrs/Miss/Ms/Mr (please circle)
_____

First Name
_____

Surname
_____

Address
_____

_____

                                  Postcode
_____

E-mail
_____

Send this completed page to: Mills & Boon Book Club, Free Book Offer, FREEPOST NAT 10298, Richmond, Surrey, TW9 1BR

Find out more at
www.millsandboon.co.uk/freebookoffer

Visit us Online

0112/D2XEA/REV

The World of Mills & Boon®

There's a Mills & Boon® series that's perfect for you. We publish ten series and with new titles every month, you never have to wait long for your favourite to come along.

Blaze®
Scorching hot, sexy reads

By Request
Relive the romance with the best of the best

Cherish™
Romance to melt the heart every time

Desire™
Passionate and dramatic love stories